MEDICAL
Pulse-racing passion

A Baby To Rescue Their Hearts
Louisa Heaton

The Paediatrician's
Twin Bombshell
Juliette Hyland

MILLS & BOON

A BABY TO RESCUE THEIR HEARTS
© 2021 by Louisa Heaton
Philippine Copyright 2021
Australian Copyright 2021
New Zealand Copyright 2021

First Published 2021
First Australian Paperback Edition 2021
ISBN 978 1 867 23031 1

THE PAEDIATRICIAN'S TWIN BOMBSHELL
© 2021 by Juliette Hyland
Philippine Copyright 2021
Australian Copyright 2021
New Zealand Copyright 2021

First Published 2021
First Australian Paperback Edition 2021
ISBN 978 1 867 23031 1

MIX
Paper from
responsible sources
FSC® C001695
www.fsc.org

Published by
Harlequin Mills & Boon
An imprint of Harlequin Enterprises (Australia) Pty
Limited (ABN 47 001 180 918), a subsidiary of
HarperCollins Publishers Australia Pty Limited
(ABN 36 009 913 517)
Level 13, 201 Elizabeth Street
SYDNEY NSW 2000 AUSTRALIA

Cover art used by arrangement with Harlequin Books S.A.. All rights reserved.

Printed and bound in Australia by McPherson's Printing Group

A Baby To Rescue Their Hearts

Louisa Heaton

MILLS & BOON

Louisa Heaton lives on Hayling Island, Hampshire, with her husband, four children and a small zoo. She has worked in various roles in the health industry—most recently four years as a Community First Responder, answering 999 calls. When not writing Louisa enjoys other creative pursuits, including reading, quilting and patchwork—usually instead of the things she *ought* to be doing!

DEDICATION

To the real baby Cassidy—stay strong.
And to my dad. I will always love you. xxx

CHAPTER ONE

SOPHIE FIGURED THERE were three different types of men in the world.

The first kind she knew very well. Those men told you that they loved you, that you were the centre of their world, their beating heart—but then they left you because you'd become 'complicated' or 'needed more' or they thought they'd found someone *'easier'*.

The second kind were the nice guys. Those were rare—in short supply. In fact, she wasn't sure they truly existed, having never met one herself, but she'd heard her friends talk about them. The boys next door, who never seemed to be anything special at first, but were always snapped up by other, luckier women, before you realised who'd been living under your nose all that time.

And then there was the third kind. The kind who were often seen posing as half-naked firefighters for calendars, holding a cute puppy whilst their biceps, pecs and six-packs gleamed with oil. All square jaws and designer stubble, with perfect white teeth and a sexually charged smoulder.

And one of those was currently walking into her ambulance station.

'Wowser...' she breathed, trying to hide her stare, pretending to check the equipment in the back of her rapid response vehicle, occasionally peeking over the roof as if to confirm that he was actually real and not a hallucination.

His green paramedic uniform fitted him very well. A little too well, in fact. Surely it was against the law to look that good? Or maybe it just fitted him perfectly but her pregnancy-induced hormones, which had been starved of male attention for months and months, were transforming what she could actually see. Sex-starved goggles, rather than beer goggles…

He was the big three—tall, dark and handsome—with a killer smile that did strange things to her insides as, from behind her car, she watched him conversing with her boss over by his office.

She couldn't hear their conversation and she was curious. She *was* expecting a student paramedic to join her for a couple of weeks—but there was no way this guy was the student she was expecting! In her experience students were younger, fresh out of the lecture hall, their faces filled with eagerness and apprehension. Nervous. Anxious.

This guy was sure of himself, confident and more mature, and possibly in his thirties. The prime of his life. No doubt he was virile and physical and…

Taken. He's taken—obviously! I mean, come on, look at the guy!

She blew out a calming breath. Probably he was someone from higher up the chain who'd suddenly decided to do an inspection, or something. Nothing to do with her. Nothing that—

Her boss, Pete, laughed at something the guy said and nodded in Sophie's direction.

She dipped down beneath the roof of the car, cursing silently. Had they noticed her staring?

That would be embarrassing.

She yanked open the drawer that held the adult masks and counted them once again, her mind racing at what was going on as her cheeks bloomed with heat and desire. She'd expected a lot of things from pregnancy, like a huge belly and puffy ankles and weird food cravings, but these sexual feelings all the time… It was typical that she turned out to be one of *those*, when there was no bloke around to sort them out for her!

Was the new guy from head office or something?

Was he here to tell her she'd have to go on maternity leave early?

Because she refused to! She would work for as long as she could. Now that she was on her own she couldn't afford to take time off for longer than she needed to— and besides, she still felt fit. She could lift, she could run, she could do CPR…all the things required of a rapid response paramedic. It would be madness to take someone with her skills off the road and tell her to go and knit bootees or something.

'Hi.'

She jumped, and banged her head on the roof of the car, wincing and feeling her cheeks colour. Rubbing at her head, she peered over the top. 'Hey.'

Firefighter Calendar Guy stood by the driver's door, smiling at her. 'You okay?'

'I'm fine, thank you." She rubbed hard at her bruised scalp. "Can I help you?'

'I'm Theo Finch.'

Theo. Of course. A guy like him *would* have a beautiful name. Something that rolled off the tongue…that would sound perfect as she breathed it out, her lips caressing the name as they brushed against his neck…

Sophie cleared her throat. 'Pleased to meet you, Theo. What can I do for you?'

She could think of many things he could do for *her*, and her brain thoughtfully provided the imagery for all of those and more as she tried to appear nonchalant and carefree and as innocent as a nun.

'I'm your student. I'm shadowing you for the next month?'

She almost laughed. A nervous, hysterical laugh that would have sounded as if she deserved to be assessed by a mental health clinician. But she managed to hold it in.

This guy was her *student*? How the hell was she supposed to concentrate and do her job with *him* around?

'My student? I'm sorry,' she said with a laugh, 'I was expecting someone more…'

'Green-looking?'

She smiled. They all looked green. It was the uniform. But she didn't want to look at his uniform. Moulded as it was to his masculine, muscled form. Because all that made her think about was what lay beneath it…

She tried to work out how she would cope with this new development in her life. Realised she would just have to deal with it. Besides, he wouldn't be interested in her in *that way*. She looked like a beached whale, and men like him dated sylph-like girls with big hair, big boobs, talon-sharp fake nails and no real eyelashes of their own.

And, for the record, she wasn't really interested in him, either!

I've sworn off men. My life is just going to be me and my daughter. That's it. Nothing else needed. Except maybe one hot night occasionally, because why not?

She was a grown woman. She had needs.

She looked at him more intently, her gaze taking in his dark-lashed blue-green eyes, the beautiful curve of his lips, the fine dark hair covering his muscled forearms.

I need to get a grip. That's what I need.

'Hi, I'm Sophie Westbrook.'

Theo had been waiting for this day for a long time. He'd always been one of those guys who'd never quite thought about what he wanted from life, growing up. There'd never seemed time to be worrying about career choices— not when he'd had to be the man in his family and help look after his ailing mother and three younger sisters.

A career had seemed like something *other* people talked about, and when he'd had to meet with the careers advisor at his secondary school he'd told the softly spoken woman behind the large glasses that he'd probably just look for some menial work to fit in around helping run the house.

The advisor had told him that he was something called 'a carer', and that he was entitled to support, but somehow none of that had actually panned out. His mother had not been a woman to accept charity, so Theo had simply carried on carrying on—until his mother had died and his sisters had flown the nest and he'd gone to an army recruiting office and signed up.

But his time in the army, following in his father's footsteps, had not been what he'd hoped it would be. He'd thought he would find routine and rules—something that would take care of him for a change. Instead he'd found himself caring intensely for his new family—the other soldiers in his battalion. Losing some of them in Afghanistan had been brutal—totally unexpected—and he'd left before he could lose any more.

You're a carer.

Those were the words he kept hearing, over and over in his skull, and he knew them to be right. It was all he'd done. But how to do that in life, without getting attached to people?

He'd considered becoming a doctor, but the training lasted years and years and he wasn't sure he had that in him. Being a nurse was something he was familiar with, but the idea of being on a ward and getting to know his patients over time, caring for them, worrying about them, seemed too much.

He'd had enough of sitting by someone's bedside watching them die, trying to convince them to take their medicine and holding their hands through nights of pain and discomfort. It hurt too much. He'd known he needed something different. Something less attachment-forming. So he'd decided on being a paramedic.

He'd get the drama, the adrenaline rush that he was used to from being in the army, and he would get to care for people, to try and make them better, and then he could walk away. No long-term commitment needed. No getting to know someone before watching them die. No having to deal with that loss. If a patient died on him? Yes, it would be sad, but not as upsetting as losing someone he'd come to care for deeply.

The first few weeks of university had been fascinating, and now he was here on his very first placement—and it was with a rapid response paramedic. Just the kind of thing he imagined doing himself. Working solo in a vehicle like this, or maybe being a paramedic on a motorbike?

And he'd been placed with *Sophie*.

She was cute. In fact, she was more than that. His first thought had been that she was strikingly beautiful. Dark blonde hair that fell in waves to her shoulders, large blue eyes, a slightly wonky smile that was wide and caused her eyes to gleam, and...

Sophie came out from behind the vehicle and the first thing he saw—couldn't help but see—was her enormous abdomen, swollen with a baby.

'You're *pregnant.*' Then he coloured at stating the obvious!

She smiled. 'And you've just made your first assessment and diagnosis. We'll make a paramedic of you yet.'

He laughed. 'I'm sorry, I—'

'Is my being pregnant a problem for you?' She was looking at him curiously, her head tilted to one side in a challenge.

'No!'

'Good."

'I'm sorry, I didn't mean to blurt that out. I just wasn't expecting—'

'To be lumbered with an elephant?' She smiled.

Theo let out a breath and then laughed, holding out his hand once again. 'Can we start over? Hi, I'm Theo.'

She reached out to take his hand and laughed. 'Sophie. Pleased to meet you, Theo. Now, shall I show you how we check the vehicle to make sure it's roadworthy before we go out on shift?'

He was very relieved that she'd allowed him her grace. He couldn't believe he'd been so clumsy to start with. He was lucky that she was as kind as she was. 'Yes, please.'

He let go of her hand reluctantly, noticing she wore no ring on either hand, before following her to the rear of the vehicle.

'First we do a stock check and make sure the oxygen and Entonox tanks are full and any medications are well within their use-by date. There's a checklist here that we work through.' She pulled out a clipboard and gave it to him. 'I've already gone through it, but we'll go through it again as it will be good for you to check with me and familiarise yourself with the whereabouts of each item, in case I need you to find something for me when we're out on a shout. Okay?'

He nodded and pulled his pen from his sleeve pocket, feeling happier now that they were getting down to business, after the awkwardness of before.

Sophie had barely pulled out of the station and signed on for duty with the control room when a call came through. A young girl had been thrown from her horse.

'Six zero two, responding,' said Sophie.

'Thank you, six zero two. HEMS seven four eight also en route,' said the calm voice over the system.

'You see that button there?' Sophie pointed at a switch on the dashboard.

'Yes.'

'Press it.'

Theo reached forward and depressed the switch and the sirens began to sound. 'Blues and twos.' He smiled.

Sophie checked both ways at a junction before cutting through the traffic, making sure that everyone knew they were there and had stopped, or were stopping, before she pulled out and began to drive down the road towards the motorway that would get them to Cobham the fastest.

At this speed she had to concentrate, because—unfortunate as it was—not everyone on the roads responded in the correct manner when an emergency vehicle was coming up behind them, lights blazing and sirens blaring. She'd lost count of the number of drivers who never bothered to look in their mirrors and didn't get out of the way. And if she'd got a pound for every driver who had cut her up or refused to let her pass she'd be a millionaire by now, sitting on a baby-soft couch at home being hand-fed grapes by a half-naked Adonis, whilst another bronzed god wafted her with an ostrich feather fan.

'Hopefully you've never travelled at these speeds before?' she asked Theo.

'On a road? No.'

She guessed he meant that he'd been in a plane, or a high-speed train, or something. 'By the time you've finished your placement with me you'll be more than familiar with some of the mistakes other drivers make. If I had my way, I'd make it part of the practical driving test to have to deal with emergency vehicles whilst out on the road.'

'They're that bad?'

'Like you wouldn't believe! Lots of people are very good at pulling over and getting out of our way, but sometimes they pull over in the wrong place—like on blind corners, forcing us to go head-on into the other lane, not knowing what's coming. It slows down our response time, and response times are everything.'

'We have to get there within seven minutes?'

'For a category one call, yes.'

'What are those, usually?'

'Anything considered life-threatening or something that might need immediate intervention.'

'And is getting there in seven minutes always doable?'

'It depends on many things—traffic, time of day, roadworks...'

'Lots of variables come into play?'

'They most certainly do.'

'Do you think we'll get to this call on time?'

She glanced at the clock on her dashboard. 'Most definitely.'

It was a matter of pride for Sophie and all the other paramedics she knew who worked damned hard to meet response times, ensuring not only patient care, but also the safety of themselves and other road users.

'Have you had much experience of patient care?' she asked.

It would be good to know if he had. He was older than the students she usually mentored, so it was likely he had seen more in life. Experienced more. Hopefully he wasn't the type to faint at the sight of blood.

'Some.'

Had she noticed a hint of terseness in his voice? 'Good. When we get there, you must wear a jacket that says you're an observer. You can help me carry equipment and things, but no rushing forward until I've assessed the situation and know that it's safe for us to approach. At *any* call—okay?'

'I know. They gave us health and safety lectures at university.'

'Lectures are one thing. Real life is another. Especially when all your instincts are screaming at you to forget safety and just get in there and help.'

She saw him nod in her peripheral vision.

'What sort of danger would you expect at this call?' he asked.

'Well, she's fallen off a horse, so the horse might still be around. We'll need to make sure it's contained—especially if HEMS are going to be landing.' He'd know that

HEMS was the Helicopter Emergency Medical Service. 'Any good with animals?'

He gave a small laugh. 'Not really had the opportunity.'

She smiled. Theo was easy to talk to when she didn't have to look directly at him. She could pretend he was just another guy. Just her work partner. Her student. He was here to learn, and as long as she stuck to educating him and nothing else, she should be absolutely fine. *Keep things serious...no flirting.* That was doable, right? Looking directly at him was another thing. Looking into those come-to-bed eyes of his would be distracting.

The turn-off for Cobham came into view and she indicated, checking her mirrors and watching the traffic on the slip road before cleaving her way through the centre at the lights to take the turning they needed. Thankfully, the drivers there got out of her way, and she quickly zipped past a big supermarket on her left and drove through Cobham cautiously, before taking the road she needed for the farm they'd been called to on the outskirts. Her GPS system showed her that she was about a minute away, and above her she could see a helicopter coming in from the east.

Tipton Farm was atop a small hill and had a long, rutted driveway which she drove down cautiously, trying to avoid the potholes and puddles. To one side was a field of cows and on the other a crop of some kind that she couldn't identify. It stood quite tall—almost waist-height, if she had to guess.

At the end of the driveway, a woman flagged them down. 'Harriet is down there!' She pointed to a small path.

'Thank you.' Sophie drove towards the path and

parked. 'This is where we disembark,' she told Theo. 'Hope you've got a strong back—the bags weigh a ton.'

She quickly radioed through to Control to say that she'd arrived on scene, and then she got out of the vehicle and opened up the boot. She passed Theo the jump bag and equipment she thought they might need and grabbed a pair of gloves as well.

'Ready?' She took a moment to smile at him, and was rewarded with a dazzling smile that did things to her insides.

Concentrate.

She quickly looked away as they began walking towards the patient. In front of them was a small huddle of people, gathered around somebody on the ground. A woman held a beautiful chestnut-coloured horse by its reins off to one side.

The people stood back to make space for her and Sophie quickly assessed the situation. Her patient—Harriet—was lying flat on her back, covered in some coats that had been laid over her. She wore a riding helmet, which was good, but she looked pale. The ground seemed solid and there didn't appear to be any hazards that might harm anybody.

'Could we get rid of the horse? The air ambulance will most probably land in this field next to us, so it would be safer for all involved if it was back in its stable.'

The woman holding the horse nodded and began to lead the animal away.

Sophie put on her gloves, crouched next to her patient and smiled. 'Hello, Harriet, my name's Sophie and I'm a paramedic. How old are you, sweetheart?'

'Fourteen.' Harriet's teeth chattered. Most probably from shock.

'Can you tell me what happened?'

As Harriet spoke, telling Sophie how her horse had been walking quite sedately down the path when it had been startled by a deer jumping out from the underbrush and had thrown her off onto her back, Sophie was assessing her patient's body by eye, mentally working out the height of her patient's fall, how the impact might have happened and what she would need to check for.

'And what hurts…if anything?'

'My back and my hips.'

'And if you had to rate your pain from zero to ten, with zero being no pain and ten being the worst you've ever felt in your life, where would you say you were?'

'About a s-s-six?' Her teeth were still chattering.

'Okay, Harriet, you're doing wonderfully. I'm just going to check you out, so you'll feel me touching you, but I'll try not to hurt you. Is that okay? Don't nod—just say yes or no.'

'Yes.'

Sophie began her primary survey of Harriet. The helmet was not cracked or broken, but that didn't mean Harriet hadn't taken a blow to the head when she'd landed. She felt nothing out of place in the girl's neck or shoulders, arms or legs, but there was tenderness, as Harriet had mentioned, around her pelvis. It was possible it was broken, or there was an injury to her back.

She reached into her bag and got out her SATS probe and slipped it onto Harriet's finger. Whilst she waited for it to give her the result she got out the Entonox—a mixture of nitrous oxide and oxygen.

'Just breathe in and out for me…this should help with your pain.'

Behind them, she could hear the *whump-whump* of the

helicopter's blades as it got closer, and she could feel the downdraft as it lowered to the ground.

She carried on with her assessment. Harriet's oxygen levels were good. Her pulse rate was a bit high, but that was understandable in this situation. She'd had an accident. She was scared. In pain. She didn't know what was going to happen.

Sophie tried to shield Harriet from the worst of the downdraft and then, as the engine whined, she took hold of Harriet's head and held it still. 'Some nice doctors are about to arrive now. They'll most likely ask you a few questions, and then they'll want to put you in a collar to support your neck and get you on a spinal board for a trip to the hospital.'

'In the helicopter?'

Sophie smiled. 'Absolutely. Ever been in one before?'

'No.'

'Well, you're about to.'

Sophie glanced up to look at Theo and make sure he was okay. He was doing as she'd asked. Standing back and observing, looking at the patient on the ground with a mixture of concern and apprehension.

The HEMS doctor arrived and she gave a brief handover of her findings and let him take control. He was the senior on the scene, though as she was the one with cervical control of Harriet's neck she would be the one to control her log-roll onto the spinal board that was arriving.

'Theo? You need to watch how we do this so next time you can help.'

'I can help you now. I did this in the army.'

The army? Okay, so that explained the proud way he walked, the upright posture, the confidence. 'Okay, you can grab her legs. You know where to hold them?'

He quickly positioned himself by Harriet's legs and placed his hands in the right position, giving her confidence in what he'd said.

'Good. Once we've got the pelvic brace on we'll need you, okay?'

'I'll be ready.'

The HEMS doctor quickly tightened a brace around Harriet's pelvis. 'She's secure.'

'Okay, let's roll to the right on the count of three, then. One, two, *three*.'

They rolled Harriet so that the spinal board could be placed underneath her. Then, on another count, they rolled her onto her back. Sophie checked with her small team to make sure everyone was happy before they log-rolled her to the left and back again.

'Right, we're just going to get you all strapped in, Harriet, and then you're going to go in the helicopter with Dr Howard—okay?'

'Thank you.' Harriet smiled and giggled slightly. It was a nervous giggle, but at least it showed the Entonox was doing its stuff.

'Mum and Dad? Harriet will be going to Kingston Hospital. There's no room for you in the helicopter. Are you able to make your own way there?'

Her parents nodded, looking anxious.

Sophie reached out to lay a hand upon the mother's arm. 'She's in good hands.'

'She's all we've got…'

Sophie wished *she'd* had parents who had worried as much as Harriet's parents seemed to. She was a lucky girl.

With the HEMS team and Theo, she helped carry Harriet across the field to the waiting helicopter. The HEMS doctor swapped Sophie's Entonox for their own and gave her back her canister. Then she and Theo hurried back to their vehicle and began packing their equipment away.

'How did you find that?' she asked him, smiling, hoping that he had loved it as much as she did.

'It was good!'

'You enjoyed it?'

'I did. Which is strange when you think about it. Enjoying someone else being in pain…'

'But we're here to help. Without us they'd be in a lot more pain or distress. You enjoyed watching someone receive help and feel better. Not the fact that she was in pain.'

He nodded. 'Yeah… You think she'll be okay?'

'I hope so. She had feelings in all four limbs…could move her toes. We can only hope she's just suffered bruising from the fall, but there's always the possibility that there are injuries we couldn't see.'

'And that's why we prepare for the worst?'

'But hope for the best. Yes.'

A car passed them. Harriet's parents on their way to the hospital.

Sophie and Theo both waved. Then she turned back to consider him. Her interest in him was rearing its head once again. 'So…the army, huh?'

He nodded. 'Yeah.'

'What made you leave?'

Theo shrugged. 'I'd had enough.'

Okay. Short and sweet.

'Didn't you enjoy it?'

'I did, but…'

He looked away from her then, and she saw a darkness in his eyes that made her wonder if he'd been hurt in some way.

'It was just time to make a change,' he said.

She nodded. Something had affected him. She could tell. Something he didn't want to talk about. It intrigued her to know that this stunning man at her side might look as if he had no troubles in the world, and as if his life was as perfect as his hair, but in reality he was just as screwed up as the rest of them.

'Was it a hard adjustment, being a civilian again?'

'A bit. But a friend of mine got me a job as a rock-climbing instructor, so that's what I was doing up until going to university.'

'You like being active?'

She smiled, imagining him climbing the sheer face of a mountain. Bare-chested, his beautiful trim waist holding a cascade of ropes and clips and…what were those things called…? *Carabiners?* His muscles would be straining and flexing under his skin, droplets of sweat dripping down his—

'I do.'

'You look like it.'

She'd said the words without thinking. Now he would think that she'd been staring at his body—which she had. But he didn't need to know that.

She felt flustered. 'I mean, I can tell you do a lot of physical things.'

Oh, God, it's getting worse! Shut your mouth, Sophie!

Fortunately, he just smiled at her.

'You go to the gym a lot?' she asked, feeling embarrassed.

'Yes. I do. You?'

She rubbed at her abdomen. 'Oh, sure! Can't you tell?' Sophie laughed in disbelief at herself. 'I used to. But I'm more of a swimmer, to be honest.'

He glanced down at her belly. 'So no doubt the little one will be, too?'

She grimaced. 'Not so little. She feels enormous already and I've still got weeks to go.'

'She? You know it's a girl?'

Sophie nodded. 'I wanted to know. So I could plan… get things sorted. I like to know what's going to happen ahead of time—that way I can account for contingencies and things going wrong.'

'Are you a pessimist?'

'No. I like to think I'm a realist. Life so far has taught me that just when I think I've got everything sorted, and my life is on an even keel, something will come along to ruin it. Anyway, enough about me—let's get this stuff sorted.'

She felt as if his questions were leading her down a route to where she'd end up spilling all her personal secrets, and she didn't want him thinking that she was a great mess of a human being who had screwed up entirely.

He was her student and she was his mentor. He didn't need to know anything about her. Not really. Realistically, he'd be in her life for a short time and then he'd go. All she'd be to him was a memory.

She wanted him to look back at that memory with fondness. To smile when he recalled her, the rapid response paramedic he'd done his first placement with, and remember how much fun she'd been. Not to think of it as a time he'd spent with a mentor who'd done nothing but complain about her life and whinge. Besides, that wasn't who she was. She tried to remain upbeat. Because anything else just led to depression and self-pity and she refused to go down that road.

Sophie showed Theo how all the equipment they'd used went into a clinical waste container. Then she restocked the jump bag and got Theo to check the level of Entonox the way she'd showed him back at the station.

'It's half full.'

'Okay. Let's get going.'

They got back into the car and Sophie radioed through to Control that they were free from the scene and available.

'Thank you, six zero two. Everything all right?'

'All good. Patient with HEMS. Suspected back or pelvic fracture.'

'Poor kid. Let's hope she's okay.'

'I hear you.'

'Are you available to attend an RTC on the A3 near the Esher turn-off?'

'We most certainly are. On our way.'

'Thank you, six zero two. Safe travels.'

'Thank you, Control.' Sophie smiled at Theo. 'When we get back towards the centre of Cobham, do you want to light us up?'

'Sure.' He nodded.

Sophie began the slow drive down the farm's bumpy driveway that tested the suspension of the vehicle, and it wasn't long before the blues and twos were creating a clear passageway for them through the mid-afternoon traffic.

CHAPTER TWO

THEO HAD ENJOYED his first day with Sophie. In fact, he was pretty amazed by her. She was so on the ball, professional…and, boy, was she fit for a woman in the latter stage of her third trimester!

She could carry hefty bags of gear, run up flights of stairs, help lift patients and control onlookers who wanted to get in the way as if it was nothing. It was almost as if there were times in the day when she seemed to forget that she was pregnant. The only sign that she was, was her huge belly, and the habit she had of occasionally having to chew on some red liquorice, which she'd just admitted was a craving at the moment.

'I know all about pregnancy cravings,' he told her.

Sophie looked at him. 'Oh?'

'My younger sisters all had them when they were pregnant.'

'How many sisters?'

'Three. I'm the oldest and the only boy.'

'So you're an uncle? To how many?'

'I have four nieces and two nephews—and let me tell you red liquorice is a nice, normal craving compared to some of the things my sisters wanted to eat.'

'Such as?'

'Leonora craved cheesy puffs in chocolate ice cream with her latest, Hazel wanted fishfingers on waffles, but it was Martha who craved sticks of chalk.'

'Chalk?' Sophie laughed.

'Yeah. The doctors said it was something called pica?'

'I've heard of that. So I should be thankful I'm normal, then?'

He nodded and smiled.

'First time for everything, I guess.'

They were checking the car before handing it over to the next paramedic for the night shift.

'You seem normal to me,' he said.

'You don't know anything about me.'

'I know some things.'

'Like…?'

She stopped to consider him over the roof of the car and he couldn't help but notice that, even though they'd just completed a nine-hour shift in which they'd attended call after call, Sophie looked just as good as she had first thing that morning.

He paused to think, wanting to keep this professional. 'I know that you're very good at your job. You're a good teacher. You explain things very well. I know you're heavily pregnant but you don't let it affect you at work.'

He noticed her smile and suddenly wondered if he'd gone too far, giving his attractive female colleague compliments… He needed her to know that he wasn't interested in her in that way, even if he did feel attracted to her. Perhaps if he showed that he knew she was unavailable…

'I hope when you get home you can have a good rest. Put your feet up, let someone cook you a nice meal…'

'Fat chance of that. I live alone.' She smiled wryly. 'What about you, Theo? Who do you go home to?'

'No one.'

She seemed to consider this for a moment, and he wondered what was running through her head. And why was *she* alone? For some reason the idea of that made him feel a little sad. Did she not live with the father of her child? Surely that would change when the baby arrived? Or was she going to be a single mother? That didn't seem right to him either.

Sophie was such a nice person. Surely she was in a relationship? He needed her to be in a relationship. Because that way she was totally unavailable and he didn't have to worry about pursuing someone he shouldn't.

'So, we're *both* sad and lonely people,' she said.

'I thought you weren't a pessimist?' he argued.

He didn't plan on being sad or lonely tonight. He planned on going out. Meeting up with a couple of the younger guys from uni. Seeing how everyone else's first shifts had gone. Drinking a few beers, maybe. Not too many. Meeting a nice girl… Someone available. Someone temporary. Someone to have a laugh with.

He wouldn't have a late night. He wouldn't be a naughty boy. He was on an early shift with Sophie tomorrow morning and needed to be at the station for seven a.m.

Sophie shook her head, still smiling, and he began to wonder if this was just a mask she put on at work.

'I'm not. Not really,' she said.

Suddenly he wanted to discard his plans for the night and suggest to Sophie that she join him. They could go out to a decent gastro pub or something. Grab a bite to eat, get to know each other a bit more…

Only he didn't. This was his first day, and she was his mentor, and she was heavily pregnant and he didn't need to involve himself with her life or her problems. He needed to maintain a distance. This was professional between them. Her being pregnant and single screamed issues.

'Good. Well…thanks for today. It was great. I'll see you tomorrow morning.'

'Yes. Thanks, Theo. You did well.'

He nodded. 'You too.'

He raised a hand and began to walk away, realising as he did so that he really didn't want to go. Something about Sophie made him want to stay. To talk to her a bit more. Learn a bit more about her.

Why was she alone? Where was the father of her child? What had happened?

Questions that he really ought not to ask on the first day of meeting her, but questions he somehow wanted answers to.

But Sophie was not his problem. She was his mentor. Nothing else. He needed to put her out of his mind.

They hadn't had much opportunity to talk today. The shift had been pretty full-on and most of their chat had been about the calls themselves, the patients, the trust policy and the like. Only occasionally had they ventured into personal territory, and even then it had been pretty light, such as the conversation about his sisters and their pregnancy cravings.

He hoped to talk to her a bit more tomorrow. Make it clear that he was not only interested in the job, but in her as a person, too. That he was a nice guy.

By the time he got home he still hadn't shifted the feeling that he'd wanted to stay with her, and all he could think about was the way her face looked when she talked about her cases. The way she sometimes tucked her hair behind her ears when she was concentrating on her driving. The way she tilted her head when she looked at him, as if she were curious and intrigued about him, too.

He liked that. The fact that she didn't make him feel like just another student. That she saw him as a person.

He had to admit that if he'd met her in a pub, or a club, he would most certainly have asked her out. If she wasn't pregnant, of course! Clearly she had something going on there, and he didn't want to get mixed up in whatever was going on with the father, but…

There was something about Sophie.

He couldn't put his finger on it. Couldn't name whatever it was. He just knew that he had to know more about the woman he was going to be spending his days with.

Theo woke before his alarm the next morning and got up quickly, feeling eager to get to his morning shift with Sophie.

He'd spent a weird night out with his friends. He'd been surrounded by people he liked, sharing a drink or playing a game of pool on one of the pub's tables when one came free, but he hadn't felt *present* in their company.

His mind had been elsewhere.

At one point he must have been staring into space, because his friend Marty had given him a nudge and asked him if he was okay.

'Yeah, sure! Just thinking about today. Processing it, you know…'

'You sure you weren't thinking about Sophie?'

He'd blinked. Laughed. 'Why would I be thinking about her?'

'I was at the same station as you, mate. I saw her with my own eyes, you lucky so-and-so! My mentor isn't as pretty to look at, with his frizzy hair and his beer belly. You've hit the jackpot, mate.'

Theo had taken a sip of his beer. 'It's not like that. Besides, she's pregnant. She's with someone.'

Marty had simply raised his eyebrows. 'That's not what my guy says.'

He and Marty had talked about her? 'What did your guy say?' He'd been intrigued.

'That she got dumped. That she's really hung up on the father and a bit of a cold fish.'

Theo had dismissed that. 'Sounds like she once turned your guy down and he's just bitter. She's not like that. She's really nice.'

He and Marty hadn't spoken any more about their mentors after that, choosing instead to discuss the cases they'd seen and what they'd been allowed to do. But all night he'd pondered on what Marty had said about Sophie being hung up on her baby's father.

Was she pining for him? Hoping he'd come back to her? And why did it irritate Theo that some of the others had been talking about her behind her back? She was really nice—she didn't deserve that. Especially if some bloke had dropped her like a hot rock, leaving her with a child to look after.

He took a shower and got ready, then drove his car to the ambulance station, grabbing some breakfast from a petrol station on the way. Whilst there, he picked up a packet of red liquorice without really thinking about it, and walked into the station to find Sophie already by the car, about to work through the checklist.

'Morning, Theo.'

'Morning. Want me to do that?'

'You remember how to do it?'

'I do.'

'Knock yourself out.'

She smiled at him and he smiled back, careful not to let her happy face mean too much to him. He wasn't here to make Sophie happy. Not in that way, anyway. He was here to get an education. Get through his placement and move on.

He reminded himself of the first items on the clipboard and checked the stock, signing with his initials and dating everything, noting that Sophie had now opened the bonnet and was checking the oil and then, afterwards, the tyres and the lights.

It took them just a few moments, working together.

He closed the boot. 'All present and correct.'

She smiled. 'Good. Checked the oxygen tanks?'

'Two full tanks and one that's three-quarters full.'

'Perfect.'

He slid into the passenger seat and put on his seat belt, before pulling his little gift from his shirt pocket. 'I got you this.' He passed her the red liquorice, feeling a bit awkward.

'Oh!' She laughed. 'You didn't have to do that! That's so sweet of you.'

'It wasn't a problem.'

She put the liquorice into the compartment that sat between them. 'I'll have that later. Right! Are you ready?'

'Yep.'

'Good. You can call in to Control and get us rolling.'

He liked it that she was letting him do things, and he was pleased that he'd made himself remember their call number. He picked up the radio. 'Control, this is six zero two. We're clear and ready for calls.'

'Thanks, six zero two. Have a good shift.'

'You too.'

He put the radio down and smiled at Sophie as she started the engine and rolled out of the ambulance station. He had a good feeling about today. At that moment he felt as if nothing in the world could ruin his good mood.

He had no idea that their first patient—or rather their first patient's relative—would change all that.

They'd been on duty for over twenty minutes before their first shout came through from Control. An elderly woman in her eighties having breathing difficulties, a known COPD patient.

Sophie hit the lights and sirens as they drove quickly to the address in Kingston upon Thames. As always, her mind raced ahead to the possibilities of what she might need to do when attending her patient.

'Do you know about COPD?' she asked Theo.

'Chronic Obstructive Pulmonary Disease.'

'But do you know what that actually means?'

'Patients with COPD have difficulty with their breathing and oxygenating properly.'

'Good. But we can't be railroaded into thinking that just because this patient has COPD, this is a respiratory issue. The patient's age means this could also be cardiac, and we need to think about possible comorbidities—medical conditions that usually occur at the same time as another condition,' she explained.

Theo nodded. 'But treatment would be to give her oxygen, right?'

'Once we've checked her SATs and found out her usual

range of oxygenation. We don't give COPD patients full-flow oxygen because of oxygen toxicity. It causes them to retain carbon dioxide, so we need to maintain a low pressure of oxygen in the blood. We give them just enough oxygen to keep their usual levels of saturation, which is generally between eighty-eight and ninety-two per cent in a COPD patient. The oxygen canisters flow at fifteen litres on full, so with this patient we'll start at two litres and see how she goes. When we get there you can put the SATs monitor on her finger and get out the oxygen and an adult mask. You remember how to attach them?'

Theo nodded.

She had confidence that he understood all the risks. He'd been invaluable yesterday. Calm, assured. He had shown no sign of panic at any of the calls they'd attended, and had kept family members reassured. She had no doubt that he would follow her instructions to the letter.

They entered the outskirts of Kingston and the traffic pulled over to get out of their way as they headed down a small close, pulling up outside their patient's home. It was a narrow, terraced house, neat and tidy, with a front garden filled with pots and a newly painted front door.

Theo helped her carry the equipment out, and before she could knock on the door it was opened by a young woman. 'Come in, come in. It's my nan. She's…' The woman looked past Sophie and noticed who she was with. *'Theo?'*

Theo looked startled, and Sophie knew a whole lot of words and thoughts and feelings were not being made clear as the two looked at each other. The young woman looked shocked, and Theo didn't look very happy at all… *uncomfortable.*

But if there was anything these two needed to say to

each other they'd have to do it later. There was an elderly lady here who needed help. And, although Sophie felt sure that there had been something between Theo and the young woman, she went to move inside the house.

She frowned as the other woman just stood there, blocking the way, still staring at her student. She turned to look at Theo and noticed a look of grim determination on his face. *Enough!* If these two had a history they could sort it later.

'Could you show us where your nan is? Is she upstairs?'

The young woman nodded, finally stepping aside to let them pass.

Sophie hurried up the stairs, trying to ignore the way her baby had suddenly started kicking violently in her belly. It was as if she was trying to kick down the walls of her confinement. She had to push her hand down hard, just beneath her ribs, to get the baby to stop for a moment. She didn't need this. Her patient was what mattered here. But for some reason all she could think about was how Theo and this woman knew each other. Friends? Romantically involved?

None of my damned business.

Sophie turned into a lavender-painted bedroom to find an elderly woman sitting up in bed, her chest making huge movements as she tried to breathe in air. She looked quite pale, and was most definitely breathless. The young woman behind her—the one who knew Theo—had done the right thing in calling for help.

Sophie smiled at the old lady, laying her jump bag down on the floor. 'Hello, my lovely, my name's Sophie and I'm a paramedic. I've got Theo with me, and he's a student. Can you tell me your name?'

Sophie glanced behind her at Theo, to tell him that she would need the SATs probe, but he was already kneeling down, unzipping the bag to get it out for her.

'Diana… Dodsworth…' the elderly lady breathed.

'And how long have you been like this, Diana?'

Sophie watched as Theo slipped the probe onto Diana's finger. It took just a moment to show that Diana's oxygen levels were at eighty-four percent.

Can you get the oxygen? she mouthed to Theo, but he was already on it.

'Your oxygen levels are a little low,' she told her patient. 'Do you know what you usually run at?'

'About ninety,' said the young woman, leaning against the door.

'Thank you. And what's your name?'

The young woman glanced at Theo. 'Jen.'

'Any other medical conditions I should know about?' she asked Jen as she helped put the oxygen mask over Diana's face and turned on the flow at a low level.

'Type two diabetes. High blood pressure and emphysema.'

'All right.' She turned back to Diana and laid her hand on the patient's. 'You just take nice steady breaths for me, okay? Any chest pain?'

'A little.'

'Okay. We'll set up for an ECG, just to be on the safe side. Theo, can you pass me the electrodes?'

She set about placing the electrodes discreetly on Diana's chest, wrists and legs, and told her to lie still whilst the ECG machine took a reading. Sophie tore off the strip of paper and scanned it carefully. Normal sinus rhythm, which was good. This was most definitely an exacerbation of a respiratory issue. A flare-up of emphysema, which was a long-term progressive disease of the lungs. It caused shortness of breath due to the alveoli in the lungs becoming over-inflated and damaged and therefore unable to work properly.

'I'm just going to take your blood sugar level,' she told Diana.

Theo was already passing her what she needed.

Two days in and he was working well with her. Knowing the way she worked, what she would need next, ready to pass it to her. He was doing well as a student and she was impressed. Plus, he wasn't letting whatever was going on between him and Jen affect him.

Sophie cleaned Diana's finger and took a small sample of blood to analyse. It came back normal.

'And now your blood pressure...' She fastened the sphygmomanometer cuff around Diana's thin arm. 'Keep breathing for me. You'll feel this tighten around your arm, but it shouldn't hurt.'

Diana's blood pressure came back slightly raised, and her pulse was fast, but that was to be expected, considering the fact that she couldn't breathe very well and was probably afraid. It was terrifying to have to call out an ambulance. Nobody wanted to go to hospital.

Sophie checked her patient's oxygen levels. The low-flow oxygen was helping, bringing Diana's levels back to nearly ninety per cent. 'You're doing much better now, Diana. Nearly got you back to normal!'

'I didn't expect to see you again, Theo,' said Jen suddenly.

Sophie turned to look at the young woman, then glanced at Theo.

'No.'

A man of few words.

'How do you two know each other?' Sophie asked, feeling intrigued now that her patient was stable.

'He was my boyfriend,' Jen said, looking at Theo with what looked like some unresolved anger. 'Now he's my ex.'

Intriguing, all right. But still not my business.

Sophie looked back at Diana. 'Well, my lovely, you've got a decision to make. When the ambulance gets here you can decide if you want to go in to be checked at the hospital or stay at home. It's totally up to you. I've got your levels back to normal, but we'll need to see what happens when we take you off the oxygen. Shall we try to do that?'

Diana nodded and removed the mask as Sophie turned the nozzle on the oxygen cannister to zero.

'Just sit and breathe normally. I'll leave the SATs probe on your finger and we'll see how you do.'

'Okay.'

Sophie turned back to look at Theo. 'So why did you two break up?'

Curiosity had got the better of her. Theo was stunning, and he seemed kind and hard-working and considerate. He listened to her when she talked, and he appeared to be empathetic. He'd been in the army, for crying out loud! And Jen appeared to be the very type she'd imagined Theo going out with. Young, slim, curves to die for... The kind of woman who took three hours to do her hair and make-up before leaving the house and who ought to have shares in fake tan.

Unlike me. Most definitely unlike me, Sophie thought. *I think getting ready to go out takes ten minutes. A quick brush of my hair, a bit of mascara, some lip balm and— boom! I'm out the door.*

Jen gave a short laugh, but there was no humour in it. 'Because Theo runs at the first sign of commitment. One hint that I wanted to talk about us getting serious and he disappeared from my life faster than a bank robber in a getaway car.'

Theo shook his head, as if silently disagreeing, but said nothing.

Sophie looked at him curiously. A commitment-phobe, huh? Well, she knew the type. All too well. She'd known there had to be *something* wrong with him. And unfortunately, men like him were *not* in short supply. It was disappointing. She'd been beginning to think that Theo might be different from Connor.

Never mind. I'll get over it.

Outside, Sophie heard the tell-tale engine sounds of the ambulance arriving. She glanced at Diana's SATs. 'Your levels keep dropping, Diana, so my advice to you is to go into hospital, but it's your choice.' She placed the oxygen mask back onto her patient's face and turned the flow on. 'Could you let the other paramedics in?' she asked Jen.

Jen turned and hurried down the stairs.

Sophie glanced at Theo and raised an eyebrow. He passed her the keypad to finish off inputting the details that he hadn't been shown how to do.

'I think... I'd better go in... I'm on my own here... Jen only visits when...she can.' Diana glanced at Theo. 'You broke her heart, you know.'

Theo looked sorry.

The thud of footsteps coming up the stairs told Sophie that the cavalry had arrived, and she stood up, groaning at the stiffness in her knees, before handing over to the ambulance crew. Josh and Sam were a good pair. She had no doubt that they would look after her patient very well and have her laughing and smiling by the time they pulled up outside the hospital.

Sophie and Theo stayed whilst Diana was wrapped up, strapped into a carry-chair and taken outside to the ambulance. Jen clambered in with her after locking up the house, and the ambulance pulled away after switching one of Sophie's empty oxygen cannisters with one of their full ones from the store they kept on board.

She didn't mean to poke her nose into Theo's business, but the question just came out... 'So, what happened there, then? Between you and Jen? She seemed quite bitter.'

'We just weren't right for each other. We wanted different things.'

'Like what?'

He shrugged. 'I think she saw more of a future for us than I did.'

'You weren't looking for a future?'

He sighed as he helped store the bags away and closed the boot of their vehicle. 'She wanted to move our relationship on a lot quicker than I did. We'd been going out for just a couple of months. I thought it was just casual fun, but she started talking about wanting me to meet her parents. About moving in and getting a cat.'

'A cat?'

They got into the car and pulled on their seatbelts.

'A rescue cat. She had this idea that we should go to a rehoming centre and pick the oldest, mangiest cat they had and give it a new life.'

'And...you don't like cats?'

'Cats are fine. Rescuing a cat is even finer. But how could we give one a stable home when I didn't even think *we* were stable? She wanted to show the world how happy we were. But I wasn't in the same place. I thought she was just someone I was having fun with when I had free time. I didn't see a future between us. I thought I'd made my feelings clear from the start. So, we had all these arguments… I kept trying to pull away and she kept holding on. She pushed for too much and I wasn't ready.'

'So, she was moving faster than you?'

He nodded. 'I just wasn't the right person for Jen, and she's bitter about it because all her friends have settled down and she's still single.'

Sophie nodded, considering for a moment. Then she called through to Control and made them aware that they were clear of their last job. 'Do you think you'll ever settle down with someone, some day?'

Theo bristled and shook his head. 'If I'm honest? No. I like my life as it is right now. Uncomplicated and free. I don't need anyone else to worry about.'

He sounded terse. But what right did she have to be upset by that? She barely knew Theo. She understood what had been driving Jen, though. The pursuit of happiness. The dream. Lots of little girls grew up reading about princesses and their magical love stories, how one day their prince would come. And when everyone around you seemed to be settling down and finding that happiness you so desperately sought yourself… Well, it did things to you. It made you hungry for what you wanted and sometimes you made poor choices in trying to find it. Attached yourself to the wrong type of people.

Jen had done so. As had Sophie.

But people were entitled to want different things. Not everybody could want the same destination in life.

She'd thought Connor wanted the same things as her.

But she'd discovered much too late that they'd had different dreams about the future. Here she was, towards the end of her pregnancy, looking forward to being a mother and settling down, raising her child in a home full of love, and yet Theo, who was roughly the same age, wanted the exact opposite. A life of freedom where the only person he had to look after was himself.

Was that selfish of him? Or wise? Because every time she'd got involved with someone it had led to heartbreak. *Her* heartbreak. She'd not even been able to rely on her parents, and they were the two people in the whole wide world a person should be able to trust the most. If they could let you down, why wouldn't everyone else?

'Good for you,' she said now, as if she understood. But to be truly honest she didn't—not really. All Sophie wanted was to be loved. Unconditionally. And she wanted to love someone back with a love that was so deep and so passionate. She wanted to share her life with someone who would make her laugh and smile and cry…someone who would move her…someone who would hold her and comfort her and protect her.

Theo wanted none of that. But what pleasure was there in a life lived alone?

Angrily she ripped open the packet of red liquorice that Theo had bought her and took a huge bite of one long string. The sweetness, the taste, was a loving caress within her mouth, and made her feel a little bit better. But as she drove away from Diana's house, she tried to decipher why Theo's life choices should make her feel so unsettled…

CHAPTER THREE

THEO STOOD UNDER the shower, letting the hot water hit his face and run down his body. It had been a long day, which had gone wrong the moment they'd attended that first shout, where they'd found Jen—his ex-girlfriend.

He'd tried to be polite when talking about her to Sophie. He hadn't wanted to come across as someone who told tales when the other person wasn't around to defend themselves, but somehow, since that call, he'd sensed that Sophie seemed a little different. A bit brusquer in her dealings with him. A bit more tense. Less willing to crack a joke with him.

They'd attended a call to a fire, where it had been reported there was someone still stuck in a house. That had turned out to be untrue, but they'd waited at a safe distance as the fire brigade had put out the flames and he'd tried to engage Sophie in conversation.

'Do you get called to many fires?' he'd asked.

'Some.'

Sophie had been looking at the house, chewing on her liquorice, watching the flames as they rose higher out of the hole in the roof where part of it had collapsed. All around it the fire officers had been working frantically, hoses positioned strategically.

'I guess you've seen some terrible things?'

'It's part of the job.'

She had been abrupt. Brisk. Still not looking at him.

He had started to feel he'd done something wrong and had tried to work out what. Had it been something to do with meeting Jen? Was Sophie angry at the way he'd treated her? Spoken about her? Why? Was it a female thing?

'I guess you have to learn coping strategies to deal with the stress,' he'd said.

She'd said nothing for a moment. Then, 'You can ask for counselling if you need it.'

'Have *you* ever needed it?'

She'd looked at him then. Shaken her head. Chewed her liquorice. 'No.'

Plumes of grey-black smoke had billowed into the sky overhead, turning everything grey. The whole street had come out to watch the fire, huddling their loved ones closer to each other behind the safety lines taped up by the fire crew.

Theo had watched their faces. Seen the relief, the gratitude that it wasn't them that this had happened to, and also the guilt at feeling such gratitude, the curiosity and the need to see the terrible thing that was happening.

Sophie had been dumped, Marty had said. But she hadn't mentioned the father of her child once. In fact, she'd barely told him anything about herself except for the fact that she lived alone. He could be totally barking up the wrong tree, but what if she felt that she'd once tried to give everything to a prospective romance, but the guy hadn't? She'd said she lived alone, but what did that actually mean?

'Do you have someone? Someone special?' he'd asked,

glancing once more at the families behind them, as if thinking of them.

Sophie had pursed her lips as if considering her answer. 'Depends what you mean by "special".'

'What about the father of your baby?'

Sophie finally turned to look at him and gave him a wry look. 'He wasn't ready for commitment. He wanted to be free from responsibility. Said it would be all too much for him, having a child. That he still felt like a child himself. He couldn't *wait* to get away from me. Good riddance, I say. Best I found out sooner, rather than later.'

So, he had guessed right. He'd left Jen when she'd wanted more and the baby's father had left Sophie when *she'd* wanted more. Needed more from him. She felt abandoned and she probably figured Theo to be the same kind of man.

But he didn't feel the same as this other man. He couldn't imagine he'd be so irresponsible as to get a woman pregnant and then walk away! He didn't particularly *want* the responsibility of a child, but if he made one then he'd damn well do the right thing! Whoever the father of Sophie's baby was, he was a different kind of man entirely, and Theo definitely felt they couldn't be compared. Their situations were different.

But he hadn't known how to say that there and then, as they'd watched the fire. Sophie was obviously still hurting, no matter how much she pretended she was fine, and he'd wondered how raw the pain was.

Pregnancies lasted nine months, if they were carried to full term, and if Sophie had found out about the pregnancy when she was around two months, then the father of her child had only recently left her. Within the last year. Was she getting more and more scared as the birth loomed? Had she imagined having someone to hold her hand as she went into labour? The father?

Now she knew she would have to face labour and the birth alone. Raise a child alone. And what about her career? It was going to be difficult for her to juggle the two. He didn't know her very well, but from what he did know, he thought she'd give it her all.

The water felt good on his neck and shoulders as he turned under the spray, and he allowed it to pound down on the tense muscles in his back too.

He hadn't known what to say to Sophie to reassure her that he was nothing like her baby's father. That even though he wasn't a man who sought out responsibility, who wanted his life to remain free and unencumbered by complicated relationships and burdens, he was still a good guy. Honourable and kind and trustworthy.

Perhaps if I can't tell her, I can show her.

He would show her what a good guy he was. That even though he was a man who didn't want to settle down yet, she could still depend on him. That he could be there for her—not just as her student, but as a great colleague and an amazing friend.

Relationships between a man and a woman didn't all have to be about sex or love. He liked her. *Really* liked her. It wouldn't be hard at all. And, even though he thought she was an incredibly attractive woman, the romantic element wouldn't be a problem because he would never get involved with her in that way.

She was about to be a mother. A single mother. All they could have together was friendship.

Sophie woke still feeling tired after a difficult disturbed night's sleep. The baby had tossed and turned for hours, poking and prodding at her internal organs—more often than not her bladder, meaning she'd had to keep getting up and going for a wee. It was as if the baby was testing her perimeter for weaknesses.

'You'll find your way out one day. Just not yet, okay?' she said as she rubbed at her abdomen and yawned.

Getting out of bed proved to be a bit of a problem. Her pelvis really ached, especially down low at the front, so she took things slowly as she headed downstairs to get breakfast.

In the kitchen, she grabbed some juice and some cereal and, not for the first time, noticed Connor's favourite bowl, still sitting at the bottom of the stack at the back of the cupboard. He'd forgotten to take it when he left and she kept meaning to throw it out, but something made her keep it.

Why? He was hardly going to come back now, was he? He'd made it quite clear that a future with her and their baby was not the kind of future he'd envisaged for himself. Not yet, anyway.

'I do want kids, Soph, just not now! We're too young! I'm just getting started in my career!'

Nice to know that his job prospects came before she did. Before their *child* did.

Sophie was used to feeling second-best—even third-best, at times. She'd always been damned well determined that her own child would never feel that way—and what had happened? Connor had dumped them both. Her child wasn't even born yet, and he hadn't considered either of them important enough to remain on his radar.

His desertion had made her feel as if *she* was the one who had let her child down by not being able to keep its father. Not being good enough. But she was damned if he was going to make her feel that way.

Her daughter would see a strong mother. A resilient mother. Not one held back by the tragedy of a lost love the way her own mother had been.

Sophie's daughter would need her. Love her. Want her. Be proud of her. Rely on her.

Until she became a surly teenager, knowing her luck.

At least I'm good at my job. I help people. I save lives. I make a difference. People might not want to stick around me, but I make them live another day if I can.

Whilst she waited for her kettle to boil she grabbed a piece of liquorice from the packet that Theo had bought her yesterday. It made her think of him. Of her reaction to him when he'd first walked into the ambulance station. The way he could make her laugh. The way he often made her smile. How hot he was, with that body, those perfect teeth, that hypnotic smile that just made her want to stare at him and stare at him until the trance was broken.

But the things Jen had said… The things *he'd* said… They had confirmed that he was just like Connor, only better-looking, which made it all the more disappointing, because those thoughts were like a bucket of ice.

Just once, would it hurt for her to come across a guy who didn't think of his own needs first? Someone selfless and giving and loving and trustworthy? Someone you could trust one hundred per cent to turn up and not let you down? Someone you just knew would be there for you no matter what?

Was it too much to ask?

She took her coffee upstairs, grimacing slightly at the ache in her pelvis as she climbed the stairs. What was that? Had she got out of bed wrong? Strained a muscle? She hoped it wasn't the beginning of that SPD thing she'd heard about... Symphisis pubis dysfunction was a condition caused by stiffness in the pelvic joints either at the front or the back. It wasn't harmful to the baby, but it could be incredibly painful for the mother, and make it difficult to get around.

She'd been doing fine up till now. She'd felt as fit as a fiddle. Some days she barely remembered she was pregnant until she got home and noticed her ankles beginning to swell, and then she'd sit with her feet up, watching a show on the television.

Sophie was loath to take painkillers. Besides, it was probably temporary anyway, and she needed to get dressed and get to work. Once there, she'd forget anyway, as her patients' needs and concerns always superseded her own.

It didn't take her long to get ready, and she was soon out of her house and on her way to the station. The sun was out in full force today, and she could tell it was going to be a really hot day. The sky was a beautiful azure blue, and totally cloudless, and she had a really pleasant drive to work, with her radio on, singing away.

As she pulled in, she saw Theo, and noticed her heart beat a little faster. How many times was that going to happen? When would her body get used to the sight of seeing him and calm the hell down?

She grabbed her bottle of water and saw him wave at her from across the car park, and then he began striding over.

'Okay, Sophie, play it cool,' she told herself, swinging her legs out of her car and trying to stand up.

The pain in her pelvis shot an ice pick through her and she knew she must have winced or gasped.

'Hey, you okay?' He was at her side in an instant, worry etched into his face as he grabbed her hand and arm, helping her stand straight.

Embarrassed, with her skin burning from his touch, his proximity, the way he seemed always to be there for her, she pulled herself free and took a step back. 'I'm fine! Honestly. Just a bit stiff today, that's all.'

'You're sure?'

'Of course I'm sure.'

He didn't look as if he totally believed her. But that was his problem. Not hers.

'Come on. We need to get a move on.' She pushed past him, trying to saunter casually into the station, but someone perhaps ought to have told her that an eight-and-a-half-months pregnant woman couldn't *saunter* anywhere.

He caught up with her and walked alongside. 'You looked like you were in pain. Were you having a contraction? Braxton Hicks?'

Sophie was irritated with herself for giving that impression, but she laughed it off. 'It was just a twinge.'

'My sisters all got twinges like that towards the end of their pregnancies. It's the body preparing itself for labour. But if you're having problems you need to tell your midwife—there are things they can suggest to help.'

She stopped in her tracks and faced him, amused, her hands on her child-bearing hips. 'Are you a fully-fledged paramedic?'

He looked directly at her, as if wondering where this was going. 'No, I'm not.'

'Are you a doctor?'

'No.'

'An actual midwife?'

He shook his head, smiling now. 'No.'

'Then you're not qualified to give me any advice. Now, I'm perfectly fine—so jump to it and complete those duty checks!'

He smiled at her as she started to walk away. He called after her. 'Are you an army major?'

Sophie stopped and turned. She raised her eyebrows, knowing the game was about to be played on her. She smiled. 'No.'

'A drill sergeant?'

'No.'

He saluted. 'You certainly sound like one.'

She couldn't help it. She imagined herself standing in front of a line of raw recruits, bellowing orders at them, telling them off for stepping out of line. And Theo looked so cute in his paramedic's uniform, saluting her as if she was his captain or something. She smirked. And when he laughed, she found herself laughing, too.

'I guess I asked for that. Honestly, Theo!' She gave him a gentle shove and he laughed again, playfully rubbed at his arm. 'You do make me smile.'

He laughed, his face full of warmth and kindness and charm. 'Good.'

And just for a moment she found herself staring at him, wondering what it might be like to kiss him. To have him hold her. Touch her.

What the hell am I doing?

She turned away, annoyed with herself. Because she'd begun to stare—and what was the point of that? The wishing? The hoping? Theo was like Connor. He didn't want commitment, he didn't need the burden of another man's child, and he most certainly was not interested in her!

* * *

They were just about to drive away from the station when one of the other paramedics, Ross, flagged them down.

'Hey, guys. Just wanted to give you a reminder about tonight. The Wheatsheaf? Seven-thirty?'

Sophie frowned, then realisation dawned. 'Of course! Your thirtieth birthday party. Don't worry, I hadn't forgotten.'

Ross smiled at her. 'No, of course not. I'm sure baby brain isn't a real thing. Why don't you come along, Theo? The more the merrier.'

Theo was happy to be included in the celebrations. 'That'd be great. Sure!'

Sophie turned to him. 'Oh, you don't have to if you don't want to. I know you've probably got assignments and essays to write for uni.'

'You make it sound like you don't want me there. I can take a night off.' He leaned forward, past Sophie, to shake Ross's hand. 'I'll see you there.'

Ross nodded and began walking away.

Theo glanced across at Sophie. 'Will you need a lift? I'd be happy to pick you up and take you home again.'

She shook her head. 'You don't have to do that. You'll want to enjoy yourself, and if you're driving you can't have a drink.'

Was it her nature to push all men away, or just him? He'd hate to think it was only him having this effect on her.

'That's okay. I don't need to drink to have fun. It's no problem. Let me pick you up. I think you mentioned you live in Berrylands, right? It's on my way to The Wheatsheaf—it makes practical sense.'

'Oh…well…um…thanks. That's very practical of you.'

'No problem. Ready to go?'

She stared back at him. 'I am.'

He watched as she picked up the radio and told Control that they were ready for duty.

'That's great, six zero two. We have a job that's just come in. Sounds like a hypoglycaemic attack. Thirty-one-year-old woman. Flat Eight, Paradise Heights, Ewell Road, Tolworth.'

'Show us as being on our way, Control. Six zero two out.'

'Blues and twos?' Theo asked.

She smiled. 'Hit the switch.'

He fastened his seatbelt as Sophie drove them out of the ambulance station. Once again, he marvelled at the powerful engine of the car as she roared down the A3, smoothly passing the vehicles that got out of their way. She showed a brief moment of irritation when someone in the fast lane didn't bother looking in their rear-view mirror and didn't get out of the way for a few seconds, but eventually the driver saw them, raised his hand in apology, and pulled into the middle lane to let them pass.

'Tell me what you know about hypoglycaemia,' Sophie said as she drove.

He racked his brain for facts. 'Er…low blood sugar… mainly affects diabetics.'

'Signs and symptoms?'

'Turning pale, sweating, shaking, fast heartbeat, confusion…patients could pass out.'

'How do we treat?'

'Try and get them to drink or eat something sugary. Test their blood sugar. Give oxygen if conscious?'

'And if they're unconscious?'

'Recovery position and monitor.'

'Good. You're doing well.'

'I've got a good teacher.'

She smiled at the compliment.

Ahead of them the Tolworth Tower loomed large. They weren't far away now.

As they pulled up outside Paradise Heights Theo got out of the car quickly and grabbed the jump bag, then waited for Sophie to get out. She was most definitely struggling a little today, and he wondered if maybe she ought to take it easy a little bit. She had to be very late in her pregnancy now. Why hadn't she stopped working? He was all for women working until they needed to stop, but surely she had to be feeling the effects of being so heavily pregnant? His sisters had used to get swollen ankles and backache and nausea if they'd tried to do too much.

There was a flight of stone steps up the side of the house to flat number eight. They both climbed it and a man opened the door as they reached the top.

'She's in here. I've given her a fizzy drink and a chocolate bar.'

They followed the man inside the dark flat and Theo quickly took in the shabbiness of the place. There were no proper curtains up at the window, just a stained sheet held by pegs to a curtain rail. No carpet to speak of, only a tatty rug in front of the electric fire that was fixed to the wall. The air was stale and musty.

On a torn couch a woman lay, half propped up by cushions, looking pale and shaky. 'I'm feeling a bit better, I think.'

'What's your name?' Sophie asked.

'Melanie.'

'And how old are you, Melanie?'

Theo already knew the answer. It had come in with

the call description. Sophie must be checking that Melanie was thinking clearly. He'd heard that some diabetics could be quite muddled after losing consciousness.

'Thirty-one,' said Melanie.

'And what's the date?'

Melanie thought for a moment. 'I never know the date. Ask me another one.'

Sophie smiled. 'Who's the Prime Minister?'

The patient told them.

'Good. Now, I'm just going to let Theo check your blood sugar and your SATs for me, okay?'

'Okay.'

Theo was thrilled that Sophie was giving him an opportunity to do the assessments on the patient himself. It showed she trusted him, and he liked that.

It soon became clear that Melanie was doing much better and her levels were almost back to normal.

'I don't think there's any need to take you into hospital,' Sophie said. 'Are you usually good on your blood sugars?'

Melanie nodded. 'That's the one thing I am in control of. But my parents aren't very well. I spent all of last night there and I simply forgot to eat.'

'Well, you won't do that again, hopefully.'

The patient laughed. 'Definitely not! I don't want to feel that way again—it was horrible. Thank God I've got Simon here to look after me.'

When Theo and Sophie got back to the car, Theo couldn't help but ask the question. 'You say you live alone, but you must have someone you can call to look after you? You know...like family? When you really need someone.'

Sophie looked awkward. 'Who do *you* have?'

'If I needed to call on someone, I have three younger sisters, all desperate to stick their noses into my private life.'

He looked at her expectantly. Surely she had *someone*? Surely she wasn't really alone? Or was she a private individual who didn't think she needed to share details of her life with her student?

'I have friends,' she said.

'Friends?' He pushed down the boot lid and went round to his side of the car to get inside.

Sophie didn't look at him as she pulled her seatbelt around her large pregnant abdomen.

'What about the baby's father?'

'What about him?'

'Well, surely, he must want to—?'

'Connor gave up every right to pretend that he's a responsible, reliable person when he walked away from us.'

Theo felt bad for upsetting her. 'I'm sorry. I shouldn't have pushed. I was just... Look, not all men are the same as him. You can rely on me, if that helps at all.'

Sophie laughed out loud, as if what he'd just said was the most ridiculous thing she'd ever heard in her life. 'I thought you didn't want any responsibilities?'

Theo smarted. 'I'm not suggesting we move in together. I'm saying I can be someone who's good in a crisis. Someone you could call.'

And he was. He was proud of that fact. He'd stepped up to look after his sisters when they'd needed it. Protected them. Raised them. He'd stepped up in the army. Protected the men in his troop. And he was the kind of man who was always there for his friends if they needed it.

His relationship with Jen had been moving at warp

speed when he'd only ever wanted some casual fun. He'd thought he'd made it clear to Jen at the beginning what he was prepared to give—but, like most of the girls he'd dated, she'd said she understood and then tried to change his mind. Change *him*.

Sophie shouldn't judge him over one relationship that had gone sour.

He wouldn't mind helping Sophie if she needed it. They were hardly going to be an item, and as a friend, he could be there for her if needed.

'You're my teacher. My friend. And you said you could call on your friends. I *am* reliable. If I wasn't, do you think I would turn up every day? If I was unreliable, don't you think I would have dropped out of the army earlier? Given up on my paramedic degree? I know how to commit to people I'm friends with, and I'm not a cold-hearted bastard, no matter what you may think.'

The cynical smile dropped from her face and she grew serious. 'Theo, you don't have to prove anything to me. We'll be together a month—no more than that—and there'll be no need for us to keep in touch after you've finished your placement. I don't expect to, either. You'll forget me and get on with your life. Just as you want.'

Did he detect a strange tone in her words? Her lack of belief in him saddened him. He was nothing like Connor. No, he didn't want responsibilities—but he was nothing like the father of her baby.

Stubbornness made him add, 'I'd like us to keep in touch.'

She started the engine. 'Fine. But time will tell what you'll do, won't it?'

For some reason Theo was feeling inordinately irritated that she thought so little about his level of commitment.

I'm a good guy!

'You know what? I'm going to make you a bet.'

'A bet?' She raised an eyebrow.

'That I can be relied upon. That I can look out for you. That I can be there if you need me. That I'll stick around longer than this placement and, hell, even hold your hand in hospital as you give birth, if you want. Because that's what friends do.'

She laughed out loud. 'I don't think I want you by my side as I give birth!'

'Why not? I was with one of my sisters as she delivered little Leo. Not at the business end, I might add, but I was there. I'm not squeamish. I'm a good guy, Sophie. I'm not like—' He stopped himself from saying it.

'The father of my child?' She smiled as if she wanted to believe him but didn't. 'You'll never be able to do it,' she said, sounding quite sure of herself. 'I'm sure you're a good friend, but a guy like you doesn't want to hang around with a single mother who has a newborn baby in tow. Especially one that isn't his.'

'Wow... I had no idea you thought so little of me.'

She glanced at him, looking a little guilty about what she'd just said. 'All right, Mr Finch! I hereby take your ridiculous most-definitely-will-fail bet that you be my best friend for...let's say one year? That should be plenty of time for you to get fed up and leave me behind on my lonesome. Especially when there's a screaming baby attached to me and my house stinks of dirty nappies. You want me calling you in the dead of the night, crying because I can't get my baby to latch on and I don't know what else to do? You're on!'

That sounded terrifying. But it was too late to back

out now. He'd made a big thing of this and she'd called him on it.

'Deal!' He held out his hand, determined to show that he was serious. He knew he couldn't fail. But he also knew that she thought he would.

Well, he was looking forward to proving her wrong.

He was going to be the best friend anyone could ever have.

Screaming newborn baby or not.

CHAPTER FOUR

NOTHING FITTED. NOTHING in her goddamned wardrobe fitted! How long had it been since she'd last been on a night out? Months. When she'd not been pregnant and had been able to fit into all those figure-hugging dresses that had caught Connor's eye in the first place.

His favourite had been the red one with the spaghetti straps. It had a side zip, and she could still remember the look on his face when he'd first seen her in it. In fact, he'd been unable to wait to get her out of it.

She distinctly remembered that passionate encounter at a friend's house! Whilst everyone else had celebrated Kim and Joe's first wedding anniversary downstairs, she and Connor had been making out—up against a wall, no less! It had been as if he couldn't get enough of her, and afterwards he'd not let go of her hand, chatting with the other guests and glancing at her with a secret smile.

Back then, he'd certainly had the ability to make her head spin. Connor had seemed exciting and full of drive. She should have realised that that drive she'd loved so much about him only applied to his dreams. He wanted the top job, the promotions, the parties, the sex with the prettiest girl. And she had been the prettiest girl. Until she'd got pregnant and suddenly Connor had begun to back away. Almost as if she'd horrified him. Terrified him?

She couldn't put that dress on tonight. It wouldn't fit. And even if she did try to squeeze into it, the look on Theo's face would be one of hilarity. He'd probably curl into a ball on the floor, laughing so much—because, hey, friends took the mickey out of each other, didn't they?

Sophie slid hanger after hanger from one side of her wardrobe to the other, looking for something that was suitable for her growing abdomen and also looked as if it was party wear.

Why didn't I think to go shopping?

As she got to her last few pieces of clothing Sophie's mood was truly beginning to sour at the prospect of turning up at the party in her stretchy leggings and a tee shirt. And then she spotted, on the last hanger, a bottle-green maxi dress that she'd forgotten all about.

Perfect!

In fact, it was so perfect, and so unexpected, she almost cried in relief at finding it. Now she could look forward to going out tonight! To showing that she might be at the end of her pregnancy and look like a beached whale, but she could still pull off some style.

She took the dress out of her wardrobe, checking to make sure it was clean, and hung it up on the outside of her wardrobe door as she sat in front of the mirror and tried to decide what to do with her hair. She wanted to make it look as if she'd made an effort for Ross's birthday without going overboard and making all her colleagues think she was on a date with her hunk of a student.

Relationships between colleagues weren't frowned upon in the ambulance service. There were even one or two married couples who worked together that she knew.

It was rather that relationships weren't...*encouraged*... And she most certainly didn't want to do any encouraging of her own. There was a line with Theo. One she'd drawn all by herself. And she was determined, no matter how attracted she was to him, not to step over it.

What was she going to do with Theo? He'd promised her support and reliability, but she knew he'd only made that promise so that he didn't lose face.

And she knew that if she'd not been about to become a new mother, but had instead been a hot single woman whom Theo had asked to take to a party, she'd be going full war paint mode—shaved legs, painted nails, perfume, skin-tight dress, heels...

Fancy matching underwear...

She almost felt resentment that she wasn't that hot young single woman any more, because if she was then Theo would be just her type. The guy who looked amazing. The one she always fell for, even knowing it would end badly, because that was what happened to her all the time.

Men like Theo didn't stick around for women like Sophie. They left her. Like Connor had. Like her father had. And all the other men who had been in her life looking for some quick and simple fun.

Way to put a downer on the night, Soph.

Perhaps she should wear her hair up? A few sparkly clips... Nothing fancy. Something to make herself feel good. This didn't have to be about attracting a man—it could be about making herself feel amazing. And why shouldn't she?

She opened her make-up bag. She didn't normally wear it, but tonight she would.

Lipstick? A small bit of mascara? Oh! And a squirt of this perfume will do.

She took off her bathrobe and slipped into the dress. It felt so nice not to have any constriction around her waist. There was a small pair of kitten heels that would go well with the dress, so she put those on, and found a silver bracelet and a long, low necklace, too.

There. Do I pass muster? Effort made, but not too much... I want to have some dignity, don't I? This is a party, after all.

She twisted this way and that in front of her full-length mirror and had to admit she looked pretty good! For a pregnant heffalump, anyway.

The ring of her doorbell told her that Theo had arrived.

Theo. Her new support system.

Her heart sped up a little at the thought of him seeing her. At work it was okay. She could hide behind her uniform and not be seen as a woman. But this was different. They wouldn't be working together tonight, and their relationship had shifted into this new dynamic. This friendship.

Theo was funny, incredibly attractive and *single*. And he was taking her out—as a friend—to a party. They weren't attending a call, or an emergency. They would be chatting. Laughing. Sharing jokes.

Oh, please, God, don't let there be any dancing!

Sophie loved to dance. It made her happy. But to do so with Theo...? She could handle being close to him when he sat next to her in the car as her student and he was learning, but tonight he would be her equal and the rules would be different.

The doorbell rang again.

I'd better answer it, or he might think I've gone without him.

Could she do that? Pretend not to be in? But what would the point of that be? He'd still find her at the party. She couldn't ignore this. She had to get her head together and calm down and just remember that he was fulfilling a bet. Nothing more. He'd be full of enthusiasm at the beginning, but he'd fall away as everyone else did—and, hey, that was fine. She was used to it. She would cope, as she always did.

So why did a small part of her hope so badly that he wouldn't?

What would her life look like with Theo permanently in it?

What if this bet truly worked out and he turned out to be the best friend she'd ever had?

Nah. Not possible. Think of what Jen said. Theo bails.

'I won't be a minute!' she called out. There. She'd let him know she was here. That she hadn't run out on him.

Why am I so nervous? It's just Theo! He's nothing to me. This isn't a date.

That didn't help. In fact she just felt more nervous.

There was nothing else to do but open the door and let him in. She would just open it and pretend to look for something in her handbag. Not actually make eye contact, pretend the evening was nothing… She'd walk away from him and fetch her mobile from the kitchen counter top, and then he wouldn't compliment her, or fib about how beautiful she looked. She would try to ignore, or derail, all that awkward stuff.

Because, let's face it, I'll be coming home alone tonight.

Sophie walked towards the door, fully intending to act

casual. But as she got closer to the door her nerves really kicked in and the baby began kicking too.

She placed a quivering hand on her belly and pulled the door open.

Theo stood there, looking so incredibly handsome and model-like in dark jeans and a fitted black shirt that he almost took her breath away. It wasn't right that a man should look so beautiful. So attractive. So edible.

'Wow! You look…' He seemed lost for words, too. 'Beautiful!'

Sophie blushed, hoping it was just her cheeks colouring and not her neck and chest going blotchy. Something about his reaction really pleased her. She might feel as if she was the size of an elephant, and she had begun, on occasion, to waddle like a duck, but it was thrilling to discover that a handsome man like Theo thought she looked beautiful—no matter how many animals she thought she resembled.

Of course he could be lying, but…she'd take the compliment anyway.

'Thanks. That's very sweet of you. You scrub up quite well yourself.'

From behind his back, he pulled a perfectly pink single rose. 'This is for you.'

A flower? She hadn't expected that. She lifted the bloom to her nose and it smelt heavenly. But she had to force herself to remember that this wasn't a romantic overture. He probably felt he couldn't turn up at her door empty-handed. It was just a thing. A token. It didn't *mean* anything.

'I'll put that in water.'

She took it through to the kitchen, aware that her heart was racing like mad as she fiddled with a small bud vase, trying her hardest not to be clumsy and smash it all over the floor. She filled the vase and added the rose, then collected her handbag and went back to the front door.

Theo still stood there, smiling, and he held out his arm for her to slip hers into. 'Shall we?'

Sophie smiled. 'Let's go.'

Why the hell did I let my pride force me into that stupid bet?

Sophie looked stunning. Simply stunning. Wholesome. Womanly. Full of curves. Her dress emphasised many pleasing features—the length of her neck, her delicate shoulder bones, an enticing décolletage—but most of all it enhanced the colour of her eyes, the way she looked at him. Demure. Nervous. With a shy smile.

That smile was *everything*.

The bloom of her belly beneath the dress had not sent him running in the other direction, as he suspected he would if he'd met her in a club or somewhere. Her pregnancy had seemed to draw him in. Draw him towards her, accelerating his desire to protect her and claim her.

He'd had to fight the yearning to move closer, to feel her baby bump against him, draw her lips to his…

Instead he'd presented her with the rose that he'd almost not brought in case she misconstrued it as something else.

They were hardly going on a date, and he'd made it quite clear that he wasn't a guy looking to get into a relationship. But, seeing how amazing she looked, feeling how much he suddenly wanted her, he was afraid for the first time since meeting her. So far his relationships with women had started well, but they always went sour when the women realised he didn't want to progress things as they did. And Sophie was a prime example of a woman who would want to progress things.

She was pregnant. About to be a mother. If she was looking for a man, she would be looking for someone to be a permanent fixture in her life and her baby's, and that wasn't the future for him.

He'd done all that. He'd taken on the responsibility for children who weren't his own—his sisters. When his father had abandoned them…when their mother had got sick. He'd become the man of the house, he'd looked after everyone, he'd kept them safe, fed them, clothed them. He didn't want to do that again. Because at the end of the day even his sisters had left him. Flown the nest, found men of their own, started families, leaving him behind.

He told himself that this was what he wanted. Freedom. And besides, Sophie had made it clear herself that there was to be a distance between them. She showed no signs of being attracted to him. Well, no overt ones. He'd caught her stealing glances at him when she'd thought he wasn't looking. Caught her considering him…sizing him up, almost. He was used to women looking at him. He knew they found him attractive. But relationships were built on more than looks, and neither of them wanted to progress something here.

Giving her the rose had given him time to recover as she'd turned to take it inside, and he'd stood there on her doorstep, sucking in some deep breaths and having a quiet word with himself as she found a vase.

Get a grip, man. Seriously.

By the time she returned, he'd plastered on a confident smile, and he offered her his arm and walked her out to his car—which he'd had cleaned after his shift.

He walked her to the passenger door and, like a gentleman, opened it for her.

'Thanks.'

'My pleasure.' He walked round to his side of the vehicle, trying to steady his breathing.

Normally Sophie was in the driving seat.

Tonight would be different.

The radio was playing some nice songs and the windows were down for their short drive in this summer evening to The Wheatsheaf, where Ross was holding his thirtieth birthday party. Theo managed to find a space in the car park and pulled into it.

'Stay there,' he said, getting out and going around to the passenger door and opening it. He held out his hand. 'My lady.'

Sophie laughed. 'Thank you, kind sir.'

It felt good, even if for that brief moment, to have her hand in his. But once she was standing and had gathered her bag he let go and walked with her into a private room at the pub, where they were greeted and cheered by a large group of off-duty paramedics who'd already had one or two drinks, by the sound of things.

They went over to the bar. 'What would you like to drink?' he asked.

'Oh, that's okay. I can buy my own.'

'Let me get these first ones.'

She nodded. 'All right, thank you. A fresh orange juice with lemonade, please.'

'Coming right up.'

He ordered two, as he was driving, and then they went to find a seat with their colleagues and friends, before heading over to the small buffet, where they could get sandwiches and sausage rolls and crisps.

It was a good crowd. Raucous. Loud. Full of tall tales and laughter. Music played in the far corner, where a DJ was mixing some tunes and people were dancing. One or two of their colleagues were discussing shouts they'd been on years ago, stories full of humour and disbelief at what some people got up to in the name of fun.

He found his gaze often drawn to Sophie. To the play of lights across her face, the way she laughed, the way she told stories of her own.

'I got called once to a man who had had an epileptic fit in an amusement arcade. I was working with another paramedic, on an ambulance, and we drove there like bats out of hell as an update on the call had come through, saying that the man was unconscious on the floor. Well, we got there, and found him lying on the carpet next to the one-armed bandits. He was just coming to. But next to him was this woman playing the slots. We asked her if she'd seen what had happened and she said she had—because she was his wife! She told us that he was sensitive to flashing lights and would come round eventually. So, we crouch down and get him sitting up, and as we do some coins fall out of his pocket. I scooped them up and passed them to his wife for safekeeping, and she thanked me and fed them straight into the machines! Seriously! If you know your husband is a photo-sensitive epileptic, then why take him to an arcade? It's ridiculous!'

And so the evening went on, with each paramedic trying to outdo the other with tales from work.

Theo found himself laughing and enjoying himself, but the thing he liked the most was the way Sophie would keep turning to look at him and they would smile at each other as if…

As if what?

Each time she looked at him like that he felt something he couldn't define. It was confusing.

But then everyone decided to get up and dance before the night was over and he found himself holding out his hand to her. 'One dance can't hurt.'

'I'd love to. But I weigh half a ton! It'll probably be safer for your toes if I stay sitting down.'

'I survived a car running over my foot once. I'm sure we'll be fine. Come on!' And he took her hand and escorted her to the dance floor.

There was a fun number on, but he kept it low-energy, holding her hand and slowly twirling her round now and then, like a ballerina in a jewellery box. Then he pulled her towards him and they danced together, until the DJ announced that they were going to end the night with something slow.

That wasn't their jam. They were friends. They didn't need to slow-dance together.

But he felt awkward about walking her back to her seat. That would seem dismissive. So he decided to ignore all his loud, screaming thoughts, telling him to stop what he was doing right now, and he took Sophie's hand in his and laid his other hand on the small of her back.

He could feel her baby belly pressed up against him as they swayed in time with the music. He felt tense. Too aware of how close she was. How good she smelt. Her perfume was heavenly. Not overpowering, but light and floral.

He made himself relax. It was just a dance. A way to end the evening. He smiled at a sensation against his stomach. 'I can feel your daughter kicking me. Do you think she's telling me to back off?'

Sophie rested her head upon his shoulder. 'Maybe.

Or she could just be telling me she wants something decent to eat.'

The buffet that the pub had provided was practically all gone. 'I could get you a bag of pork scratchings,' Theo said, 'but she'd probably be better having something more substantial.'

'I'd kill for some fish and chips.'

'You're really hungry?'

'I'm starving.'

That was it. His gentlemanly instincts kicked in. 'If we go now, we can pick up some proper food on the way home—before they close.'

She nodded. 'Sounds good.'

'Come on, then.'

He kept her hand in his, almost without thinking about it, as he led her off the dance floor. They said their goodbyes to Ross and the rest of the team, citing the excuse that pregnant feet needed to rest and saying that they hoped he'd had a good birthday.

Theo tried to ignore the cheers and catcalls they received as they walked away together, but both of them were laughing as they emerged into the cooler night air.

'What are they like, huh?'

He opened the door for her once again, waiting for her to be safe inside the vehicle before getting in and driving them to a local fish and chip shop. He bought them both food and they sat in the car, eating with tiny wooden forks.

'Oh, my God, this is just so good!' said Sophie, closing her eyes in ecstasy.

The aroma in the car was one of salt and vinegar, but he had to admit it was very good. Just what he'd needed after a few hours of nothing but orange juice and some snacks.

'Agreed. Baby happy?'

'Mmm!' She laughed and popped another chip into her mouth.

He'd had a good night. It was funny, really. He spent ages pursuing fun and excitement with his friends—rock-climbing, white water rafting, paintballing, going to clubs—but the simplest of pleasures could come from the simplest of things. Good food with a friend who made him smile. He didn't do that enough.

He couldn't remember the last time he'd just sat and had a takeaway with a woman. He'd certainly never done it with Jen, who had only considered food worthy if it was presented well in a five-star restaurant and would look good with perfect lighting in a photo. Usually her food had gone cold by the time she'd finished taking endless pictures, and so had his, because he didn't like to start his meal unless whoever he was with had started theirs. It was a manners thing.

He liked it that Sophie had no such high pretensions and was simply sitting next to him, clutching her bag of chips, with salt and grease all over her fingers.

'So, Theo, tell me—why did you join the army? Had you always wanted to?'

He thought about how best to answer. 'My father was in the army. He loved it. Sometimes I think he loved the army more than he loved us. I don't remember seeing him very often, but I do remember that when he did come back I had this feeling of…joy and wonder. Here was this man in uniform, fatigues, whatever…a *real* soldier—and he was my dad! I so wanted to be like him. I think… I think I thought it would help me understand him more if I became a soldier, too. That somehow he would know and it would bring him back to me.'

'Back to you? Is your father not around, then?'

He shook his head and scrunched up his empty bag. 'No. My father loved the adventure of travelling the world. We were just a port in a storm. One of many, it turned out.' He heard the bitterness in his voice.

Sophie frowned. 'I don't understand.'

'My father had not just a woman in every port, but *families*. Lots of affairs...lots of illegitimate children. It devastated my mother and she divorced him as soon as she realised. Then she got sick, so I very quickly became the man of the house, looking after my mum and my younger sisters. I really missed him coming home. I really missed having a dad. Once my sisters had flown the nest and I had no responsibilities, I joined the army in the hope that it would bring him back to me.'

'And did it?'

'No.' He smiled ruefully. 'As far as I know he's living with his latest girlfriend in Buenos Aires.'

'Don't you feel like turning up at his door and confronting him?'

He shook his head. No. 'Why would I chase after someone who doesn't want me?'

That must have struck a chord, because Sophie went silent. Thoughtful. And that was when he remembered that the baby's father—Connor—had not wanted Sophie or their child.

'It's a hard thing to accept,' she said. 'You give your all to someone and sometimes it's just not enough. Not what *they* want. It's like my mother. Whatever I did was never good enough to catch her attention. Never good enough to be important. You can't make someone love you, I guess.'

She scrunched up her own paper bag, all finished.

'No.'

He drove her home, taking her hand to help her out of the car and walking her up the path towards her house to make sure she got in safely.

'Well, I've had a lovely night, Theo. Thank you.'

He nodded and smiled. 'I have, too. It was fun. You've got a great bunch of friends, there.'

'Paramedics can be a better family than your real one sometimes.'

'The army's the same. I've got some good friends I'll have for a lifetime.'

She smiled. 'Well, thank you for bringing me home.'

'My pleasure. It's what friends do.' He smiled.

She reached into her bag for her keys. Paused. Turned and faced him. 'Do you want a coffee before you go?'

He thought about leaving. How he'd feel on the drive home.

Talking about his father always made him feel alone. And what she'd said about her mother had intrigued him. It sounded as if they'd both had a parent who was distracted by other, more interesting things.

It would be good to spend a few more minutes in Sophie's company. Chat to her... He liked her a lot. 'That'd be great—if you're not too tired?'

'I'm good. Come on in.'

He followed her into her home. It was warm and inviting, with some lovely bits of art on the walls—abstract pieces, awash with colour and vigour. He could imagine the artist just throwing paint at the canvas and then smudging a brush through it in insane strokes.

A black cat was curled up on a chair, and it opened one lazy green eye to assess him briefly before becoming bored.

'That's Magellan. He's the boss of this house. God knows how he'll react when I bring a screaming baby home. He likes his peace and quiet.'

Sophie stroked his head and he began to purr. She kicked off her shoes, groaning at the pleasure of being barefoot, and padded into the kitchen.

He followed her.

Sophie tossed her bag onto the table and grabbed a couple of mugs from the kitchen cupboard. 'Normal or decaf?'

'Whatever you're making.'

She smiled. 'Decaf it is. Take a seat.' She pointed at the kitchen table.

He sat and watched her move around her kitchen with ease. His gaze dropped to her belly. She clearly didn't have long left. Somehow, the dress she was wearing made her look a little bigger than she did when she wore her uniform. He figured it was because it was loose and flowing, but the sight of her blooming and glowing, filled with new life, made him smile.

'What's so funny?' she asked.

'Nothing. So, you're looking very…pregnant. You mentioned Magellan might not be ready for the baby. Are you, do you think?'

She let out a long breath. 'I think so. As much as I can be. I've got all the equipment in. Nappies, clothes, baby wipes, car seat, pram… Oh, and a cot upstairs that I've got to construct—which'll be fun, because I'm useless at following instructions. It'll probably look like a piece of torture equipment by the time I'm done with it.'

'Want me to take a look?'

'Oh, I couldn't ask you to do that!'

'It's no bother. I'm good with my hands.'

Did she blush at that? He thought she did.

He smiled. 'Good at making things,' he clarified. 'I could deconstruct a gun in less than ten seconds.'

She considered him, her head tilted to one side. 'What about putting it together again? Any spare parts left over?'

He laughed. 'Thankfully not. And it always worked again, too.'

'All right,' she said, passing him his mug of coffee. 'I'll let you do the cot.'

'Now?'

She shrugged her shoulders. 'If you want.'

'Lead the way.'

She led him upstairs and he kept his gaze on her bare feet, so that he wasn't staring at her bottom—even though he wanted to. He couldn't help it. He knew he was attracted to her. But she was out of bounds. He liked being with her—that was all.

But he hated saying goodbye to her each day, and then, tonight, he'd had one of the best nights he'd had in a long time—including some great fish and chips on the way home. He knew it was the person he'd spent the time with who counted, and there was something special about Sophie. He wanted to help her. Protect her. Care for her.

It was weird. He never usually felt like this. He could feel stirrings within himself that he'd not expected. It was probably because she was reminding him of how he'd felt when his sisters had got pregnant. It had been a very obvious sign that they were with other men now, and he wasn't needed any more. They were starting new lives. Moving on. And, although he'd dreamed of having his own freedom and being without responsibilities, it had been hard to take that step back and not interfere.

He was used to being a carer. Didn't like the letting go part. He couldn't help it. But sometimes he needed to remind himself that he didn't need to take on anyone else's issues—and Sophie had *plenty*.

But she was a beautiful woman. There would have been something wrong with him if he hadn't noticed. And her being pregnant wasn't putting him off the way it might have at the beginning, before he'd got to know her. The fact that he'd spent a week or more with her now made him feel as if he knew her quite well, and every day he liked her more and more.

Sophie led him into a small room. It was painted white. There was a rocking chair with a foot-rest in one corner, filled with stuffed animals in pale colours. There was a changing unit, piled high with folded baby clothes, and against the wall a large cardboard box—no doubt filled with the pieces of the cot.

'Is that it?'

She nodded, leaning in the doorway. 'You sure you want to do this now?'

'No time like the present. You could go into labour at any moment.'

'Are you saying I'm huge, Theo Finch?' She said it with an amused tone.

He smiled at her and raised his mug of coffee as if in salute. 'Hugely unprepared. What if you had the baby and came home with no cot to put her in? Would you leave her in her car seat whilst you tried to put it together?'

'I'd find a way of making it work.'

'I'm sure… But this is easier—and besides, all that's

waiting for me at home is my bed and the prospect of a day off tomorrow, so I can have a late night.'

He turned to open the box and missed the look on Sophie's face that spoke of her tumultuous thoughts.

'Thank you. Shall I leave you to it?' she said.

He turned to face her. 'You can talk to me, if you'd like. Here, let me move all those cuddly toys and you can put your feet up.'

He scooped up all the plushies in one go and set them down on the floor, away from where he'd be working. Sophie settled into the rocker with a sigh, resting her hands on her swollen abdomen.

Theo got busy pulling out all the pieces, locating the instructions and checking that he had all the screws, nuts and bolts needed for the project. The pack helpfully included an Allen key.

'Seems straightforward enough. If only life came with instructions…'

She laughed. 'We'd all screw up less.'

He gathered the first two pieces for assembly. 'When did you screw up?'

'When I chose the father of my baby.'

'Were you trying to get pregnant with Connor?'

Sophie shook her head. 'It was an accident.'

'Then you didn't know that he was a bad choice. You picked him as a partner—not a potential parent.'

'But I *thought* he'd be a good parent. How wrong could I be? Ouch! She's kicking me. Probably telling me off for bad-mouthing her father.'

'Can I?' He indicated that he'd like to touch her belly to feel the baby.

She blushed a delightful rose colour. 'Sure.'

He smiled back as she took his hand and guided it

over her bump to where the kicks were. He concentrated, waiting to feel something, and then—*bam!* A little kick. Right in the centre of the palm of his hand.

'Wow! She's strong.'

Sophie agreed. 'She is, isn't she?'

When he became aware that maybe her hand upon his and his hand upon her belly was perhaps a little more intimate than he'd been expecting, he pulled his hand free to continue building the cot. He was glad to be able to look away from her, because his cheeks were flaming hot.

What was the matter with him? He'd hardly been drinking—he'd been on orange juice all night! Or did vitamin C make your head woozy? He'd have to check on that later.

But for now he carried on, screwing into place all the slats to go under the mattress. That was the longest part of the process. After that it could only have been maybe thirty minutes or so before Sophie had a completed cot.

'What do you think?' he asked with pride.

'It's amazing! Thank you.' She held out her hand and he helped her up into a standing position.

'Tell me whereabouts you want it.'

'Over in that corner, please.' She pointed.

He hefted the sturdy cot over to the corner and then picked up all the toys he'd moved earlier and put them inside.

'How does it feel to know that a baby will be sleeping in here soon?'

Sophie suddenly looked so uncertain, so apprehensive.

'What's wrong? What did I say?'

She seemed to think for a moment, as if deciding whether to share her innermost thoughts with him. Then, 'What if I do it all wrong?'

'What makes you think that'll happen?'

'My mother was never the greatest role model for being a mum. What if I'm like her? Distant? Not interested in my child? I want to continue to do my job. What if my child feels pushed away, the way I felt with my mother?'

He didn't really think. He just went straight over to her and pulled her into his arms for a hug. 'Hey, it'll be fine.'

'I know. I just...'

For the moment they continued to hug. Theo could understand her fears. If all she'd known was a mother who didn't seem to notice her, then of course she might feel she'd turn out the same way. But sometimes having a bad parent showed you how you *didn't* want to be. Made you determined to walk an alternative path and do things differently. *Better.*

He squeezed her tight, loving the way she felt against him, all soft and her hair scented with shampoo. It felt good to hold her. To make her feel better. To assuage her fears and worries.

What would it be like if this were *his* baby in her belly? If this was *their* home and he was the one waiting for this baby to be born so that he could hold it too?

The feelings he felt were so terrifying he almost pushed her away, but he knew he couldn't do that. He would never be so cruel. And besides, this wasn't about him. It wasn't his baby. He had nothing to worry about. So why was he holding her? Comforting her?

I shouldn't be doing this.

Sophie must have felt the change in him, and she lifted her head to look at him, as if to check that he was okay.

Theo looked down into her eyes. Such a deep blue. Like a clear Caribbean sea. She held such wonder in those eyes of hers. Such concern. Such hope. Such…desire? He looked at her mouth, at her lips parting as she breathed.

Would it be wrong to take advantage of this moment? Should he be a gentleman and walk away?

'Sophie, we shouldn't do this…'

He saw her glance at his mouth, and he wanted to kiss her so much it almost tore him in two! But she wasn't his. Wasn't meant to be his. And this wasn't how friends should be with each other.

So why was his body telling him to throw caution to the wind and friendship be damned? Telling him that kissing her would be the most wonderful thing in this world?

'No, we shouldn't…'

But her words didn't match her actions. He could see it in her glazed eyes, her dilated pupils, that she wanted him to kiss her, and the temptation to do so was so strong he wasn't sure if he was strong enough to walk away.

Then he felt her daughter kick him again, and it was like a bucket of cold water thrown over him.

He *couldn't* kiss her. This wasn't just about her! There was a baby involved. A little baby girl who would need her father. And he wasn't that. And he couldn't make Sophie's life any more complicated than it already was.

If he was her friend, as he kept insisting that he was, he needed to walk away. To hell with this attraction. This need. This want.

With sadness and deep regret, he took a step back.

'I'm sorry, Soph.'

CHAPTER FIVE

SOPHIE WAS IN a state of disbelief. She had been in his arms, pressed against him, enjoying the feel of him, the warmth, the sense of safety she'd felt. He'd asked her about how she felt about becoming a mother, and just for a brief moment she had felt absolute terror. Had shared with him her innermost fears, practically blurting them out, needing to say them. Get them out in the open.

At work, in front of other people, she managed to maintain a calm façade—she was a woman who could roll with the punches. She was strong…she could cope. It didn't matter that Connor had deserted them.

But at home, alone, she often worried over her doubts. Especially late at night and as the time for her to give birth became imminent. It could happen tonight, tomorrow, the next day…and then her entire life would be different.

She wanted to be the best mum she could be to her daughter—but what if she wasn't? What if she was like her mother? She'd left as soon as she could. Bolted the second she'd thought Sophie was old enough to look after herself, not realising that Sophie had been doing that already for years.

Even when her mother had been around Sophie had

been a dutifully quiet child, knowing that she would never get the attention from her mother that she craved. She had learned to take care of herself at an early age and her expectations of her mother had been low.

How would she make sure she could meet her child's needs? Or even her own, when she had a child and a career to take care of? In that moment when Theo had asked her it had all seemed too much. And for him to hold her like that had been everything. He would never fully know or understand just how much she had needed to be held in that moment. To be taken care of by someone else.

And then he'd nearly kissed her.

She'd wanted it. Oh, how she had wanted it! To feel him press his lips against hers… To give in to her desires and to hell with the consequences…

But Theo had been the stronger of the two of them.

Perhaps that was a good thing? Someone had needed to be sensible there.

No. Let's face it, he was probably trying to save me any embarrassment. He wouldn't be interested in someone like me. I clearly come with a whole truckload of baggage.

She stepped away from him now, reluctantly letting go, but nodding frantically. 'No, of course not. It was just a silly moment. It's late…we're both tired…it's been a long day.'

He stared at her then, and she hated his scrutiny.

'I ought to go. Leave you to it,' he said.

She nodded. 'Yes. Thank you for doing the baby's cot. I really appreciate that.'

'It was no problem.'

She pushed past him and headed down the stairs, hearing his footsteps behind her. Her cheeks were flushed with a raging heat, and when she got to the bottom she opened the front door wide, glad of the cool air that blew in.

'Well, goodnight, Theo.'

'Night, Soph.'

Another brisk nod. 'Drive safe.'

He passed her, stood on the front path and looked back. 'I will. Take care.'

'You too.'

And she closed the door, sinking back against it, registering what a huge mistake the pair of them had just evaded. Theo might be hot, and he might be the kind of guy that filled her dreams, but in real life Theo wanted no more commitment from her than Connor did.

He'd told her enough times that he was there to be her friend, but even that, she believed at heart, was in doubt. Men like him didn't stick around for women like her. Especially now she'd revealed her deepest, darkest fears. He must think she was going to be a right flop as a parent. It was pathetic, really.

How could I have been so stupid?

No. They'd both had a lucky escape. There was no point in falling for her hunky student, no matter how good-looking he was and how erotic her dreams about him might be.

She had no time or place for men who only wanted fun.

She was about to become a mother.

Good mothers put their children first, and that meant not having casual guys hanging around, dipping in and out of her bed.

She needed to put some distance between herself and Theo, so as not to be tempted again.

* * *

Sophie had had a bad night's sleep. She'd tossed and turned constantly, unable to get into a comfy position, as her mind had helpfully replayed that moment in her baby's nursery.

What the hell would have happened if they'd kissed?

Well, apart from feeling amazing at the time, I think afterwards would have been pretty embarrassing!

Would it have stopped at a kiss? Would she have wanted more? Would he?

They both knew where they stood. She wasn't looking for a new man and Theo most definitely wasn't father material. He was a fun-loving guy who wasn't looking to settle down and who didn't do commitment, which she'd thought made him safe to be around.

But maybe they ought to have adult supervision now, after spending the night laughing together and dancing? An old-fashioned chaperone? Because she had to face it: she wasn't just dealing with normal physical attraction here. These damned pregnancy hormones had a part to play, too. It was as if she wasn't really herself, but had been taken over by an inner demon that wanted and yearned and desired.

There was a spark between them. It was undeniable. She knew he'd felt it, too, before common sense had kicked in—and thank God it had!

She smiled now, as she put her breakfast things into the dishwasher. They were okay. Neither of them had done anything they shouldn't, and they would carry on as normal when they met again.

All she had to do today was grab her swimsuit and a towel and get ready for her pregnancy aqua fitness class.

She went every weekend and had been going since she was about six months pregnant.

It felt good to be in the water. It supported her body—especially her heavy belly—and she always felt wonderful afterwards. Plus, it was a bonding experience. She was getting to know some other mothers-to-be, and one or two of them were going to be single parents, like her. She'd talked to them after class, found out how they were going to cope. But each of them seemed to have someone to call on. Someone to be a birth partner. Someone to help in those first few difficult weeks.

It made her feel less alone to have these new friends, but at the same time it made her see how isolated she really was. A lifetime of being independent and looking after herself had somehow kept people at a polite distance. She had her paramedics family, but she needed to have a postnatal family, too—because when this baby came she wouldn't be able to hang out at the ambulance station or meet her colleagues when they dropped their patients off at the hospitals. They'd be gone. Working. Theo would be back at university.

She'd have to start letting people in. Trusting them.

But how did you do that?

How did she put trust in other people when all she'd ever done was only trust herself?

Theo found himself clock-watching. He'd last seen Sophie just over eleven hours ago and already he missed her. He found that to be something that disturbed him greatly.

She was someone he considered just a friend. He didn't want to get attached to this beautiful woman. She was about to become a mother. Her whole world would shift and change, her priorities would become different, and he could not expect that a relationship with her would be successful because he wasn't looking for the type of commitment that Sophie and her daughter, would need. Plus, there was all her history with the baby's father, and from what he had heard none of that was really settled...

But he couldn't stop thinking about her.

Why was that?

He thought about how he'd felt each time his sisters had been pregnant. He'd worried about them. Had asked them to phone him the second they went into labour so he could be there. It had seemed the natural thing to do. He'd been like a father to his siblings after their actual father had deserted them. He'd been their carer. Their protector. He'd nursed his mother through her last days, trying to hide as much of it as he could from his sisters, and the burden he'd been under had been immense.

All that fear, all that pain, all that grief...he'd kept it all under wraps to protect his sisters, leaving almost no time to take care of himself because he had Leonora, Hazel and Martha to worry about.

And yet there was this unwanted physical desire for Sophie. Something that pulled at him. Which, again, blew his mind—because, if he'd been told a few months ago that he would want to kiss or fall into bed with a heavily pregnant woman he would have looked incredulous and laughed his head off. That was not the type of woman he looked for when he wanted to share some adult fun on occasion.

Perhaps it would be best if he maintained some sort of professional distance?

No. I made that stupid bet with her that she could depend on me for at least a year...and I don't break my promises. I'm not my dad.

He couldn't walk away—not now. Not like Connor had. Not like her mother had. Not like his own father had.

He knew how painful it was to be the one left behind. How it made you feel. Unworthy. Unloved. Unimportant. As if you weren't good enough to stick around for.

Maybe once his placement with her was over he would start to distance himself? For his own protection. He didn't need to go making any stupid mistakes with a mother-to-be! Imagine how complicated *that* would be! No, he would finish his placement, keep in touch on occasion, as promised, and maybe just send Christmas cards or something? Back away slowly. Not get too involved. Do what he did best when things got complicated with women.

So why did having these particular thoughts make him feel so bad? It wasn't as if he was walking away from the mother of *his* child. Her baby was nothing to do with him! She'd been in that situation before he'd even arrived on the scene.

Maybe he felt so rubbish because he'd promised to be reliable, someone she could trust, and already he was thinking of his exit strategy?

I'll just play it day by day. Besides, she might be the one to get rid of me!

They might have a huge falling out—who knew how she felt this morning, after last night's near miss? She was probably already regretting it. She might even be the one to let *him* off the hook! To tell him to forget the bet, that it didn't matter any more, that all bets were off and he could go back to his normal life.

And then he would be able to walk away without feeling any guilt. Start again. Find someone single—

someone who wasn't already writing a birth plan would be good.

He sighed, knowing that wouldn't make it better either, and then did what he always did when he got confused. He called his little sister Martha.

'Hey, it's me.'

'Hey, you. How's it going?'

He smiled at the usual greeting. 'Fine.'

'Oh-oh. I don't like the sound of that. Come on, spill—who is she?'

Theo sighed. 'Sophie.'

'Sophie? As in *paramedic* Sophie? The one you're doing your training with?'

'That's the one.'

He waited for the barrage of abuse.

'Are you stupid? Wait! Didn't you say she's hugely pregnant?'

'Yeah.'

'Wow, Theo! It doesn't take you long, does it?'

He smiled.

'You haven't…um…you know…done the deed?'

'Of course not! She's pregnant.'

'So? A woman doesn't stop being a sexual being just because she's about to drop a sprog.'

'You have such a poetic way with words, Marth. Remind me again what you do for a living?' Martha was an English teacher, with aspirations to write a book. 'Nothing happened. We just…nearly kissed.'

'How do you "nearly" kiss someone?'

'We were going to. I backed off at the last minute. It's too complicated.'

'It certainly is. I would have thought she'd be the last type of woman you'd get the hots for.'

'Yeah, me too.'

'I'm sure everything's fine. You didn't do it. You thought with your head, rather than that other thing you guys have got going on, and for that I'm proud of you.'

'Thanks. I think…'

Martha was silent for a minute and he could tell she was mulling something over.

'What?' he asked.

'Have you ever thought that…?' She sighed. 'I don't know… That maybe one day you would *want* to settle down? With a family? You did a great job with us, and sometimes you just seem so…'

'What?'

'Lonely.'

He said nothing. It wasn't a thought he wanted to entertain.

'Look, I've got to go. Leo is waking up and he'll want a nappy-change.'

'All right.'

'You make an excellent father-figure, Theo. To other people's kids. I'm just saying it in case you need to hear it.'

Theo smiled. He wasn't meant to have a favourite sister, but Martha definitely came close.

'I love you, Martha.'

'I love you, too.'

CHAPTER SIX

Sophie was feeling apprehensive on Monday morning. She'd had a whole weekend free of Theo, wondering how he might be with her when they met again. Not that they'd actually done anything. No one had stepped over a line, no rules had been broken, but… But she had stared deeply into his eyes, hoping, clearly *asking* for his kiss, and she'd not been able to stop wondering how far it would have gone if Theo *had* kissed her…

She knew he was a guy who wanted nothing more from a woman than to have a bit of fun on a temporary basis, so technically she'd had a lucky break. It was good that he'd stopped it when he had, because they might have slept together, and then he would have expected everything to be normal.

She didn't need the complications of dealing with the aftermath—the awkwardness, the not being able to meet each other's eyes, the knowledge that once he'd got the grand prize he didn't want to be with her any more.

He'd made it quite clear that he wasn't the settling down type and yet… She couldn't help but wonder. Theo had the look of a guy who would be good in bed and good with kids. And being pregnant, being flooded with hormones that made her want and need, that was an explosive cocktail.

When he'd held her close she'd felt the heat of his body, the solidity of it, his hardness against her softness. She'd smelled the scent of him. Felt security within his arms. His gaze had matched hers when her lips had parted, almost tempted...

It's a good thing that nothing happened.

At his usual time she saw him arrive, and he gave her a huge smile as he approached.

Sophie let out a sigh of relief.

Good, it wouldn't be awkward. Thank God for that!

'Morning. You ready for another full-on week?' she asked.

'Yep! Are you?'

'Always.'

They both checked the vehicle, adding some extra supplies they might need, and then called in to Control that they were ready for calls.

One came in almost immediately.

'Six zero two, we've got a category one call. Male, age unknown, breathing difficulties, found collapsed in the street.'

Control gave them the approximate address and they hit the lights and the sirens.

'What do you think it is?' Theo asked.

Her mind conjured up many things. 'Breathing difficulties could mean anything. Joe Public can't always accurately describe what he's witnessing, so it could be someone having an asthma attack, it could be cardiac-related, or respiratory, or something else entirely. He could be drunk and passed out.'

She concentrated on driving them safely through the

traffic. If someone was having breathing difficulties seconds could be vital in saving a life, and she needed to make sure her focus was on the road, on the other drivers, bikers, and even on pedestrians, who were sometimes known to absently step into the road, seemingly without hearing the siren or seeing the lights blazing and coming towards them. Mobile phones had a lot to answer for…

They pulled up next to a crowd of people, gathered around a man in his mid to late twenties who was slumped up against a shop window. He didn't look good. He'd obviously been sick, and the onlookers had a mix of disgusted, pale expressions as they gawped at the scene, intrigued by what was must be an interesting event on their way to work.

'I've been trying to move him so I can do CPR,' said a young man wearing a grey suit, holding his hands out in front of him, covered in the man's excretions.

Sophie put gloves on and knelt down to lay two fingers against the patient's neck to check for a pulse. 'Has he been able to communicate with you? Do you know his name?'

'No, I just found him like that. He's cold and…stiff.'

Sophie looked up at Theo and shook her head. They were too late. By the look of this patient—his clothes, the marks on his arms—this young man had succumbed to the misuse of drugs. It was a very sad scene.

'Could you get one of the blankets from the car, Theo? And can you get—sorry, what's your name?'

'Jack.'

'Can you get Jack something to clean himself up with?'

Theo got various things from the car, passing paper towels and antibacterial gel to Jack before he covered the patient with a blanket and stood by whilst Sophie she called in to Control, asking them to notify the police that they were with a dead body.

'Already en route, six zero two.'

'Thanks, Control.'

'Are you okay?' Control asked.

'We're good.'

'And your student?'

She looked at Theo. He seemed all right. This wasn't any way for anyone to start their week, but Theo was no green student still in his teens. He was a fully-grown man and he'd been in the army. Surely he'd seen a dead body before? His face looked stern.

'He's okay. But if anything crops up I'll notify you.'

'We'll tell your station, so when you get back he can be assigned someone to talk to if he needs it. And we'll let his university know.'

'That's great. Thank you, Control.'

The ambulance service was very good at looking after their own. A lot of hardened paramedics were used to seeing death, and some even developed a gallows humour to deal with it. But every time they dealt with a death Control would still check on the team involved, to make sure they were okay and give them time off and counselling if they needed it.

Theo was trying to keep the growing crowd back. 'Is there anyone here who recognises him? Saw what happened?' he was asking.

Sophie smiled inwardly. He was doing the right thing. They needed the crowd to move back because the police would want to examine the area. It was an unexpected death on a public street, so they would want to take statements from the onlookers. Theo was going to make a great paramedic. His instincts were in the right place.

Eventually she began to hear the wail of police sirens, and soon they were surrounded by officers and the crew of the ambulance that would be needed to take the body to the nearest hospital morgue.

Once they'd given their assessment to the police and handed over the case, checking one last time to make sure that Jack was okay, they packed up and got back into the car.

'You all right?' she asked Theo.

'Yeah. I'm good. Are you?'

She nodded. 'Have you seen a dead body before?'

He nodded. 'Unfortunately.'

'Do you want to talk about it?'

He shook his head. 'Just army stuff. I'm all right.'

'You're sure?' He didn't look all right, she thought.

'You see death in the army. Stationed overseas—in Afghanistan…other places with active shooting—you almost expect it, in a way. Harden yourself to it. You're fighting for a cause. You know you're there to try and do the right thing. You forget that not everyone can cope with that type of stresses.'

She understood. 'Who did you lose?'

His voice softened. 'A good friend. Matt. Matty-Boy, we all called him.'

'What happened?'

'I would have said it was nothing out of the ordinary for us. We were infantry. We'd been in skirmishes, fire-fights, ambushes. The usual. We dealt with it in our downtime by playing footy, cards, making jokes, riling each other up. We thought we were fine. We kept an eye on each other…made sure we were all okay.'

He paused briefly.

'One night, after a skirmish in which we found an entire family had been killed, Matty-Boy took his own life.'

'Oh, Theo…' She couldn't imagine how he must have felt.

'I didn't see the signs. I thought he was okay. He seemed okay. Until he wasn't.'

'Is that why you left the army?'

He nodded. 'It added to it. The guilt I felt at missing the signs…it ate me up for a while.'

She wanted to lay her hand on his. To show him that she was there. That she cared. That she understood how he was hurting. But she was afraid to. What if it was misinterpreted? It was so soon after last night…

Dammit! He's hurting.

She laid her hand on his, wrapped her fingers around his. Squeezed. 'If you ever want to talk about him I'd love to hear about who he was. What he meant to you. His life…'

'Thanks. I'm okay, though.'

And he pulled his hand out from under hers.

She tried not to feel hurt at the small rejection, but knew her previous assessment of him had been correct. He was strong. That was good. He would need that in this job. He was able to separate his feelings and control them, not let them overwhelm him.

'Let's grab coffees to go. Get some breakfast.'

He smiled. 'Great idea.'

She drove them to a small supermarket where they quickly bought what they needed, and they were on their way back to their vehicle when Control called in with another job. Multiple units, including the fire brigade, were being dispatched to an address where two patients had been found together, collapsed in their front room. One female in her seventies and an male who was eighty.

'Odd…we don't often get two people together like that,' Sophie said, already trying to imagine in her head what had happened.

The address wasn't far from them, and they managed to get to the property within six minutes of the call coming in.

'Grab the jump bag and the oxygen,' she told Theo.

They'd arrived first, and a young woman in her forties was waiting for them at the door. 'They're in the lounge. They're breathing, but I can't wake them up!'

Sophie rushed in, her eyes scanning for danger. Had there been a break-in? An attack? If so, she had to be mindful that the assailant might still be there, or that a weapon might be around. But nothing looked disturbing except for the fact that there was an elderly couple, each in their respective chairs, completely unconscious, their faces pink.

The gas fire was on, as it had turned a little cooler… Carbon monoxide poisoning? Carbon monoxide was tasteless, had no smell, and it was colourless. If the fireplace was faulty it might have been issuing out poisonous fumes within the room.

As Sophie rushed to check for pulses, she turned to Theo and the woman. 'Open all the doors and windows!'

'What's going on?' asked the young woman.

Was she their daughter?

'It could be carbon monoxide. Can you turn that fire off?'

The woman hurried to do so.

'Theo, I'm going to need you to help me carry these

two out of here. We'll do airways and oxygen once we've got them outside. It's too dangerous for us to stay.'

She was thinking about her baby. If it *was* carbon monoxide poisoning—which she strongly suspected—what effect might it have on her growing child?

The pinkness in her patients' faces was a dead giveaway. Carbon monoxide, once breathed in, would enter the bloodstream and mix with a person's haemoglobin in the blood cells that carried oxygen around the body to form carboxyhaemoglobin. When that occurred, the blood wasn't able to carry the oxygen the body needed, therefore causing cell and tissue death.

Theo shook his head. 'No. You two get out now! Go on—I can't have you in here. I'll get them out one by one.'

'But I'm the senior para—'

Theo grabbed her arm. 'You're *pregnant*,' he said. 'Your rank means nothing in this situation. Now, go!'

He was right. But she was fighting against her training, which drummed into them the fact that you never approached a patient or a scene without checking for your own safety first. She should be the one protecting Theo! Not letting him sacrifice himself for these two patients. He was the student. The observer.

But she'd barely detected a pulse in the man…it might already be too late!

In the end her training was no match for the instinct she felt to protect her unborn child and she hurried out, pulling the other woman with her, only to find that outside a fire engine was arriving, the crew jumping out, dressed and ready for action.

She quickly apprised them of the situation and two firemen rushed in wearing breathing apparatus to help Theo bring out the first patient. The rest of fire crew brought out the second and laid her on the grass next to Theo and Sophie, who applied oxygen masks to their faces and turned them on full.

The elderly couple weren't looking great. Completely unconscious.

An ambulance crew loaded the patients into their vehicle and went screaming off into the distance just as a firefighter came out, removing his mask.

'We've switched the gas off at the mains. Looks like there was a blocked flue in the chimney. You've both been exposed to the gas, so you really ought to go and get yourselves checked out.'

'Okay.' Sophie nodded and looked at Theo. 'You okay?'

'I feel fine—it's just not the start to Monday morning that I'd expected.'

Neither had she. After such a great Friday night spent with Theo, and a wonderful relaxing weekend, she'd expected the usual high-octane week of racing from call to call, but to get a death straight away and then this...

And now they would have to go to hospital to get themselves checked out. That would take her and her vehicle off the road, and they couldn't afford to be a crew down. And what about Theo's training? He'd lose a whole day.

She'd been exposed for...what?...a minute? Was that enough to harm her? Or her child? She couldn't take that risk. That was what was most important here.

At the hospital, a doctor checked them over.

'Could it harm my baby?' asked Sophie. 'I wasn't in the property for long.'

The doctor nodded in understanding. 'We'll check your bloods, but for now I want you both to have some oxygen therapy.' He attached masks to their faces and turned on the flow. 'I'm sure your baby will be fine. It's long-term exposure to carbon monoxide that we worry about, and you say you were only in the room for less than a minute? Let's keep you on the oxygen for a short while, and then we'll carry out an ultrasound, just to be on the safe side.'

Sophie nodded. 'Do you know how the couple are?'

The doctor shrugged. 'They're still alive. They appear to have been exposed the night before, plus they're both smokers, so the levels in their blood will be high. We might have to try hyperbaric therapy if they're to survive this.'

An oxygen chamber...

'How long do we have to wear the oxygen masks?' Sophie asked.

'Not long. I'll just check the carboxyhaemoglobin levels and if they're really low, or non-existent, then you can go.'

'Thank you, Doctor.'

He nodded and left.

Sophie looked at Theo, appreciative of how he'd thought to protect her and her baby. 'You were great back there, you know?'

'I was just doing my job.'

'You were putting the patients first.'

'So were you. I had to order you out of there.'

She nodded. He had. He'd stepped right up, knowing he was the stronger one of the two of them—the one who could risk remaining in the room a little longer than her. She appreciated what he had done for her and her baby. He had proved again that he could be relied upon.

Sometimes being a first responder you forgot that you

were always the one running *towards* danger, when everyone else was running *from* it. But Control was very good about her current situation, and only sent her to jobs where she could play the part of rapid response paramedic. She knew she would always have back-up. Knew that others would be right behind her.

It was easy to forget how dangerous life could be—and she had a precious little one on board whom she needed to think about, too. Maybe she should slow down? Consider exactly what she should be doing now? Change her mindset from thinking just about herself to becoming a *mum*. A job that came with a whole new set of dangers and risks and worries…

'I don't leave people behind,' he said.

Of course. Army guy. He would have been committed to his fellow soldiers. They would have had a code. They would have been honourable. They'd have looked out for one another.

Theo, even though he was the trainee, the subordinate, had been the one to order her out of the house to keep her and her baby safe. To stop her from inhaling any more of the carbon monoxide than she had already. He'd put her first. Her baby first. She could never thank him enough for that.

He was going to make a fantastic paramedic. Whomever he got paired with would totally be able to rely on him, she had no doubt. She'd worked alone for so long, she'd almost forgotten that she didn't need to be the one in charge all the time—that on occasion she could rely on and trust someone else to look out for her.

She wasn't a lone ranger. She had Theo and Control and the whole ambulance service watching her back.

In that moment, looking at him as he sat with an oxygen mask clamped to his face, she felt her feelings for him grow. She could actually feel them. Could feel gratitude and appreciation and love for what he had done swell within her.

He was a good man. A kind man.

She thought of him out in Afghanistan, fighting, finding his friend Matty-Boy dead, all the things he must have seen, the things he must have gone through. Experienced.

He was brave.

He was a man she felt she could trust professionally, and that was what you needed when you worked in a team as paramedics. You had to know that you could rely on your partner, and Sophie knew that she could rely on Theo.

But personally…? On a romantic level…?

She knew she wanted him to be right for her, but she also knew that they didn't stand a chance. They might both have been abandoned by a parent, but they wanted different things because of it. He was in her life but he was a mayfly—a beautiful thing that would only last for a short time. She should appreciate him whilst he was with her.

'You know…we've never really had a chance to speak about what nearly happened the other night,' she said.

He turned to look at her, his hand clutching his oxygen mask.

'I know I really wanted to kiss you, and I think you really wanted to kiss me,' she went on. 'At least, I hope you did. I hope I'm not so unattractive like this that you would recoil.' She laughed, feeling almost embarrassed.

'You're beautiful, Soph. Pregnant or otherwise. Don't let anyone tell you anything different.'

She smiled behind the oxygen mask. He made her feel glad.

'And, for the record, I wanted to kiss you very much.'

She nodded, staring at her hero in the other bed and feeling glad that he was by her side as a partner, even if it was just at work.

She knew that if she were to keep him in her life he'd need to understand that she wasn't going to be like those women in his past who'd got clingy. She was nothing like that—even if she did find herself wondering what it might be like to be with him.

But that was just stuff and nonsense—hormones and her baby brain, looking for dreams and perfection and happily-ever-afters when she knew that she could never have that with Theo.

She would just have to bask in his presence temporarily. Enjoy the brief time she would share with him before he moved on and became someone else's hero.

She would cope with his loss.

She'd dealt with loss her entire life.

It had become an old friend.

Theo breathed in his oxygen. So they'd almost kissed? So what? It didn't mean anything. It had been a brief weakness. They'd both gone a little too far after an evening of fun together, creating the illusion of something else that wasn't truly there. It had brought them close, and then he had built her baby's cot, comforted her when she'd got scared. It had been a moment, that was all.

So why did he feel that he was somehow letting her down? And not just *her*, but also himself? Was it because she was pregnant? Was it because he felt as if he'd messed with a woman he really ought not to have? She was going to be a mother! She had a life and a history with someone else—this Connor, the father of her baby.

Even if he wasn't around, he was still there, lurking in the recesses of her mind. She might think things were over for her and Connor, but what if that all changed when the baby arrived? People did that. Didn't realise what they'd lost until it actually became a reality. What if this Connor had simply failed to connect with the fact that Sophie saying *'I'm pregnant'* meant that there was going to be a real baby he would have to deal with one day? Once his daughter was born, he might feel differently. Who knew?

And when this other man eventually came crawling out from under the rock where he'd been living for the last few months, finally having admitted his mistake, did Theo really want to have developed *feelings* for this woman? Feelings he would then have to deny?

Absolutely not!

Theo didn't need *complicated*. He didn't need the problems that getting involved with a woman who was having a baby by someone else would bring.

She was going to have a baby. A brand-new baby girl who hadn't been let down by the world yet. She was completely innocent, and she deserved to have the best start in life possible when she was born, to be brought into the world by people who loved her.

Sophie might think things were over with Connor, but Theo knew differently.

His sister Hazel had split with her partner once. She had told everyone that it was all over between her and David, that he was an idiot, and a child, and she would have nothing to do with him ever again. But they had a son together, and when that boy had been admitted to hospital with suspected meningitis—thankfully it hadn't been—it had brought Hazel and David back together again and they were a family now. Happy and content.

Theo didn't want to get in the way of something that might not yet be over. But still…despite his rules about not getting involved…he was finding it really hard to tell himself that he needed not to think of Sophie in *that way*.

It was difficult, because he'd really enjoyed that night they'd spent at Ross's party, and he knew her quite well now, and he liked everything he saw. She was intelligent, dedicated, funny. She made him laugh and smile and he looked forward to every shift he had with her—didn't like having to say goodbye each evening.

He kept finding his thoughts running to her. What was she doing? Where was she? Was she all right? Was she happy? It was important to him that she be happy. And, weirdly, he found that he felt an intense, irrational anger towards this Connor for having hurt her. For having royally screwed up an opportunity to be with this wonderful woman who was having *his baby*, for crying out loud! Was the man *stupid*?

When the doctor came back and told them that the carboxyhaemoglobin levels in their blood were barely traceable, and they could go, with relief, the pair of them removed their oxygen masks and thanked the staff for taking care of them.

'Next time you come here just bring us *other* patients. Don't be the patients yourselves, you hear?' the doctor said with a smile.

They promised they would do their best.

'We've got a trauma call for you. Fifty-two-year-old male, fallen from a ladder, suspected broken arms.'

Arms. Plural. Ouch!

Sophie drove to the address and could see their patient lying on the paved driveway by a ladder. A woman, probably the patient's wife, came scurrying up to their vehicle as they got out.

'He fell off the ladder taking down the Christmas lights. I told him to get them down months ago, but he wouldn't listen.'

Sophie pulled on gloves as she walked towards the patient, Theo following behind with the jump bag and Entonox.

'You don't look like you've got long to go,' said the woman.

'I'm imminent.'

'You should be at home, putting your feet up.'

Sophie smiled. She got that a lot. But she'd go stir crazy at home. Working was much better—even if it did tire her out. All her scans and blood tests and BP checks told her that she was doing fine, and it wasn't as if she was ill. She could still do her job.

'What's your husband's name?' she asked.

'Jeff.'

'Any medical issues we need to know about?'

'Does lazy-itis count?'

Sophie smiled as she knelt down so that Jeff could see her. He was face-down, but she could see a bad graze across his cheek.

'Hello, Jeff. I'm Sophie, and I've got my colleague Theo here, too. Can you tell me what happened?'

'I was taking down the damned lights and the ladder must have slipped.'

'You put your arms out to break your fall?'

'Yeah. Felt something go…heard something crack.'

'What hurts the most?'

'My arms. My right knee.'

'Okay...and if you could rate your pain from zero to ten, with zero being no pain and ten being the worst...?'

'Definitely a nine.'

Sophie looked to Theo and mouthed *Entonox*.

Theo got the canister and the mouthpiece ready. Ideally, they liked the patient to hold the mouthpiece, but on this occasion the patient's arms were out of commission, so Theo kept hold of the mouthpiece so that Jeff could breathe from it.

'Nice deep breaths, mate,' Theo said. 'You can breathe out as well as in...breathe through it.'

They were going to need help, log-rolling this patient. Because of the fall he might have a neck or spinal injury, and with Theo controlling the Entonox, and Sophie pregnant, they would need extra hands—and soon.

She radioed through to Control and asked them what the running time was on the second crew with an ambulance.

'En route, six zero two. ETA two minutes.'

'Thanks.' She knelt down again to explain the situation to Jeff. 'I'm going to give you a painkilling injection. It will help until they get here, okay? All you need to do is breathe, try to relax, and don't move anything.'

After giving him the injection, she tried to check out the rest of his body. They'd need to get a cervical collar on him, but that would be impossible until the extra help arrived. His arms were most definitely broken, and she thought he'd either broken his kneecap or maybe even his lower leg near the knee joint from his impact with the paving slabs from such a height.

When the ambulance crew arrived she smiled to see

her friends Ross and Cameron. In a co-ordinated effort they managed to log-roll their patient and get the collar on, plus two arm splints and one on Jeff's right leg. Then Ross and Cameron loaded Jeff into their vehicle.

'You look after yourself, Jeff, all right?' she told him.

Jeff smiled, despite the pain he was in. 'Will do. Looks like those lights will have to stay up all year, huh? You can tell the missus I won't be going up any ladders any time soon.'

Sophie smiled in return. 'It's not that long till Christmas again, anyway.'

Theo closed the ambulance doors and then they both cleared up their equipment and got everything loaded back into the vehicle. There was about an hour left of their shift, and without any calls coming in Theo asked her about their previous patients.

'Do we ever get to find out how they're doing?'

'Occasionally. If we end up at the same hospital we can always ask.'

'I thought I'd be fine, not knowing how the story ends, but as it turns out I'm curious.'

Sophie glanced at him and smiled. 'It happens—but you can console yourself with the fact that you got there first, you treated someone and got them the help they need. You began their story. Everything after that is out of your hands. You have to learn to let go.'

He nodded, but she could see he was clearly thinking about something.

'Did you choose to be a paramedic because you thought you wouldn't have to get involved?' she asked him.

He shrugged. 'Maybe a little. I thought I could care

for people a little bit and then just let them go on their merry way to hospital, my part done.'

'Is that what you're used to? Only having a bit-part in people's lives?'

He was silent. Clearly the question made him uncomfortable.

'If it makes you feel any better, that's what I'm used to. This works for me,' she said.

'But you reached out once. Tried to be more than a bit-part in Connor's life.'

'I thought he was *"the one"*.' She shrugged. 'Turned out I was wrong.'

'If only people came with bright neon signs flashing above their heads—that would make it easier, don't you think?' he asked.

She looked at him, considering. 'Don't you ever find yourself wondering what if…? I mean, what if you've already walked away from the woman who could have been the absolute love of your life?'

Theo laughed. 'I'm hoping that I'd be clever enough to recognise her.'

'And if you did? Would you finally settle down, do you think?'

He seemed to think about her words. 'I don't know.'

'Not even for true love?'

Theo went quiet again. Clearly, she'd made him think. What was he so scared of? Was it just of commitment to one person? Was he one of those guys who was so in love with the idea of playing the field that he couldn't bear the idea of settling for just one woman? She hoped not. She hoped he was more than that. Because it seemed like he cared so much! His heart was in the right place with his family, and with his patients, but what about when it came to his own heart? Was he afraid to give it to someone?

'I just find it hard to understand,' she said. 'All my life I've wanted love. Craved it, even. I was so independent as a child. Dutiful, never getting into trouble, never wanting to bother my parents with having to pay attention to me. It was like I kind of knew they weren't capable of it, you know…? So when I grew up I was ready for love. I'd been starved of it for years. Maybe that was my mistake? Seeing it in Connor because I wanted to. I wanted to see something that wasn't there, when in actual fact I'd fallen for a man who was just as incapable of showing me love as my parents were.'

'Are they both still alive?' Theo asked.

'Mum is. As far as I know. My dad died when I was young.'

He frowned. 'I'm sorry to hear that.'

'He died when I was seven years old and my mother left when I was eighteen. It was like she was waiting for me to be old enough so she could go, and she left me as soon as I moved out to university to study for my paramedic degree.'

'But you keep in touch with her?'

'Sporadic phone calls, but that's about it. It's hard to talk to her sometimes. She doesn't seem to hear anything I have to say. Always full of what's happening in *her* life. *Her* adventures. *Her* dramas.' She frowned. 'But what about your parents? You haven't really spoken about them much.'

'After my mum divorced my father, she got sick. She died after a long battle with multiple sclerosis. That's why I had to do everything for everyone. Mum couldn't if she was going through a bad phase, and as the oldest I kind of took charge. I had to.'

'Did you resent it?'

He shook his head. 'No. I'd do it all again. It brought me and my sisters really close together. We were a group. A band. We relied on one another, we looked out for one another, and we stuck together. Whenever one of us needs help, we call the others.'

'Is that how you ended up being at the birth of your nephew?'

He laughed, remembering. 'Yeah.'

'That must be nice, having such a close family. I can't imagine what that's like. Maybe you don't look for love because you already have it. With your sisters. I was an only child. Always alone.'

'Perhaps your mother acted the way she did because she couldn't handle losing her husband so suddenly and so young?'

Now it was Sophie's turn to frown. 'Maybe...'

'It must have been hard for her,' he said. 'Losing her husband and then having to look after a little girl when all she wanted to do was fall apart?'

'Maybe,' she said again.

She hadn't considered that. Not really. She'd just known that her dad had died and she'd got nothing from her mother in the way of comfort. In the way of attention. She'd felt starved of both from the get-go. Even before her dad had passed away.

'They were very much in love. I remember her telling me how much she loved him.'

'She must have been devastated, then. There's nothing worse than thinking that you have all this time with someone, only to discover that it's over before you know it. Your parents loved each other deeply. You had that. That's something. My parents were always distant. My father was hardly ever at home. When my mother divorced him it was almost a relief that he wasn't coming back, so that we could get on with our lives. Stop sitting there and waiting for someone to come home who didn't want to be there.'

She sighed. 'Families, eh? They sure know how to screw you over.'

And she couldn't get the thought out of her head that he was missing out on being with someone special. Someone as gorgeous and kind as he was. Why did he insist on being alone? He deserved to find someone special, even though it wouldn't be her.

'Maybe none of us know what we're doing...' He said. 'Stumbling our way through life, hoping we're making the right decisions. Once you have your daughter, you'll have that love you seek. It's already there—you're just waiting for her. Maybe even Connor will see the error of his ways.'

She laughed. 'I doubt that very much. And even if he did, would I want to know? He's already proved to be unreliable. I can't depend upon him the way your sisters depend on you.'

'You might feel differently afterwards. When the baby's here.'

Sophie doubted it very much. Connor had ruined his chance of being in a happy family with her and their daughter. But what would she do if he wanted shared custody or some contact? She'd have to give it to him, surely? What would that be like? Having to let her daughter go and spend time at her father's every week? Would he want her every weekend? Once a month? Never?

Perhaps she ought to find out if he'd even thought about this? Was it worth giving him a call? Was it worth reminding him that the time to change his mind was nearly at hand?

Just as she was about to think they might not have any more shouts that shift, the radio blared into life and Control told them they were needed at a road traffic accident.

She sighed. 'Would you like to do the honours?' she asked Theo.

He smiled and pressed the button for lights and sirens.

CHAPTER SEVEN

THAT WEEKEND, SOPHIE finally managed to get Connor on the phone. 'I was beginning to think you were ignoring my calls,' she said, rubbing at her swollen belly as the baby kicked frantically within her.

'Have you had it?' he asked abruptly.

It?

No *Hello, Soph, how are you?*

'Our daughter? Not yet.'

She tried not to sound angry. They needed to keep this civil. She didn't want her baby to pick up on the animosity that there was between the two of them. It wouldn't be fair. Their daughter was not a bargaining chip, or an asset to be passed around in a war. But she hated the fact that he'd used the word *it*. As if their baby was just some random object and not a precious, much wanted child.

'Then what do you want?'

'Well, I was hoping we could talk about things.'

'Like what?'

My God! Whatever did I see in this man? He used to be charming, right?

'About the future. About what's going to happen after the baby's born.'

'You mean money?'

'No, I don't mean money! Though I guess that will have to come into it sooner rather than later. I'm talking about when she's born—about if you'll want to see her and, if you do, what sort of contact you'd want.'

'I hadn't really thought about it.'

'Really?'

She couldn't believe this! Ever since they'd broken up, just over half a year ago, she'd thought of nothing else but this baby and she'd imagined—hoped—that beneath Connor's selfish exterior there might lurk a streak of love or a sense of duty towards the baby that he'd helped create.

He knew her due date. He'd stuck around long enough to find that out. Surely his mind had been drifting more and more to what would happen when his child was born? Or did he truly not care? How could she have once thought that this man cared for her? Was her radar so far off? Had she been so desperate for love that she'd taken his confidence, his swagger, his apparent ardent desire for her, as something else?

'It's been a difficult time for me, Sophie.'

'Difficult for *you*?'

'You wouldn't understand. I've had to make some huge adjustments since we broke up.'

'Since you walked away, you mean?'

There was a silence. Then, 'I'll pay child support. I spoke to my boss and he gave me a small pay rise after that deal I brokered, so paying maintenance shouldn't be a problem.'

'And will you want to see her?'

Another long silence. One so long she almost thought that maybe he'd put the phone down and walked away. But then she heard him let out a sigh.

'I don't know…'

'Well, you don't have long to figure it out. She's due in a couple of days, in case you've forgotten.'

'Of course I haven't!'

'Haven't you?'

Her anger seeped out. She couldn't help it. She was frustrated. Where was the man she'd thought she was in love with? And did she really want her beautiful daughter spending time with a man like him? She'd be better off spending time with Theo.

She felt strange, thinking that, then dismissed it. Hormones again. That was all. It was totally wrong even to think that Theo could be in any way shape or form a father to her child. Or even an influence. He simply wouldn't be around. He'd made it clear what he was to her. He hadn't even wanted to kiss her!

But…

I wish that he had. He's ten times the man Connor ever was. At least he's been honest with me from the start.

'I've got to go,' said Connor. 'I've an important call on the other line.' And he put the phone down.

Sophie threw her mobile phone across the room in frustration. An important call? Was she and the future of their daughter not important enough for him?

Boy! She'd royally screwed up with him.

Could she ever trust herself again to find a good man?

And did she even want to find one?

No.

Yes.

Perhaps they were all the same as each other?

But what about Theo?

What about him?

Her anger with Connor had burnt out any real possibility that there was anything there. And why would she want it, anyway? *Why?*

And then the tears came. Floods of them, ripping through her like knives, and she sat on her couch, hiccupping her way through her breathing, as she wiped her nose on soggy tissues before throwing them across the room, to join her phone.

She didn't want to be wasting tears on Connor.

I'm not. I'm crying because I'm sad for my daughter.

The call to attend a pedestrian versus car came through, and Sophie got them to the accident site less than four minutes later.

Theo went to grab the jump bag and the Entonox as Sophie pushed her way through the milling crowd, all of whom seemed to be standing there, filming everything on their mobile phones.

He frowned. He was beginning to notice this more and more since working with Sophie, but this wasn't something they'd brought up in any of his lectures at university yet—how to deal with the general public, who often thought an accident was a good bit of footage to put on their social media sites.

He tried to ignore them, pushing through to get to their patient.

They found a little girl sitting in the road, crying, with a nasty laceration on her lower leg. The car driver stood next to them, crying her eyes out, obviously shocked and upset. She motioned to Sophie and Theo that she was fine and that they should check out the little girl first.

'Can you tell me what happened?' Sophie asked the woman holding the little girl's hand.

'I'm her mum. We were walking to school. Well,

Keeley was skipping… As she got to the junction I shouted to her to stop. She turned…but she must have been too close to the edge and she fell backwards and hit the car.'

Theo was relieved. On the way to the job Sophie had told him that when calls came through like this, they had to assume the worst. That a pedestrian had been hit so hard by a vehicle that they'd been thrown into the air and over it. That injuries could be life-threatening. To get here and find that it was a low-speed impact and that this little girl hadn't been thrown anywhere was very reassuring.

'We're going to need some bandages,' Sophie said, pulling on her gloves. 'Hi, Keeley. My name is Sophie, this is Theo, and we're going to make you feel better, okay? Can I have a feel of your leg? You can stop me if anything hurts.'

Keeley continued to cry, but also nodded.

Theo watched carefully, noting how Sophie assessed the leg, her fingertips probing along the bones, checking her kneecap, her thigh, her foot. Checking for pedal pulses. Then she did the other leg.

'Did you bang your head, Keeley?' she asked.

'No.'

'I'm just going to check the rest of you, is that all right?'

Keeley was only sniffing by the time Sophie had finished doing her primary assessment.

'How is she?' asked Theo.

'I'm satisfied that the leg injury is the only problem.'

Theo passed her the bandages and she began to wrap the leg.

'You need to wrap the wound tight enough that it compresses the bleed, but not too tight that it damages the tissue beneath.'

He nodded. He knew about pressure bandaging. He'd applied it a couple of times in his life whilst serving in the army, waiting for medics. Stopping blood-loss could save a life. Lose too much and the body could go into shock.

Sometimes just the sight of their own blood could send a person into extreme shock. Thankfully, Keeley seemed made of stern stuff.

'You're being very brave, Keeley,' he said. 'Tell me what your favourite subject is at school.'

She sniffed and wiped her nose on her sleeve. 'PE. Netball.'

'What position do you play?'

'Centre.'

'Wow. You must be a really important player!'

Keeley smiled. He was so pleased to see the little girl smile he looked at Sophie, and caught her smiling, too.

'What else do you like doing?' he asked.

'I like baking. I want to be on that show on TV, but Mum says I'm not old enough.'

'Maybe try for the kids' version?'

Keeley nodded. 'Am I going to get stitches?'

He shrugged. The doctors at the hospital might stitch the wound, or they might choose to close it with glue. That wasn't his call, and he didn't know enough about it to say what the doctors would do once they'd had a better look at the wound and cleaned it. It would depend on how clean the edges were, how deep the injury was... whether anything beneath it had been damaged.

'Do you want stitches?' he asked.

Keeley shook her head. 'A cast would be cool, though.'

'So everyone can sign it?'

Keeley smiled again.

'Tell you what—let's put one of these on you.' He grabbed one of the gloves he kept in his pocket and put it on her hand, then he signed the back of it. 'Get people to sign that. I bet Sophie will sign it, too.'

Sophie did so—just as the ambulance arrived. As she handed over the case to the other paramedics, Theo stood to double-check on the driver of the car.

'What's your name?'

'Teresa. I saw her at the corner. I thought she'd stopped. But then she fell and...'

She burst into tears again and Theo rubbed at her shoulder to reassure her. 'Are you okay? Anything hurt?'

He saw the police arriving and waved them over. It probably had been a simple accident, but they'd need to take a statement, and most definitely would breathalyse this poor woman.

'I'm fine. I'm just...shaky.'

'The police will want to have a word with you, okay?'

She nodded. 'Absolutely. Whatever I can do to help.'

He left Teresa in their capable hands to go and say goodbye to Keeley before she was taken away. He clambered up into the ambulance and smiled at the little girl. 'Some people will do anything to get a day off school, huh?'

'Look, Theo!' she said. 'Danni and Neo have signed my glove, too!'

She held out her hand for him to see and he smiled at the smiley face one of the paramedics had drawn on her glove.

'Brilliant! You look after yourself, you hear?'

She nodded, and he waved her goodbye, stepping back out of the ambulance so that Keeley's mother could get in.

He found Sophie waiting for him. She had a broad smile upon her face.

'You did brilliantly back there, Theo. You really put her at ease. Went the extra mile. I'm very proud of you.'

'Thanks.' He smiled back at her, trying to be professional despite being inordinately pleased with her praise. He pulled his gaze away to watch the ambulance that carried Keeley drive away.

'You're good with kids, aren't you?' she said.

He shrugged. 'I try.'

'Your nieces and nephews are very lucky indeed.'

He looked back at her. Heard the wistfulness in her voice. Was she sad? Was she upset? Her smile had gone. She looked quite forlorn. Was she still worried about what kind of parent she'd be? He really didn't think she had anything to worry about. Clearly she wanted to be the best mother she could, and after seeing Sophie with her patients he couldn't imagine her being anything less than exemplary.

He wanted to tell her that. Pull her close and give her a hug. But look at what had nearly happened the last time he did.

Could he console her?

There was only one way to find out.

She needs a hug!

He reached out and pulled her in close against his chest, smiling when he heard her let out a long sigh and settle against him, her arms around his waist.

It felt *so good* to be held by Theo, his strong arms wrapped around her, holding her close. It was as if he was protecting her, keeping her safe, so that she could just relax for a few minutes and let someone else have the burden of worry.

Almost her entire life she'd felt as if she'd been looking after herself. Her dad dying when she was seven years old had changed everything. She'd loved her dad very much, and for him to just be there one day and not the next…gone…

It had been a massive heart attack, and he'd been dead before he hit the floor, her mother had said. And her mother hadn't been much help to her afterwards, as she'd been grieving too.

Her mother had turned to other things to make her happy. Other people. Chasing the happiness she thought other people had, forgetting that she had a child who wanted more love than she was providing.

Sophie had just got on with being a little girl. Trying hard at school, working hard for herself, knowing that her mother was never that impressed with her grades, or her spelling test results, or how high she was on the reading ladder. She'd quickly learned that if she wanted to be happy then she would have to find happiness herself, the way her mother did, so she'd surrounded herself with good friends and made sure she had a good rapport with her teachers, who'd all liked her.

When Sophie had got older, and had been excited about going to university, her mother had announced that she would be going travelling and selling the house to pay for it. Sophie would need to find her own place to live at the end of her first term if she wanted to 'come home'.

It hadn't been a problem. In fact she'd been so self-sufficient by then it had almost been a relief that her mother had left, because she'd been worried about her.

Her mum had been getting more and more depressed, saying that she felt stuck at home, having to be there to look after Sophie, and that she felt she needed to spread her wings and enjoy life before she got too old to enjoy anything.

Sophie had struggled to understand before, but since talking to Theo she'd begun to think that perhaps her mother hadn't been as bad as she remembered. Perhaps it had been just her mother's way of dealing with the loss of her beloved husband? Sophie knew a bit about loss. She had felt it when Connor had walked away without a backward glance. Okay, he hadn't died, but her dream of what her future might be had. Maybe she'd been too harsh on her mother? Maybe they had more similarities than she'd ever imagined?

Connor had swept Sophie off her feet, with his suave suits and expensive tastes, and he'd been so unlike anyone she'd ever known she'd fallen in love with him, thinking she'd finally found the one person who would stand by her side.

She had been hypnotised by his attention to her, his glamorous lifestyle...

And then he'd left, when life had got too hard. Too complicated.

By a child.

Her mother had been left alone just as suddenly. She'd been in shock. And maybe...just maybe...she'd looked outside herself to find the happiness she'd so desperately sought?

Had Sophie helped her with that? When her mother had pulled away, what had Sophie done? She'd tried to get her attention initially, but then she had just maintained that distance. Had helped it along by not really communicating with her mother. By standing alone.

Sophie knew how to look after herself. She'd been doing it for so long. Theo holding her like this, looking after her, well…it felt *good*! Even if it was only momentary.

'Six zero two? Are you clear of scene? Only we've got another job for you. Forty-two-year-old female entrapment, six minutes away from your current position.'

Control brought them back to reality and the radio blurting out was enough for them to break apart.

Guiltily, she smiled at Theo and then grabbed the radio. 'Yes, Control, we're clear of the previous scene. Show us as attending.'

She listened to the address carefully, already mapping out the route she'd need to take in her mind. 'Entrapment' could mean anything. What was the woman trapped under? Was she conscious? Was she bleeding?

'Pelican Place, Kings Road. Police, fire brigade and an ambulance crew also en route, six zero two.'

It was definitely something serious. And on the Kings Road… She knew that area. It was mostly housing. A new development was being built there. Was that Pelican Place? She'd driven past it a few times, but hadn't really had time to take in the name. If it was, then this could be a big job. Building sites were dangerous places.

'Call Control and ask them if HEMS is attending,' she told Theo, wanting to know if a doctor was going to be there.

But the helicopter was busy on another call.

Traffic was quite light as they raced to the job, and as soon as they arrived they were met by a foreman who was waiting with high-vis jackets and hard hats for them to wear.

'What's happened?' Sophie asked as she donned everything.

'We had the timber joists all set up for doing the roofs and… I don't know…they somehow came down without warning and trapped Annie.'

'Is she conscious?'

'Yeah, but she's in a lot of pain.'

No doubt.

The foreman led them through the site to their patient, who seemed to be trying to smile and joke through her pain with her colleagues, who were all gathered around.

Sophie turned to the foreman. 'The police, the fire brigade and an ambulance are on their way. Can you get someone to wait for them and lead them here?'

He nodded, and ordered a couple of guys to go and wait for support.

Sophie got down on her knees and smiled at Annie. 'Hi, Annie. I'm Sophie and this is Theo. How are you doing?'

She winced. 'My back hurts.'

In the distance, Sophie heard sirens. Good. Back-up would be here soon. They'd need help to lift these roof joists off Annie in a safe and controlled way. Her colleagues had done what they could, placing coats over her and trying to keep her warm. Shock frequently made a patient feel cold.

'And how's your breathing? Can you take deep breaths?'

Annie gave a little shake of her head. 'Think I might have cracked a rib or two…'

Theo had opened up the jump bag and was getting out

the equipment. As soon as he heard Annie was having trouble taking big breaths he passed Sophie her stethoscope.

Placing the buds into her ears, she listened to Annie's chest. Both lungs sounded good, so she didn't think they had a punctured lung to worry about.

'Right, I'm just going to have a feel of your bones. If anything hurts you tell me and I'll stop, okay?'

'Okay.'

Sophie carried out a primary assessment and found no obvious breaks anywhere—though Annie did complain about a pain midway down her back where the main joist had hit her. Sophie was worried she had a fracture there. But it was good that Annie could still feel all four limbs and was able to wiggle her toes and move her hands. There didn't seem any risk of paralysis.

She looked up and saw the ambulance crew arrive, along with a small group of firefighters. She quickly apprised them of the situation and the fire crew set about working out how they were going to lift the joists off Annie without causing any more damage.

Annie was being a star. It had to be frightening to be in her position, and yet she was taking it like a champ. Laughing. Smiling. Not complaining. Sophie liked her a lot.

She managed to get a cannula into her arm and give her some morphine. 'That should keep you comfortable whilst we wait to get this wood off you.'

'What do you do, Annie? Are you a bricklayer?' Theo asked.

'Scaffolder.'

'You don't mind heights, then?'

'I love heights. Love climbing things.'

'Me too. I'm a rock-climbing instructor.'

Annie beamed. 'No way! What's your latest climb? I did Rainshadow last summer.'

'You did? Amazing! Sophie, we've got a real star here. Rainshadow at Malham Cove is one of the most difficult climbs in the UK. Even I haven't done that route yet.'

'Are you going to?' Annie asked, grimacing.

'I think I'm going to have to now. Got any tips for when I do?'

'Just take it steady, man. Enjoy every moment and conserve your strength. The end part at the summit takes everything from you.'

'Okay, I'll remember that.'

The fire crew had created a rope and pulley system that would safely lift the joists off Annie, and Sophie watched as Theo reached out to grab Annie's hand.

'We're not leaving you, okay?'

'Okay.'

Sophie smiled. He was so good with patients. He was going to make an amazing paramedic. One she would be glad to work with if he chose to stay in the south-central area.

Would he? She was enjoying seeing him every day. Enjoying being with him. To think of him going made her feel sad. She didn't like it. They hadn't spoken about his future yet. She had no idea what he planned to do when he qualified.

Maybe I haven't asked because I'm scared he'll say he's going?

With the joists lifted and the site secure enough for them to work in safety, Sophie, Theo and the other para-medics log-rolled Annie onto a spinal board and finally got a cervical collar around her neck.

The police got everyone to back away and give Annie some privacy as Sophie used scissors to cut off her clothes and check for any injuries that hadn't been seen when she was on her front, but it appeared that Annie had been lucky—if luck was what she'd had in the first place.

'Will she be okay?' asked the foreman.

'We'll know more when we get her to the hospital,' Sophie told him. But it was looking good to her, and she didn't think there was any chance of paralysis.

Theo and the fire crew helped carry Annie off the site to the ambulance. Sophie waddled after them, rubbing at her sore back and feeling glad to be standing up again as her knees were beginning to feel it.

They always told you that as a paramedic: *Don't kneel anywhere...you'll regret it.* Because sometimes there could be questionable stuff on the floor at people's homes and at accident sites. But sometimes it was impossible *not* to kneel.

Sophie recalled once, at the very beginning of her career, she'd forgotten this rule at the house of a drug addict, and when she'd knelt down next to the patient she'd knelt on a carpet wet with urine. Her colleague had laughed at her afterwards for her wet knee patches, and she'd had to change, but Sophie had just been glad it hadn't been a needle.

She'd remembered after that never to kneel again. But because of the pregnancy she'd been doing what she had to, to be safe as well as comfortable.

She winced and rubbed at her belly.

Theo frowned. 'Everything okay?'

'Yeah...just Braxton Hicks, I think.'

'Does it hurt?'

'No, it's just really tight. Uncomfortable.'

He nodded. 'Perhaps you need to take it easy? Sit down for a moment?'

'I'm fine. Just spent too long in one position, that's all. I need to loosen up.' She began to shake out her arms, wiggled her feet around.

'But you'll tell me if you need a minute?' he said.

She nodded. 'Of course!'

His concern for her was more than a little disconcerting. She didn't want to tell him that she was feeling a little bit of pain. Like cramping, quite low, beneath her bump. It couldn't be the start of anything, right? It had to be cramping from sitting in a weird position.

Him caring for her, holding her, hugging her, making her feel safe and protected—that was the dangerous thing! She was beginning to like it too much. Was starting to crave it. Having him be all concerned and trying to look after her was making her antsy, and if she wasn't careful she'd be falling for this guy hard.

Sophie got into the driving seat and yanked at the seatbelt irritably. Every day she seemed to need more and more belt! She was getting huge now, and totally understood why some women were fed up by the time they reached their due date.

And having a kind, caring hunk of a guy looking out for you when all you were used to was looking after yourself was *not* the kind of emotional trap she was looking to fall into right now!

CHAPTER EIGHT

SOPHIE OPENED THE contacts list on her phone and dialled the number she wanted. It rang for a brief while before being answered.

'Soph?'

Her mum's voice sounded so clear. Almost as if she were in the next room. And suddenly Sophie ached for her in a way she had never felt before. Her eyes filled with tears and she had to swallow hard to be able to talk.

The Theo effect in full action—making her *want*.

'Hi, Mum. How are you?'

Suddenly she wanted her close. Wanted to tell her everything. About Connor. About the baby.

'I'm doing just great! I haven't heard from you in a while.'

'No, I've had a lot going on.'

Pregnancy. Growing your grandchild.

How was she to tell her this? It would be so out of the blue! Especially so close to her delivering. She regretted the distance between them, both geographically and emotionally. Had her mother simply taken the cue from her daughter that she wanted space, so stayed away? Barely called?

'Me too. Justin and I have just got back from a two-week holiday in the Algarve.'

'Justin?' She'd not heard that name mentioned before. And her mum had gone on holiday with him?

'Didn't I tell you about him? Oh, he's fabulous! Tall, dark and handsome. Works in the travel industry—so we're often flying here, there and everywhere. We went to Las Vegas a couple of months ago. I bet he could get you a good deal, if you and Connor want to go somewhere nice.'

Sophie sucked in a breath. This was the easy part. *Let's tackle this one piece of information at a time.*

'Connor and I aren't together any more, Mum.'

There was a brief pause. 'Oh! Well, plenty more fish in the sea, eh? Look at me! Now, I've got to go. I'm getting ready for a meal out and I promised I wouldn't keep Justin waiting too long. You're doing okay, though?'

It was a rhetorical question. Not one that her mother expected her to answer in detail. Sophie could just imagine her mother's horror if she suddenly decided to say, *Well, actually, I'm not, because I'm pregnant and about to become a single mother...* and then launched into a massive diatribe about how alone she felt now. How she regretted their history. How she wished her life was different.

Sophie tried her hardest not to cry. Not to let tears fall or let her mother hear the upset in her voice. And suddenly she felt doubt about telling her. She just couldn't and she didn't know why.

'I'm fine.'

'All right, sweetie... Well, take care! Toodaloo!'

'Bye, Mum.'

But her mum had already rung off.

Now the tears came. The crying. It all just seemed too much. She was feeling so alone in the world. No mum, no dad, no Connor, no Theo. Just herself. Herself and her daughter.

Why am I always left on my own?

Was there something inherently wrong with her? Something unlovable that made people feel they didn't want to stick around? Even Theo had warned her about what he wanted from the very beginning—and what had she done? Fantasised about the guy and developed feelings for him, despite telling herself not to. It was as if she was punishing herself with people who weren't emotionally available. Why did she do that?

She decided that from this point on she wouldn't do it any more.

I'm going to live my life for me and my daughter and to hell with everybody else! If they can't be there for me, then I'll be there for me.

The silence in the house made her promise seem empty.

'What did *you* do at the weekend?'

Sophie was trying her hardest to ignore the cramping she was feeling. It had been coming on and off all morning, but she had a shift to do, and for some reason it made sense to her to ignore what might be happening.

She was thinking that if she could put off giving birth for just a few more days, then somehow she could make things right between her and Connor, so that their daughter would be loved deeply—though separately—by both of them.

'We went to a sports park and did some climbing,' Theo replied.

'We?'

Dammit, why did I ask that? It's none of my business who he spends time with.

'Some of the guys at the rock-climbing place.'

Guys. Men. Okay. So he hadn't spent time with any women.

Not that his personal life was any of her business. She shouldn't resent his freedom. Or was it more that she resented the fact that he was free of her? Another example of him living his life quite happily.

She reached into the middle compartment under the dashboard and brought out a string of red liquorice. She balled the whole thing up into one tight ball and popped it in her mouth. If she chewed, then she wouldn't say anything that might show her anger right now.

Sophie had woken up angry. Had woken up feeling that she was a different woman somehow.

She knew she had to take responsibility for the situation in life she found herself in. It was no one else's fault. She was the one who had made bad choices throughout, looking for love with men who weren't available. It might have something to do with her dad dying, and her abandonment afterwards by her mother, but if she wanted to be loved then she had to love herself first—and that meant a bit of tough love.

She'd given herself a stern talking-to, and now she was sitting there, trying not to count how long this pain was lasting, as in the distance there was a strange boom.

Sophie frowned and looked at Theo. Had he heard it?

Theo looked at her, his face full of concern.

He had.

* * *

That boom hadn't been a good sound.

He glanced at Sophie and she grabbed the radio to contact Control.

'We're getting multiple calls coming through. Some kind of explosion at the Corn Exchange in Kingston.'

'Show us as attending.'

His mind whirled at what might have caused that noise. He hoped it wasn't a bomb. Control had said an explosion. Terrorism? Gas? No one knew. But he could hear Control summoning all available resources to the site, and he had no doubt that the police and the fire brigade were on their way, too.

He felt himself go into soldier mode. It was a certain mindset on a rescue mission. *Do what you can. Rescue those who can be saved. Come back later for the others.*

He had no doubt that whatever they were driving towards, it was going to be a big job. A turning point in his life that he would never forget.

Beside him in the car, Sophie drove intently, one hand rubbing at her underbelly.

'Baby kicking?' he asked.

'Um…yeah.'

He frowned, worrying about her. She'd been odd since the weekend, and he'd been noticing more and more that she was feeling discomfort as she got closer and closer to her due date.

'You know, no one would think less of you if you stood back from this.'

'Why would I be standing back?' she asked tersely.

He sighed. 'You're heavily pregnant, Soph. This could be dangerous.'

'It's dangerous for everyone—and besides, I'm fine. You don't have to look out for me, okay?'

Had something happened at the weekend? Had she realised how her world was going to change? How she was no longer going to be just Sophie, paramedic, but Sophie, *mother*? Perhaps she was still worrying about whether she'd be able to do it?

He figured that might be it. She hadn't been a mother before and, from what he understood, her own mother hadn't exactly been an exemplary model. He knew what it meant to be alone. To raise yourself. How you became dependent upon yourself and made your own decisions. Sometimes that could make you a little *too* independent. Made you snippy with people who tried to help.

But everyone winged it as first-time parents. Babies didn't come with a manual—you went on instinct. And generally people tried to help you.

Traffic was building as they got closer and closer to the town centre, and sometimes the lights and sirens weren't enough to clear a way through the streets. Sophie had wound down her window and was waving at people to get out of the way. At one point they found themselves stuck, with literally no place to manoeuvre, and Sophie cursed and swore, using words he'd never heard her use before.

He got out of the car and ran to the front of the traffic that was stopped at a red light, where he began to instruct everyone where to move to. Slowly but surely he created a narrow lane for the car to drive down, and Sophie stopped to collect him.

'Thanks.'

'No problem.'

They raced forward again, then hit another load of

traffic. He could now see people moving away in their hordes from the city centre, which was was filled with a mix of dust and smoke.

Sophie parked where she thought it was safe and they both got out and began to run as fast as they could towards the Corn Exchange. Theo was faster than her but he stayed with her, constantly looking back as she tried to run, holding her belly before her.

The building looked as if it had exploded outwards. There was glass everywhere, tables and chairs from the coffee shop strewn all over the pavement, and one or two people sitting there in shock, some with dirt and blood trickling down their faces. A lone teddy bear lay discarded in the middle of the road.

'Theo.' Sophie pointed to indicate that he should help those he could see and get them away from the Corn Exchange in case there was a second blast.

He passed her the smaller jump bag, so that she would have supplies to treat patients, and then ran towards the first person he saw: a woman with long dark curly hair and a laceration to her face from the hairline down to her eyebrow.

'Let me help you—let me take a look.' He knelt beside her and took her hand in his and gave it a squeeze. 'You're okay. I've got you. Do you know what happened?'

'I… I don't… I was sitting having coffee. I was working on my— Oh! My laptop!' She turned to try and find it, tried to get up and look for it.

Theo kept her in a seated position on the kerb. 'Don't worry about that for now. It can wait. Let's get you sorted.'

As he got bandages and saline to wash the wound from

his jump bag he glanced around him, saw Sophie attending to a man whose arm she was putting into a sling.

He glanced back at his own patient. 'What's your name?'

'Gemma.'

'Hi, Gemma. I'm Theo.'

She managed a weak smile at him. 'Am I bleeding?'

Gemma was clearly in shock. A lot of these people were going to be.

In the distance he heard the very welcome sound of more sirens. That was good. They were going to need a lot of extra hands here—a lot of ambulances. There were so many people with cuts and injuries, and there might be people trapped inside with more serious wounds. No one had any idea of what had caused the explosion, or if there was any danger of another one. They'd need the police and the fire brigade to secure the area.

Gemma's wound was jagged and deep. After cleaning it with saline, Theo applied a pressure bandage around her head and helped her walk further away from the Corn Exchange.

He sat her down on the ground near their vehicle. 'I want you to wait here, okay? Don't move and don't go looking for your laptop—it's not important.'

'Where are you going?'

'I've got to help the others.'

She nodded, understanding. 'Okay.'

He ran back towards the scene, eyes scanning quickly, trying to judge who needed him the most, and afraid that his skills would not be up to par for what might be needed from him. But it was all hands on deck, so he figured his basic skills would have to do. Besides, reinforcements were on their way.

He spotted a man with a little boy. He was trying to pick a shard of glass out of the child's leg.

'Stop!' he called out, running over.

The shard was large, and he had no idea how much was embedded. It could just be the tip—but what if it was something more? If this piece of glass had torn through an artery, then the little boy could bleed out.

The man faltered and looked up. 'But he's hurt!'

'I know—but if you pull that out it could make it a lot worse.'

The little boy was strangely quiet. Shock.

'What's his name?' asked Theo.

'Kyle.'

'Okay, Kyle.' Theo knelt to face him, tilted his chin up with his finger so that Kyle would look at him and meet his eyes. 'I'm Theo, and I need you to listen to me, okay?'

The boy stared back, saying nothing, his eyes blank.

'We're going to have to leave that in until we get you to hospital and do a scan or an X-ray. So I'm going to wrap a bandage *around* the glass, but I don't want you to touch it or move it, okay?'

He was really concerned. There wasn't much blood around the wound. If the glass was tamped down on an artery Kyle could bleed out in seconds.

'Were you outside the coffee shop?' he asked the father.

The man nodded.

'What happened?'

'I don't know. One minute we were sitting there, enjoying our drinks, the next—*boom*—we were being thrown into the road.'

Theo wrapped Kyle's leg and glanced around him to see what Sophie was up to. He couldn't see her from where he squatted on the pavement, but behind him he saw other emergency vehicles arriving, paramedics and firefighters running in all directions, and he felt a swell of relief.

Standing, he waved over to the first ambulance and headed over to the paramedic. It was Ross. 'Hey, man. We've got an injury here, and another woman with a facial laceration over by our vehicle.'

'Okay.'

'Sophie is…' Theo looked around and caught a glimpse of green uniform disappearing into the building behind a team of firefighters.

He swore, grabbed his equipment bag, and broke into a run.

'Soph!'

Theo's voice right behind her reassured her.

'Theo. There's a young woman over there who needs help. Looks like facial lacs, maybe some embedded glass—can you get her out?'

He looked about for the woman and began scrambling over the rubble and broken glass to get to the patient. 'What are you going to do?' he asked.

'I think I heard something. A child. A cry from back there.' She pointed to a doorway that led further into the building.

Beyond all the other noise—the coughing, the crying, the hubbub from the observers who'd been beginning to gather—she alone had heard the noise as the firefighters beside her had clambered over rubble in their breathing equipment.

And it was a noise that had called to her.

The cry of a baby.

Medical back-up would be coming—she could hear the reassuring sounds of sirens fighting their way through the streets of this town. She had Theo with her, the fire crew. All she had to do was quickly run in, grab the baby, and she'd be out again in a matter of seconds.

She would be saving a life. She couldn't leave a baby in there. It could be hurt. *It could be dying.* It hadn't even started to live yet!

'Be quick,' Theo said, giving her a look as he helped the stunned young woman to her feet and began to guide her out.

She nodded, her feet already beginning to carry her forward, waddling in the fastest run she could do in her condition. She felt another cramp coming on and winced. She'd had one earlier in the car and had thought it was maybe because she was sitting in a funny position. This one had to be because of all the adrenaline filling her— and even if it was something else, she would have plenty of time to go and find one of the other paramedics and tell them once she was out of there…

It could be something else.

Braxton Hicks weren't meant to be painful and these cramps were.

She had to be in labour.

Sophie clambered over a splintered broken table to get inside, her eyes adjusting to the dark, dusty interior. The coffee shop was in complete disarray. Almost destroyed. There were chairs everywhere, broken china cups and plates on every surface, and yet, strangely, a cake sat on a counter completely whole, its icing accompanied by debris from the roof.

She coughed, feeling the dust in the back of her throat. 'Hello?'

The crying continued. It was coming from the back. There were abandoned coats and boxes which she had to climb past, getting closer and closer to the crying, and finally finding the source of the noise. A baby in a pushchair, still strapped in and completely unharmed. It was probably crying because of the noise of the explosion. Or because it wanted to be picked up. It must be terrified. Was the mother the woman that Theo was helping?

'Sophie! Have you found anything?'

Theo's voice, right behind her, had her picking up the baby and turning around with her in her arms. 'Yes!'

'Give her to me. Let's go.'

She passed the baby over to him, wincing as another pain came and clutching at her abdomen.

'We need to get out of here. Come on!' He held out his spare hand.

'You take her out, get her checked. I'll be right behind you.'

He nodded and began to make his way through the mess and out of the café.

Sophie took a moment to breathe through her contraction, putting her hands on her knees for support. It completely took her breath away, the pain enveloping her entire abdomen so that she couldn't move. Couldn't follow Theo and the baby.

She stood upright again when it was over, relieved, and even smiled at herself. It was happening. The baby was coming. She was going to be a mother!

She took a step forward, and then saw smoke beginning to issue from a back room. Something was burning. She could hear it. A crackling noise.

'Guys?' she called out, hoping one of the firefighters was close enough for her to signal to.

As she started to walk out through the coffee shop, she noticed a storeroom of some kind. There were some canisters there. They were right next to the flames.

Gas? She didn't know, and she didn't have time to react. She turned, wanting to run, wanting to tell the firefighters that there was a dangerous area to secure—and then there was another loud boom and something knocked her off her feet. The ground disappeared and she fell into a deep, dark hole, landing awkwardly, feeling a pain shooting up her leg before she passed out.

Theo had just handed the baby to a paramedic when behind him there was another explosion. He covered the baby and the paramedic with his own body, then turned around, looking for Sophie.

Had she got out?

She'd been right behind him!

'Soph…? *Sophie!*'

He ran back towards the Corn Exchange, but the firefighter coming out of the building held him back. 'You can't go back in there.'

'My colleague's in there!'

'We need to make sure this building is secure.'

'She's heavily pregnant! She was right behind me!'

The firefighter looked grim. 'Okay. I think I saw her before the second explosion. But *we* go first—understand?'

Theo nodded. He thought the second explosion had seemed smaller than the first. Or was that just wishful thinking? He could kick himself for not checking that Sophie was following him, but he'd been in such a rush to get out of there, to get the baby some proper help, that he'd assumed…

Never assume! Always check! Hadn't his corporal told him that?

Theo looked despairingly at the building. If something had happened to Sophie he'd never forgive himself.

It took every ounce of self-control he had not to follow the firefighters in, and when they came back out empty-handed the lump in his throat almost threatened to stop him from breathing.

The fire chief came over to him. 'Okay, we've found her, but she's trapped.'

'Is she all right?'

'She says she's fine, but her leg is caught under some concrete and she thinks it's broken. She's asking for Theo.'

His heart sank and he felt sick. 'That's me.'

'The floor's collapsed and she's fallen through to a room below. We'll need to secure the safety of the floor before we let anyone in.'

'Let me down there. I'm a rock-climber, an ex-soldier. She knows me, and she can tell me what to do when I get down there with some equipment.'

'There's a doctor on his way via helicopter, isn't there?'

'But he's not here yet—and I am! Please! You said she asked for me.'

The fire chief seemed to think about it. 'All right, seeing as she wants you. We'll give you the equipment to help free her leg, so you can splint it.'

He nodded, glad to finally be of use, to put right this wrong and help Sophie—bring her to safety as he should have done after he'd helped the baby. He'd never forgive himself if he didn't do this.

It was his fault for leaving her behind.

* * *

Down in the dusty dark, Sophie tried not to cry or feel alone. She seemed to be in some sort of basement under the coffee shop. She'd landed on the floor and her right leg was trapped beneath a slab of concrete wall. It hurt badly, but it was nothing compared to the intense contractions she was experiencing. And—she glanced down, wincing—her waters had just broken.

I can't give birth down here! Not like this!

This was not the way she'd planned on bringing her daughter into the world! She'd pictured a beautiful clean, white hospital room. Some music playing. Soft lighting. Maybe even in a birthing pool! Candles. Someone mopping her brow. Midwives softly coaching her through contractions. Gas and air…

Not *this*. Not this dirty, dusty basement with a hole in the roof above her and smoke and rubble all around! With the stench of dirt and stone and cloying smoke.

Not alone. Never alone. I deserve more! Goddamn it, I deserve better than this!

'Sophie?'

Her heart almost stopped in joy at hearing his disembodied voice above her. 'Theo?'

'It's me. I'm coming down.'

'Be careful!'

'I've got an entire fire crew making sure I am.'

She looked up and saw him being lowered down through the small gap, climbing ropes and pulleys attached to his waist and hips. Carabiners held bags of equipment below him as he descended, and as he got closer and closer towards her, she began to cry.

'Oh, Theo!'

'I'm down!' he called to the firefighters above, unclipping himself and all the equipment. Then he went over to her, knelt down and wrapped his arms around her. 'Sophie!' He pulled back, frowning, looking down at the wetness around his knees.

'I'm in labour, Theo. My waters have broken.'

He looked grim. 'Okay…we're gonna get you out. We have time. You've not had any contractions yet, right?'

She nodded, biting her lip. Feeling guilty. 'One or two.'

'Sophie!' he admonished her. 'How many? How often?'

'I've not been counting. But I've had them all morning and they appear to be coming every few minutes.' Then she looked at her leg and winced. 'I'm also trapped.'

'I've got stuff to get you out. A jack to help lift the concrete so we can free you. And then we're going to haul you up out of here.'

'Have they got a pulley strong enough?' She smiled, trying to joke. She wanted to be brave. Like Annie had been, trapped beneath those roof joists, joking to her colleagues.

'For a little ole thing like you?' He smiled back and began pulling the equipment out of the bag the fire crew had given him. One piece was like a car jack, and he wedged it beneath the slab of concrete that was pinning her lower leg.

'I think I've broken my tib and fib.'

'You might not have, though.'

'I can feel it, Theo. Even if the fall didn't break it, the wall crushing it certainly did. And what about compartment syndrome?'

Theo shook his head. But she knew that compartment syndrome was a condition in which increased pressure could build up in an affected part of the body, resulting in insufficient blood supply to the tissues.

'You've not been trapped long enough for that, have you?' he asked.

She nodded. 'It's a crush injury—'

And then another contraction came, and she had to close her eyes and breathe through it. She felt Theo take her hand, could feel his thumb caressing the back of it, hear his soothing words coaching her through her breathing. His strength, his presence, helped her.

When it was over, she opened her eyes again and smiled at him. 'I'm glad you're here.'

'I'd like to say, *Me too*, but—' he looked around them '—I can think of better places we could be doing this.'

His radio crackled into life with a disembodied voice. 'How are you doing down there?'

Theo depressed the button on the radio with his thumb. 'We're okay.'

'We've got everything stable up here, so whenever you're ready...'

'Thanks.'

Another contraction hit, this one much stronger, and Sophie stared at Theo in shock as she felt the urge to push. *What?* This couldn't be happening! Already? Most first-time mothers took hours and hours, if not days, in labour.

'Theo, I think I need to—' Her voice was cut off by the primal groan that issued from her throat and she couldn't help it—she bore down.

'Sophie? I need you to look at me, okay?'

She opened her eyes, fear flooding her body, panic encroaching fast. She was stuck underground, her leg trapped, possibly broken, and her baby was trying to come into the world at the same time. This shouldn't be happening. Not this quickly. Not here. Not in this terrible place!

'If you're going to push, then I'm going to need to see what's going on.'

She shook her head. Not because she didn't want him to look, but because she couldn't believe this was happening. 'I'm scared!'

'I know you are. But I'm here, and I know what to do. We're going to get you out of this—do you hear me?'

He reached into the bag for scissors. She knew that with her leg trapped there was no way he was going to get her trousers off easily. He cut through the fabric from the ankle all the way up her leg to her hips, including her underwear, and clicked on the radio.

'I'm going to need someone to send down a couple of blankets, stat.'

'Will do. Is she going into shock?'

'She's about to give birth.'

Another contraction hit and Sophie sucked in a huge lungful of the dusty, dirty air and bore down as much as she could. The pushing helped. It somehow helped to push the pain away, made the pain a useful tool rather than something to be endured.

When it was over, she looked at Theo in exhaustion.

'I can see the baby's head. She's got hair.'

Sophie wanted to smile, but another contraction was coming and she had to deal with that.

Beside her, Theo stood and caught the blankets that were being passed down, and when her contraction was over he got her to lift her bottom so that he could place one clean blanket beneath her and one above her, over her groin.

She felt better about that. There would be some dignity, at least. Something was clean. Her baby wouldn't slither out onto a cold, concrete floor, but would instead feel softness.

'Soph, the next bit is going to hurt. I think you're going to crown with the next contraction or so...so when you feel that burn, you push through it—okay?'

She nodded. 'I forgot you've done this before. You delivered a baby. Your sister's.'

'Little Leo. But I hardly delivered him. I just stayed up by Martha's head and let her crush my fingers.'

'Leo and Theo.' She breathed in, smiling, resting her head against the wall behind her. 'I'm glad I'm not calling my daughter Cleo.'

He smiled and nodded. 'What a family we'd make, eh?'

She looked at him then. She thought he seemed to want to say something else, but then another contraction began.

Sophie sucked in the biggest lungful of air that she could and pushed down into her bottom. She could feel her baby moving through her. It felt as if she was pushing all the bones in her pelvis out of place, as if her skin was stretching so thin it would tear, and she cried out.

'Sophie, just pant! Pant it out! That's it. That's perfect. Okay, her head's out. Do you want to feel her?'

She reached down and— oh! She could feel her! Her daughter! It was nearly over.

'One more push, one more...'

When the pain came again she pushed as hard as she could and gasped as her daughter slithered out into Theo's waiting hands.

He scooped her up and placed her on Sophie's belly,

draping her in a blanket and rubbing the baby's back, as her child burst into lusty cries.

Above, she heard clapping and cheering and yells of congratulation, and she cried as she wrapped her hands around her baby and bent to kiss her head. She did have hair! Lots and lots of dark hair. And she looked a good size, too.

'Well done, Soph,' Theo said, clamping the cord with two scissor clamps, then cutting it.

She couldn't believe it! She'd done it. Her baby was here and she was perfect. She checked everything—ten fingers, ten toes. Then she hurried to undo her uniform top and held her daughter skin to skin, not caring about anything else. She felt as if she could stay there all day, just holding her and watching her. The broken, blown-out basement room was forgotten.

Theo was smiling at them both. There was something in his eyes that she couldn't understand, but she didn't try to. All her thoughts were on her beautiful baby daughter. They needed to get out of here.

Then Theo turned, glanced at her leg. 'Soph...? I've still got to free that leg.'

She nodded. 'Okay.'

'It's gonna hurt.'

She knew that. But right there and then she felt as if she could get through anything. 'Just do it.'

He nodded.

Sophie held her daughter tight and used every ounce of her inner strength to breathe as she felt him wedge the jack under the concrete slab. He glanced at her once last time, to make sure she was ready, and she nodded. He began—and as the concrete was lifted and her mangled leg was revealed she almost passed out from the pain.

CHAPTER NINE

SOPHIE LAY IN her wonderfully clean hospital bed, in a room that contained no dust, no smoke, no rubble, and truly felt blessed. Her daughter was healthy and perfect.

The doctors wanted to keep them both in for a while—not only to make sure neither of them had picked up any infection from the dirty basement, but also to let her leg heal after the lengthy surgery she'd had to put in a plate and screw back together the comminuted fractures of her lower leg bones. Both her tib and fib *had* been broken, although thankfully neither of the breaks had gone through the skin.

She'd had surgery and given birth and now she needed to rest, and she was looking forward to bonding with her daughter Cassidy.

Leaning over her cot, Sophie tried to work out who her daughter looked like. She'd read somewhere that babies tended to look like their fathers right after birth, to help the male parent bond with his child, but the only thing on Cassidy's face that looked even a little like Connor was her nose, and a little around her eyes. Everything else looked like Sophie as a baby. At least in the photos she'd seen of herself.

Cassidy made a small mewing sound in her sleep and

Sophie smiled, aching to pick her up again and hold her in her arms. But she knew, as an only parent, that she did not want to create a rod for her own back if she taught Cassidy that she would be picked up every time she made a cute sound.

Instead, Sophie lay back against her pillows and looked out of the hospital window. She could see brown trees and green grass, and those colours had never looked more beautiful. She supposed she ought to call her mother and let her know about Cassidy.

She'd not even had the nerve to tell her she was pregnant! But she couldn't let her mum live without knowing that she was a grandmother. Who knew? It might make her come and visit. She hadn't seen her mother in ages…

And she supposed, reluctantly, that she ought to tell Connor. He deserved to know his child had been born, even if he didn't care for either of them.

But the person she longed for the most was Theo.

Where was he?

The doctors had told her that he had remained by Cassidy's bedside for hours, watching over her whilst Sophie was in surgery, and that he'd wanted to wait by her side in Recovery afterwards too, but the nurses had sent him home to get some sleep, eat and change his clothes.

She felt she had so much to say to him. She wouldn't be able to express enough in words to thank him for looking after her and standing guard over Cassidy, whilst Sophie could not. How could she ever thank him enough for that?

She knew that he hadn't wanted to watch over anyone else's children ever again. That he was a free spirit. And she wanted to be able to say that she knew that before he vanished from her life for good.

Because she certainly wouldn't hold him to that *friends for at least a year* promise he'd made in jest. It wasn't fair on him—not when she knew he didn't want this, or anything she had to offer him. It would be unfair of her to expect him to want her because of what they'd been through together.

He'd helped her give birth. Had delivered Cassidy safely. She would always remember him with fondness even if he did walk away from them both.

And yet the thing she feared the most was that he wouldn't show. What if she never saw him again? What if he figured he'd done his part?

The ambulance service would probably place him with another mentor to finish off the last few days of his placement and he'd be busy, he'd forget her, and…

Sophie wiped away a stray tear.

I have to let him go.

If you love someone, let them go—wasn't that what they said? Whoever *'they'* were. You let them go. You put their needs above your own because you loved them. Because that was what love was about. Being selfless.

Theo had done it with his sisters, hadn't he? He'd let them leave the nest and find partners and leave him behind because he'd wanted them to have happiness. He'd always wanted them to have happiness—it was why he had cared for them when his mother had got sick.

If you love someone…

Did she love Theo?

I guess in a way I do. Probably for all the wrong reasons—but that's just me falling for the wrong guy again.

It was time to stand on her own two feet and be the mother that Cassidy needed. To fully focus on her daughter and not have her heart fretting and yearning for a man it couldn't have.

Why do I even think I want Theo, anyway? Just because he's kind? Because he makes me laugh? Because he's brave and strong? Because he makes me feel good? Because he protected my child when I couldn't? Because he brought her into the world? Because I suddenly can't imagine my life without knowing I can talk to him whenever I want to?

'Damn it!'

Sophie reached out to the box of tissues at the side of her hospital bed and dabbed at her eyes before wiping her nose. Sensing her distress, Cassidy began to awaken, her face pulling into a pout, before earnest crying began.

Sophie bent at the waist to reach out and lift her up into her arms. Glancing at the time, she saw that Cassidy was due for her next feed, so she unbuttoned her top and offered Cassidy her breast. The baby latched on almost instantly and began to suck. It felt strange, but beautiful and natural. She felt as if she was doing the one thing she'd always wanted to do. Being a mother.

She took the time to appreciate everything about her daughter. Her fluffy dark hair, the softness of her skin, the lashes resting upon her chubby cheeks, the shape of her lips. How gorgeous she was, and how much she loved her already.

Could I love anyone else as much as I do her?

Probably not.

But she knew of someone who came really close to deserving that level of love…

Knowing that he was never to be hers, she pushed the image of Theo's face out of her mind and focused on what mattered right now.

Her beautiful daughter.

* * *

His first thought upon waking was, *How many hours have I been asleep?*

Theo checked his mobile phone and saw that it was just gone eight o'clock in the morning, so he must have slept for a good eight hours. And he'd needed it after yesterday.

He'd spent so long living off adrenaline after the blasts, taking care of the casualties, running after Sophie into that devastation and finding her trapped, helping her deliver her baby girl...

He smiled to himself as he thought of that beautiful baby girl and the look on Sophie's face when he'd handed her daughter to her.

That was love. Pure love.

And he'd been envious.

He'd felt the same way at Leo's birth. Watching Martha take her son in her arms, seeing that love in her eyes, that connection they instantly had and knowing that it wasn't his, knowing it wasn't something he could be part of.

It had been a shocking emotion for him to acknowledge.

And he had feelings for Sophie, whether he liked to admit them or not. He'd found himself thinking of what it might be like to be with someone like her. He admired her. Her strength, her skill, her intelligence, her determination. The way she cared for people.

And he was most definitely attracted to her.

To see her on that concrete floor, rubble and devastation all around her, sitting there holding her newborn daughter in her arms... He'd wanted to sit beside her, drape his arm around her shoulder and just hold them both. Be part of it. Be part of something bigger than himself.

He'd felt envious of the adventure they were about to go on as a new family, and had known he would be left behind. He'd watched over his sisters and had to let them go when they'd found partners and had children of their own. Now he would have to do the same with Sophie.

I almost felt like the proud father myself.

But that wasn't what he wanted. A family...

Or was it?

Sophie had asked him once what he would do if he found true love and he'd not known the answer. Right now, he'd probably want to grab it with both hands—but he couldn't do that with Sophie. She wasn't his. Would never be his. She had a baby now. Had other priorities. She would put her daughter first in all things. And there was a father lurking in the dark shadows who hadn't played his hand yet, either. Theo knew he would play it at some point.

Knowing Sophie—being with her, talking to her—had made him realise that he had always defined himself in the past by what he could be to others. Whatever they'd needed from him, he had given it. After his sisters had left, he had decided to take the time to find out who he was by joining the army. He'd thought it would put him through tests and trials and make him who he was meant to be—but he'd just found himself giving to his army family, too.

Was that what he was really meant to be?

Part of something bigger than what he was alone?

He'd tried to stand alone. Had forced it to happen many times—leaving Jen being one of those occasions.

He'd needed it. To discover who he was, what he was, and what he wanted.

Was that Sophie?

This was playing with his head. He'd behaved a certain way for so long…to suddenly have these different thoughts, ideas and wants was confusing. Because if he did want Sophie and her baby, what was he to do? It was one thing to look after his little sisters—he was related to them through blood, after all—but totally another to take on another man's child.

And yet when he'd looked down at Sophie's daughter he'd felt something. Happiness. Pride. Love.

He knew he was capable of love, but was he capable of maintaining it? His own father hadn't managed it, and Theo had kept all his relationships short on purpose—not wanting to commit, not wanting to go with the flow, because he was afraid. There were no certainties with relationships. How many did he know that had problems? Too many. How many successful relationships had he seen?

And yet people still got into relationships all the time—and not just simple ones. Complicated ones. Because they had the hope and the belief that they could make it through whatever was to come.

Theo was a man who had climbed rock faces, conquered mountains, run towards gunfire and exploding buildings. He tried. He worked hard. And most of all he didn't like letting people down. He didn't like leaving people behind.

He never wanted to be anything like his father, so it was easier not to even try to be one. Why tempt fate when there were no certainties?

He thought again of how Sophie had looked with her

baby. How he had felt looking at them…how much he had wanted to be a part of their little family.

He could have that one day.

If he was brave enough.

But not with Soph. Not right now, anyway.

She had her relationship to sort out with Connor.

Theo threw off his bedclothes. He would take a shower, grab a bite to eat, and then he would go and visit Sophie and her baby girl in hospital. Make sure they were okay. See if there was anything she needed.

She'd need help in these early days, what with her leg and everything. He'd help her out. Do what he could. And when she got more mobile, he'd start to take steps back. Give her space. Let her live her life.

So why does the idea of stepping back feel so wrong?

'A *grandmother*?'

Her mother's shock reverberated down the phone.

'Are you sure?'

Sophie laughed. 'Well, there's a beautiful baby girl in my arms, so…yeah, I am. And you are a grandmother. I'm sorry I didn't tell you before…everything was just mixed up and crazy. I didn't even want to tell you that Connor and I had broken up.'

'Well… I don't know what to say. What are you going to call her?'

'Cassidy.'

'Oh, I like that.'

Sophie smiled. 'Good.'

She'd wanted her mother to know so badly, and now that she did she wanted her mother to want to see them. To say that she would come and see them both. Visit.

Look after them for a bit whilst she got over the birth and the surgery.

Wasn't that what mothers did? Came to cook or clean or fold laundry whilst the new mother and her baby got to know one another? It would be nice not to go back to an empty home. Nice to think that maybe, just this one time, her mother would do the kind of thing that mothers normally did.

But she knew her mother. And since talking to Theo she had begun to see what had happened in the past in a different light. They'd both been grieving. Both had coped with the death of a father and a husband in different ways.

'I would love you to see her, Mum. I've been thinking about how things have been between us in the past and I want to rectify that. Maybe you could come visit? What with the broken leg and everything, I'm going to need an extra pair of hands...'

It was worth asking, wasn't it? She never knew—her mum might change.

'I can't, Soph. I've got responsibilities here.'

Her mother sounded sad to be saying no and Sophie nodded silently, trying to understand. But with all the hormones surging around her body she found herself trying not to cry. She understood. But she also wanted her mum with her so badly! She wanted her to put her arms around her and hold her close and tell her how proud she was of her! She'd hoped they might take this opportunity to get to know one another again and grow closer, now that Sophie had had time to think about all they had gone through.

'I've got so much on my plate here. There are people here I can't let down.'

'I understand. It's fine…honestly. I'll send you some photos.' Sophie wiped her eyes with her hospital gown.

'That'll be great—and I'll get to see her sometime. It's not like she's going to go away, is she? When I'm free again…maybe nearer Christmas… I'll try and get down to you both.'

'Great. We'd love to have you for Christmas. Bring Justin. It would be nice to meet him.'

'I'd love that. And I'd love to get to know you again. You and I…we messed up, didn't we?'

Sophie nodded, saying nothing.

'I love you, kiddo. I'll see you soon, okay? Bye!' and then she rang off.

Sophie held the phone in her hand, wondering how on earth she was going to cope at home if she had no one to help her whilst she hobbled around on crutches. Taking care of a newborn would be hard enough, but to deal with a broken leg, too…? Would they even let her leave the hospital unless she could prove she had support?

She hoped her mother would come to mend things between them. They'd mentioned it briefly. Both acknowledged it. Perhaps that had been the problem all along? Neither of them had been able to admit there was a problem, but until they did, they couldn't fix anything.

But now she felt she understood her mother a little more. Her mum had been lonely. Grief had left her alone and looking at a child who had her father's eyes. It must have been difficult. She'd loved Sophie's dad very much. And she'd spent the rest of her life chasing love, trying to find it with others. And she'd done it without Sophie.

Maybe that had been the wrong way to do it, but now, with both of them willing to try and fix things, at the right pace for them both, then maybe they had a chance at the kind of relationship Sophie had always hoped for.

It took Theo ages to find a parking spot. He found himself wishing he had the rapid response vehicle, so he could park anywhere and not spend twenty-five minutes driving up and down the rows of cars, waiting for someone to pull out so he could quickly nip in. Not to mention the outrageous parking fee he'd have to pay when he finally emerged from the hospital again—but he wasn't going to let that worry him too much.

He hoped Sophie would be awake when he got to her room. The last time he'd seen her she'd just come out of surgery, and she'd looked so small in that bed, so vulnerable, he'd felt a pain in his chest. When the nurse had suggested he go home to take a break, and said she'd keep an eye on Cassidy until Sophie woke, he'd accepted. Gladly. The strange feelings assailing him had not been making sense at all.

He buzzed the door at the unit and spoke over the intercom, telling them who he was there to see. Like a shield, he held a box of chocolates and a teddy front of him as he headed to Sophie's room. Peering through the window, he saw that she was awake, sitting up in bed, with one hand upon her daughter as she slept.

A huge smile crept across his face. He gave a quick knock and then pushed the door open. 'Room for one more?'

'Theo!' Sophie beamed at seeing him, and he headed in and placed the gifts beside her, not knowing whether he ought to kiss her on the cheek or not. He made the sudden decision to do it anyway, but kept it brief, telling himself not to do anything stupid like breathe her in, or anything like that.

'How are you feeling?' he asked, sitting down.

She shrugged. 'Bit rough. But I think that's the anaesthetic. They said I might feel sleepy for a day or so.'

'How's the leg?'

'Fixed.'

He nodded. 'And Cassidy?'

Sophie smiled. 'She's wonderful. Do you want to hold her?'

He wanted to—very much—but every time he had before, when Sophie had been in surgery, he'd found himself imagining what it would be like if she were his.

'Oh, I don't think I should—'

'You delivered her. You should at least have the honour of giving her a cuddle after coming to our rescue.'

Theo got up from his seat at the side of the bed and walked round to Cassidy's cot. Cassidy was awake now, but yawning, her arms above her head as if she were stretching. Gently, being careful to support her head, he scooped her up into his arms and stood there gently rocking her, smiling down at her. She was gorgeous!

'She's beautiful...'

'Yes, she is.'

He stood there for a moment, just enjoying having Cassidy in his arms, then after a bit went back to his seat and settled down with the baby in his arms.

'Have you told Connor she's been born?'

'Yes.'

He looked up at her. 'And when's he coming?'

'He's not.'

Theo frowned, feeling annoyed that this idiot of a

man could walk away from such beautiful souls. 'Did he say why?'

'No. He thanked me for telling him and then said he had to go. That he'd send me some money for "nappies and things".'

Theo wanted to swear. But to do so with a baby in his arms felt wrong. 'Have you told your mother?'

Sophie nodded, but didn't smile. In fact, she looked close to tears.

He got up and walked around her bed to the cot. He laid Cassidy down before grabbing a tissue box from the side of the bed and passing it to her. 'Is she not coming either?'

Sophie shook her head, dabbing at her eyes. 'Said she was busy. That she might make it down for Christmas.'

'Then who's going to look after you?'

'I'll manage. I'll find a way. I'll—'

'I'll help.'

The words were out without him even having to think about them. For her to be so let down by Connor and her mother was appalling! And who else could she ask? She had friends, but they were all paramedics, too, and they wouldn't be able to take time off work. Theo figured he could take a couple of weeks—he could make the time up later—and after that… Well, he could bring in reinforcements. There was no way he was going to let her do this alone! It was what friends did. They were there for each other.

'No, Theo. I couldn't ask you to jeopardise your studies.'

'No jeopardy. I can make up the time. As long as I fulfil the required number of hours on placement, it doesn't matter when I get them done. I can help you out for a week or two. And my sisters will help—I know they will. Don't you worry about anything. I'll sleep on the couch,' he added, to clarify.

Not that he needed to. They were just friends. She wouldn't expect anything else of him—he'd made his position clear.

'Theo...you're so...so good to me. Thank you.'

He smiled at her, feeling good about his sudden decision, even though his logical brain was screaming internally at him—*You're doing what?*

CHAPTER TEN

SHE'D NEVER IMAGINED returning home like this—on crutches, hobbling up her front path whilst, behind her, her student carried Cassidy in her car seat. It wasn't meant to be like this. She'd never imagined coming home truly alone, having figured Connor might show up out of guilt, at least! Or her mother… But the less said about her, the better.

Of all the people she could rely on, it was Theo.

Handsome, caring, lifesaving Theo.

A man she couldn't have.

A man you don't want. Remember?

Though right now she was struggling to remember why. Something to do with commitment and responsibilities? But if that was the case then what was he doing here? Was he just being reliable and dependable, as he'd promised?

Of course he is. It couldn't possibly be anything else.

Theo didn't want this kind of responsibility full time! He was doing this out of pity, or something. Kindness, maybe.

'It's good to be home,' she said.

'I bet.'

Theo placed Cassidy down in the middle of the floor

in Sophie's living room and they both just stood there for a moment, looking down at her.

'What do we do with her now?' she asked.

Theo shrugged and said nothing, but then a bubble of laughter escaped him and, before they knew it, they were both laughing hysterically.

Sophie hobbled over to her sofa and flopped down, propping her crutches against the wall.

'Cup of tea?' Theo asked.

'Oh, yes, please. The stuff they serve you in the hospital tastes of dishwater, at best.'

'It's a ploy—to make you go home quicker.'

'Well, it worked.'

With Theo making himself at home in the kitchen, Sophie found herself staring at her daughter, fast asleep in her car seat, and wondering just what kind of life she was going to give her. Her own experiences of life had taught her that she was always second-best, or not worth staying for. How did she want her daughter to feel? How did she want her daughter to grow up? She would do anything not to let her daughter feel that way, and that had to start now. Cassidy would know that she was loved.

But one parent would have to be enough, because Sophie really didn't see her ever having two...

'Here you go.' Theo brought her a cup. 'She'll be ready for a feed soon, won't she?'

Sophie smiled. Theo knew their routine already. The time they'd spent in the hospital together had really focused him, and she'd marvelled at how dedicated he was to seeing to their needs. What would she have done without him?

But I can't rely on him for ever. He won't be here long.

'Yes, she will,' she said.

'Well, I'll go and unpack everything upstairs whilst you take care of that.'

She was breastfeeding, and she'd noticed that Theo would discreetly disappear whenever she needed to feed Cassidy. He didn't need to. She would cover herself with a shawl or blanket if she wanted to. But she said nothing. Theo was coping with this in his own way and she didn't want to start telling him what to do. He wasn't her partner. He was just helping out.

Theo got Cassidy out of her car seat and laid her in her arms.

Sophie felt her heart expand every time she looked at her. Every time she held her. Cassidy made her happy. So did Theo—but she figured that was just postnatal hormones trying to make her feel she was in a happy family, even though she knew it wasn't real.

As Cassidy latched on Sophie found herself unexpectedly wiping away a tear. The midwives had said she might feel emotional for a little while. Her body had been through a lot. It had been very traumatic. She'd been trapped, frightened, at her most vulnerable.

The fact that she was doing so well was all down to Theo.

Where would I be without him?

The doorbell rang, startling them both out of sleep. It seemed both he and Sophie had nodded off on the sofa—Theo looked at his watch—for about an hour.

'Dinner's here.'

Sophie struggled into an upright position. 'You ordered takeaway? I'm not sure I want spicy food whilst I'm breastfeeding—'

'Not takeaway.' He smiled. 'My sisters, remember?'

He almost laughed at her confused frown, then hurried to the front door and opened it wide.

'Theo!'

Hazel, Leonora and Martha all stood on the doorstep, armed with trays and dishes of food that should last him and Sophie a good week. His heart swelled at seeing them, and he gave them each a hug before inviting them in and leading the way into the lounge.

'Soph? Meet my sisters—this is Martha, that's Hazel, and Leonora on the end.'

Sophie beamed a smile. 'Hello.'

'They've brought food, so that we don't have to think about shopping for the first week. Plus...' he smiled '...it's also an excuse for them to come and spy on the woman who's wickedly blackmailed me into staying and looking after her child.'

'Theo! That's not true!' said Martha, blushing, giving his arm a gentle, playful shove. 'Well, maybe a little true—but come on! It's not every day our dear, determinedly single brother shacks up with a woman and a baby, is it? You'll have to excuse us, Sophie, we're a little protective. Of course we wanted to help out, but admittedly we were curious, too.'

Sophie laughed. 'I get it. Don't worry—I'd probably do the same thing, too, if I had a sibling.'

Leonora passed her tray to Theo. 'Well, don't just stand there, brother mine. Put the kettle on whilst we chat to Sophie and coo over the baby.'

Theo looked to Sophie, to make sure she was okay being surrounded by his protective family, and she gave him a small wink and smiled, so he headed into the kitchen.

It was good to see his sisters again. He'd not really

seen them since his placement with Sophie on rapid response. They'd spoken on the phone, obviously, but it wasn't the same as spending time with them. He'd almost forgotten how they could be when they were all together. He jokingly referred to them as 'The Coven' when they were away from their husbands and children and the wine began to flow, but it was affectionate. He loved them to pieces and hoped Sophie would like them too.

He'd asked if they wouldn't mind helping out with a dish or two, but he'd certainly not expected them to all descend at once! Not that he minded…

From the living room he heard cascades of laughter from all four women, and he thought he detected his name being mentioned. When he took the cups of tea through Martha was regaling Sophie with a childhood tale of Theo getting nettle stings all over his backside, because he'd been running around naked in their back garden and had fallen into a wild patch.

He felt his cheeks colour, but he laughed with them, because Sophie seemed to be enjoying every minute of his sisters telling her things about him she didn't know—from the time he threw up after eating all their Halloween sweets one year, to the time he held Martha's hand whilst she gave birth, because her husband hadn't been able to make it through the traffic. They also told her about how Theo had sat with Hazel and her partner David as they'd watched over their son in hospital when he'd got suspected meningitis. His dedication. His strength. His commitment to them.

He sat there mostly saying nothing, blushing sometimes, his gaze meeting Sophie's, watching her smile, watching her laugh. She fitted in with them so well, and she regaled them with some tales of her own of their time together in the rapid response vehicle.

He hadn't realised just how proud she was of him.

He felt happy. Content.

And that frightened him—because he knew happiness and contentment always got taken away from him. He'd always thought his dad was the centre of his world, until he'd learned that he was leaving. He'd thought he could look after his mum and keep her safe, until she'd succumbed to her condition and died. He'd thought he'd be able to look after his three sisters and keep them safe for ever, until they'd each flown the nest and left him behind.

Even the army—the one place where he'd thought he'd have a family—had disappeared the day he'd lost Matty-Boy and it had begun to hit home that he always lost those he allowed himself to get close to. Letting his guard down, always ended with him getting hurt.

Even this—what he was experiencing now—was a mirage. It wasn't really his. Sophie wasn't his. Cassidy wasn't his. He was only here as a stopgap, helping her out—it wasn't *real*.

The thought cast a pall which he tried to ignore.

He smiled when he felt he ought to.

He kissed and hugged his sisters goodbye and closed the door after waving them off.

When he got back inside the living room, to see Sophie about to feed Cassidy once again, he made his excuses and said he was going to grab a quick shower.

He could see that Sophie was worried about him.

Had she noticed a change in him?

Well, she didn't need to worry.

He wasn't hers to worry about.

Which was something they both needed to keep in mind.

CHAPTER ELEVEN

SOPHIE HAD *LOVED* Theo's sisters. To see the bond between the siblings had made her yearn for the same thing, wish that she'd not been an only child. But then, if she'd had a brother or a sister it would have been one more child to be ignored by their mother, so it was best that it had been just her.

Though it might have been a little less lonely...

She envied the relationship Theo had with Martha and Leonora and Hazel. They were so close! And she'd loved having them here. Such a noisy, but loving group...

Would Cassidy ever have a sibling? It might be nice for her to have one, if they could be anything like Theo and his sisters were together, but that would entail trusting a man enough to be in her life and she wasn't sure she could do that.

Theo was the closest she'd come to letting a man back into her life again, and she could see he would make a great father—

No! Stop it!

Maybe this was a bad idea, having Theo so close all the time? So available? So giving of himself? It didn't tally with all that he'd told her of not wanting commitment, and yet here he was! Unless he thought of her as family? A kind of sister, perhaps?

Now, why does that thought depress me?

'Because I don't want him to see me as a sister, do I, Cassidy?' she said quietly, picking up her daughter. 'I want him to see me as a woman.'

Cassidy opened her mouth, rooting for a feed.

'I don't know why. It's just how I feel and…and I think that's okay. Because he saw me as his boss and his mentor, and then he saw me give birth, for crying out loud. You can't get any more intimate than that, huh?'

He saw me give birth.

She'd read somewhere online that some men didn't want to watch their wives give birth in case it put them off having sex with them. Which seemed a ridiculous, misogynistic thing for any man to say.

She wondered if men really were so fragile that they needed to maintain the fantasy that their wives and girl-friends' vaginas were only for their sexual pleasure—not a place that could get torn or ripped as a baby squeezed itself out. She almost laughed. It was ridiculous, whatever it was.

Theo had watched her give birth and he hadn't looked appalled or embarrassed. He had been concentrating on the task at hand, had tried to maintain her dignity, and he had marvelled at the new life she had brought into the world.

Besides, he's not sexually attracted to me. We almost kissed that time, but he stopped it. Saved me from embarrassing myself. And, quite frankly, I'm embarrassing myself still now, if I even think that for one moment he's thinking of me in such a way!

* * *

Theo couldn't stop thinking about Sophie. She was in his head constantly.

Was she feeling okay?

Had she taken her painkillers?

Was her leg comfortable?

Did she need anything to eat?

Did she need help getting upstairs?

What did she think of his family?

Had she enjoyed the visit with his sisters?

Why did he feel that they had something special between them when she winked at him?

Why did he enjoy her smiles?

Why did her happiness and contentment make *him* feel so good?

His mind was whirling with all the possibilities and he couldn't quite get a fix on his emotions.

When he'd said he'd help out he'd meant it, figuring that sleeping on her sofa for a few weeks wouldn't be a problem. He could help out with laundry, do the shopping, run errands, hold the baby on occasion when Sophie needed a break... But he found himself doing a whole lot more. Looking at Sophie in snatched moments. Thinking about her. Wondering if he could reach out and just take her hand... What it would have been like if he'd kissed her that time...

He'd not been able to get to sleep at all tonight, tossing and turning on the sofa, and now he could hear Cassidy crying.

Cassidy slept in a cot attached to the side of Sophie's bed, so he knew that Sophie would be able to reach her and see to her needs in the night. Each evening he made sure that the changing bag was full, so if Cassidy needed a nappy-change Sophie could do that, too, without having to get out of bed.

But Cassidy wasn't stopping crying.

He could hear Sophie, trying to soothe her, but for some reason Cassidy continued to cry, wailing and screaming as if nothing was going to settle her.

As soon as he heard Sophie getting upset, too, he threw off the blanket and pulled on some jogging bottoms and raced upstairs. He paused outside Sophie's room, about to knock gently on the door.

Would she be offended if he suggested that he help? Would she think he was implying she couldn't cope on her own? He'd hoped that by setting up her room each night he was empowering her to be the mother she wanted to be, that it was only her leg in a cast that was stopping her.

But Cassidy sounded miserable—and Sophie did too.

'Cassidy, please stop crying. I don't know what you want!'

Theo knocked and popped his head inside. 'Are you decent?'

He held his hand over his eyes in case she was in a state of undress, or trying to feed Cassidy without a blanket covering her modesty. Not that he'd be bothered by seeing her breastfeed. It was the most natural thing in the world. But he was aware of his intense sexual attraction to Sophie, so that made him respect her.

'I'm fine. But she won't stop crying, Theo!' And she burst into tears, too.

Theo rushed over. 'Does she want a feed?'

Sophie shook her head.

'A nappy-change?'

'I just changed her.'

Sophie grabbed a tissue from the box at the side of her bed and noisily blew into it.

'Want me to try and settle her?' he asked.

Sophie nodded, and Theo stooped to take baby Cassidy from her arms.

Poor Cassidy had a bright red face, wet with real tears, and her little body felt tense and rigid with her frustration.

Theo stood upright and placed her against his shoulder and gently began to rock her, singing a song that he remembered his dad singing to him. A song that he'd heard his sisters sing to their babies when they wouldn't settle.

'Two little men in a flying saucer...'

He bobbed up and down as he rocked gently from side to side, and it took a moment, but eventually Cassidy began to settle, her crying lessening to become sniffles, then nothing, as she enjoyed the rocking, bobbing motion of his body and began to relax against him.

'I don't believe it...' Sophie whispered.

'It's a magic song. Don't tell anybody—it's a secret.'

'Where did you learn how to do that?'

'My sisters. My nieces and nephews.'

At that moment Cassidy let out a deep belch, and Theo's eyes widened as Sophie chuckled in her bed, her eyes glistening with happy tears now, not sad ones.

'You're very good with babies,' she said.

'I've had a lot of practice.'

'Thank God you're here.' She smiled. 'I'm never going to let you leave.'

He smiled, but the thought scared him a little. This was only meant to be temporary, right? But a real part of him was considering the possibility of being here and looking after little Cassidy for a long, long time. And with that came the thought of what might happen between him and Sophie.

And if he allowed it to happen…if he got comfy, if he let his guard down…would it all be taken from him?

Sophie was out of bounds and Cassidy already had a father. This wasn't his child and Sophie wasn't his girlfriend! Babies played games with your mind. They made you reconsider things…they made you wonder *what if?* They made you want. They made you question your life choices.

What if Sophie and I were an item?

He wouldn't let his mind go there.

He couldn't.

Sophie stood in front of the fridge, trying to decide what to choose for her and Theo for lunch. After his help with Cassidy the night before they were both tired, and she wanted to thank him by getting him something to eat for a change. Normally Theo cooked for them.

Looking inside the fridge, she could see she had a choice of Martha's macaroni cheese or Hazel's vegetarian lasagne. She opted for the lasagne and, whilst it was heating in the oven, began to prepare a salad.

It was a bit of a nightmare, constantly hobbling from the chopping board to the sink, to rinse vegetables in the colander, but eventually, with a drizzle of balsamic and a garlic tahini sauce, the salad looked great. She even sprinkled some sesame seeds on top for presentation.

Then she stopped to consider how she might carry two plates of food and a salad into the living room.

I'll set it up on the kitchen table and we'll eat in here.

She made them a cup of tea each, and placed a jug of water on the table, too, then went to fetch Theo. But when she hobbled into the living room she noticed that Theo was reclining on the sofa, fast asleep, with Cassidy resting on his chest, fast asleep, too!

Bless... They look so sweet together. Like father and daughter.

Only he wasn't Cassidy's father, was he? Connor was. The slimeball who had dumped her when she'd discovered she was pregnant and hadn't even bothered to turn up at the hospital. *That* was the man she'd chosen as a partner. The man she'd believed would bring her a happy-ever-after. Clearly her decision-making processes couldn't be trusted.

Why couldn't she have met Theo first? No, he didn't want commitment of any kind, but at least he'd been honest about it up-front and, despite that, here he was after only knowing her for a few weeks, living in her home and helping her take care of her child.

He'd stepped up. He'd committed. Whether he wanted to accept that or not.

But he was just a friend, and moments like this one would be rare.

With that thought in mind she pulled her mobile from her pocket, opened up the camera and took a picture of the snoozing pair.

It was a perfect photo. Theo's arms were wrapped protectively around Cassidy, his head to one side, as he caught up on the sleep he'd lost last night helping her out. And helping Cassidy. Her daughter looked totally content. As if the two of them were meant to be.

Only I can't have him. We can't have him.

'Theo...?' she said, her voice just above a whisper. She didn't want to make him jump. 'Theo?'

Slowly his eyelids opened and he squinted, looking for the source of the voice and smiling when he saw her.

He glanced down at her daughter on his chest. 'Sorry. I shouldn't have fallen asleep like that. What time is it? Want me to prepare lunch?'

Sophie smiled. 'No need. I've done it. I've come to tell you it's ready.'

'Should I disturb Sleeping Beauty here?'

He rubbed Cassidy's back and she snuffled and snuggled further into him as he scooped her against his shoulder and carried her over to the bassinet, slowly laying her down and tucking her in. She went right back to sleep.

'Mission accomplished.'

'Lunch is in the kitchen.'

'I'll be right there. Let me wash my hands.'

She hobbled her way back to the kitchen on her crutches and laid them against the wall as she sat at the table. Moments later, Theo joined her.

'Must have been more tired than I realised,' he said.

'That's okay. You obviously needed it.'

'Why don't you take a nap this afternoon?' he suggested. 'I'll take Cassidy out for a walk in her pram… get some fresh air.'

'Thanks.'

Why was he so kind and considerate? Why was he exactly as she'd imagined her partner might be as she raised a child? Taking it in turns with her, giving her time to sleep, to rest, sharing the responsibilities equally and without blame? *Why?*

'Except the health visitor is coming this afternoon at four,' she added. 'So you'll need to be back by then so she can see Cass.'

He nodded. 'Okay. This looks great, by the way.'

'It does. I must phone your sisters later and thank them again.'

'Haven't you already done that?'

'I know… But I like talking to them. It's like having sisters of my own. Mind if I adopt them?' She laughed.

'Be my guest. They'd love that.'

The lasagne was indeed delicious, and they both had second helpings. Theo made her stay seated whilst he cleared everything away, and she watched him intently, wondering why a man who was as adamant as he was against commitment seemed to be so good at it.

'You're a good man, Theo.'

He smiled as he loaded plates into the dishwasher. 'Thanks. I try.'

'No, I mean it. I could get used to this… I have to keep telling myself it's temporary. That I'm only *borrowing* you. I know I'll be okay afterwards. You know…on my own… But it'll be odd not having you around.'

He dried his hands on a tea towel and looked at her, saying nothing. 'Well, until you're back on both feet I'll be here, so you won't be losing me just yet.'

But she would lose him one day. There was no doubt about it. And she could feel the day approaching. Getting closer and closer.

It was like being stalked by something terrible. Another man she had begun to love would leave her.

It was uncomfortable to know that it wasn't just because she needed him—she was a strong, independent woman and always had been. It was the knowledge that she *wanted* him to stay.

But she couldn't bring herself to say it out loud, Because if she did that would make her vulnerable, and she didn't want to see the pity in his face as he tried to let her down gently.

She didn't want to be like her mother—chasing happiness and love in other people. Her happiness had to come from within herself, no one else, and yet here she was pining over a man.

Just as she'd told herself she would never do.

CHAPTER TWELVE

THEO WAS OUT, walking Cassidy in her pram, and his mind was going over and over what had been said after lunch.

Of course he'd love to stay! These last few days with Cass and Soph had been some of the best days of his life! They'd laughed, they'd cried, they'd watched over Cassidy, parented her like a real couple.

Babies were intoxicating—especially babies like Cassidy, with her cute smile and her wispy curls that were just the softest thing Theo had ever touched.

But he was terrified of what was happening. This yearning to stick around was becoming impossible to deal with, and everything was still so uncertain. Soph had heard nothing more from Connor—but what if he turned up suddenly and Sophie fell back into his arms? Theo would be ejected…he'd lose them both. Of course he'd step aside to give Connor a chance to bond with his daughter. She was Connor's, not Theo's! He had to remember that.

Sophie wasn't the one borrowing *him*—he was the one borrowing *them*, playing at being a happy family again, reclaiming the past he'd had with his sisters before they'd married and had children, putting off in his head what would have to happen in the future, when it got snatched away again.

They could be taken from me at any moment.

Connor could knock on that door and that would be it. Over. Done. *Adios muchachos!*

He knew how that would feel and it scared him to death. Already he was in too deep with Sophie and her daughter, and he knew he had to back away soon. This was all too familiar—this caring for other people, knowing he would lose them, that they had never been his in the first place. His dad hadn't belonged to him, his mother had been lost much too soon, and each of his sisters had flown the nest.

He remembered that feeling he'd felt deep in his heart when he'd stood in the house all alone.

I never want to feel that way again.

But how to step away without upsetting Sophie?

How to leave without destroying the friendship and the relationship they had created?

Perhaps if he took baby steps towards giving her independence? She was getting around much better on her crutches now, she was doing well, and if he got his sisters to check in on her that would give him time to get back to his studies. To complete his placement hours.

He couldn't forget that he had a career that had been put on hold whilst he was playing at being a family man!

This wasn't his life.

It was never meant to be.

Tormented, he got back to Sophie's house with Cassidy just as the health visitor arrived, and he invited her in, calling for Sophie.

'I'm in the kitchen!'

He smiled, parking Cassidy in her pram in the hall. She was still asleep. 'You get some rest?' he asked.

'An hour.'

'Health visitor's here.'

Sophie hobbled into view. 'Oh, hi! I'm Sophie.'

'Nice to meet you. I'm Michelle.'

'Shall we go through?' Theo suggested.

With the two ladies settled, Theo offered to make a cup of tea.

'Oh, nothing for me, thanks,' said Michelle. 'I had tea at my last lady's house.'

Sophie shook her head. 'I'm fine, too.'

Theo settled down on the couch next to Sophie.

'Well, it's nice to meet both of you… How have you been, Sophie?' Michelle asked.

'Not too bad. The leg can be a bit of a hindrance, but apart from that I'm coping well.'

'Good—that's good. And how have you been feeling within yourself? Mood okay?'

Theo sat listening as Sophie and Michelle talked. Sophie wasn't alone with Cassidy. She had her midwifery team at the end of the phone, she'd got a health visitor she could call on at any time, and there were his sisters! Hazel and Sophie in particular got on really well. And of course, somewhere there was Connor. Maybe Connor's family. And Sophie's mum. Plus, she had her friends in the ambulance service. It wasn't as if he was going to leave her in the lurch.

But he knew he had to leave her sooner, rather than later—before he got ousted by someone else. Taking control of his leaving was preferable to suddenly losing them, and it wasn't as if he couldn't keep in touch! Though for a little while he might have a bit of a break…because seeing Sophie and knowing he couldn't have her was going to be a little problematic…

'And you're Dad?'

Theo tuned back in. 'What? Me? Oh, no!' He laughed. 'No, not at all… Just a friend, helping out. I'll be gone soon. Sophie's coping really well.'

He somehow needed to say it out loud. Let her know his intentions. Announce where he was, what he needed to do.

Make it clear so it's no surprise.

He didn't look at Sophie.

So he didn't see the look on her face.

He was going to leave soon.

The words slammed into her chest like a wrecking ball and she had to swallow hard and look away, pretending to straighten some magazines on a side table so that Michelle or Theo wouldn't see how affected she was by those words.

But she couldn't have been that good at hiding her feeling, because Michelle said, 'Theo, would you mind if I have a word with Sophie in private? Just to ask a few personal questions?'

'No problem. I'll check on Cassidy…take her upstairs.'

Sophie watched him go. He sounded so cheerful.

Because he'd made up his mind to go?

Did he not realise how much she needed him? Not just because of Cassidy, but because…

She loved him.

Sophie turned to look at Michelle with tears in her eyes.

'Are you okay?' asked the health visitor.

She sniffed. 'Yes. No. It's just… I knew he was only

here to help me out temporarily, but he's been so good…
I don't know what I'm going to do without him.'

'You should tell him how you feel.'

'I can't. I know it's not what he wants. *We're* not what
he wants. Not really. I'd hate to put him in a position
where he feels trapped into staying. And besides…' she
laughed '… I'm full of hormones. I don't know how I really feel.' She sniffed. 'Theo has done *everything* for me.
It would be so easy to think he's the answer to it all. Did
you know he delivered Cassidy?'

Michelle nodded. 'I read the notes.'

'Theo isn't the type to settle down.' She smiled
through her pain. Wiped her eyes. 'He doesn't want the
responsibility of a family. What if I put myself out there
and ask him to stay and he leaves anyway? I can't be
abandoned again, Michelle. I can't!'

'Well, only you and he know how you really feel.
Maybe you should start talking about the future? See
what he has to say?'

'I know what he'll say. He just said it to you. He's
going to leave soon. And I'm not chasing him.'

Sophie chatted with Michelle for a bit longer, but then
the health visitor had to leave. Sophie walked her to the
door and said goodbye, knowing she'd have to talk to
Theo, who was still upstairs.

But the fear of having him walk away from her, of
having him abandon her, was just too painful to bear.
She loved him. She knew she did. But he didn't want
this. He'd laughed just now when it had been suggested
he was Cassidy's dad and he'd mentioned leaving soon.

Perhaps it would just be best if she offered him an
easy way out?

'Theo? Can I talk to you?'

She didn't want this conversation. Not ever. But she knew they had to have it. Had to have it now, before she went insane with all the *what-ifs*. Theo was already thinking of leaving—he'd said it himself—but what if he felt he couldn't raise the issue without upsetting her?

Well, she'd make it easier for him.

He appeared at the top of the stairs. 'Has she gone?'

'Yes. Look, we need to talk.'

He sighed. Nodded. 'Yes. We do, don't we?'

She watched him trot down the stairs. Waited for him to get to the bottom.

'I've asked so much of you, Theo. And you've given me everything I've ever asked for in helping me look after Cassidy. But you have your own life. And it's unfair of me to keep you from living it. You've put your career on hold for me. So I just want you to know that I'm ready.'

She needed to know what her future would be. Needed to plan. And she couldn't do that with Theo here, making everything so uncertain. If she planned this—if she took control—then she wouldn't be left behind. Not if she did the pushing away. It was for the best. For both of them. He was probably only staying here out of guilt, and that wasn't fair on him, either.

'Ready for what?' he asked.

'To do this on my own.' She took a deep breath, squared her shoulders. 'Thank you for everything. I've learned so much from you. So much about myself. My mother. The past. And I won't be like her—chasing happiness from people who aren't ready to give it. I've always looked after myself and I'm going to be fine on my own. *We'll* be fine. Honestly. You can leave us now.'

CHAPTER THIRTEEN

AT FIRST HE wasn't sure that he'd heard her right. But the look in her eyes told him everything he needed to know. Steely. Sure.

Had she needed him to go a long time ago and he'd been holding on like a needy child, desperate not to be left on his own again?

That was silly.

The very things he feared were the things he kept telling people he wanted—independence, no commitment, no responsibilities, to be a free agent.

And here they were, being offered on a plate.

He'd be able to walk away with no repercussions. Go back to uni, catch up with his placement hours at the weekend, make sure he met his targets and passed his year. Go back to being Theo, the man he'd thought he wanted to be.

Only now it was being offered to him he wasn't sure he wanted it at all.

And yet I did want it! Just this afternoon, I was thinking of how I could get my independence back!

But it wasn't what he truly wanted.

What he wanted was Sophie. And Cassidy.

He wanted a family and a home.

And, though it was terrifying to admit it, he knew that if he didn't speak the truth right now he would regret it for ever. He would lose them. Just like he'd lost everybody else. But there was a chance here to have something he wanted, and he ought to fight for it.

If she said no, then he'd walk away. But she'd asked him once before: *'If you met the love of your life would you want to settle down?'*

Back then, he'd not known how to answer, but right now he knew the answer.

He was damned sure of it.

'I don't want to leave.'

What? What did he mean?

'Theo, honestly… I'm fine, I don't need you to—'

'I don't want to go.'

This was confusing. Wasn't she giving him what he wanted?

'I don't understand…'

'Neither do I. But I've been thinking about this. Thinking about it a lot. I need you to know how I really feel, and I'd like you to listen. If you still want me to go afterwards, then I will, but I need you to listen first. Will you do that?'

She was shaking. Trembling. She had to adjust her weight on her crutches as her heart pounded madly in her chest, hoping he wasn't about to make this even more painful than it already was.

'I know what I've always said about relationships. That I don't want to settle down…that I don't see myself as being in a committed relationship. But I think that's because I've never truly been in one before where love like this has existed.'

'Love like this?' she whispered, almost afraid of the answer, but also desperately needing to hear more.

'The kind of love I have for you. And for Cassidy. I know she's not mine. And I know I can never be her real father. But I would very much like to be your real boyfriend. Your real love. The man who gets to love you every day, through thick and thin. The man who gets to see you first thing in the morning and last thing at night. The man who gets to hold you in his arms and never let go. I know you might not want me like that. I know you may think that I'm not reliable. But I am. I can't imagine walking out of that door, knowing that I can't be with you, knowing that you can only be my friend. But if that's what you need me to be—a friend—then I'll take that if that's all I can have. Being here with you and Cassidy has made me feel complete. It's made me feel whole. I want to build a future for the three of us, no matter what happens, no matter what complications or difficulties there may be ahead—because being by your side makes me the strongest and luckiest man in the whole world.'

Tears were streaming down her face. Happy tears. And her heart felt so swollen with joy in her chest that she thought it might burst right open and shower the world with rainbows and sparkles.

'You love me?'

He nodded. 'I do.'

'Oh, my God, Theo...'

She looked down at the floor, trying to gather her thoughts, trying to gather herself, to process the enormity of his statement.

This is everything I've ever wanted!

'I was trying to tell myself that I had to be happy for you to leave. I kept telling myself you were on loan and that what we had wasn't real, that we were living in a world of make-believe. I tried so hard not to fall for you, Theo, but you made it difficult! Being so sweet with me, with my daughter… I couldn't have asked for more. But I love you, and I found myself wanting more. I did. I wanted you. Wanted you to stay. And I thought by offering you a way out I'd be protecting my heart from the pain of losing you.'

He stepped closer, stroked her cheek, looked deep into her eyes. 'You don't ever have to lose me.'

She smiled, laid her hand upon his, looked up into his face. 'So, tell me again that you're staying.'

He smiled. 'I'm staying.'

'For ever and ever?' Now she caressed his face, staring longingly at his lips.

'For eternity'

'Then kiss me and don't ever stop.'

Theo smiled and slowly, tenderly, pressed his lips to hers.

EPILOGUE

'DA-DA-DA-DA-DAH!' CASSIDY BEAMED a smile at Theo as he walked in through the front door and chuckled at his surprised expression.

'She's been saying that all day.' Sophie pressed a kiss to Cassidy's cheek. 'She's been saying it all morning—like I'm nobody and I haven't been pandering to her every whim for the past eight hours.'

He put down his backpack, which looked as if it contained all the books from the university library, gave Magellan the cat a quick stroke as he pressed up against Theo's legs, and scooped Cassidy from Sophie's arms.

'Yes, sweetheart, you're saying Daddy. *I'm* your daddy. Who's a clever girl then, eh?'

Sophie watched as he inhaled her perfect scent and nuzzled his nose into the wisps of dark hair that were beginning to curl. Then he held out an arm for Sophie and hugged her tight, too.

'How's your day been?'

'Fine. I had my last appointment with the orthopaedic surgeon today and he's happy with my leg. I don't need to go back and see him any more. And he said I can start thinking of going back to work on a phased return.'

'That's great!'

'It's certainly a relief.'

They walked into the kitchen, where Theo put Cassidy down on her playmat and handed her one of her building blocks. 'Something smells good,' he said.

'African stew with new potatoes and baby vegetables.'

He went up behind her and wrapped his arms around her waist, planting a kiss on the back of her neck. 'What made you think I was talking about the food?'

Sophie laughed and turned to kiss him. 'Oops, my mistake!'

She felt so happy. Life was wonderful and she couldn't imagine anything better. She and Theo and Cassidy were the perfect little family.

Even Connor was behaving—doing his part and occasionally seeing his daughter at weekends. It had been a shock to finally hear from him, though it had quickly turned out that it had been because Connor's mother was badgering him to do the right thing, so that she could see her granddaughter on occasion.

'When does your mum get here?' Theo asked.

Sophie's mum was coming to meet her granddaughter. They'd seen each other in video calls online, but never face to face. Sophie was looking forward to seeing her mother's eyes light up at seeing and holding her granddaughter for the first time.

'I'm picking her up from the station at nine.' She glanced at the wall clock. It was nearly seven.

Theo smiled. 'Two hours. I can think of something we can do in two hours. We could do it twice. Maybe three times!'

Sophie laughed. 'But dinner's ready! It'll be ruined.'

'It'll keep—and besides, there's something I want to do first.'

He smiled and reached into his pocket, pulling out a small velvet box. He opened it to reveal a beautiful solitaire diamond ring, sparkling and catching the light.

'You have my made my life so complete. I could never have imagined that I would be so happy, and I don't want anything to ruin what we have. I love you and Cassidy so much and I want to show that to the world. Sophie Westbrook—would you do me the honour of becoming my wife?'

He sank to one knee.

Sophie gasped, clamping her hand over her mouth as tears beckoned. Happy tears. Disbelieving tears. Joyful tears. Of course she would marry him!

'Oh, my God, yes! Yes, I will!'

He smiled and slid the ring onto her finger, standing to press his lips to hers and embrace her within his arms.

She was his.

She and Cassidy both were.

The love they shared was beyond anything she had ever experienced before.

And now it was for ever.

* * * * *

The Paediatrician's
Twin Bombshell

Juliette Hyland

MILLS & BOON

Juliette Hyland began crafting heroes and heroines in high school. She lives in Ohio, USA, with her Prince Charming, who has patiently listened to many rants regarding characters failing to follow her outline. When not working on fun and flirty happily-ever-afters, Juliette can be found spending time with her beautiful daughters and her giant dogs, or sewing uneven stitches with her sewing machine.

DEDICATION

For Dot.
You're missed beyond measure.

CHAPTER ONE

DR. TESSA GARCIA leaned against the bar and slid the back of her heel out of the four-inch peep-toe shoes she'd crammed her feet into. The shoes had been uncomfortable when she'd purchased them three years ago, but she didn't remember them being such torture devices.

What had possessed her to wear them?

The same ridiculous urge that had driven her to give in to Lily's plea that she come tonight. Tessa had hoped that this outing might stem the loneliness that clawed at her when she collapsed into bed. At least for an hour.

She should have known better. But she'd wanted to believe she might still have a place with these people.

That she wasn't completely alone.

Tessa glared at the martini sign hanging from the bar. The former dive bar had been revamped over the last year. The pathetic-looking burned-out neon bar signs were now upscale artwork. But the worn bar and exposed brick walls were still the same. Likely a design aesthetic Tessa didn't understand—or maybe the new owners had run out of money during their revitalization effort.

Revitalization. Tessa hated that word. Out with the old, in with the new—the phrase applied to people, too, apparently.

A cackle went up from the patio, and Tessa hated the

heat coating her cheeks. She didn't belong here now. This had always been Max's place. His social circle, his night to shine. She'd been a girlfriend, and then a wife, but never a friend. That realization sent more regret washing through her.

They'd divorced a little over a year ago, though they'd inhabited the realm of uncomfortable roommates instead of spouses for far too long. She and Max might not have been able to save their union, but she hadn't thought the women she'd considered friends would also be casualties of their failed marriage.

But they were all married to Max's college buddies. God, Tessa wanted to slap herself. She should have been smart enough to make that connection.

Maybe if she had spoken to anyone outside the hospital in the last month besides food delivery people...

Tessa's eyes looked to the ceiling as her foolishness washed over her—again. The people in the corner had all stared when she'd popped in, the press of pity in their gazes as they tried to pretend it was fine that she'd stopped by. Even Lily's bright exclamations hadn't been able to cover the pink on her cheeks as her eyes darted between Tessa and her ex-husband's new bride.

Her divorce had been easy—at least on paper. Her lawyer had called it textbook. She and Max had divided their savings account, sold the starter home they'd purchased and said goodbye to their shared lives. It was the *after* that had rocked her.

In all her failed attempts to make him happy, Max's hobbies and dreams had taken precedent. When she'd suggested hiking or visiting the botanical gardens, or even hanging out in the backyard where she'd cultivated a relaxing green space, he'd balked. He'd point out that she was always asking him to do more than his share of things. That she should want to do what he wanted, since he was handling everything at home so she could advance at the hospital.

That hadn't been the full truth. He'd done slightly more than half the chores and complained every step of the way. But she'd given in every time. That still rankled.

Her father hadn't appreciated being asked to do anything for his family, either. Tessa's mom had always made excuses for him—just like Tessa had for Max. Tessa had watched her mom try everything to hold on to her marriage. Then she'd watched the catastrophic aftermath.

She'd witnessed all of it, and rather than protecting herself, Tessa had given in to a man's desires, too, hoping that by ceding her likes, her friends, *her dreams*, Max might look at her like he had when they first started dating, hoping that she could have the happy family she'd always craved.

As an only child, Tessa had longed for siblings. For a home life that didn't rock between stony silence and angry shouts. Tessa had wanted to believe her union would differ from her mother's. But life rarely produced fairy tales, and the Garcia women always seemed to end up alone.

At least she had a thriving career as a pediatric attending at Dallas Children's Hospital. Her ex-husband hadn't been able to strip that from her, though he had stolen the promotion they had offered her at Cincinnati Children's.

Maybe Tessa should have moved without him. But she hadn't been willing to admit what, deep down, she'd already known. Her marriage had been over long before they'd finalized the divorce decree.

She'd put so much of herself aside for Max, and what did she have? A closet full of colorful scrubs—and comfy shoes. And no one to grab drinks with. No one to see a movie or go to the botanical garden with. No one at the other end of the phone. *And no senior attending position.*

Hell, she'd even given up the garden she'd cultivated so carefully because Max had wanted to sell their home. Instead of fighting or making a sound argument for why she should purchase it, Tessa had just consented to the sale.

Her townhome didn't have a lot of extra space for a garden. Tessa harrumphed as she spun the ice around her cup. She'd been so focused on finding a spot close to work—and away from her ex—that she'd rushed the purchase. But she had her independence, and she would never let a man dictate her path again.

"I didn't think Max and Stephanie were coming." Lily's cheeks were red as she fanned herself and waved for another drink. "I swear, she's barely old enough to be in here." Lily dramatically rolled her eyes to the ceiling as she leaned against the bar.

"Mmm-hmm." Tessa kept her gaze focused on the ice melting in the glass that once held club soda. Lily might not be drunk...yet, but the wife of her ex-husband's oldest friend was tipsy enough to repeat anything Tessa might say.

At least the bubbly blonde had interrupted Tessa's pity party.

"It was nice to see you. Guess I probably shouldn't—"

She bit back the last part of that sentence, but Tessa had no problems filling in the silence. This would be the last time she was invited.

A martini appeared in front of them, and Lily sighed. "If I hear one more word about college sports..." Her first sip almost emptied the fancy glass. She laid her hand on Tessa's arm and then flounced back to the patio.

College athletics might not be interesting, but, apparently, neither was spending time with an ex-wife who didn't know her place. Lily clearly regretted the multiple texts she'd sent begging Tessa to show up tonight.

Not that it really mattered.

Over the years, girlfriends had come and gone, and now she was the first wife who was being booted from the group. It was past time for her to go home.

"Those heels look like hell."

She sighed. Flirting in a bar had never been her scene, but flirting in a bar where her ex-husband and all his friends were drinking felt like an extra level of desperation.

And she was not desperate. Lonely, but not desperate. *Never desperate.*

"I've already asked for the check and am going home to get out of these torture devi—" Her tongue froze as she met the honey eyes next to her.

God, he was gorgeous! His dark hair was trimmed, but a bit of a five o'clock shadow accented his firm jaw. His arms were muscular without looking like all he did was grunt in front of a gym mirror and drop weights on the floor.

Clearing her throat, she held up her empty glass and tried to push the unexpected arousal away. The man before her was extraordinary.

"Just let me strike out. Then I can tell my sister I tried and go home myself." He winked before waving over her shoulder. "If you want to throw the ice in my face to make it look really convincing, she will definitely let me off the hook."

Tessa laughed and had to stop herself from leaning closer. "I've never thrown anything in someone's face. But now I kind of want to."

"The option stands." Two dimples appeared in the Adonis's cheeks. "But if you keep laughing, it won't be believable—though I wouldn't complain. Even with the air-conditioning, this place still feels like an outer ring of—"

He caught the last word, and Tessa beamed. "Not from Texas, then?" The question slipped between them, and she gripped her glass. She hadn't meant to drag out this encounter, but she suddenly didn't want it to end.

She really needed to make some new friends…or set up a dating profile on one of the apps the single medical professionals were always discussing. *No.* She was not interested in that.

But what was five extra minutes in this hellhole, if it was with the dreamboat before her? At least he'd give her something delicious to think about in her lonely bed tonight.

"Originally, yes. But I've been out of the state for years. I forgot how hot it was in Dallas in June." He leaned over her shoulder, then shook his head. "She just gave me a thumbs-up. Ah, well, I can still tell her you told me to take a hike in a few minutes. I'm Gabe."

"Gabe?" The subtle shift in his voice tickled the back of her brain. Her gaze wandered his chiseled cheeks, and the bite of recognition stole through her. *It couldn't be…* "Gabe Davis?"

Tessa blinked as she tried to reconcile the stunning hunk before her with the teenager who'd spent a summer working with her in the Tinseltown theater. The honey eyes and smile were the same, and her mood lightened even further as he tilted his head and raised an eyebrow. He'd been cute then, and most of the staff had swooned over him.

Tessa had, too. They'd even shared an impromptu kiss late one night.

Then he'd disappeared.

She gave her best fake smile, "You forgot to tell me you'd like extra butter layered in your popcorn. *Of course* it's not too much trouble to get you a fresh one."

"Tessa Garcia!"

Gabe's deep chuckle rumbled through her, and this time Tessa didn't stop herself as she leaned closer. "I'd heard you left Texas. I assume it was for someplace cooler, given your hatred of this lovely June evening."

She bit the inside of her cheek as that piece of information floated out. She hadn't gone looking for him... not really. He'd been a recommended friend on social media, and she'd clicked on his profile once. Just for nostalgia's sake.

There'd been a picture of a lot of snow and a notice that he only shared his information with friends. She'd almost pushed the bright blue request button, but she'd resisted. Barely.

"I was in Maine. Just moved back." A shadow passed over Gabe's eyes as he signaled for the bartender, but it disappeared quickly.

If she'd had something other than club soda in her glass, she might be able to pretend the haunted gaze had never existed. But she was at a bar avoiding her ex-husband and his friends, so who was she to pass any judgment?

"Can I get a Coke and—" he turned to Tessa "—I owe you a drink for saving me from my sister's matchmaking schemes."

"Club soda with lime." Tessa pursed her lips as the barkeep barely kept the smile on his face. She'd worked in a bar through college and knew their tab wasn't enough to keep the great service coming. Still, she laid some extra on the counter as he put the two cups in front of them. "To cover the first club soda."

The man's shoulders relaxed a little, and he added an extra lime before passing them the drinks.

"If you're up for it, why don't we see if there are any seats on the patio? Get you off those dastardly high heels."

"My ex-husband is back there with his new wife." The words slipped from her lips, and Tessa could have throttled herself. The last person she wanted to talk about was her ex. But she also didn't want to sit back there talking to Gabe while all the people she'd thought were her friends either ignored her or studied this interaction.

"I really was getting ready to leave when you walked up. It wasn't a lie." She raised the drink to her lips, enjoying the bubbles tickling her nose. "Pathetic, I know."

"Nope." Gabe shook his head. "Plus, this saves me having to politely pretend I'm not sweltering back there while we nurse our nonalcoholic beverages and try to figure out how long we have to play catch-up."

He tilted his glass toward her, and his dimples sent another rush down her back. Pressing her fingers to her lips, she shook her head. How did this man make her swoon with just a few minutes of conversation?

"What if I want to catch up?" The question surprised her, but it was the sincerity behind it that nearly made her knees buckle. She wanted to catch up with Gabe. Wanted to know what the gorgeous, clever man—whose sister was thrilled he was talking to someone in a bar—had done for the last two decades.

Maybe discover why he'd disappeared after they'd kissed. *No.* That was not a question she was going to ask.

They'd had fun working behind the concession stand at the theater and goofed off more than they probably should when the theater was dead on the weeknights. But they hadn't gone to the same high school. Their final

flirtation, which had led to her first kiss, had felt like…
well, it had felt like the rush of first crushes that only
teenagers could experience.

She still remembered being hurt that he hadn't warned
her he was quitting. If it had been a few years later, cell
phones and social media could have transitioned their
flirtation into a more genuine connection. But those
things had still been just over the horizon.

"I wouldn't mind playing catch-up. Do you want to
down that drink, and we can head to another place?
Someplace where your ex isn't around?" The ridges of
his cheeks darkened as he made the offer.

Was he as out of practice at this as she was? Tessa
doubted anyone could be as rusty in the dating field as
her. She and Max had met in their freshman dorm and
dated all through college. They'd married just before she
started med school, and he'd gone to work in finance.
She'd been off the market for most of her adult life.

"My place is just around the corner. I have wine and a
patio that overlooks the community pond." Heat engulfed
her body as she met those sultry eyes again. "I… I… I
just meant that it's a good place for me to dump these
shoes. And then you can come back to your sister after
a drink on my patio."

Nope… There was definitely no one rustier than her
at this. And she wasn't even trying to flirt. Well, maybe
a little, but not like "invite a stranger back to your condo
fifteen minutes after he buys you a club soda."

He took a sip of his drink, and her breath caught as she
watched him mull the offer over. If he said no, it would
be fine. Better than fine—it would be the right answer.
But Tessa didn't want Gabe to say no. She wanted him
to want her—at least for a night of friendly conversation
on a condo porch.

How long had it been since someone outside the hospital wanted to spend time with her? Tessa didn't want to calculate that answer.

"Sure," Gabe finally stated. He looked over her shoulder again and smiled. "But just so you know, I'm telling my sister this went perfectly and counting it as a date. That will get her off my back for at least the next three days. Maybe even an entire week!"

Laughter again bubbled in Tessa's chest. How had he taken the most awkward moment ever and made it seem like she was helping him? And how was this gorgeous man still single?

He grinned, dimples deep in each cheek before heading to speak to his sister.

Another round of laughs echoed from the back corner, but most of its sting had evaporated. She laid another couple of dollars on the bar and spared one more glance at the over-the-top decor, then let her mind wander to Gabe's delicious dimples. She could get lost in that smile.

Maybe for more than one night.

That thought sent a cold bead of sweat down her back. She was not interested in dating anyone—even if she was more than a little tired of curling up with a pillow each night.

The position for senior emergency room attending was opening in a few weeks. Assuming the rumors were true.

And she'd learned the hard way that men did not appreciate a successful woman. Oh, they claimed to. Max had said he loved Tessa's drive for success. Asserted that her being so successful made them a power couple—a term Tessa hated.

Then his finance career had stagnated following several poor business decisions and the recession. When he was laid off, Max had grown increasingly agitated by his lack of job prospects. She'd understood, but after he accepted another position, their relationship had still raced toward its explosive end.

Particularly when she'd been offered the senior attending job at Cincinnati Children's. He'd refused to even consider moving for her job and suggested that it would be too much of a commitment if she wanted to start a family anytime soon.

So she'd stayed. Given up the promotion hoping that her sacrifice could repair the divide that had widened between her and her ex. Instead, he'd filed for divorce, claiming Tessa didn't need him for anything besides housework.

It had been a BS excuse—particularly considering he'd married again before the ink had dried on their divorce decree. But it was proof that many men couldn't handle being equal partners in a relationship. They always wanted to be more than their partner. And Tessa didn't have the time to wade through the dating landscape to figure out the good from the bad.

She licked her lips as she subtly checked out Gabe's beautiful derriere. If her heart thumped a bit as Gabe leaned over to tell his sister he was going to Tessa's place for a short while, that was just a symptom of loneliness and nostalgia for an old crush. A one-night escape.

Nothing more.

"I won't wait. You can just order an Uber." Isla's grin was too wide, but Gabe didn't want to disappoint his sister with the truth. He and Tessa were just catching up… which didn't explain the heat running through him, or his willingness to go back to her place.

She was uncomfortable at the bar. Her tanned skin had reddened after she'd invited him to have a drink on her patio, her gaze refusing to meet his. If any other person had made what sounded like such a bold request, he'd have found a polite way to demure. To redirect the conversation to something humorous, something that didn't sound like a direct refusal.

Gabe had only approached Tessa at the bar because he'd assumed the walled-off brunette would shut him down. She'd barely acknowledged the three men he'd watched confidently stride over to her. She'd raised her near-empty glass and waved them away.

He'd watched her lift her feet out of those absurd spikes and been certain she was about to call it a night. And the clock hadn't even struck eight. She'd been perfect.

All he'd needed was a refusal. Then he could pretend to be off his game for the rest of the night. That part would have been the truth.

Gabe Davis had been off his game for the last six years. If life had gone according to plan, he'd have been celebrating his fifth wedding anniversary to Olive this year. Maybe even have a toddler or two to keep their life busy.

But life hadn't followed the plan—it had shredded it. Something Gabe should have been used to. He'd learned at sixteen that the movie version of family and love was a fantasy.

A sitcom reality that drove advertisers to Saturday-morning cartoons and after-school specials. That laid the groundwork for kids to believe in happily-ever-after, leaving them vulnerable to the heartbreak that life seemed all too willing to deliver.

But instead of rejection at the bar, he'd found Tessa Garcia, the girl who could make a slow shift fly by in giggles and fun. Tessa had been a bright ray of sun at a dark time.

He'd applied for a job at the theater two weeks after his mother announced over pot roast that she'd finished her family experiment.

His mother had loved her career and the accolades that came as she climbed the corporate ladder more than she'd loved her children, and significantly more than she'd loved the man she'd married. But it was the word *experiment* that time hadn't driven from his mind. That still sent fury through him.

He'd shadowed his mom, always praying that he'd earn a bit of her praise. Of her love. Trying to earn things that other mothers gave so freely to their children. But his acts of service had earned him nothing when she'd packed her bags.

He should have quit almost as soon as he started. The theater had sent him home far too often on slow nights, and Gabe needed the money to help his dad. But he'd stayed because working with Tessa had made him happy. For a few hours he could forget the turmoil of his life at home.

He could still remember finally working up the courage to kiss her after they'd closed one night. It had been the highlight of his high school experience.

But the veterinary clinic had called the next day to offer him the afternoon and weekend front desk assistant position, starting immediately. He hadn't been able to turn that down.

His father had already been working two jobs and asking him to drive Gabe to the theater had seemed selfish, particularly when he didn't know her schedule. By the time he'd finally earned enough to buy a rusted-out car that barely ran, she'd left the theater, too.

He'd gone to the football game when her school played his—the only one he'd ever made it to—but if Tessa had been in the crowd, Gabe hadn't been able to find her. He'd left feeling defeated.

When she'd recognized him tonight, his lonely heart had lit up. The freckles on her cheeks had lifted as her lips turned up. The pretty young teenager had turned into a stunning woman. And a night of catching up was all his heart craved.

"Have fun." Isla's laughter was bright, but Gabe didn't turn around.

He could spend as much time as he wanted with his sister. Reconnecting with Tessa at a bar felt...well, he didn't know how to explain the emotions darting through him.

After the offer had spilled from her lips, Gabe had watched Tessa's eyes dart to the corner. He'd waited a moment, expecting her to withdraw the offer, disquieted by the twinge of longing rushing through him. When she hadn't, Gabe's heart had sped up—just a tick. He hadn't felt that brush of anticipation in so long.

He didn't want to let it go—at least not yet. "Ready?"

"To get out of these?" She gestured to her feet, where red spots were forming on the edges of her big toe, and the back of her heel had to be rubbed raw. "Absolutely!"

"Are you going to make it?"

Tessa sent one more glare south and then shrugged. "No other choice."

For a second Gabe considered offering her a piggy-back ride. It was something they'd done more than a few times on slow nights at the theater, racing down the halls, keeping their laughs as quiet as possible for the dozen people seeing movies on a random Tuesday.

He'd enjoyed every moment of her pressed against

him. The thrill of her cheek against his as they passed life-size movie cutouts.

Such an offer would be absurd now. They were adults, not goofy teens in the throes of first crushes. No matter how much the urge to help her pulsed through him.

That was just his nature. Gabe was a helper—all his siblings teased him about trying to do everything for everyone. Stacy often reminded him that he didn't have to do everything, but he enjoyed it. Gabe needed to be needed. And it had been so long since anyone had needed him.

It was just that side of him calling to Tessa, wanting to offer an old friend some comfort. If his heart yearned to see if her laughter still sounded the same or if her cheek pressed against his could bring joy back to his life, well, that was just a symptom of nostalgia. He didn't believe the lie his brain was feeding him, but it didn't matter. He would not do anything to break the evening's spell.

The walk to her condo lasted less than ten minutes, and he let out a breath as she stopped in front of the Boardwalk Complex. The most expensive condos in the Dallas area. The developer had bragged in more than one interview that he'd always dreamed of making a property worthy of the most expensive spot in the Monopoly game. It was exactly the type of place his mother would love.

What does Tessa do for a living to live here? He braced himself for opulence as he stepped through Tessa's heavy front door.

But the entry was bright and airy—nothing like his mother's upscale unit where she'd fretted over her breakable finery the few times he and his siblings had visited. A stack of gardening books was piled next to the gray couch, and a bright yellow blanket popped with color. The condo had a light floral scent that sent a thrill through Gabe. The home felt like home.

Which was impossible—and unsettling.

When was the last time he'd felt like anywhere was home? In the months before Olive's passing. Their apartment could have mostly fit in Tessa's spacious living room, but it had been a happy place.

Another wave of nostalgia rushed through him as Tessa grinned and pulled him toward her kitchen. The pinch of longing he hadn't felt in forever bloomed in his chest—again. He was lonelier than he'd realized.

"I have Diet Coke, water and wine." Tessa's voice was soft as her dark eyes held his.

What was he doing here? Gabe had never gone back to a woman's place right after meeting her. Except he knew Tessa, sort of…

But was the memory of teenage Tessa the only reason he was here?

Gabe didn't wish to investigate that question. Clearing his throat, he tried to ignore the flutters in his stomach. "Wine sounds great, but get out of those heels first. Point me in the direction of the bottle opener and glasses. Might as well let me earn my keep." Gabe's fingers brushed hers as she handed him the chilled bottle. Her warmth ran up her fingers to his. Such a minor touch that was over too soon.

Get it together. The innocent touch was nothing—really. This was a friendly catch-up session. A way for two lonely people to feel less alone for a few hours.

"Thank you." Tessa raised out of the heels as she pointed to a cabinet. "But these monstrosities—" she glared at the heels as she lifted them up "—are going directly in the trash! No woman should be subjected to such pain."

Gabe chuckled as he pulled two glasses down. "I think my sister Isla may have just shuddered." At Tessa's confused look, Gabe continued, "She's a buyer for a very fancy department store. She worked for years to become their main shoe buyer."

"Well, you are free to tell her that these are evil!" Tessa's laugh was deeper now, but it still had the lilting edge at the end he'd craved so long ago. The part of Gabe that had been mostly silent since Olive's departure burst open.

Handing her a wineglass, Gabe tipped his own up, trying to ignore the dangerous combination of ancient feelings and new desires. "To old friends and comfortable shoes."

Her dark eyes shimmered as she met his gaze and raised her glass to her lips. "The patio is this way." Her hand gripped his and her gaze floated across him again before she dropped it.

Did her palm tingle, too? The connection had been too brief and too long all at once.

"So, what brought you back to Dallas? Too much snow?" Tessa crossed her legs as she sat on the wicker love seat on her patio.

Gabe slipped in next to her, aware of how close the beauty by his side was. His neck burned. And he couldn't pretend it was the heat of the evening, particularly with the bright umbrella covering them with shade while the sun set. Her soft scent mixed with the evening breeze, calling to him. The intimacy of the setting was thrilling.

And terrifying.

Maine had been Olive's home. And he'd happily returned with her after they'd graduated from nursing school. But it hadn't felt like home with her gone. And after so many years, he'd finally felt ready to leave. The yearning to return to his home, to find a new life—whatever that meant now—had finally sent him back to the Texas heat. Swallowing the cascade of emotions floating through him, Gabe knew there was no way to articulate all those thoughts.

"The snow is not that bad." Gabe didn't directly answer her question, but the response was safer.

At least he thought it was, until Tessa playfully shivered and drew a millimeter closer to him. Her full lips were tinged with red wine, and the urge to dip his head to hers made it hard to breathe. Gabe lifted his glass, never taking his eyes from Tessa. "What is it with Texans and hating snow?"

"It's cold." Tessa held up a finger as she continued to tick off her reasons. "It's slushy. It makes driving difficult. It's cold."

"You already said that one."

"It bears repeating!"

Tessa's hand tapped his knee, and Gabe pinched his wineglass to keep from laying his hand over hers. What was wrong with him? He yearned to make her laugh, to see the hint of a dimple when her lips tipped up. To pull her close.

A small voice in the back of his brain wondered if he should take his leave—chalk the evening up to nostalgia and move on. But it was easy to ignore when Tessa smiled.

He leaned closer. "What Texans don't understand is that snowy weather just means you have to cuddle closer." The flirtation escaped his lips. Gabe watched an emotion he wanted to believe was desire flash in Tessa's eyes.

"I guess that could be true." Her tongue ran along the edge of her lip as she closed a bit more of the distance between them. "But the heat can be—" her gaze darted behind him before she pulled back "—sensual, too."

True… Gabe's tongue refused to form any more words as he stared at the woman across from him. This wasn't catching up, and discussing Maine's snow versus Texas's heat shouldn't make him want to kiss her. Shouldn't make him want to run his hand along her waist…shouldn't make him want so many things.

"I missed you when you left the theater. After we…" Her cheeks bloomed as she tilted her wineglass back. "You were my first kiss."

The words were so soft that Gabe wondered if Tessa had meant to say them out loud. "You were mine, too. I even went to the Trinity versus Bell football game senior year, hoping you'd be there. I wanted to apologize for vanishing. To explain that the job I got paid better and started immediately. To ask for your number." Gabe grinned. "If only every teen had had a cell then."

"If only…" Tessa took another sip of her wine, then set it on the table.

"If only…" Gabe repeated, setting his wineglass next to hers. Without the glass in his fingers, his palms itched to reach out to Tessa. The urge to follow a path that might lead somewhere ignited in him. Gabe crossed his arms, trying to redirect the desire.

It didn't work.

"So now, on to the major questions." Tessa's smile was infectious as she shifted beside him. "Why is your sister trying to set you up at a bar?" Her nose twitched. "You were cute when we worked together, but…" She gestured toward him. "I can't imagine you having trouble getting a date."

No. Gabe hadn't had any trouble getting a date, or he likely wouldn't have, if he'd had any interest in the dating scene. But his heart had gone dark after he'd lost Olive. An empty shell had occupied his chest for years. When it had finally started beating again, Gabe hadn't known what to do. But getting involved with someone new had held little appeal.

So what was he doing here?

"I was with someone for a long time." Gabe's heart hammered, but the sting of loss was muted now. Grief never vanished, but you learned to move around it. And with time, the memories, like Olive's bright laugh and her good heart, came easier. She would have loved Tessa's commentary on high heels. "She passed away."

Warm hands found his, and the cavity in his chest lit up again. Tessa's presence called to him in a way he'd never expected to feel again. His thumb rubbed along the edge of her wrist, just enjoying the connection.

"I'm so sorry, Gabe."

"Thanks. It's been over six years. The pain is distant now, but Isla wants to see me happy again. Of course, her idea of happy is me giving her more nieces and nephews to idolize. I guess Stacy's and Matt's kids aren't enough to sate the great Aunt Isla."

"You're an uncle!" Tessa squeezed his hand again.

Tessa's pressure was light, but it grounded him in a way that Gabe hadn't felt for years. *Six years.* The sensation was comforting—one more surprising element to add to tonight's growing list.

"Yes. My brother Matt has two young boys, and Stacy has two preteen girls and a three-year-old daughter who drives them all batty." Being nearby to help his siblings with their growing broods had been part of Texas's siren call, though Gabe wasn't needed for much.

"That's lovely," Tessa sighed.

"When you are goaded to approach a stranger in a bar, it doesn't feel that way. Though tonight worked out better than I could have hoped." That was the truth. Isla had probably texted everyone the moment he left. How would they feel when he told them that this was just catching up with an old friend?

Except it felt deeper.

That was a dangerous thought. And one that Gabe didn't wish to examine too closely. Everything had seemed easy from the moment he'd stepped up to Tessa at the bar. If he tried to unravel the mix of thoughts and emotions, it might get messy. At least for tonight, he just wanted to enjoy Tessa's company—for as long as she wanted him here.

"I meant the family meddling." Tessa sighed. "I'm an only child. I haven't seen my father since I was seven, and my mother passed when I was thirteen. They were both only children, too, so no cousins to speak of. I used to daydream about having a huge family." She grinned. "About sisters I could tell secrets to. Or a few brothers who might want to protect me."

Protect me. He felt his lips dip. Everyone should have someone to look out for them. Someone to run to when the world tilted unexpectedly.

"Children's imaginations are something, huh." Tessa rubbed her fingers on her lips and looked over his shoulder before meeting his gaze.

"I'm sure the Davis clan would adopt you." The offer hovered between them as Gabe smoothed his thumb along her wrist, again. The connection electrified him, and Gabe couldn't have dropped it even if he'd wanted to.

It wasn't an errant statement, either. He was sure that Stacy and Isla would willingly welcome the woman before him into their friendship group. If his sisters adopted Tessa, he'd get to see her often, too. That held so much appeal—and sent a thread of worry dancing through him.

Tonight felt like the perfect spell. But perfection was an illusion. If he fell for Tessa and lost on the gamble…

His heart constricted just at the thought. He wasn't sure it could survive another battering.

But he didn't withdraw the offer.

"The heat of the day is finally breaking." Tessa didn't address his suggestion, but she didn't let go of his hand, either.

"And at ten o'clock!" Gabe chuckled. *Somehow they were back to the weather.*

Tessa picked up her half-full wineglass and stared at the lukewarm contents. "Maybe we should have opted for the soda." She let go of his hand and uncurled her feet.

Gabe opened and closed his palm, trying to chase the sensation of emptiness away. The night was ending, as it should, but Gabe desperately wanted to pause time. To sit here with Tessa for hours, watch the sunrise and just be with her.

As she stood, her feet wobbled, and Gabe reached for her. She landed in his lap, her mouth falling open as she stared at him. "My feet fell asleep."

Gabe pushed a tight curl behind her ear. *God, she is gorgeous.* "It's okay."

Heat that had nothing to do with the Texas night crackled between them. When her lips met his, Gabe's body released tension he hadn't even realized he'd been holding. Tessa's fingers were heavy on his chest as she deepened the kiss.

The taste of wine lingered on her lips. This wasn't the innocent young kiss they'd shared as teens. This was deeper, electric, and the longing buried within it drove him close to the edge.

Tessa... All his senses lit with longing. *Tessa.*

She pulled back, and Gabe had to reach for all his control not to pull her close again.

"Do you want to go inside?" Tessa bit her lip as her fingers danced across his chest, each stroke sending another jolt through him.

"Yes." There was nowhere else he wanted to be tonight.

CHAPTER TWO

GABE'S WARMTH CARRIED through her as Tessa led them up the stairs. Her breath caught as she saw her bedroom door. She wanted Gabe, he wanted her, and they were single. She needed to lose herself, feel desired, cared for.

At least for one night.

His lips grazed the back of her neck, and the final flutters of nervousness floated away. Turning in his arms, Tessa locked her hands behind his neck and kissed him. His arms tightened around her as his mouth captured hers.

This wasn't a flirtatious test kiss. This was demanding and needy. It was everything, and her body reacted in ways she hadn't experienced in years—maybe ever. Her fingers caressed his back, loving the feel of his body as he molded against her.

They fit perfectly.

It was a ridiculous thought, but it sent shock waves through her as his fingers ran along her sides, each stroke growing bolder before he finally traced his thumb across her nipple. Even through her top, his touch burned. His lips trailed along her neck, and Tessa thought she might explode just from the heat of his lips. "Gabe..."

His name on her lips brought his honey gaze to hers.

"Tessa." He dropped a soft kiss along the edge of her jaw. "Do you want to stop?"

The safe answer was yes. She'd never gone to bed with a man on the first date. And this couldn't even qualify as that. But going to bed alone—again—had no appeal when there was such a stunning, sweet man before her. "No. Do you?"

His smile lit up the room. "No, I most certainly do not."

She slipped her hands under his shirt and lifted it over his head. Her breath caught as she stared at his chiseled abs and the dark hair that ran from just below his belly button under his jeans. He was amazing!

"You are beautiful." The compliment slipped between them, and Tessa wanted to slap herself. That wasn't a compliment for a man—was it? *Hot* or *handsome*—those were the words she should have used.

Nerves fluttered across her belly, and a heat that had nothing to do with Gabe's fingers stroking her arms cascaded across her. Max would have hated being called beautiful.

Striking was another word she could have used. Of course, now that the wrong word had slipped out, she could think of so many right ones. How could she be so out of practice at this?

"I mean—"

Gabe captured her lips before she could offer any explanation. When he pulled back, he ran a finger along her cheek. The gentle gesture made her bones melt.

"You're beautiful, too. So lovely."

The whispered words ignited deep inside her. It had been ages since anyone had called her beautiful.

Gabe's lips trailed along her neck. "I think we're both a little nervous."

"It's been a while," Tessa conceded.

"Well." His hands were warm as they slipped under her blouse. "What if we just go with what feels good?" His hand ran along the base of her bra, and Tessa's breath caught. "Does that feel good?"

"Yes." The breathy word echoed in the room, and Tessa let the worries slip away again. "But it's not enough." She yanked her shirt off and stood looking at Gabe, drinking in his admiration.

"Gorgeous." The tips of his lips curled up before he dipped his head to the top of her breast. "You are perfect, Tessa."

Perfect. That adjective had never been ascribed to her—at least not outside the hospital. But it pierced her, and a small part of her heart clasped it. Even if no one else ever said it again, she could treasure this one moment.

Her breath quickened and knees weakened as he dropped more kisses along the edge of her bra. The sensations scored across her as his fingers trailed ever closer to her nipple, but never quite close enough. Reaching behind her, Tessa unhooked her bra, reveling in Gabe's sigh as he gently sucked each of her nipples. The backs of her knees hit the bed, and she grinned as Gabe carefully laid her back.

His heated breath sent shivers along her skin as he slowly kissed his way down her stomach. He paused just above her waist and looked up. Their eyes connected. She unbuttoned the top of her skirt while he stared at her.

Was it possible to have such an instant connection with someone? To crave his touch?

His lips trailed fire as they traveled along the insides of her thighs. Her panties dropped to the floor, and she gripped the sheets.

"Tessa?"

When he lifted his head, Tessa sat up and grabbed the waistband of his pants. "It doesn't seem fair that I've lost all my clothes, and you haven't." His jeans slid to the floor, and she let her hands linger on his tight backside. He really was gorgeous.

As her fingers slid to the waistband of his boxers, Gabe gripped her wrist. "I want you, Tessa. Badly." He kissed the interruption from her lips. "But I still have plans."

"Plans?" Her heart skipped as she held his gaze.

His thumb grazed her nipple, and she shuddered. "I want to see you melt with pleasure." His fingers slid up her thigh, almost to her center but not quite. The heat scorched her, but it still wasn't enough. He licked each nipple before moving his way down her body—again.

Tessa arched as he drew closer to where she wanted him—needed him. "Gabe," she panted as he finally slipped a finger deep inside as his tongue teased her.

Dear God!

She wanted…needed more. "Gabe, please."

"Plans," the whispered word held so much promise as Gabe increased the pressure—barely.

Tessa arched again as waves of sensation crested over her. She lost herself in the feelings, the thrills his hands and mouth created as Gabe drove her closer and closer to the edge. "Gabe!"

Gripping his shoulders, she pulled him toward her and captured his mouth as she slipped his boxers down. Had she ever wanted someone so badly?

She rolled him to his back and reached into the side drawer. The condom box was stuffed in the back. She'd purchased them a few years ago and found them in the box she'd simply labeled "nightstand" after moving in.

It felt like forever, but when she finally slid down Gabe, her body took over.

His hands clasped her waist as he drove his hips toward her. Then he slipped his finger between them. The pressure made Tessa gasp.

"Tessa."

Her name on his lips was thrilling. "Gabe, Gabe... Gabe." His hips raised again, and Tessa crested into oblivion.

Tessa's breathing was light as he held her. Gabe pressed a soft kiss to her shoulder, simply relishing the feel of her next to him. He couldn't explain the rush of the connection between them, and he wasn't sure he wanted to.

Particularly after midnight. If he thought too much, he might rush from her bed. *Or get too comfortable.*

He ran his hand down her side. Her skin was so soft. The urge to touch her, to hold her, was burying itself deeper within him. Perhaps he should kiss her goodnight and slip out—but that held absolutely no appeal.

He'd tried dating a few times since Olive passed, but his ability to feel connected to another had felt broken. Because he'd been broken.

He'd accepted that belonging to another person had ended—before it had even started, at least for him. Tragedy ripped away part of your soul, but he still had so much to be happy for. He might not be complete anymore, but being Uncle Gabe, a skilled nurse, an excellent brother and a good son was enough.

It was.

But tonight, he'd wanted more. Craved more. With Tessa, he'd felt almost whole for the first time in forever.

For a few precious hours, laughter had come easy— and it had been real. Not the forced chuckles that he'd become so adept at. He hadn't had to remind himself to smile. He'd simply enjoyed each moment.

Because of the woman beside him.

What did that mean? Probably nothing.

Gabe's heart skipped in his chest. He should just enjoy this time by her side.

She let out a soft sigh, and his name followed. *His name…*

Gabe's heartbeat felt like it echoed in the dark room. His soul cried at the small connection. How did something so insignificant touch such a deep part of him?

"Tessa." His lips trailed along her neck.

Tessa moaned as his hand skimmed along her hip. She rolled over, and her dark gaze met his. Her eyes were hazy in the dim room, but the desire building there made him smile. *She* made him smile. *Tessa.*

"I didn't mean to wake you." The words were soft— and mostly true. He hadn't meant his touches to awaken her. But he wasn't sorry as her lips met his.

"I'm not sure I believe you." Tessa's long fingers stroked his chest, diving deeper with each exploration, "Did you want something?"

The question felt more profound than it should have, and Gabe's tongue was unable to form any reply. When her lips moved down his body, he let the question drift away in the fog of exultation.

Gabe's arm was heavy as Tessa slipped from the covers. His breath hitched, and all the flutters and questions she should have contemplated last night rushed toward her. The connection they'd had was electric, but she didn't know him. Not really.

They'd never even addressed the questions that one

usually answered on a first date. *What do you do for a living? Hobbies? Future plans?*

No, they'd flirted over the weather. *The weather!* How had such a superficial conversation led to explosions in her bed?

Whatever had pulled at them, she needed a few moments of distance. Even though her body wanted her to wake the gorgeous, kind Adonis with kisses. And more.

So much more!

Pulling on a pair of shorts and a tank top, she headed for the kitchen. She needed coffee and a bit of space. What did one do the next morning? She'd never had a one-night stand.

But what if she didn't want this to be a one-night stand?

That thought sent thrills and panic racing through her. She and Gabe had an easy connection and chemistry that ignited desires deep within her. But that didn't necessarily mean anything.

She rubbed her arms, hating the uncertainty warring within her. Emotions were dangerous, and getting hurt seemed to be the natural order of the world. At least for the women in her family.

She stopped at the base of the steps and listened for any sign that the striking man was awake. The memory of his fingers running down her skin sent longing and heat rushing through her. But instead of returning to him, Tessa started for the kitchen.

Love was a chemical reaction. A dopamine high that vanished with time. She hated that thought, but her father had abandoned her mother when the family life he had claimed to need no longer excited him. And the high had evaporated years before Max had demanded a divorce.

Even with the pain it had witnessed, her heart still

cried out for more. Maybe the organ was just a glutton for punishment as it whispered for her to consider that Gabe might be different?

Her phone buzzed, and Tessa frowned. She wasn't on call this weekend.

Dr. Lin told me he's retiring on our shift last night. His last day is in three months. His senior attending position should open in a few weeks. You're a shoo-in!

The text from Debra, the head nurse, made her smile. Tessa hopped from foot to foot. She wanted to burst with the news!

Now Tessa's heart was racing for another reason.

What would Gabe think?

She felt her lips tip down again. That errant thought was unacceptable. She'd known Gabe for six months when they were teens and now for one lovely night as adults. But she was not searching for the approval of any man regarding her career. *Not again.*

Tessa read the text again. *Senior attending...* Her skin bubbled with excitement. She wanted the promotion. It was the perfect chance to prove to herself that compromising her promotion in order to try to save her marriage hadn't dealt her career any setbacks.

She was the best choice, but that didn't always matter. She'd served as Dr. Lin's replacement when he'd had to have rotator cuff surgery last year, but she was younger than at least two other colleagues she knew would be interested.

And a woman.

Her gender shouldn't matter—but it did. She'd been asked questions throughout her career that her male colleagues had never faced. Particularly when it came to her plans to start a family.

People assumed her male colleagues had spouses, or ex-spouses, to look after their children. That they wouldn't need family leave. That they could operate at their best, even if they went home to a half a dozen children every night.

That wasn't an assumption that was granted to a woman of childbearing age. *No.* They had to prove that having a family wouldn't make them *less* of a physician.

For years, she'd said that she had no plans to start a family right away. There wouldn't be a need for maternity leave just yet. But she hated the answer. Hated being asked it. Hated answering it. Hated the emptiness that it always highlighted in her home.

She loved children. Tessa had never considered another specialty. Her mother had left med school after discovering she was pregnant with Tessa. Her dream had been permanently diverted, but she'd fostered Tessa's fascination with the human body and the healing arts.

Even as a teen, Tessa had known pediatrics was her calling. Taking care of children—big and little—made her happy. But it wasn't the same as coming home to a few of her own.

Rubbing her arms, Tessa tried to push away the pinch of unhappiness that always floated around her whenever she thought about how she had two extra rooms in this town house, and neither was a nursery or a playroom.

She'd always dreamed of having children. Of being the mom that hers hadn't gotten the chance to be. And she was sure she could be both an excellent mother *and* a wonderful doctor.

At least the question of a family was one she could

answer easily now. With her divorce behind her, she wouldn't be having children anytime soon.

Maybe at all.

Pain sank into the room, and Tessa had to force her lungs to expand. Biting her lip, Tessa closed her eyes and tried to focus on what she had. And how fulfilling those things were.

Her job. The prospect of a promotion. Her condo. Rediscovering herself after the divorce. She had more than many people. *Focus on the blessings you have.* Wallowing because everything she wanted hadn't come to fruition wouldn't make a family magically appear on her doorstep.

Her eyes wandered to the doorway. Last night's memory would always bring a smile to her lips. *Gabe.*

Tessa could fall for him, and that was terrifying. It would be nice to let the connection that had been so easy last night bloom. Get lost in his good heart and stunning dimples.

But there was always a cost to caring for someone. Her mother had paid the ultimate price for lost love. And if Tessa hadn't been so willing to make Max content, she would already be a senior attending.

No, Tessa wasn't prepared to pay for love and affection—not again. No matter how much a piece of her lonely heart cried out for it.

Dr. Killon is already talking about taking on extra shifts!

Debra's new text sent Tessa's eyes to the calendar. It was common for doctors to pad their résumés with extra shifts when coveted positions were opening. Luckily her calendar was completely clear. There was no one and nothing to stop her from working as much overtime as she could.

She looked at the empty last two weeks of the month and sighed. She should be excited that she didn't have to move anything around. That she could focus on this dream…but those blank dates highlighted a loneliness that cut deeper than she'd expected.

She lifted the page to look at the next month and stared at the block of leave she'd blotted out. She'd never worked on her birthday. Not out of any desire to celebrate the occasion; she hadn't celebrated the date since she was thirteen.

Tessa never did anything other than visit her mother's grave—which bore the date of Tessa's thirteenth birthday, too. But if the competition for the promotion was coming up, her mother would understand if Tessa broke that personal rule this year. After all, her mother hadn't gotten to chase her dreams—but Tessa could.

For both of them.

I can't wait to call you Boss!

That text forced away the pain.

Gripping the phone to her chest, Tessa spun around. She could do this. She could!

"Such a bright smile in the morning." Gabe grinned before his arms wrapped around her belly. Then he dropped a kiss to her cheek.

Maybe she didn't have to have an empty social life?

"A job that I have wanted for forever is finally coming open. My colleague was letting me know." Tessa brushed her lips against his.

"A job opportunity has you dancing around the kitchen

this morning?" Gabe's voice dipped. His hands loosened on her hips.

Tessa tried to ignore the pinch of anxiety that pulsed in her back. *It's early and he hasn't had coffee. That wasn't a frown.*

These were the excuses she had lived with for so long with her ex. And she was not going to pepper them in this morning.

"Yes." Tessa nodded. "It's the thing I want most." That wasn't exactly true, but her connection with Gabe was too fresh to mention that she also wanted a family. A few kids to call her Mom. A happy home. Those desires were buried deeper—and harder to achieve than a promotion.

"A job," Gabe repeated before he shook his head.

This time he definitely frowned.

"Last night was fun." Tessa hated the words as they tripped from her lips. Fun didn't describe last night—or at least not completely. Amazing, rejuvenating, exciting… the start of something.

Except something had shifted in the morning light. Did he regret their night together? Or had the fact that she was excited about a promotion changed everything?

Gabe's phone buzzed, and he smiled as he read the message. "My sisters are not so patiently wondering where I am. We usually meet up for breakfast on Saturday." He pushed his hand through his hair.

Tessa gulped down the desire to ask if she could come. She would not tie her friends to a man again—even if Gabe remembered his offer to let his sisters adopt her last night. "It was good to see you again." Those words felt wrong, but she didn't know the protocol for this.

She grabbed the notepad sitting on her counter and quickly jotted her number down. Gabe looked at the note and smiled before pulling the pad from her fingers.

His touch still sent fire licking up her arms, but she had a terrible feeling that he wouldn't call.

And that would be fine.

Her heart sighed as he passed the notepad back, his number scrawled across it. Then he pocketed her number. *Maybe he'll call after all.*

"I should probably get going." Gabe pursed his lips, looked at his phone, then back at her.

For a moment, she thought he might ask her to go. Instead, he dropped a light kiss to her cheek. After a night of passion, it crushed her.

But she was not going to let it show.

"It was good to see you, Gabe. Really." Tessa wrapped her arms around herself, the crumpled note with his number wrapped in her fist.

"It was good to see you too, Tessa." Gabe dropped another chaste kiss on her cheek, then he walked out.

CHAPTER THREE

PAPERWORK WAS NEVER-ENDING in the medical world. Tessa checked off another box on her tablet, trying to keep her mind from wandering to Gabe Davis. She'd alternately promised herself that she'd call him or throw his number away for the last two days. Not that throwing his number in the trash would offer her any relief.

She knew that number by heart now.

But every time her fingers hovered over the call button, the flicker of emotion he'd shown as she talked about the promotion stilled her fingers.

She'd seen a similar look before. Max had worn it for years. Before he'd given up the pretense that he didn't hate her success.

Gabe's face floated through her memory again, and Tessa wished, for the hundredth time, that that morning had gone differently. That he'd invited her to breakfast or asked when he could see her again instead of just exchanging numbers. That she hadn't witnessed the spark of uncertainty. That somehow their one night could transition to a fairy-tale story they'd tell their grandkids—minus a few details.

But life wasn't a fairy-tale. How often did she need to remind her heart of that?

Tessa's mother had married her father after a whirlwind romance. Less than four weeks after meeting her father, her mother had found out she was pregnant with Tessa. Her dreams of med school and becoming a surgeon had evaporated. But Tessa's father had immediately proposed and sworn he wanted to be a husband and father. That they could make it work.

He'd taken a promotion and moved their growing family from Houston to Dallas. Her mother's dreams had shifted from being a top physician to being the best wife and mother she could be. But it hadn't been easy. Tessa could still recall her practicing stitches on oranges—just for fun.

But they'd made do, and Tessa had never doubted that her mother loved her more than anything. Then her father had packed his bags to start a new business—one that he didn't want his wife or child to help him with. Last she'd heard, he was running a successful restaurant in upstate New York—with his fourth or fifth wife.

Her mother had believed in love. Even after setting aside her dream career to raise Tessa, and after her husband's abandonment. Even after taking on two jobs to make ends meet after her father's child support payments routinely failed to materialize. After watching her world implode, Tessa could still remember her mother saying that love was the most important thing. That it would all work out.

Except it hadn't.

Tessa had tried to take her mother's optimism into her own marriage, hopeful that she could have a love that lasted forever. But she hadn't gotten it, either.

Gabe wasn't Max or her father. At least, she was pretty sure he wasn't. But that dash of uncertainty she'd seen in his eyes had kept her from calling.

And he hadn't called, either. That stung.

"Dr. Garcia, have you met our newest pediatric nurse?" Debra, the head nurse on the unit, always walked the recent hires around, introducing them to their new colleagues. Most of the time, it didn't happen on their first day, and they already knew at least a few of their colleagues. But it was a Dallas Children's Hospital rite of passage. You weren't a full member of the staff until Debra had shown you off.

Tessa turned to smile at the new arrival, excited to focus on something besides paperwork or Gabe Davis. Her lips went numb. Gabe was standing next to Debra. She saw a glimmer of hesitation pass through his honey eyes before he offered a brilliant smile.

Had he missed her as much as she'd missed him? Why hadn't he called?

Neither of those were appropriate questions for the hospital.

"This is Dr. Tessa Garcia." Debra smiled at Gabe before turning her attention back to Tessa. "Nurse Gabe Davis."

"We met at a bar." The words blurted from her mouth. If there was a more embarrassing way for this reunion to go, she didn't want to find it.

Debra looked at her, and she saw the questions flickering in the woman's gaze. Tessa considered Debra a friend. She'd listened to her complaints when Max packed his bags and had declared him unworthy and suggested drinking away his memory. Tessa had thanked her, even enjoying the few jokes Debra had made. But lately, she'd been a little too interested in Tessa's lack of a dating life.

"What I mean—" Her cheeks were hot as she tried to find the right words, any words to follow her first statement as Debra cocked her eyebrow.

"We worked at a movie theater together in high school." Gabe turned the bright lights of his smile on Debra.

Tessa saw the happily married grandmother swoon.

"We ran into each other a few nights ago, and Tessa tried to convince me that the Dallas heat is preferable to the snowy locale I just came from."

"Snow!" Debra shook her head, horror drenching her features. "Not for me."

Tessa placed a hand against her cheek, grateful that it wasn't stinging with heat as she replayed where her last conversation about snow had led. Gabe's gaze met hers, and the draw she'd felt a few nights ago pulled at her. *He's here.*

"It's good to see you again, Tessa. I mean, Dr. Garcia. Always knew you were destined for great things!" His smile was deep as he nodded toward her.

His voice struck her, and Tessa barely kept from leaning toward him, her body aching with the memory of his touch. Her lips were desperate for one more kiss, even as her brain tried to remind her that he hadn't called.

"She *is* destined for great things!" Debra's voice echoed as she turned to lead Gabe away. "She's going to run this place someday—just wait and see." Debra looked over her shoulder and winked at Tessa.

Her stomach skittered and her body lit up as she let her gaze linger on him for a moment. How was she supposed to work with him?

By being a professional! Her brain screamed the command, but her heart wasn't sure. She'd certainly inherited her mother's romantic nature; unfortunately it hadn't earned either of them a happily-ever-after.

"I need help! Please!" The scream echoed from the room where a teenager was waiting on stitches following a skateboarding accident.

Gabe raced toward the room as the mother stepped out, carrying her younger daughter, his heavy footsteps pounding against the floor as he reached the mother.

"Please!" Her wail echoed down the halls.

Tessa saw several nurses motion for the other patients to stay in their areas—not an easy ask in a children's emergency room where little ones were already anxious and curious.

"Give her to me, please." Gabe's voice was firm as he reached for the young girl. His jaw tightened as he took the child. "Empty room?"

"Seven," a nurse from behind Tessa yelled.

Closing the distance between them, Gabe and Tessa quickly walked toward the empty room while another nurse tried to calm the mother enough to get details. "What do you think? I saw your face shift."

"Her breath is sweet. If she's in diabetic ketoacidosis, then we need—" Gabe dropped the statement as he laid the child in the bed. "Your orders, Doctor?"

Leaning over the small girl, Tessa could smell the sweetness of her breath, too. "Get me an IV line ready." She turned to the drawer and grabbed the blood-sugar-testing kit that was kept in each room. "Her blood glucose level is five-eight-six."

Any glucose level over four hundred was dangerous. But once you got over five hundred, you were dealing with a medical emergency. If they didn't get her sugar levels down, she could go into kidney failure or a diabetic coma.

Gabe nodded and immediately started working to secure a line in the girl's arm. A bag of fluids was hung on the hook. She looked so young and tiny in the bed as Tessa and Gabe worked to stabilize her.

"Her heart rate is steady." Tessa turned as Wendy, another nurse, walked in. "We need two units of insulin, and put another two on standby."

Wendy nodded and raced off.

The heart-rate monitor beeped, and Gabe looked over Tessa's shoulder. She knew he was making sure he knew exactly where the crash cart was. But they were not going to need that today. *Not today.*

A small sob echoed by the door, and Tessa turned. The girl's mom was standing just inside the threshold. "Do you have a history of diabetes in your family?" Her voice was steady but firm. People reacted to stress differently, but right now, they needed as many answers as possible.

The mother's eyes widened, and she shook her head. "No. No." She stifled another sob and squared her shoulders. Tessa had seen many parents do the same. Once the initial shock passed, they often fortified themselves to do whatever necessary for their children…and fell apart in the cafeteria when they were on a "coffee break" a few hours later.

"Okay," Tessa responded. Type one diabetes usually ran in families, but it could happen without any known genetic connection, too. "Has she been thirsty lately? Or complaining of headaches?"

Wendy stepped into the room and passed Gabe the insulin injections, then quietly took her place on the other side of the child's bed. A nurse's uncanny ability to enter the room silently or with as much ruckus as necessary depending on the situation never ceased to amaze Tessa.

"Rebecca is always thirsty. But the heat—" The woman's lip trembled. "I just thought—"

"This isn't your fault." Gabe's voice was firm as he triple-checked the line and readied the insulin injection that Tessa had ordered.

"Nurse Davis is right," Tessa agreed. "When you are

fortunate not to have a history of diabetes in your family, often you learn by having your child fall unconscious. Luckily, your son was here already."

The woman wrapped her arms around herself as she stepped closer to the bed where her daughter was resting. "Will she be okay?"

"We've given her rapid-acting insulin. It will take around thirty minutes to take effect, but it should stabilize her. Then we'll monitor her blood sugar and use regular insulin to keep her stable." Tessa nodded toward Wendy. "Nurse Hill will stay and monitor her insulin every fifteen minutes for me. We have extra shots ready if necessary."

Tessa waited until Rebecca's mother looked at her. "Once her insulin comes back up, she will regain consciousness and likely be scared."

Her mother swallowed and then looked toward the door. "My son—"

The poor woman had been through too much today. This was one area where Tessa could alleviate a few of her worries. "I'll make sure your son's stitches are done, and he's sent in here. Rebecca will need to spend at least tonight with us, and we'll arrange for you to start counseling with the diabetic specialist tomorrow, too."

"Thank you." The woman wiped a tear away and slipped her hand into her daughter's.

Once they were in the hall, Tessa turned to Gabe. "Nice work. You saved us valuable time."

Gabe's gaze fell on the door to Rebecca's room, and a small shudder rippled across his shoulders. Tessa ached to rub the worry lines from his forehead.

She needed to get control of herself. They were at work; she should not be concerned with the tension radiating from him. But something about Gabe called to her.

"My sister Isla is diabetic. A few weeks after my mom left, Isla started complaining of headaches. Dad was busy and…" His gaze flitted to the door as his voice died away.

"Anyway, we found out the same way they did—though we had to follow an ambulance and it took over an hour to figure out. She suffered permanent kidney damage. I will never forget the smell of ketoacidosis." He rocked back on his heels. "At least it saved us time today."

Tessa nodded, unsure what to say. The frown lines on his cheeks made her ache. As an only child, she couldn't really understand the closeness Gabe had with his siblings, but she knew what it was like to be scared for someone you loved and unable to change anything. At least individuals with well-managed diabetes could live close to a normal life, though Rebecca would always need to make sure she was monitoring her body.

"Want to help me stitch up a skateboarder?" Tessa tapped her shoulder against his. It was a small connection, but her body vibrated as she pulled away. Apparently, even that friendly gesture was too much. *And not nearly enough!*

"Of course." Gabe's dimples hit her again.

Tessa felt a warmth slip through her. Any of the nurses could help with stitches. But Tessa wasn't ready to give up the time with Gabe. That was dangerous, but she didn't care. She was glad he was here. She'd wrangle her heart later.

Gabe's skin was on fire, and his mind was racing. Tessa was here. Here! If he focused, he could still feel the ghost of her touch on his shoulder.

His brain tried to keep his sprinting heart in check. He'd spent the last two days hoping she'd call, but nervous about pressing Send himself. When he'd come downstairs, he'd seen her do a little dance in the kitchen.

After their night together, Gabe's soul had soared that she might have enjoyed his presence as much as he'd enjoyed hers. That she might want to see what happened next.

And maybe she did!

But the excitement had been over a job—probably the senior attending position here. He'd worked two shifts and already heard multiple doctors and nurses discussing the potential opening.

His mother had danced in the kitchen like that once, too. He'd come down the morning before she packed her bags to see her swaying on the linoleum. She'd hugged him and told him that great things were coming. Except those things hadn't included her family.

She'd given him a list of things that needed done. And Gabe had done them. Hoping that he could earn a place in her new life.

Gabe was the only one who answered his mother's infrequent calls. She only ever called if she needed something, but Gabe hadn't given up hoping that she might want more of a relationship with him.

Tessa wasn't his mom—except she'd said this position was the thing she wanted most.

If Gabe was ranking his life goals, career progression would be on the list. Most people wanted to be successful. But it wouldn't be at the very top. Nothing would ever unseat his family.

But Gabe hadn't been able to drive away the longing to reach out to Tessa. He'd wanted to see if she might like to grab dinner, go hiking. He'd even wondered about the job she wanted. It had made her smile, a huge, warm smile, and he'd ached to know more.

He just longed to know Tessa. Gabe wasn't sure what to do with those feelings. But now wasn't the time to work through them.

"Ready?" Tessa's voice jolted him from his thoughts as she stopped in front of the door where he'd grabbed Rebecca.

"Is my sister going to be okay?" The boy's voice wavered, but he didn't break eye contact with Tessa as they stepped through the door. The teen's face had multiple abrasions, and his left arm was in a splint. He had to be in pain, but Gabe could see the worry coating him, too.

He'd worn that look often after his mom left. He'd worried over his father's exhausted features, over his siblings, over all the changes. It had taken him years to conquer the anxiety it created.

Then Olive had started complaining of headaches. She'd been so strong and independent. She'd blown it off as wedding and work stress, and he'd pushed away the worry that something was wrong, too.

Logically, Gabe knew that even if they'd discovered the aneurysm before it burst, there was little chance she'd have survived, given its location. But worry and guilt weren't things that you could easily wash away with logic.

And Gabe hated seeing it mirrored back to him with the young boy before him. There was nothing he could do for Olive now. But he could help the young man sitting on the exam table—after they addressed his visible wounds.

"Rebecca is going to be okay. But she's spending the night with the wonderful doctors and nurses upstairs."

Tessa's response released a bit of tension from the child's shoulders.

"Right now, though, Nurse Davis and I need to take care of you. Can you tell me your name?"

"Sam." The boy's lip trembled, but he stuck his chin out. "I want to see my sister."

"Not until we have you sewn up." Tessa smiled, but her voice was firm.

Even though the kid was still just a kid, he was at least three inches taller than Tessa and probably weighed at least fifty pounds more, too. But he looked so young as he glanced from Tessa to the door.

She examined his un-splinted arm before meeting the child's eyes. "I know you want to help your sister and your mom."

Tears welled in the boy's eyes, but he didn't drop his chin. "They need me. Dad's gone—" The statement was low and cut off by a sob he caught before it fully erupted.

"You can't help if you're not okay, Sam. Can't pour anything out of an empty cup." Tessa sat on the edge of the bed as she held up a light to examine the cut on his cheek. "I think we can just get by with a butterfly bandage on this one."

Gabe swallowed as she patted the boy's leg. The hospital was busy, but this was a child trying to be more than he was. Gabe understood that drive—and knew how tired Sam was. How tired he was going to continue to be. Tessa was taking extra time; making sure he knew that he mattered, too, was a balm that would soothe the boy for weeks, maybe even years to come.

Pediatric emergency room doctors were often judged on how quickly they fixed and released patients. And the metric was not weighted to give slow docs the advantage. At his last hospital a physician had been promoted because he was so efficient that his average time with a patient was less than twelve minutes.

It was not something Gabe thought should be rewarded. Stitches shouldn't take more than a few minutes. But Tessa was not rushing this simple interaction.

A lump formed in the back of his throat as Gabe pulled out the material for Tessa to stitch up the cuts on Sam's arm. That empty cup analogy was a line his sisters had repeated to him after Olive passed—when Gabe had tried to keep everything together while he was falling apart.

He'd been so used to helping others, to being needed, that he hadn't known how to ask for help—hadn't wanted it. Hadn't wanted to admit how lost he was.

That you can't keep trying to pour out of an empty cup was true. But following through with the sentiment was a lot harder for some people. And Gabe guessed Sam was like him. He would put everyone before himself and avoid his own wants—and needs—to make sure his mom and sister had as much as possible.

When Tessa stood to wash her hands, Gabe squatted, so he was looking Sam in the eye. "I know it feels selfish to put yourself first."

Gabe saw Tessa's head turn toward him out of the corner of his eye, but he kept his focus on Sam. "Anything you do for yourself, that makes you happy, takes time away from helping your mom and Rebecca, right?"

Sam sniffled and held up his splinted arm. "And it costs Mom money." He scowled at the appendage, and Gabe's heart broke. He'd crashed his skateboard. It was an accident, not a massive crime. But Gabe could see the loathing in the young man's eyes. That kind of thinking could worm its way deep inside and destroy so much.

"I've been there. I crashed my bike when I was seventeen. Ended up with a head injury, and it cost my dad almost a thousand dollars to make sure I hadn't cracked my skull." Gabe waited until Sam met his gaze before continuing, "But you're still a kid. A very helpful kid, I bet. But a kid. You aren't responsible for carrying everything. Dr. Garcia is right—you can't help if your well is completely drained. Trust me on that."

Pulling back, he watched Tessa stitch up Sam's arms. She talked in low tones about superhero movies and skateboards—two topics Gabe was stunned to realize she had so much knowledge of and was willing to spend time on. If metrics were being monitored for the senior attending position, too many extended interactions like this one could cost her. But she never cut off a question or rushed the stitches. They were going to heal with minimal scaring.

When the stitches were complete and she'd secured the bandage to his cheek, Tessa asked another nurse to walk Sam to his sister and mother.

"Gabe?"

He turned. Her dark eyes held such compassion *and* the emotions he'd seen the other night. Now was not the time to discuss what had happened between them, though. If Tessa wanted to talk, she had his number.

And he had hers.

"Do you think counseling would help Sam?"

Would it have helped you? That was the second question he saw dancing in her eyes. She might not realize the depth of his connection with the boy's circumstances—though maybe she did—but she'd seen it. The recognition of a soul trapped in the same cycle that caught many people in its lonely trap.

"I think so. But if money is tight—" Gabe shrugged. His father would have loved to have placed all his kids in counseling to deal with their mother's abandonment. Would have given them everything if he could have afforded it. "It will be the first thing to go if bills come due."

Tessa nodded and bit her lip. "I'll pull a favor from

Dr. Gendler. With Dr. Lin retiring, everyone is looking for a leg up. He'll probably want—" Her words drifted away. "It's important that Sam get help."

So there would be a high price for the favor. "But you want the job, too." Gabe's voice was low as he stared at the woman across from him.

"Not at the cost of my patients." Tessa's eyebrows rose as she clicked through the tablet, closing out the notes on Sam's case. "No job is worth that."

His heart sang at that simple phrase, and he wanted to pummel himself. He should have called. Should have invited her to breakfast. Should have taken a risk.

But maybe it wasn't too late.

"This is quite the change of venue from the Tinseltown theater, huh? But it's nice to be working with you again, Gabe."

"You too, Dr. Garcia." Gabe beamed. "Dr. Garcia. That has a very nice ring to it, you know. It suits you."

The look she gave him lit up the hallway. "Thank you." Tessa let out a soft laugh. "That means a lot." She started toward the nurses' station before turning. "It really is good to see you here, Gabe."

There was a touch of something in the way she'd said his name, a softness that warmed his heart. For an organ that had been silent for so long, he wasn't certain exactly how to proceed now. His gaze locked on her as she walked away. Dr. Tessa Garcia. He smiled. Gabe was excited to be working with her again, too.

CHAPTER FOUR

TESSA JIGGLED HER tray and looked over the heads of individuals in the cafeteria. Dallas Children's pancakes were fan favorites, always drawing a larger number of staff and patients. But there was only one person she was looking for this morning.

Gabe...

Her body still lit with excitement and more than a touch of need whenever she was with him. They'd settled into a pattern of friendly chats when their shifts were slow. But it didn't sate Tessa's need to be near him.

The night of passion they'd spent together seemed to have been a fleeting moment. They never discussed it, though its presence seemed to hover in the rare uncomfortable silences that dogged their talks. And as each day ended, it seemed harder and harder to bring up.

But avoiding Gabe wasn't an option, either—at least not one that Tessa planned to exercise. He'd burrowed deep inside her, and her heart refused to relinquish its quiet what-if questions. Though she tried to remind herself that she was done listening to that voice.

"You look deep in thought."

Gabe's warm tone ripped across her and she smiled.

God, she had it bad.

"What are you so focused on this morning?"

You. Tessa set her tray across from him and slid into her seat, determined not to mention that truth.

"Just thinking about how Dr. Lin hasn't even officially put in for retirement, and Dr. Killon is already lobbying for the job. He certainly has a high opinion of himself." Tessa carefully monitored Gabe's features, but he just plopped another bite of pancake in his mouth.

Gabe seemed to be the only employee uninterested in discussing which physician was the most likely replacement for Dr. Lin. Despite attempting to keep away from most of the talks, Tessa had been locked into more than a few gossip sessions regarding the future competition. Gabe's refusal to engage in the discussion was usually refreshing, but sometimes she really wanted to know his thoughts. *And whether he thought she'd be a good choice after working with her for a few weeks.*

This was an easy topic, though. Dr. Killon was inexperienced and showed little care for his patients. Gabe was still in his first month of employment, but he'd worked several shifts with the man. He was the last person anyone should want to replace Dr. Lin.

"Really, Gabe? No thoughts?" Tessa raised an eyebrow, hoping to draw some commentary from him on the job opening, wishing there were a simple way to know if her reaction to it was why he hadn't called.

His honey eyes held her gaze, and Tessa had to remind herself to breathe.

"Tessa—"

Before he could finish that statement, something hot and sticky slid down Tessa's back. The heated syrup burned a line down her spine.

Then hands pushed into her, and a tray clacked to the floor. The owner of the liquid fell to the ground.

A cry of alarm echoed in the crowded cafeteria as Tessa turned to find a teen seizing.

She moved quickly. Pushing back at the curious on-lookers who were gathering, Tessa slipped next to the young man's side. She heard creaking and looked up to see Gabe climbing over the table to reach her and the patient. That was an effective way to get through a gathering crowd.

"Help me turn him on his side." Tessa nodded to Gabe as he helped shift the boy. Then her eyes went to her wrist. They needed as accurate a time count as possible.

"Make way!" a voice called.

Debra and Jackson stood by with the portable crash cart. Tessa turned so she could keep a better focus on her patient and her watch. The longer the seizure went on, the more likely the teen was to suffer long-term consequences.

Or need the crash cart.

The minute hand moved on her watch, and Tessa heard Gabe let out a soft sigh. She briefly looked to him. A bead of sweat coated his upper lip, and his shoulders were rocking. But he did not let his gaze leave their patient.

Blessedly, the boy started to release. *Thank goodness.*

"One minute, twenty-eight seconds." Gabe's voice was ragged as he sat back on his heels to let the gurney through.

"I got the same," Tessa stated. Gabe's hands were shaking. *What was going on?*

Something about this patient had impacted Gabe. There was too much for her to focus on. But as soon as she knew their patient was going to be all right, Tessa was going to find Gabe. Whatever memory this had dredged up, he needed someone. And that was something she could offer him.

* * *

Gabe's body swung between hot and cold flashes as he leaned against the wall in the employee lounge. He'd helped patch up a little girl who'd fallen from her bike and needed stitches, and delivered discharge papers to another, but his mind kept wandering to the closed doors where Tessa and others were dealing with the seizure patient.

The teen had briefly met his gaze before he dropped hot syrup down Tessa's back. The world had stopped, and his breath had caught in his throat. He hadn't even been able to find the words to call out a warning. His lips had been frozen as the past raced through him.

The unfocused eyes. The drifting step. The crash. Olive had experienced each of those symptoms in quick succession the morning he'd lost her.

The aneurysm that had plucked her away had bulged, pressing on a nerve, resulting in a seizure. Then it had ruptured.

Gabe knew the odds that a boy who couldn't be over seventeen was having a seizure because of an aneurysm were minuscule. Those types of clots almost always built up over a long lifetime. But Olive had been vibrant, independent and twenty-six when one had stolen her away. There were no guarantees in this world.

"Gabe."

Tessa's soft voice sent skitters across his raw nerves. The present overtook the past as he pushed away from the wall.

"He's all right." She didn't waste any words as she stepped toward him, her face open and concerned—for Gabe.

"Did he have an MRI?" Gabe's voice sounded off, and he crossed his arms. Olive had been fine for a precious hour after she'd seized. He'd sat next to her in the ER, trying to keep her spirits up as worries mounted. When she'd screamed from the pressure suddenly pressing through her skull, Gabe had known what it meant.

And been unable to do anything other than hold her hand as she slipped away.

Tessa's gaze flickered, and Gabe wondered if she could see the roller coaster rushing through him.

"No, I didn't order an MRI." She kept her voice calm as she carefully watched him. "You're so pale." She took a deep breath and placed a hand on his chest as she held his gaze. "Breathe with me." She inhaled, held it for a second, then waited for him to follow her.

Her soft scent chased through him as the present pushed the past's panic aside. His heart raced, but that was because of Tessa's light touch. When she stepped away, he hated the distance between them.

"He's an epileptic. The new medication his neurologist prescribed is not managing it as well as hoped. He was actually here under observation as they weaned him off it and restarted his old regimen. He got hungry and went for pancakes without asking.

"Teens, right?" She let out a soft laugh.

The sound sent a touch of longing through him. For the hundredth time, he wished he'd called her. That he hadn't let his fear still his fingers.

"I'm glad he's all right."

"Your girlfriend died of a seizure?" Tessa followed Gabe to the small window, her presence sending a wave of contentedness through him.

Gabe swallowed the twisting emotions as he stared out at the parking lot. He would always miss Olive. There was a hole in his heart that no one could fill. You learned to accept that a piece of you was gone, but grief transformed. It morphed. It became easier to hold others, to think about opening yourself up to another. At least that was what the books he'd been given following Olive's passing had said.

He hadn't felt that…until he met Tessa. Today the past had flitted into his future, and it hadn't been the debilitating pain of her loss that had driven his concern over the teenager. It was the aftermath that Gabe feared for another family.

As a pediatric nurse, he'd helped stabilize many seizure patients, but usually after the seizure started. Witnessing the start had thrown him because the teen had so perfectly mimicked her symptoms.

"Olive was my fiancée." Gabe let out a breath and squeezed Tessa's hand, grateful that she had seen how the episode had affected him. And sought him out.

"But I lost her to a brain aneurysm. She seized about two hours before. The symptoms were identical to the teen before…" He let the last words go unsaid. "I'm glad the patient is going to be all right."

"Winston. His name is Winston."

"Of course you know his name." Gabe forced himself to release the pocket of air he'd been holding.

A frown line creased Tessa's forehead. "Of course. I just left his room, Gabe."

"True." He offered a smile. "But not every doctor focuses so closely on their patient. I suspect if Dr. Killon had treated him, he wouldn't be able to tell me his name. He also wouldn't have noticed someone else's distress."

Gabe had heard all the rumors regarding Dr. Lin's position. The man hadn't even officially put in his retirement request, and people were acting as though his last day had already occurred. Gabe hadn't wanted to feed into that rumor mill but when Tessa had asked him about Dr. Killon this morning, he should have responded.

Should have joked that he didn't want to see the man running anything—anywhere. They were colleagues and friends now—a little workplace discussion about something Tessa cared about should have occurred.

The tips of her lips twisted up.

He enjoyed seeing her happy.

"That's true," she conceded, "but he would have correctly diagnosed his problems."

"Yes." Gabe took a deep breath and looked into the dark eyes that called to him. "But a senior attending should care about more than just the condition."

The look of joy that flitted across her face made Gabe wish he knew a way to bridge the gap that had opened since the night he'd spent at her place.

He wanted more than passing conversations in the hallway. More than the friendly waves and smiles. So what if she was interested in a promotion? That didn't mean that she'd choose it over everything else. She cared about her patients, and the staff.

His mother only cared about herself. She never looked at others as anything other than pawns to help drive her own desires. He'd let his fear keep him from seeking something that made him happy.

"How's your back?" It wasn't the question Gabe wished to ask, but he'd find a better place than the hospital break room to ask her out. *And soon.*

"Sticky." Tessa laughed as she stepped to her locker. "Very sticky!"

Tessa stepped into the elevator and leaned against the wall. Her day hadn't been terrible, but she'd run from patient to patient with no downtime. Her toes ached in her shoes. She was looking forward to comfy socks and an easy evening.

"Hold the elevator!"

Tessa put her hand to the door, stopping the sensor. Fingers grazed hers before pulling back, but her body lit with recognition. *Gabe.*

"Thanks." He grinned as he stepped into the elevator with her.

He leaned on the other wall, several feet from her, but Tessa's body called out at the close confines, aching to bridge the distance. To see what he'd do if she invited him to dinner.

It would be nice to have someone over to dinner. To have a house with noise that didn't just come from the television. To spend time with people outside the hospital.

To spend time with Gabe.

Swallowing those desires, she shifted her messenger bag. "No problem. I know what it's like to want to get home. A little peace and quiet after the craziness here."

Gabe shrugged. "That might be nice, but I'm still couch surfing at my sister's place. Stacy's girls don't really do peace and quiet."

That would be nice to come home to, too. Sticky faces and loud noises. Belonging. *Family.* Tessa pushed that need away before she could mention that she'd love to come home to sticky faces and loud noises. No need to further embarrass herself.

"I'm constantly fending off her oldest's karate moves. She may be almost two feet shorter than me, but I am pretty sure Brett could pin me with ease!"

Tessa laughed as the elevator doors opened to the parking garage, wishing she could extend the interval with Gabe. He always found ways to make her smile. Real smiles, not the fake fixtures that had become her mask during the final years of her marriage.

"I'd love to watch you dodge her. I bet it's a sight to see." Tessa caught the desire to ask if she could come over sometime—but barely.

Get it together!

Her body heated as Gabe's dark gaze held hers. He cleared his throat and stepped from the elevator.

Gabe turned. "What are your evening plans?"

Her stomach flipped as she shrugged. "Reading up on hydroponic gardening." *Nothing that can't be rescheduled.*

His dimples appeared as he stared at her. Hope fluttered in the dimly lit garage.

Gabe put his hands into the front pocket of his backpack and pulled out a set of keys. "How—" His faced shifted as he looked away. "That sounds interesting. I'd like to hear more about it sometime."

An awkward pause erupted between them. Time extended as she looked at his chiseled features.

Why didn't you call? The question reverberated around her brain as they stood together.

The elevator dinged behind her and the spell binding them broke.

"Have a good night, Tessa and Gabe," Debra shouted as she walked toward her car.

"You, too!" Gabe called as Tessa waved.

"Enjoy your book." Gabe tipped his head as he spun his keys around his fingers.

"Watch your back around your niece." Tessa pulled her keys from her bag, too.

His deep chuckle sent need cascading through her.

"Always." He winked and walked away.

She let out a breath, trying to calm her heart rate.

Want to get dinner? See a movie? Why were those phrases so hard to utter? If he said no, Tessa would at least know.

But no also meant he really wasn't interested—and she wasn't ready to lose the bright bit of hope her heart was clinging to.

"I'm headed to the coffee shop. Do you want me to grab you something?" Tessa offered as she stepped out of a patient's room.

"I'd kill for an iced caramel macchiato!" Gabe's step picked up as he moved beside her. He still hadn't figured out the perfect way to ask her out. It should be simple. *Want to grab dinner?* But he wanted it to be...*epic.*

To be something she wouldn't turn down.

Tessa grinned, but her eyes weren't as bright as they normally were when she met his gaze before she offered a pretend shudder. "I asked if you wanted coffee. Not a cup of sugar."

He loved sweet drinks, but it was the company Gabe craved, not caffeine. He leaned as close as he could in the hospital and whispered, "You might like it if you tried it."

The twitch in her lips lifted his spirits even further. He was happy when he was with her.

"I think I'll stick to my regular."

Gabe shuddered as she winked, the playful exchange putting an extra bounce in his step. How Tessa gulped down cup after cup of black coffee was beyond him. He might like and sometimes need the caffeine boost, but it could be done with a little chocolate or caramel drizzle!

"Any word on the job?" Gabe tried to keep the question light. He'd never understand the craze this position was causing among the doctors. But he was trying to be supportive. It mattered to Tessa.

And she'd be great at it. Gabe knew that, but he was still concerned that she was pushing herself to the edge. Over the last few weeks, she'd been at the hospital during each of his shifts. And on most of the days he wasn't here, too, according to the other nurses.

It was one thing to love your job, to want the best for your patients—Gabe understood that drive because it rumbled through him, too—but living at your job, focusing only on it, was a recipe for disaster. But he wasn't sure how to bring up the worry—or if it was even his place.

But surely a friend could point out that Dallas Children's Hospital was not a person. That it couldn't love its employees. When one moved on, another would be hired. Even Dr. Lin, who'd been a senior attending for almost a decade and a half, could be replaced easily enough. Shoot, people were talking about his replacement before he'd officially announced his last day.

"No word." Tessa frowned as they reached the coffee shop.

The line was longer today than usual but Gabe didn't mind. A few extra minutes with the woman beside him was a joy.

"I'm worried they might look to an outside hire." She pressed her fingers to her lips.

Gabe bumped his shoulder against hers, hating the dip of concern he saw floating in her features. Dr. Lin had only told a few people he was retiring; he hadn't made anything official. There was nothing the hospital could do yet.

"Not that Human Resources will ask me, but I think hiring one of our doctors would be best."

"You'd be a good resource for them." Tessa looked at her hands before meeting his gaze. Emotion floated there that made his knees weak.

Did she feel the electricity that connected them, too? Did she still lie awake at night thinking of their time together?

Tessa leaned a little closer, and her scent made Gabe want something very different from caffeine.

"You notice things. You listen better than anyone I've ever met, and you genuinely care about the patients and staff. Actually, you probably care about everyone you meet."

"Life's too short not to make everyone feel special." Gabe grinned. A look passed over her face that he couldn't quite understand. Before he could ask, they'd reached the front of the line.

"Happy birthday, Dr. Garcia." A resident waved and raised his coffee toward them.

Birthday? Why hadn't she'd said something? The hollow in his belly expanded. He'd have gotten her a card.

Or used it as an excuse to plan a birthday dinner. It would have been the perfect opportunity to see if she wanted to test out the feelings that still seemed to crackle between them.

"Thanks." Tessa waved before staring at her shoes.

"Well, let me buy the coffee today. After all, I didn't realize we were celebrating." Gabe ached to throw an arm around her shoulder, but that was too much. *And yet not enough.*

"We aren't." Tessa's words were tight, and the flinch along her jaw nearly stilled his feet.

What had he said? Gabe hated the tension stringing through her. "Tessa?"

"Medium house blend, black." She held her badge up to the scanner and stepped aside to let him order his drink without looking at him.

"Large caramel macchiato with an extra shot of

espresso." Gabe pressed his badge to the scanner, too, before moving to her side. Her lips were pursed, and her gaze was far away. What was he missing?

Birthdays should be a day of celebration.

His father had always made a big deal of birthdays. Even when money had been tight, a birthday cake decorated in the birthday boy's or girl's favorite color always materialized on the hand-me-down kitchen table. Balloons purchased from the Dollar Store were taped to the wall, and the entire family sang to—or rather belted at—the newly aged member of the group.

Even now, his siblings had a tradition of trying to be the first to call on someone's birthday. The silly tradition had gotten so out of hand that a few years ago, a truce had been declared that no one could start the call until at least five in the morning in whatever time zone the birthday person was in. Only Gabe and Isla still competed to be first, but that was because Matt and Stacy preferred to sleep until a reasonable hour now that they were settling down with kids.

"So, you don't like your birthday?" Gabe grabbed his large drink and took a deep sip.

"No." Tessa lifted the coffee to her lips, but it didn't mask the subtle shake in her hands.

Most of the medical professionals Gabe knew didn't mind adding years. Once you saw how fragile life really was, you celebrated the additional laugh lines and crow's-feet that far too many people never got to earn.

"You want to talk about it?" He knew the answer before the question left his lips, but he didn't regret asking it. Gabe wanted to know about Tessa, and he wanted her to know that he wanted to know her.

"No." The word was clipped, but he saw the twitch of

her lips behind the cup. It wasn't much, but at least she knew he'd listen if she opened up about it.

She grimaced and ran a hand along her belly.

"Seriously, are you okay?" Gabe reached for her elbow as she shuddered. She had been working extra shifts; he knew how much exhaustion could bring emotions to the surface. What was going on?

"I think coffee in the afternoon just isn't sitting right with me." Her jaw clenched as she looked at the cup. "Maybe it's because I'm getting older." Tessa winked.

His chest seized as her dark eyes held his. This wasn't the place he'd planned or the perfect moment he wanted, but Gabe was done waiting. "How about we—"

"Code yellow! Code yellow!"

Tessa's eyes flew to the speaker on the wall before her feet took off.

Gabe dropped his full drink into the trash can beside the emergency room's side door. Adrenaline raced through him, but it didn't push away all the concern for the woman who hit the ER doors a second before he did.

"Seven-car pileup on I-635. At least four of the cars had families. We've got six patients incoming. More possible!" The call came up from the nurses' station, and Gabe saw the color drain from Tessa's face before she squared her shoulders.

They'd had a few bad days since he'd started working at Dallas Children's. It was always difficult when you had more than broken bones and stitches, but her panicked look as the nurse stated that the adults were heading to Presbyterian Hospital sent a chill down his spine. This was one of the worst ways to spend your birthday.

She hated this day! If there were happy memories tied to it, Tessa couldn't dredge them up.

"Where is my momma?"

The tiny voice belonged to Natalie Dreamer, the final patient on Tessa's long list of little ones who had been on Interstate 635. A church group had been carpooling to a campout. An elderly driver suffered a cardiac event and crossed three lanes of traffic. Seven of the fifteen cars in the caravan had been involved in the resulting pileup.

Bending to look at the dark-haired cutie, Tessa tried to keep her voice even. All she knew was that Natalie's father was on his way here, and her mother was at Presbyterian Hospital.

Please... Tessa sent the tiny plea into the universe, hoping that this might be the one time it listened to her entreaties. Tessa didn't want to add another tragedy to today's list of traumas. *Please...*

"Your dad will be here shortly, Natalie." Tessa smiled, hoping it seemed comforting. She'd been this child once, asked everyone where her mother was. All the smiles she'd been offered that day hadn't mattered as she'd sat in the waiting room with a tiny stuffed elephant that a nurse had procured from the gift shop. She'd clung to it, even though she'd sworn off stuffed animals as babyish in a fit of preteen drama the year she'd turned twelve.

It was the last birthday present she'd allowed herself to receive.

The door to the room opened and Gabe stepped in. His eyes were heavy with exhaustion, but he offered a bright smile to Natalie. Then he pulled a pink bunny from behind his back. Tessa couldn't quite control her recoil.

Gabe's gaze darted toward her before returning to Natalie. He was very perceptive, but Tessa hoped he'd just think she was tired. Which she was.

No matter how much sleep Tessa got lately, it was

never enough. But that was a problem for another day, too. *Focus!*

"Bunny!" Natalie grabbed the stuffed animal, snuggling it close with the arm that wasn't in a sling.

"I thought it might help to have a snuggle partner while Dr. Garcia puts your arm in a cast." Gabe made sure he was at Natalie's level as he addressed the child. It was a small thing, but children often felt more comfortable when an adult was at their level. Even after treating their share of the fifteen patients who had arrived from the car accident, Gabe didn't rush through his patient interactions.

He'd make an excellent partner and father.

The loose thought stunned Tessa as she prepared the material for Natalie's fiberglass cast. Mentally shaking herself, Tessa tried to focus on the task in front of her. But if you worked in a children's hospital, you saw more broken bones than probably any other medical professional, so she could do this routine in her sleep.

She should be thrilled that Gabe was such an excellent pediatric nurse—that he fit so well at Dallas Children's. Little boys needed to see men in caring roles—needed to know they could become nurses, too. That it wasn't just a girl job.

But Tessa wanted more than coffee runs and breakroom chats. There'd been a few times when she'd thought he was about to ask her out. Like that evening in the parking garage. But the topic always seemed to shift to something else.

Usually a question regarding Dr. Lin's position. Tessa felt her lips turn down and tried to wipe the emotion from her face. She'd been thrilled when Gabe had finally started talking with her about the job, but after previously ignoring the topic, he now broached it at least once every other shift.

Was that why he hadn't asked her out? Tessa didn't want to believe that. But she hadn't wanted to believe that her ex-husband was jealous of her, either.

She could ask him out. It was the twenty-first century. Women did that. But each time she'd considered it, her tongue had failed to deliver the words.

If he said no, she was afraid she'd lose what they had now. An easy work relationship wasn't all she wanted, but it was better than awkward silence. When he was around, Tessa didn't feel so unmoored in the world, a sensation she hadn't realized was so normal until Gabe's anchor had appeared.

Gabe's anchor? That was romantic fairy-tale stuff that rarely led to happily-ever-after. They'd had one perfect night, but that did not qualify as an anchor.

But as she looked over at him, Tessa's nerves and aching heart calmed slightly. Breathing through the pain of today was easier when he met her gaze.

"Will my cast be really pink?" Natalie's voice was soft, but it broke through Tessa's mental musings.

"Really, really pink—" Tessa grinned "—with sparkles." Having a broken bone wasn't a cause for celebration, but many kids got excited to have a fun color.

"Sparkles?" Gabe opened his mouth, pretending to be shocked by the revelation. Most of the girls who broke a limb asked for sparkle casts and many of the boys, too. Sparkles could make almost anything better. "Now I wish I had a sparkle cast."

"It hurts to get one." Natalie's eyes were damp with unshed tears as she looked toward Gabe. "I wish Momma was here."

A lump stuck in the back of Tessa's throat. Her gaze

flitted to Gabe, willing him to understand that she couldn't answer. She must be more exhausted than she'd realized. Tears threatened to spill into her eyes, too, as she looked at the young girl. She bore so many similarities to Tessa. What if today she joined the terrible club that no child should have a membership to?

Gabe sat on the table with Natalie and tapped the top of her bunny's ears to get her attention. "I called the other hospital before I came in. I have an old friend who works there. Your mommy is going to have to stay with them for a few days, but she is okay." He raised his eyes to meet Tessa's and repeated, "She's okay."

Tessa wasn't sure what strings he'd pulled to get that information, but she was grateful as she watched Natalie exhale. He'd given her the best gift possible. And a pink bunny, too!

"So, let's get your pink sparkle cast ready. That way, when your dad gets here, he can take you to see your mom." Tessa made the statement, then caught her breath. Gabe hadn't said what condition Natalie's mom was in, but she couldn't pull the words back now.

"That cast is a genuine work of beauty." Gabe grinned as Natalie held it up for inspection.

"Yes, it is," a man who looked strikingly like the little girl stated as he stepped through the door.

"Daddy!" Natalie hopped off the bed. "Look what Nurse Davis got for me!" She held the bunny next to her cast. "They're both pink."

"Imagine that." He bent and pulled his daughter close.

Tessa saw him tremble a little as he kissed the top of her head. The ache in her chest opened further as she watched Natalie's father hold her. Tessa's father had been gone for years when she'd lost her mother. She'd never gotten the hugs and comfort that Natalie's father could give her.

Tessa's grandmother had tried, but she'd been consumed with the grief of losing her only child and the added responsibilities of raising her granddaughter. She'd exited retired life, reentered the workforce and done her best for Tessa. But she hadn't been her mother.

The last person who'd held Tessa like that had been gone twenty-three years now. And this year, Tessa was officially older than her mother had ever gotten the chance to be.

"Her mom?"

Tessa felt the words leave her lips. There was no way to recapture them—but even if she could, she wanted to hear that the little girl's mom was all right. If it had been any other day, any other situation, she'd never have asked. But she wanted the confirmation that she'd never gotten as a child.

"Yes, where's Mommy?" Natalie bounced, trying to break the tight hold her father had. She was too little to understand how much he must need to touch her. To convince himself that his little girl was indeed all right—mostly.

"Mommy has broken bones like you. In her left leg. She's going to have to stay in the hospital for a few days, and she'll be in a bigger cast than you." Natalie's dad brushed a piece of hair from her cheek.

"Is hers pink, too?"

Her dad chuckled as he shook his head. "I bet she wishes it was. But nope. Just a plain white cast."

Gabe made a motion to Tessa, and she nodded to him. They needed to give this little family a few minutes together. Just before she closed the door, Tessa turned and looked at the father and daughter. Their embrace sent chills through her. How much she yearned for just the comfort of a hug. The comfort of knowing there was someone who noticed that she wasn't okay. A little wish that was so far out of reach.

CHAPTER FIVE

GABE STOOD IN front of Tessa's town house holding a box of cupcakes, hoping she wouldn't care that he'd just shown up. He'd tried to catch her after their shifts ended, but she'd vanished the second they could clock out. So he'd grabbed the box of cupcakes from a bakery by his sister's house, raced to Stacy's, showered and then come here.

He wasn't sure what was going on, but Gabe needed to see that she was okay. Something about the accident on the highway had touched Tessa more deeply than a stack of badly injured patients. That was not the memory that Gabe was going to let linger on her birthday.

Besides, even if they hated the day, no one should be alone on their birthday. Particularly after a day like today.

Medical professionals faced more bad days than most. It was a career field ripe with impressive highs. They occasionally got to witness miracles, but those highs came with devastating lows when the unthinkable occurred. Medical staffers were forced to develop coping mechanisms.

He always spent more time lifting weights when the weeks were going poorly. Not because lifting heavy things made him feel better, but because the pain in his aching muscles drowned out the other racing thoughts.

And pushing his body made him feel a little more invincible in a world where invincibility was a true illusion.

He didn't know Tessa's self-care routine, but whatever it was, she shouldn't do it alone. *Not today.*

The tears in Tessa's eyes as she watched Natalie hug her dad had cut across Gabe's heart. Tessa was hurting—aching—and he longed to reach out to her. But there wasn't an easy option at the hospital.

She needed someone. And he was done waiting for the perfect time. He was here for her—in any way she wanted.

Gabe was lucky. He had his family to walk beside him when the world turned upside down. She'd told him on the first night he'd seen her that there was no one in her life to protect her. No one to shoulder the trauma that a day like today would bring. It had troubled him then.

But it pulled at him now. If she'd let him, maybe Gabe could be that person.

Nerves chased up his spine as he made his way to her door. He wanted to be the shoulder she cried on, the one she danced in the kitchen with, the one who made her laugh and smile.

But if Tessa didn't want the same, he'd find a way to settle for being her friend. Tessa belonged in his life. He was certain of that.

The chime echoed through the door, and Gabe straightened his shoulders as his stomach flopped with nervous and excited energy.

"Just a moment." Tessa's voice sounded strange on the other side of the door, or maybe it was just the door making it sound like it was breaking up. His heart burned as he waited for her to open the barrier between them.

"Gabe?" Tessa's voice shook, and her cheeks were tearstained when her gaze met his. "What are you—"

Her gaze floated to the pink box in his hand. "Are those Maggie's cupcakes?"

"Yes." The tear streaks worried him. How long had she been crying? Maybe he shouldn't have taken the detour for pastries.

But her gaze brightened as she leaned toward the pink box. He flipped the lid open, and his soul eased as Tessa's body relaxed some.

He hadn't known which flavor was her favorite, so each of the cupcakes was different. They made a pretty display in the bubble gum–colored box. If the confectionery treats got him in the door to help her, he'd frequent Maggie's bakery more often. His nieces and nephews would love that!

"You didn't have to bring me cupcakes." Tessa offered a weak smile as she stepped back to let him in. "But I'm glad you're here."

"Today was rough." Gabe looked over his shoulder as he headed toward her kitchen. "You ran out before I could check on you. So…" He shrugged. "Figured a sweet treat might soothe away a few of the day's rough edges."

"So this isn't a birthday celebration?" Tessa cocked her head as she stared at him.

Raising his right hand, he grinned. "I promise these are only half birthday treats."

She let out a light chuckle as she grabbed the coffee cupcake and held it up. "Only half? So what's the other half?"

"You seemed upset earlier. So these are 'make sure Tessa is okay' treats." Gabe studied her as she sat across from him. Her eyes were red, and there were exhaustion pockets under them. She was tired and sad, and he was here to relieve as many burdens as she wanted to drop at his feet.

Tessa mattered to him. And he wanted her to know that. Needed her to know that.

"My mom died today." Tessa let out a soft sob as she pulled the wrapper off her cupcake. Her fingers trembled, and she set the cupcake down on its paper wrapper. Like she was afraid the confectionery wonder might tip out of her shaky grip.

Gabe's tongue was momentarily frozen as he tried to process that statement. What had she been doing at the hospital today?

"What can I do?" Gabe reached for her hand. His heartbeat steadied as her long fingers wrapped around his. He hoped he had the same calming effect on her that she had on him.

"Oh." Tessa squeezed his palm, and she didn't let go. "I meant this is the anniversary of her death. It's been twenty-three years. But this—"

She blew out a breath and stared at her ceiling for a second, trying to compose herself, like there was any shame in mourning someone years after they'd departed. He still took the day off on the anniversary of Olive's passing.

"It's okay." His thumb rubbed along the delicate skin just below her wrist. He knew what small connections to others meant. How it grounded you when it felt like everything else in the world was unhinged.

She ran her free hand under her nose and shook her head. "I'm not usually such a watering pot. I swear. I guess..." She shrugged and looked out the window. "I'm older than her today. Every birthday, starting with this one, marks a year she never saw. It feels weird. That probably sounds silly."

"No." Gabe let go of her hand and moved around the counter. He pulled her into his arms and just held her.

She let out another sob, and then another as he tightened his grip. She laid her head against his shoulder, and he felt the tension melt from her shoulders. He'd hold her for as long as she needed.

After several minutes, she let out a deep breath and pulled back. "Thanks. I needed that hug. But this is probably not what you expected when you brought cupcakes over." She tried to smile as she headed back to her seat, but only the tips of her lips moved. She reached for her cupcake and took a big bite.

"These are so good." She let out a sigh, but no tears hovered in her eyes.

"Happy to help. I'm here for you." Gabe waited until she met his gaze. "Any time you need it. I am here, hugs and all."

"Thank you." Tessa lifted the cake to her lips. "To sugar and—" her cheeks darkening "—friends."

Gabe swallowed the knot in his throat as he grabbed the double chocolate cupcake. That wasn't the term he wanted to use. But he wasn't going to push, at least not tonight.

She took a big bite of the pastry. "I love Maggie's!" She quickly finished the treat and looked at the box. "It's my birthday, and I am having another."

She sighed before grabbing the lemon cupcake. "I usually take the day off at the hospital. But with Dr. Lin's job potentially opening, everything gets monitored, discussed...dissected. I didn't want to take any unnecessary leave."

Unnecessary leave?

Recharging yourself on a difficult anniversary was not something he'd describe as unnecessary. He knew Tessa was interested in the job, but she still had years left at the hospital. If she didn't get the position, others would open. Why the focus on this one?

"Today is always difficult. But the accident—" Tessa's words drifted away as she met his gaze.

"You lost her in a car accident?"

Tessa spun the lemon cupcake around. Her gaze focused on the edible pearl beads decorating the light yellow frosting. Her mind seemed a million miles away, but Gabe wasn't going to draw her back. She'd tell him in her own time—or she wouldn't. Either way, he was here for her.

"She had two jobs, and she'd worked sixteen hours a day for almost two weeks. After my father left us, the bills were piled high and—" Another tear spilled down her cheek as she raised her eyes to meet his.

"Mom fell asleep. For just a minute, but that was enough. We drifted across two lanes of traffic. I screamed. She woke, but it was too late to course-correct. Twenty-three years ago, I waited at Dallas Children's with a broken arm, clutching a stuffed elephant that a nurse procured for me. Except when my grandma came to get me, my mom was gone." She hiccuped as she shook her head.

"I should have told Mom it was all right that I didn't have a birthday cake or present. That we didn't need to go get anything. Not that it would have mattered." Tessa hugged herself and sighed. "She didn't want her daughter to miss out on the birthday fun. She was a very determined woman. And caring."

"Just like her daughter." He was glad she had such fond memories of her mother. That the traits she used could so easily describe Tessa, too. "I'm sure she would be proud of everything you've done."

She pulled at the collar of her deep blue T-shirt before dipping her finger in the frosting and lifting it to her lips. "I like to think so. Mom was in her first year of med school when she found out she was pregnant with me. My parents married and followed my father's sales job to Dallas. She never got to be a surgeon, but I like to think my successes are both of ours.

"So how do you like to spend your birthday, Gabe?" Tessa held up the lemon cupcake. "I assume it's more celebratory than cupcakes and tears."

"Movie night." Gabe winked. "An enormous pile of popcorn and a list of streaming titles."

"Well, that sounds lovely." Her eyes met his, and he saw a touch of the sadness give way to something different.

"Name the time and place, Tessa. I'll bring the popcorn." He grabbed the mint cupcake and dipped his finger into the icing.

Tessa's eyes widened, and she wagged a finger. "You're going to regret that!"

"Did you want the mint cupcake?" Gabe playfully started to offer his finger full of icing to her before remembering that *that* was more flirtatious than the night's conversation allowed. Trying to ignore the heat in his face, Gabe devoured the icing.

Tessa grabbed his hand. The warmth from the connection burned as she held him. *Does she feel it, too?*

Her eyes sparkled as she held his fingers up. "See!" She pointed to his bright green finger and laughed as Gabe felt his mouth slide open.

"How?"

Tessa continued giggling; her laughs made his green finger completely worth it. She wiped a happy tear from her cheek and held up the cupcake. "It's called the Minty

Monster because they use so much food coloring in the icing that it stains anything it touches."

"The voice of experience?" Gabe leaned closer to her. Even with the tough conversations they'd had, the tears and green finger, there was no place Gabe would rather be tonight.

"The first time, my teeth were green for almost an entire day!" Tessa leaned closer, but still not near enough. Like they were magnets circling in an orbit, able to feel the pull of the other, but not close enough to get yanked together.

Yet.

"That cupcake is a kid and teenage favorite, so the bakery doesn't adjust the recipe. They make hundreds for Halloween. I always bring a dozen for the staff. The kids love our green mouths!"

She swallowed and met his gaze. "I really appreciate you coming tonight. It's been a long time since anyone noticed that I wasn't okay." She pushed a loose strand of hair behind her ear, and her gaze drifted to his lips just briefly. "And even longer since someone went out of their way to make me feel better."

"Any time." Gabe forced the words out. They were true. But he was in danger of getting lost in the depths of her eyes again.

Before he could follow up, Tessa reached for his hand. "You said today that life was too short not to make everyone feel special. Is that why you came tonight…to make a friend feel special?"

The air crackled around them as he searched for the right words. In the end, the words refused to materialize. So he just let his heart talk.

"Life is too short not to do your best to make others realize that they matter." Gabe rubbed the delicate skin along her wrist, grateful when she didn't pull back. "But no. That's not why I showed up on your doorstep with five gourmet cupcakes and one green icing bomb!"

She bit her lip as she waited for him to continue.

"I wanted to check on you. I *needed* to make sure you were okay." Gabe rested his head against hers, measuring the subtle changes in her breath. "You matter to me. I have wished a thousand times that I'd called you after we were together. That I'd invited you to breakfast with my family that morning. That I'd told you how much I enjoy just being near you. I've spent the last week trying to figure out the best way to ask you to dinner."

"Wow." Tessa sighed as she moved around the counter and slid next to him. "That was quite the pronouncement. I wish I'd called you, too. You matter to me, also."

His heart skipped a beat, not sure it could trust the statement. He wanted to pull her close, but there was a glint in her eye that stilled his hand.

"Can I ask you a question?" Tessa's voice was quiet as she crossed her arms.

Nerves raced around him, but Gabe nodded. "Anything."

"Did you not call because of my excitement over Dr. Lin's job?"

"Yes." Gabe let the truth rest between them. "And that wasn't fair to you. My mom left us like your father deserted you. Her career mattered more than her family. After our night together, seeing you dancing around the kitchen for a promotion made me nervous. And I'm sorry. That was wrong."

Tessa nodded, her lip twisting between her teeth. "I'm going for that position, Gabe." She pulled her arms tighter. "If that's a problem then we can just be friends. I won't hold it against you. I promise. But my ex demanded I refuse a similar position at a hospital in Ohio two years ago. I turned down that job for a man, and I won't do it again."

He blew out a breath as that truth sank between them. No wonder she hadn't called him! But he wasn't going to make the same mistake as her ex-husband. "It's not a problem." Gabe pushed a curl behind her ear. "And it shouldn't have been a problem then. I panicked."

Tessa let her fingers lace through his. "Life at the hospital is hectic, and my schedule is…" She squinted as she looked for a word.

"Jam-packed?" Gabe offered.

"Yes." She nodded. "But I want to give this a try. Give us a try."

The air rushed from his lungs and Gabe couldn't remember the last time he'd smiled so much. His heart rang with joy as his brain echoed tiny warning bells, but they were easy to ignore when Tessa was touching him.

He should reach for this. He wanted to grab this! Life was too short to wait for happiness.

"Are you free Friday night?" Gabe ached to kiss her, to taste her again, but he sensed hesitation in Tessa, and he wouldn't rush this. If he was going to risk his heart again, then he wasn't going to give Tessa any reason to doubt him.

"No." Her bottom lip pushed out as she looked at him. "But I'm free Sunday. Have you ever been to the Dallas Botanical Garden?"

"Not since I was in high school." Gabe smiled. "But I'd love to see it this weekend."

"Then it's a date." Tessa beamed as she leaned closer, her arms wrapped around his neck as she held him tight.

"Yes, it is," Gabe confirmed as he relished her body next to his. *Tessa.*

He ran a thumb along her cheek, grateful to get a second chance with this incredible woman.

When her lips met his, Gabe's body rejoiced. It wasn't the passionate need they'd experienced weeks ago. No, this kiss was comforting, and it spoke of tomorrow's promise.

It was perfect.

When she pulled back, he dropped a kiss along her cheek. "I'll see you at the hospital tomorrow."

Then he kissed the top of her head. "Happy birthday, Tessa."

CHAPTER SIX

"THIS PLACE IS bigger than I remember." Gabe's gaze wandered across the large parking lot.

Tessa bumped his hip with hers, enjoying the feel of his arm around her waist. They were on a date. Her heart felt like it might leap from her chest. She and Gabe were on a date.

"There are twenty-two gardens in all. At Christmas they set up twelve mock Victorian shops and houses to represent the twelve days of Christmas. The whole garden is sixty-six acres in total!" She bit back the other facts that wanted to pour from her lips.

This was one of her favorite places. She could recite as many facts as the volunteer tour guides who worked each of the gardens.

She'd wanted to be married here. But Max had balked at the notion. He wasn't going to contend with the garden's guests on their special day. Tessa had been hurt, but after her marriage had failed, she'd been grateful. At least she didn't have any poor memories here.

It felt right that she was here with Gabe. Tessa knew this was only their first date—their first real date, anyway—but she couldn't stop the smile spreading across her face as they crossed the threshold of the first garden.

"Sixty-six acres." Gabe squeezed her side as they wandered through the main entrance. "That's a lot of gar-den. So what other facts are popping around your brain, Tessa?"

"Am I that transparent?" She pulled him toward the Margaret Elizabeth Jonsson Color Garden.

"Transparent?" Gabe shook his head as he squeezed her waist. "You are basically bouncing. This is a place you have clearly been before—a lot, I'd wager."

Leaning her head against his shoulder, Tessa sighed as she drank in the peaceful settings. Even when the garden was full of families and picnic-goers, it always seemed like she was in her own bubble when she was here. Except now, Gabe was in her bubble, too. And that felt so right.

"I've been a member since I was a student in college. I used to come here to study on the grass yards. It's my happy place. Spring is my favorite. The tulips bloom for acres in the Color Garden. And you see everyone from brides-to-be, to girls celebrating their quinceañera, to moms and dads trying to snap the perfect picture of their rambling tots among the blossoms."

She used to dream of bringing her own small kids here. *But maybe...* Tessa pressed that bubble of hope away. This was their first date. It might feel like more because of their fiery first night, but she was not going to hope too much.

Clearing her throat, she pointed around the open space. "Right now it's got banana and tapioca plants in bloom. In a few weeks, it will be painted orange and purple with chrysanthemums."

"Really?" Gabe's gaze was focused on the field of colors before them.

Tessa swallowed the other plant information that was running through her brain. She'd had a thriving garden at the house she and Max sold. When she'd packed up her final things, she'd stood over the blooms she'd patiently coaxed from seedlings and cried. She'd driven by the house only once since her divorce and been horrified by the condition of her plants.

Except they weren't her plants anymore.

Her town house didn't really have the space for a large garden. She had a few ferns on her porch, but it wasn't the same. But she'd been doing some research on apartment gardens and she was pretty sure she could figure out a way to make a small green space happen.

"Sorry, I have a tendency to go overboard when talking plants." She pressed her free hand to her lips, willing all the things she wanted to say to stay buried.

"You don't need to apologize for being excited about something."

Gabe met her gaze and Tessa felt her spirit lift. It was such a small thing, to have someone willingly listen to her go on about the thing she enjoyed most. To care that she was excited.

"So, what's your favorite flower?"

"It's not here." Tessa leaned her head against his shoulder. Months ago, she'd come here on her own to see the tulips—and been painfully aware of how alone she was. This felt much more like an intimate day between long-term partners, and that should terrify her, but it was impossible to be worried when she was in her happy place... with Gabe.

"It's called Henry Duelberg salvia. It's drought-resistant and a deep bluish-purple. When you plant it in a bed, it will spread out, and—" Tessa watched Gabe's features shift. She always went overboard with plants. "Was that too much information?"

He chuckled and kissed her cheek. "Nope. But I was hunting for information on what types of blooms I might bring in the future that would make the smile you have right now appear."

"Oh." Tessa shook her head as they wandered towards the statues in A Woman's Garden. "I'm not sure there's a flower or plant you could bring me that wouldn't put a smile on my face. Though lantana does smell like gasoline if you brush against it, so maybe not that one."

Gabe pulled her into the shade and ran a hand along her cheek. "What if I leave it up to a florist to tell me which flowers will work, or maybe I'll grab some bundles at the grocery store? Those will look pretty enough on your table—at least until I learn the difference between lantana, salvia and roses, right?"

Learn the difference... Her eyes misted. She wasn't sure why she was so prone to waterworks these days, but she didn't care. She dropped a light kiss on his cheek. How had she gotten so lucky to be walking next to this man in her favorite place?

"Right," Tessa breathed out. But it wasn't Gabe's mention of a florist or his desire to make sure she had flowers that made joy race through her. It was his easy use of the word *future*. As though there would be more perfect moments like this to look forward to.

As a thrill rocketed through her, fear trickled behind it, too. Max had been interested early on, too. He'd never asked her favorite flower, but he'd been supportive of the garden she'd tended, helped her dig the beds and cooked dinner when she had to work late. She'd done her fair share, too, but when she'd gotten ahead, she'd asked him to take on a little more. And he'd hated her for it.

But as Gabe dropped his lips to hers, joy conquered fear—at least temporarily.

His touch was light, and Tessa craved more. Pulling him closer, she deepened the kiss. The gardens were lovely, romantic and the perfect place to kiss Gabe. Actually, the bar they'd reconnected in had felt perfect, too. She suspected every place might seem perfect when she was with him.

Gabe.

Her body molded to his as he stroked her back.

"Aren't they cute?"

Gabe pulled back and Tessa felt her cheeks heat as she caught a few knowing looks from others walking past them. She'd smiled at many lovers who'd worn expressions of contentedness, too—but never been caught kissing in the gardens herself. It was a memory she knew she'd treasure.

Before she or Gabe could say anything, Tessa's phone buzzed. "Sorry." She pulled it out of her pocket.

"No, it's fine." His voice was breathless as he turned to look at the flowers.

Knowing that she could make the handsome, sweet, generous man beside her swoon made her euphoric. She quickly glanced at the text and typed out a reply.

"Everything okay?" Gabe's fingers were warm as they ran along her side.

Slipping her phone back in her pocket, Tessa grinned. "One of the residents ran into a case today that they had some questions on. They want me to look over their notes tomorrow and give them some feedback."

An emotion played across his face that sent a bead of worry pulsing through her. Many people took work calls on their off day. "I'm always available to help."

His lips twitched before Gabe nodded. "That's nice." He kissed her cheek as they started down the walking path. His eyes were far away, though his gaze was focused on the flowers in front of them.

Another twinge of uncertainty washed through her. Was

he upset that so many people at the hospital relied on her? Had he not really meant it the other night when he said it shouldn't have mattered that she was so excited about the job opportunity? Max had done that—encouraged her to put in for promotions, then gotten upset when she got them.

No. Gabe was not Max. She would not let intrusive thoughts ruin this beautiful day and her time with Gabe.

She pointed out a few more of her beloved locations. Gabe nodded along and even asked questions. The disquiet that never quite left Tessa was silenced as they walked back to the car. Mostly.

"How did we manage to close the restaurant down?"

Tessa's laugh as they walked up to her town house door sent a thrill through him. After their day at the garden, Gabe had suggested they grab a quick dinner. *Quick.* He let out a soft chuckle, too.

"It really didn't feel like we'd been there for several hours." Gabe had made sure to leave the waiter a sizable tip for hogging the table for most of the evening. It had been unintentional, but he couldn't be sorry for it. Time just flew when he was with the woman beside him.

Tessa put her key in the door and turned the lock. Her dark eyes held his gaze as she leaned against the door. "I had the best time today, Gabe."

She leaned in, her soft kiss igniting flames of need through his body. Her fingers ran along his stomach, and Gabe ached with desire. *Tessa.*

She pulled back and let out a breath. "I…" Tessa bit her lip. Her cheeks flamed. "I know our first night…"

Gabe dropped another kiss on her lips, then he smiled. If she invited him inside, he'd gladly carry her to bed and worship each inch of her again. But there was no need to rush anything. Gabe wanted Tessa for more than a one-night fling; he'd wait however long she needed to advance their relationship. "I'm in no rush, sweetheart."

He pushed a curl behind her ear, enjoying the heat of her skin beneath his fingers. He'd wait a lifetime for the woman in front of him, though he hoped it wouldn't be that long.

Tessa laid her head against his chest and sighed. "I had the best time today. The best."

Her repetition made his insides melt. *Best.* "I did, too, Tessa."

Wrapping his arms around her waist, Gabe kissed the top of her head, enjoying the feel of her against him. Then the top of her pants vibrated.

Another text message from the hospital?

During their date, she'd gotten at least ten messages or calls from interns and residents. Gabe had worked in the medical field for years and he understood that it was a calling to many. But Tessa was so tied to Dallas Children's.

No. He was not going to tumble down the path of worry. Tessa was helping, not trying to advance herself on the backs of others. And she didn't reach for the phone as he held her.

But Gabe couldn't hold her on her porch all night. No matter how much he might want to. Running his hand along the edge of her jaw, Gabe waited until she looked at him, then he dropped another kiss to her lips.

He didn't rush the kiss or deepen it. It was soft, and comforting, and full of the promise of more. So much more.

Pulling away, Gabe forced himself to take a step back, otherwise he might never make it off her stoop. "I can't wait to see you again, Tessa."

Her face lit with excitement. "I can't wait either, Gabe. Good night."

* * *

Tessa spun the scrambled eggs around on her plate and tried to calm the tumble of her stomach. She forced herself to take another bite. Protein was important, and she was just starting her shift, but her stomach twisted again. Maybe the extra dessert she and Gabe had ordered during their extended dinner last night had been a mistake.

She enjoyed sweets, but her body was not as acclimated to the sugar as Gabe's. Electricity shot across her as she thought of him. Of their kisses on her porch.

Her body still ached with desire. Her dreams had all tumbled with images of him in her bed. Kisses and passion had lit through her sleep.

Until early this morning. After a peaceful night, she'd woken with a start from a nightmare. The remnants of the dream had faded quickly, but she remembered Gabe walking away from her after she received the promotion. It was just a product of an overactive subconscious. He'd said that he shouldn't have let the promotion keep him from asking her out. But the notch of uncertainty in the back of her mind refused to vanish.

The smell of the eggs made her queasy as she tossed her plate in the trash. Before she left the cafeteria, Tessa thought of grabbing a container of yogurt or a banana. But just looking at them made her stomach want to revolt. What was going on? Tessa rubbed her hand along her belly and started toward the nursing desk.

"Are you all right, Dr. Garcia?" Denise stared at her as Tessa reached for the thermometer.

Tessa's stomach lurched again, and she took a deep breath through her nose, trying to gather herself. "I'm not sure." She ran the thermometer along her forehead and sighed as it read ninety-eight point three. "No fever."

Her belly danced again, and she paged Dr. Killon.

He was on call today. Even with no fever, she wouldn't be able to stay if her stomach was going to betray her. Most rotaviruses didn't present with a fever, but they were highly contagious—and often carried by children.

"Maybe my stomach just really wasn't in the mood for omelets today, but I've paged Dr. Killon." Her brain felt foggy as she uttered the words. Her overactive dreams must have kept her from truly resting—though she was not sorry to have spent the night dreaming of Gabe.

Denise nodded but kept her distance. The cleaning schedule at Dallas Children's was intense, but hospitals were breeding grounds for germs. "Shame, I love omelets. I ate them every Saturday until I was pregnant with Ginger. That little one hated eggs, though you'd never know it now!"

She grabbed a chart tablet. "I hope you feel better soon, Dr. Garcia."

"Thank you." Tessa barely forced the words through her lips as Denise's statement registered. *Pregnant...that is not possible.*

Except it might be. Tessa's nails dug into her palms as she calculated her last period. Two weeks before she and Gabe had been together. They'd used protection, but the condoms had been older, and protection wasn't perfect. She'd been busy, focused on the upcoming job opportunity, but how had she not noticed that she was so late?

She pressed her hands into her side as she felt her entire body start to shake. She needed to get out of here. Needed to gain control of herself—needed to stop by a pharmacy. What was she going to do?

One foot in front of the other. The mantra did little to calm her racing heartbeat as she started toward the employee lounge. If she was pregnant, she'd be almost eight weeks along. Over halfway through her first trimester.

Her hands were clammy as she reached the lounge and pulled on her locker door.

Eight weeks along. That meant she'd spent most of her first trimester unaware of the little bean. She quickly racked her mind, trying to think through the last several weeks. She'd had alcohol the night she and Gabe… Her face heated at the memories.

Clearing her throat, she offered a short wave to a nurse as she headed for the parking garage. No alcohol since conception, but her caffeine habit had been maintained. Still, that wouldn't matter much at this early stage. And she hadn't been taking any prenatal vitamins.

Her chest tightened as she slid into the car. Prenatal vitamins were important, but many women started them after they discovered they were pregnant. The thought sent another wave of panic through her as she gripped her steering wheel. How was she calmly running through the checklist in her mind while her body was locked in terror?

She was probably overthinking this. In a few hours, she'd laugh at herself, order herself to look into stress relief tactics, and make an appointment with her gynecologist. It had been far too long since she'd seen Dr. Fillery anyway.

Her heart rocked a little at the idea that she might not be pregnant. She bit her lip as it started to tremble. That shouldn't make her upset—it shouldn't.

So why were tears coating her eyes?

Tessa forced air into her lungs as she tried to calm her aching heart. She'd wanted to be a mother for so long. To have a few little ones to come home to. But this wasn't the way she'd imagined it happening.

She and Gabe had decided to turn their one-night stand into something more. To see if the chemistry igniting them meant what they hoped. Yesterday had been so perfect, and Tessa was already looking forward to their next date. How might an unplanned pregnancy change the mixture?

And Dr. Lin was filing his retirement paperwork next week—or maybe the week after that. Though all those rumors had been false so far.

She was not prepared for a baby. This was not the right time. But her heart didn't seem to care.

Tessa rolled her free hand over the still-flat portion of her lower belly. She knew it was far too early to feel anything—assuming she even was pregnant. But she was protective of the potential life growing inside her.

Her child.

She could do this.

Whatever this might be.

The tile floor in her bathroom was cold and hard, but she didn't feel like moving. Not yet. In the two hours it had taken her to buy a pregnancy test—four pregnancy tests, actually—Tessa had managed to convince herself that she'd been overreacting. But the double blue line on three of the tests did not lie.

She stared at the unopened fourth box. The urge to open it and confirm what the other three had stated was almost overwhelming. Rolling her head from side to side, she pushed back at that desire. The fourth test would only confirm what the second and third had.

Her life was changing. *And Gabe's life is changing, too.*

As if just her thoughts were enough to summon him, her phone buzzed.

You okay? Dr. Killon said you were sick.

Her fingers shook as she laid the phone aside. She should respond, should say she was fine. But was she? *Yes. No. Yes.* The words spiraled through her mind as she pulled her knees to her chest. Laying her head against them, Tessa stared at her phone as another message popped in.

Let me know if you need anything.

It was such a sweet offer. The kind Gabe made—and meant—without even thinking. What was he going to do? If they'd known each other longer, today's revelations wouldn't cause her such worry.

Gabe was going to be an amazing father. Tessa swallowed. Assuming this was an adventure he wanted to take, too.

Wrapping her hands around her waist, Tessa tried to ignore the worry rooting its way through her mind. She didn't think Gabe would step away from her and their unexpected family. But her father had told her mother that he wanted a family when she'd discovered she was pregnant with Tessa. He'd promised to take care of them both, had professed a desire to be a family man. Then he'd abandoned them. And her ex-husband had discarded Tessa with little thought, too.

And she'd survived that, she reminded herself. She was strong, independent and caring, just like her mother. This wasn't the path to motherhood that she'd expected, but Tessa was going to show her child that they could do it all. No matter what.

Her child would never question that they were loved, wanted and treasured. Tessa laid her hands over the stillness of her belly and sighed. "I will always protect you."

At least she knew why she'd been such an emotional

watering pot over the last few days. Taking a deep breath, Tessa tried to force her racing mind to focus. There were many things she needed to figure out. Things to do. Slapping her knees, she stood up.

Picking up her phone, she called her ob-gyn and walked to the kitchen. Pulling a glass down, she quickly swallowed her prenatal vitamin and started a small grocery list while she waited on hold. Then she texted Gabe and asked him to come over.

The text was vague; she didn't want to give too much away. Particularly since Tessa hadn't figured out the right words yet. But this was not news that she wanted to relay over text or phone. He deserved to hear that he was going to be a father in person.

They were going to be parents.

Parents.

Gabe spun his phone around as he waited at the traffic light six blocks from Tessa's townhome. He was barely holding to his pledge to ignore his cellular device while in the car but he'd already memorized Tessa's cryptic texts. All four sentences.

We need to talk. Can you please come over after your shift?

He'd sent her a text back saying that he wasn't off until ten, but she'd responded to that, too.

I know. It's not something I want to put off.

Are you all right?

She'd read his last message three hours ago, according to his phone, and not responded. His hands were clammy as he gripped the steering wheel.

They'd had an excellent time at the gardens. The daytime date had spilled into a lovely evening. He'd thought it was perfect. Surely this wasn't a maybe-we-really-should-just-be-friends talk?

Could she really be having second thoughts?

Please, his soul whispered. He didn't want to give up on the possibilities his heart was painting.

He pulled into the small alley and tried to ignore the blood pounding in his ears and the tightness in his chest. What was waiting for him in Tessa's home? Gabe wiped his hands along the jeans he'd changed into after his shift, then forced himself to head to her back door.

The deck furniture where they'd sat so many weeks ago made him smile. That memory would always be good. *No matter what happened now.*

Her back door flung open, and Tessa stood in the bright light. Her shoulders were stiff, but he saw her fingers flex slightly. Something was bothering her. What had happened in less than twenty-four hours to make her so stressed?

"How are you feeling?" he asked as she stepped back to let him in. Denise had mentioned that Tessa's stomach had been upset, but Tessa looked all right now—at least physically.

A little tired, maybe. Her dark eyes met his. Worry floated across her gaze, but hope was there, too. That eased part of his concern, but only a little.

"I'm better now. Thanks for coming."

"Anytime." He hoped she knew how much he meant that. If she needed him, he'd be there for her. Gabe reached for her hand, and his heart loosened as she let him hold it.

"I'm pregnant."

The world shifted under his feet as Gabe tried to process the words. "Pregnant." His voice was barely above a whisper. "Pregnant?" He repeated. He should have said something else. Anything else, but the word just kept bouncing through his brain.

Tessa let go of his hand and moved toward the living room. "I'm sorry. I had an entire speech planned. I should have asked you to sit down." She sat on the end of the couch and drew her knees under herself as she motioned for him to sit on the other end.

She wanted him to take a seat, but not too close to her. Gabe tried not to let that sting. He was dealing with the news, but Tessa had only known for a few hours, too. Their lives were changing, but it would be okay.

He was going to be a dad. A sense of peace washed through him. *I'm going to be a dad.*

Excitement bubbled within him until he looked at Tessa's pale face. Was she not excited? This was a big change for him, but an even bigger one for her. What if she didn't want to be a mom?

Before he could let that concern take root, he let out a deep breath.

"You don't have to be involved." Tessa's voice was soft, but the words cut him. "I've worked everything out. I'll—we'll—be okay if this isn't something you want." Her fingers shook as she gripped her knees. "I know we've not discussed the future too much."

"I am not going anywhere, Tessa." Gabe was stunned as she let out a deep sigh. They'd only known each other a few weeks, but surely she knew him well enough to know that he wouldn't turn away from his child. *From her.*

Tessa nodded and pulled her knees even farther up— which he hadn't thought possible. "I know this wasn't planned. I don't want you to feel trapped. Our first *real* date was yesterday. I know we talked about another—"

"Do you not want another date? Because this news does not change that for me." Gabe slid next to her on the couch. She might not be ready to relax yet, but Gabe was here whenever she un-cocooned herself.

Tessa looked at him, her eyes watering as she held his gaze. But the edge of a smile hovered on her lips.

"Are you okay? Denise said you looked positively green this morning."

"The baby doesn't like eggs." Tessa sent a small glare down to her belly, but it was followed by a brilliant smile. "Guess it's toast for right now."

"I bet the little bean will change his or her mind in a few years."

Tessa's bright grin sent a thrill through him.

"That's what I called the baby this morning. Little bean." She pulled her knees out from under herself but didn't slide any closer to Gabe. "I know I kind of sprang this on you. If you change your mind, I won't hold you to tonight's decisions. This certainly isn't how normal get-to-know-you dating starts."

Gabe couldn't argue with that, but he didn't care. He'd always wanted to be a father. This might not be the path he'd planned to walk, but he'd never turn his back on his child, or on Tessa. He hated the doubt he still saw floating in her expression.

"I won't change my mind, Tessa." Gabe laid his arm on the back of the couch, not touching her, but he hoped she viewed the open gesture as an invitation to move closer. "I've always wanted a family." It was the truth. He hadn't thought it was possible after he'd lost Olive, but staring at the woman across from him, Gabe couldn't be anything other than excited.

They were going to be parents. Parents!

He wanted, needed, her to know that he wasn't going

anywhere. This was where he wanted to be. "I was stunned when you first told me. I'll admit I came over here fully expecting you to tell me we were not going to have another date, and I already reserved tickets for the holiday festival at the botanical gardens."

"You did?" Her mouth slipped into the small O shape that he'd found so enticing a few weeks ago. "That's months away. What if something goes wrong?"

His hand reached for hers, and his body relaxed as she let him hold it. He'd never tire of touching her. "Yes. It is months away. But I purchased them from my phone as soon as I got to my car last night. I'm banking on the future, Tessa. I want many dates between now and then, but I can't wait to see the Christmas village set up in a few months. Spending time with you is my favorite thing."

Tessa's bottom lip trembled as she slid next to him and put her head against his shoulder.

"Actually, I was wrong. This is my favorite thing. You in my arms."

Her eyes were bright as she looked up at him. "This is my favorite thing, too. And the gardens are beautiful at Christmas. All the lights…"

His hand wrapped around her belly. Over the place where the child slept. They were going to be a family.

"I managed to get an appointment with Dr. Fillery tomorrow afternoon." Tessa looked up at him, and he saw her take a deep breath. "Her office had a last-minute cancellation. I know you're off tomorrow afternoon, too. Do you want to come?"

"Wild horses couldn't keep me away." Gabe sighed as she placed a light kiss on his cheek. Tonight was as close to perfection as he'd experienced in forever. "Want to try a movie night this weekend? See if the baby likes popcorn."

"That sounds lovely." Tessa closed her eyes, and her breathing slowed down as he held her.

"Then it's a date." Gabe kissed the top of her head and leaned his head back against the wall. Life had sent them a new twist, but it was going to be okay. Better than okay!

CHAPTER SEVEN

TESSA LET OUT a yawn and grinned. The smell of break-fast was one of the best things someone could wake to.

But she lived alone.

Her eyes flew open as she sat up. The room spun. Tessa held her head and groaned as her stomach lurched.

"Tessa?" Gabe's voice was strong but laced with worry as she felt him step beside her.

"Gabe?"

What time is it? What is he doing here? Will breakfast taste as good as it smells?

A piece of bread was pressed into her palm.

What is going on?

"Try a couple small bites. Stacy swore by a slice of toast first thing in the morning to curb some of her morning sickness."

Tessa took a bite out of the corner, then looked up. He was really here. "You didn't leave?" He hadn't left after she'd fallen asleep. Had he held her all night long?

They'd slept together again—except this time it had been on her couch. Nothing physical had happened between them, so why did this action feel so much more intimate? So much more permanent?

"I was surprised when I woke up, too." Gabe's lips turned up as he sat beside her. "Not sure how we slept so soundly on your couch, but I guess we were both past the point of exhaustion." His hand lay across her knee. The warmth it carried calmed her as much as the toast.

She let her gaze linger on his hand for a minute. So many things were running through her mind as she finished the piece of toast. He was right; her stomach felt infinitely more secure.

"I should have asked before I went rummaging through the kitchen, but you were still asleep. You barely noticed when I slipped away." He pulled on the back of his neck as he met her gaze. "And with the morning sickness yesterday, I figured—" He looked at her as his words died away.

She kissed his cheek, enjoying the fact that he'd stayed more than she probably should. "You figured you'd help." Tessa smiled.

"It's the thing I do best. Gotta earn my keep." Gabe offered a silly salute. "Do you want some ham? I fried up some in case your stomach was ready for something besides toast."

"Thanks," Tessa answered as she stood. Gabe was next to her, not touching but close.

Was he staying close in case she got dizzy again?

The gesture was sweet, but Tessa felt a touch of worry. They were going to be parents, but she didn't need him to watch her every step. Pregnancy wasn't a disease; it was something women had been doing since before the written word.

"It's nice that you like helping." She leaned against him, enjoying Gabe's strength. It balanced her before she started for the kitchen. She waved him away from the cupboard as she grabbed a few plates. She could fix her own breakfast plate.

"I'm the oldest, remember? I learned early on how to

earn my keep in my large family." His eyes were bright as he watched her grab her breakfast before fixing his own. "Even before my mother walked out, I was more of a third parent to Isla. I swear she's been getting into trouble since the moment she was born."

He let his gaze wander to her belly, and Tessa's cheeks heated. He was happy about this…he really was.

"Isla is going to be thrilled to be an aunt again. She loves to dote on little ones."

She could see the pride radiating off him. Their child would have cousins and aunts and uncles to watch them. A built-in extended family.

But what would *her* place be? She'd let herself be absorbed into Max's friendship group. And when the marriage failed, she'd been pushed out. She and Gabe would always be connected by their little one, but if they didn't work out…

Why was she plotting the worst-case scenario?

Because that was what always happened. Her heart ached at that truth. Just because her father had left her mother and Max had walked away, that didn't mean that her relationship with Gabe was doomed.

Particularly if she made sure that he never felt put upon like Max had.

"Coffee?" Gabe offered as he rummaged through her cabinet.

"I can do that." Tessa got off the stool.

"Just point me in the direction of the coffee filters. It's no big deal."

"What?"

Tessa's blood iced at Gabe's statement. It was the line Max had thrown around constantly when she'd asked him for help. *It's no big deal* had been the phrase she'd learned meant he was in a foul mood, resenting that she'd asked him for help.

"I said point me toward the coffee filters. Oh, never mind!" Gabe spun around holding the stack.

He laid a cup of coffee in front of her.

"Are you okay?" Gabe's gaze hovered on her. His eyes shone with worry.

"Does the little bean not like ham?" Worry lines pressed into the corners of his eyes as he started toward her.

"No." Tessa's voice was stronger than she'd expected. "I just don't gobble up my breakfast." She smiled, hoping it covered the anxiety coursing through her.

He playfully threw a hand across his chest.

The feigning-hurt gesture almost fully lifted her spirits.

"What time is the appointment this afternoon? Think they'll let us see the little one?"

"I hope so." Tessa grinned. She'd love to see the baby. And she couldn't wait to see Gabe's reaction to their child. He was going to love seeing the dancing bean.

At eight weeks there wouldn't be much definition, but she smiled knowing they might get a glimpse of their little one.

She stood and scooped the last bite of ham into her mouth before starting toward the sink.

"I can get that." Gabe held out his hand, waiting for her plate.

"It's fine, Gabe. I can do it." The worry lines reappeared, but he stepped away. She wasn't going to let him do everything for her. No matter how nice it might feel. She was pregnant, but that didn't mean that she needed help.

And she wouldn't risk his future resentment.

"My appointment is at three at the Plano office. Only

the nurse practitioner works in the Dallas office on Tuesday, and I didn't want to wait." Tessa dried the plate and put it back in the cupboard.

"Do you want me to pick you up? I need to at least swing by Stacy's to shower and change clothes." His face brightened as he mentioned his sister.

"I have a few errands beforehand. I'll just head to the doctor from there."

"I don't mind running errands." Gabe smiled.

She wanted to say yes. To ask him to come along. But she was only going to look at maternity clothes. It was still too early for her to need much, but with her hectic schedule, it would be good to have a few things on hand while she had a chance. But picking out stretchy pants was only going to be interesting or fun for her.

Her ex-husband had grumbled even when she'd wanted to make a quick stop, and Tessa suspected this wouldn't be a swift outing. No, she was going to enjoy each moment of this experience. This was an avenue where she could spare Gabe.

His gaze raked across her, but Gabe didn't press. "I'll see you at Dr. Fillery's at two fifty, then."

"Two forty." Her throat was tight as she explained, "I have to be there at two forty to fill out paperwork." She could fill out documents without him, but she didn't tell him that. It was a little thing, but she wanted him there when she walked into the office.

"Then I'll see you at two forty." He stepped next to her, his gaze holding her steady.

Her mind was racing with a million different excitements and more than a few worries, but as she slipped into his arms, her body quieted.

She wrapped her arms around his neck and kissed him, sighing as he pulled her tight. So much had changed over the last few weeks, but her body still reacted to Gabe the same. Still seemed to call out with joy and need as he touched her.

As he walked out, she hugged herself. Suddenly two forty seemed very far away.

Gabe hustled down the stairs of the parking garage. He hadn't expected there to be so much traffic between his sister's place and Plano. He'd been back in the Dallas area for over six months, but he still hadn't gotten used to the increased traffic. Normally, he gave himself extra time to get anywhere, but getting out of his sister's house had been a trial.

Stacy had peppered him with questions when he'd arrived home. She'd wanted to know all about the woman he'd spent the night with twice. And whether they were dating. He understood Stacy's questions and the concern he saw hovering in her eyes—to a point. She didn't want to see him hurt.

But there'd been no way to explain where he was going this afternoon without also saying he was going to be a father. And that conversation would have resulted in his phone blowing up with calls and texts. Secrets were not a thing in the Davis family.

He wasn't quite ready to subject Tessa to that. The Davis clan would love her and gladly initiate her into their crazy brood. But the Davis family was so many things.

Loud, intrusive and loving beyond measure. Overwhelming didn't begin to describe his family.

Tessa would fit in perfectly.

She was a strong, independent woman. But that didn't mean that she didn't need someone to care about her. He wanted to make things easier, particularly now that she was pregnant.

But that urge had been there before he'd found out about their impending bundle. Tessa made him happy. It was as simple—and as complicated—as that.

But what if she didn't want his help?

The worry tickled the back of his brain. That was the thing Gabe did best. He thrived on making sure those he cared about knew they could always ask him for anything. But Tessa had seemed unsettled by it this morning.

He tried to remind himself that she hadn't had someone to look after her. Maybe she just wasn't used to it. But the worry still bounced around his brain as he shuffled around a car in the parking garage.

Tessa could handle anything—Gabe would never doubt that—but it didn't mean she needed to shoulder all the burdens that were coming.

He was an expert at lightening the load. He'd just have to figure out a way to show her that she could rely on him for anything. *Always.*

"You still have a few minutes," Tessa's voice carried across the parking garage.

He spun and felt the small bead of warmth that had nothing to do with the afternoon heat spread through him as she started toward him.

She stepped next to him and hesitated only a minute before sliding her hand into his. "You ready for this?"

"I think so." Gabe matched her stride as they entered the building with at least a dozen different doctor's offices. The blast of air-conditioning sent a shiver through him, and he was glad that Tessa led the way. "I'm a little nervous."

"Me, too. This isn't the exact path I saw myself on to becoming a mom." Tessa's free hand rested over her belly. "But it's exciting." She let out a nervous laugh. "Everything is topsy-turvy, terrifying, happy, and I feel like I'm grasping at marbles as they all drop around me."

Squeezing her hand, he opened the office door she stopped in front of. "I think that's almost everyone's description of having a baby."

Tessa kissed his cheek. "I'm so glad you're here."

His heart sang as he followed her. *Here we go!*

Tessa's vitals were fine, and the nurse asked her the basic questions as Gabe hung to the side. Even though they were both medical professionals, he could see the bit of worry tracing across Tessa as she looked at the heartbeat monitor and gel on the counter. He'd glanced at them several times, too.

It was important for the nurse to get all the details, but waiting to hear the heartbeat was growing harder with each passing second. She was nearing her eighth week. The first trimester was always the riskiest for miscarriage. He knew that as many as 20 percent of known pregnancies ended in miscarriage. They were devastatingly common, which made the relative silence around them sadder.

But the metric also meant that nearly many pregnancies made it to delivery. At seven weeks, almost eight, their child's heartbeat should be strong and bright. But until they heard it, they'd each wonder—and worry.

"Can you lean back for me? This may be cool." The nurse smiled as Tessa lay back.

Gabe leaned closer, his eyes moving from Tessa's face to where their baby was growing. Her belly still betrayed no sign of their impending joy. When Tessa reached for his hand, he grabbed hers and squeezed. The nurse rolled the heartbeat monitor over Tessa's lower abdomen, and they each let out a sigh as a strong beat echoed through the monitor. Then the beat adjusted. The nurse's nose scrunched, and her forehead tightened for just a moment as she lifted the heartbeat monitor. She hid her reaction, but not quick enough.

Tessa's fingers clenched at her sides.

"What is it?" Gabe asked as the nurse lifted the monitor.

The nurse didn't glance at him as she asked Tessa, "How far along did you say you were?"

"Seven weeks—almost eight." Tessa's voice was tight as she stared at the nurse.

"Great." She tapped Tessa's hand. "Dr. Fillery will be in shortly."

It took all Gabe's restraint to keep his seat and not beg her to roll the heartbeat monitor back over Tessa's belly so he could try to catch what she had. As a nurse, he knew that it was the doctor's responsibility to pass along diagnoses, but he also knew that he often knew exactly what was wrong with a child, too. You didn't work in a specialized area without picking up the most common diagnosis capability—and even some less common ones.

He also knew from the look on the nurse's face as she patted Tessa's hand that she wouldn't tell them what was going on. That was the correct procedure, but when it was your baby, the emotions swirling around you felt so different.

He'd learned after losing Olive that life sometimes didn't let you protect those you loved. But Gabe would do everything in his power to protect Tessa and their child. *Anything.*

As soon as the door closed, Tessa's scared gaze met his. "Did you hear whatever made her demeanor shift?"

"No." Gabe shook his head and moved to her side.

Her fingers tightened in his as he squeezed his eyes shut and tried to think through what he'd heard. "I was so focused on the happy sound. The heartbeat sounded strong. Fast—but that's normal at this stage." He knew Tessa knew that, but he was just trying to figure out anything.

"When she rolled it closer to my belly button, it sounded a little slower. But that shouldn't matter. Should it?"

His top knuckle cracked as Tessa squeezed his hand even tighter.

"Sorry." She released him.

Gabe pulled her hand back. "Nothing to apologize for. That's just the result of me cracking my knuckles since I was ten." Lifting her fingers to his lips, Gabe placed a light kiss on her hand. "No matter what, I'm here for you. Okay?"

She nodded her head and stared at the door. "You never realize how long this feels from the other side— huh! We run from patient to patient—usually skipping meal breaks and living on caffeine. But now I want to run out that door and scream for Dr. Fillery to march in here."

Gabe chuckled as Tessa laid her free hand against her forehead. "I'm itching to rip the door open myself. But we are going to be patient, right?"

"I guess." Tessa laid a hand across her belly. "I'm just a ball of nerves."

"A gorgeous ball of nerves." Gabe kissed her fingers again, and a bit of the tension leaked from him. He loved touching Tessa, loved the feel of being near her. No matter what Dr. Fillery came in to discuss, Gabe knew they could handle it. Maybe that was naive given how long they'd known each other, but Gabe couldn't imagine it going any other way. He and Tessa were meant to be in each other's lives. They just were.

He wasn't sure where that certainty came from. But as she met his gaze, warmth burst through him again. She was his second chance. Gabe swallowed as that thought, that knowledge, settled around him.

The door opened and they both straightened. He'd have to work out exactly what that meant some other time.

"What did your nurse hear?" Tessa rushed the words out. "Sorry, she told me her name, but I'm panicking and can't recall."

Dr. Fillery offered a smile as she pulled the portable ultrasound machine toward Tessa. "Meghan thinks she heard two heartbeats."

"Two!" The word flew from Gabe's lips and heat flooded his body as Tessa looked from him to the ultrasound machine. "Sorry."

"It's fine," Dr. Fillery stated. "It may have just been that she caught the baby's heart rate shifting." She dropped more gel on Tessa's abdomen, then picked up the ultrasound wand. "Let's take a look."

Gabe doubted that the nurse had just heard the heartbeat shifting. He couldn't imagine a nurse working in obstetrics and not being able to identify multiple babies' heart rates. It would be like Gabe hesitating to differentiate between the chicken pox, rubella and measles rash. You just knew—even if the doctor passed along the actual notes and follow-up.

It took only a few seconds for the wand to find the sac. Gabe swallowed as he stared at the images on the screen. Two babies in one amniotic sac—identical twins. He was going to be a father...to two!

CHAPTER EIGHT

TWINS! TESSA'S FEET pounded on the tile of her kitchen floor. She hadn't stopped moving since she and Gabe had left the doctor's office.

She was pregnant with twins. *Identical twins.* All multiples carried risks, but identical twins were more likely to be born early and more likely to need the NICU. More likely to result in bed rest for the mother.

Her chest seized. She laid a hand across her belly; the babies were safe right now, and she needed to focus on that. Tessa squeezed her eyes shut and tried to force all the racing thoughts from her mind.

But they refused to vacate the premises.

How was she supposed to raise two at once? Her heart pressed against her chest. Tessa pushed a hand through her curls as she tried to rework everything she'd started.

She'd measured the room she was using as an office this afternoon. Two cribs could fit in there, but it would be tight. And she'd window-shopped for a crib, a high chair and clothes while grabbing a few maternity items, but she'd focused on the safety ratings, not the cost of outfitting two at once. The day care bills alone...

Her chest tightened again. She was not going to panic. At least not any more than she already was.

And the promotion? Her skin prickled as she tried to

remember the meditation tricks she'd learned during her residency. *Breathe...clear your mind.*

Would the human resources department even consider her a candidate now?

That thought wasn't helpful, but it refused to cede its place in her brain. Technically, it wasn't legal for them to discard her résumé due to pregnancy, but there would be no way to prove it.

No. She could be a twin mom and a senior attending in the emergency room. Her maternity leave might be longer than with a single pregnancy, and the possibility of bed rest was higher. The blood pounded in her ears, and Tessa ran her hands along her arms.

Breathe.

She'd just have to double her efforts at the hospital while she could. Her mother had lost her chance for the career she wanted because of an unplanned pregnancy. But it had been a different time, and they hadn't been able to afford day care and med school.

If she hadn't acquiesced to Max's demands, she'd already be a senior attending.

But then you wouldn't have met Gabe. Wouldn't be carrying twins. Wouldn't have this incredible chance at a family.

She couldn't wish that she was in Cincinnati now.

Tessa stroked her belly where two children—*her* children—were currently growing. She was going to take care of them. She could do this. All of it.

"Tessa." Gabe's voice sounded far away. His hand was warm as he grabbed her, and her heart slowed its racing pace. His anchor stabilized her.

"We need to figure this out." Tessa's voice was ragged as she stared at him. "How are you so calm?"

"That isn't an adjective I'd use to describe myself

right now. But I'm trying to think of it as an adventure." His fingers brushed her cheek before he leaned his head against hers. "With double the diapers!"

She laughed. It felt good to release some tension. His rich scent sent a wave of solace through her. "I love how you smell." The compliment slipped from her lips. She knew that pregnancy heightened the senses, but it seemed like such a silly thing to say when they were trying to determine a path forward.

"That's good to know." Gabe pressed a kiss to her forehead. "I know there's a lot to do. And it seems scary, but can we focus on the positives for a second?"

"The positives?" Tessa raised an eyebrow. They'd gone from a one-night stand to parents-to-be, to parents-of-twins-to-be, before they'd even made it to a second date. The things that needed to be done looked more like mountains than minor to-do lists. But as Gabe held her, the panic that had been on a near-constant rise abated.

"You're healthy and our children are also healthy. Those two things mean everything." Gabe smiled, his dimples popping.

She hoped the babies inherited those!

She saw his gaze shift down her body. Tessa squeezed his hand. Then she laid it over the place where their children were growing.

He dropped a light kiss to her lips. "It's going to be okay. Our hands may be full, but we can do this—together. Promise."

His hand sent sparks along her skin, even through the light gray shirt she wore today. The connection between them crackled as it had since that first night. He seemed so certain, so sure that it was going to be all right. So sure that they had a future. Why couldn't she focus on that possibility? Maybe everything would work out for her—*finally*.

"So, what do we do first?" Tessa turned to grab a glass of water; she was still a little too keyed up to stay in one place.

"Well, we probably need to alert Human Resources."

"No." Tessa shook her head. "Dr. Lin's position is opening." She was so close to fulfilling her dream. To earning what her mother's unplanned pregnancy had stolen from her. Another chance might not open for several years. At least not at Dallas Children's. And she doubted Gabe would want to move. He was more tied to this area than Max was. Now was her best shot.

"Tessa." Gabe closed his eyes. His lips pursed.

He was frustrated—with her. A shiver of worry pressed against her spine. She wanted to keep this to themselves, at least for a few more weeks, but she hated upsetting Gabe.

She'd watched Max pull away from her whenever he was upset with her. Tessa had learned to control her emotions around her ex. But with pregnancy hormones racing through her, it was harder then ever.

Gabe hadn't reacted poorly to her tears when he'd brought over cupcakes. Hadn't gotten angry at the fear and panic she was displaying or told her to get a hold of herself. He seemed genuinely happy to help.

Maybe relying on him for something wouldn't lead to disaster? Surely he wouldn't blame you for his unhappiness? She felt her eyes widen at that thought. Gabe's eyes shifted, too—the man noticed everything.

"Tessa," Gabe's voice broke as he pulled her to him.

Before he could get any further, she offered, "I'm not through my first trimester. Dr. Fillery said everything was fine, but it's still early. I promise to alert Human Resources when I enter my second trimester."

Maybe by then a decision would have been made about Dr. Lin. She hated the thought. But she owed her mom. And she wanted to be a senior attending.

He pulled back a little and wiped a stray tear from her cheek. He smiled, "Okay. No telling HR until the second trimester."

He dropped a chaste kiss to her lips. "What if you help me look for an apartment? I can't really have the twins over to my sister's place when they're with me. Her couch was getting uncomfortable, anyway."

His statement struck her. *With him.* Tessa hadn't considered that her children would have two homes. The idea of her children being somewhere else brought tears to her eyes—again. *Hormones!*

It was ridiculous. Many people shared custody, but Tessa didn't want that—at least not when they were first born. "What if you moved in here?"

The question shot out, and there was no way to reel it back. Her heart rejoiced while her brain screamed. She had plenty of room in her town house. And the idea didn't seem so preposterous as she met Gabe's gaze.

She was on dangerous ground. It would be so easy to fall for him. *Fall for him more.*

But Tessa couldn't bring herself to retract the offer. Instead, she crossed her arms and dug in further. "I just mean, I have a spare bedroom. I was going to put the baby—babies," she corrected, "in the study since I never really use it. I want to breastfeed for at least the first few months, so they'd need to be here, anyway." The more she talked, the more this made sense.

And if he was willing to give the future a shot, she could, too.

"I know it's an unorthodox arrangement but…"

Tessa threw her hands in the air. She didn't want Gabe locked into a yearlong lease somewhere else. Didn't want her children split between homes from the second they were born. And she wanted Gabe close.

That was terrifying. But having him somewhere else made her heart ache more. Her palms were clammy as she waited for his answer.

"Why start with the traditional now? Whatever traditional means?" Gabe shrugged. "Are you sure, Tessa? If you want to take a few days to think it over…"

She didn't want to think it through. Gabe belonged here with their children. With her.

"No. I don't need a few days. We're a family now. Maybe an unusual one. But a family."

Family.

The word wrapped around her as she let Gabe pull her close again. Her heartbeat stabilized as she breathed in his scent. How long had it been since she'd belonged to a family? *A real one.* Not since the early days of her marriage to Max. As soon as he'd failed to advance at work, she'd become a competitor instead of his wife. An interloper in her own marriage.

But Gabe would never make her choose between her career and their relationship. He'd promised her.

"Family." Gabe brushed his lips against hers. Maybe this wasn't the usual path, the safe one, but for the first time in forever, Tessa's felt like her feet were on secure ground.

"We have one other thing we need to do." Gabe's grin was bright, but she thought she saw him hesitate a little.

He was always so sure of himself. The hesitation stunned her. "What?" Tessa put her hand on his chest and was surprised that it was thrumming. What was he so nervous about?

"We have to tell the Davis clan."

Tessa swallowed as she met his gaze. "Name a time and place." Then she raised her lips to his. Her life had shifted completely. But when she was with Gabe, those changes no longer seemed so frightening—in fact, they seemed perfect.

The alarm had gone off far too early for Tessa. Particularly now that she couldn't dose herself with a giant pot of caffeine fifteen minutes after her feet hit the ground. And waking alone no longer brought her any comfort either. Had it ever?

She didn't investigate that thought as she smiled at Gabe before he ducked into a patient's room. Gabe's family was helping him move in this weekend. He swore that it wouldn't take long. Apparently, even the stuff he'd moved into storage the first weeks he'd been here had only been a bedroom suite and a beat-up couch that he suggested they drop at the curb. The rental unit was close to Southern Methodist University. Gabe was confident that the battered but not broken piece would find a home in a college apartment.

"He *is* something!" Denise's statement broke through Tessa's mental wanderings as she handed her a tablet chart. "I know Gina and Rochelle are hoping that he might ask them out. I told them not to get their hopes up."

"You did?" Tessa tried to pretend that it wasn't jealousy racing up her spine. Gabe was kind, well-educated and stunning. Of course the single staff would be interested in him.

She winked at Tessa before leaning closer. "He only has eyes for you."

Tessa's cheeks heated as Denise leaned away. "Oh. Well. We're—" Her voice faltered as she tried to find the right words.

They were going to be parents and were moving in together, but they'd agreed it was too early to share a bedroom.

He promised they could move as slow or as fast as she wanted on this path they were traveling together. But that didn't leave a lot of standard definition for Tessa to fall back on in this situation.

"Don't worry." Denise grabbed another tablet chart. "Whatever it is, your secret is safe with me."

"Thank you." Tessa nodded. "I'll see to the little guy in room three."

"I know he's here for a stomach issue. But the little sister may have fifth disease." Denise swiped up on the chart she had in her hand and didn't catch the panic rippling through Tessa. "They noticed it in triage."

Fifth disease, also called erythema infectiosum, was a common childhood illness. Most kids had a low-grade fever and cold before a bright red rash spread across their cheeks, and occasionally their bodies. It was almost always mild. Except in pregnant women.

Her hands itched to stray to her belly, but they weren't discussing her pregnancy at the hospital. Fifth disease was most dangerous in the first half of pregnancy.

She'd likely had fifth disease, but she didn't know for sure. And it was nearly always asymptomatic in adults. Unless you miscarried. Tessa took a deep breath. She hadn't told anyone about her pregnancy, and the little boy had been ill for several days. She had to walk into the room. She'd take all the viral precautions she could.

"Hi." Tessa smiled through her fear as she stepped into the room. The small boy on the bed was lying on his side, holding his tummy. He looked miserable. The child's father was holding his little sister. Her cheeks were bright red, and he looked exhausted, too.

The door to the room opened, and Gabe stepped in. "Denise said you might need a hand." His nose scrunched as he met Tessa's gaze. She glanced toward the sister and saw Gabe follow her gaze.

"Hey, cutie."

Gabe bent to examine the sister while Tessa turned her attention to the little one on the table. "Can you tell me what's going on?"

The boy's eyes teared up, but he didn't say anything.

Tessa looked toward his father. "What can you tell me?"

The father looked from Tessa to Gabe, and she saw his shoulders sag even further as he looked at his child. "I don't know much. Ryan can't seem to keep food in. He doesn't throw up, but he's been in the bathroom for days. I've been working extra shifts this month." His voice wavered.

"My wife—ex-wife—might know, but she isn't returning my calls. She…" He let his words drift away.

"Okay." Tessa saw the desperation in the father's face. Heard it as he looked between his two kids. Her mother had worn the same expression in many of the memories Tessa could dredge from her mind. "What did you eat last?"

She moved to the sink and washed her hands as Ryan rubbed a tear from his cheek.

"Mac and cheese. It tasted good, but my belly hurt after. Now it feels like someone is jabbing it with knives. It's never been this bad before." Ryan clenched his teeth as he gripped his belly.

So Ryan had been experiencing the issues for a while.

"Does it hurt if you eat bread?" Tessa asked as she caught Gabe's gaze.

He held up a five as he headed for the sink, too. So he thought that Ryan's little sister had fifth disease, too. Nurses might not make official diagnoses, but every pediatric nurse could identify the different common childhood rashes. She'd double-check the rash, but if two of her nurses thought the rash looked like fifth disease, then she'd be shocked if it wasn't.

That was a worry for another hour.

Right now, Tessa was concerned that Ryan had celiac disease, or one of the other autoimmune diseases that attacked the intestinal tract.

"I don't eat bread. It makes me—" The boy's cheeks turned bright red.

"Fart?" Gabe smiled as he winked at the boy.

Ryan nodded but didn't say anything else. Most boys this age enjoyed talking about bodily functions. In fact, Tessa had participated in more conversations regarding gas with boys between the age of six and twelve than she had ever thought possible when she graduated from medical school.

If you were dealing with painful gas all the time, it could go from something silly to giggle about with friends to something you were embarrassed about really quickly. Unfortunately, there was no quick diagnosis for celiac disease. It would take a few weeks to confirm. But if they were right, then shifting his diet could bring him some instant relief.

"I think Ryan may have celiac disease. It means his body cannot process gluten. While he's here, I'm going to order a blood work panel. We'll also need to rule out a parasitic infection."

Moving around the table, Tessa squatted in front of

Ryan's little sister. "Hi, sweetheart." The little girl buried her head in her dad's chest, but she'd seen enough. Her cheeks looked like they'd been slapped, and there was a rash on her arms. Classic fifth disease presentation.

She met the exhausted father's gaze, "And your daughter has the symptoms of fifth disease."

Ryan's father blinked as his gaze shifted from his son to his daughter. "What?"

"The runny nose, pink cheeks and the rash on her arms." Tessa nodded. "The good news is that there really isn't anything to do for that except treat any symptoms if she gets uncomfortable."

"I am really failing at this single-parent thing, guys." Ryan's father kissed the top of his daughter's head.

"It's okay, Daddy." His daughter looked at him, her eyes so full of love that Tessa's heart nearly broke.

"Yes, it is," Tessa reiterated. "I need to talk to your dad real quick. But Nurse Gabe is going to stay with you guys."

"Yep." Gabe made a mock salute that caused Ryan and his little sister to grin.

The hallway was quiet as she stepped into it.

"I know I messed up," Ryan's dad started, and Tessa held up her hand.

"You didn't. You brought your son to the hospital, and kids get fifth disease all the time—literally! What's your name?"

"Adrian Farns." He wrapped his arms around himself and looked at the closed door where Gabe was probably starting to draw Ryan's blood for the autoimmune panel workup.

"I didn't bring you out here to discuss poor parenting. Negligent parents don't worry about their kids or bring them to the ER unless it's critical. You *are* doing a good job." Tessa offered what she hoped was a bright and comforting smile. "I wanted you to know that what your children need most is you."

Adrian blinked. "What?"

"You're exhausted, Adrian. That is a natural state for most parents, I know. But I think your exhaustion goes deeper."

His shoulders sagged even further. How heavy the weight of the world must seem to the man before her. "I came home to a note about four months ago. My wife— ex-wife—had left the kids with the neighbor, cleaned out the bank account and run off with her boyfriend. It's been a lot to handle."

"I bet." Tessa nodded. "I'm going to give you a list of dietary restrictions and recipes to try with Ryan to get him some relief. But I'm also going to include a list of services that can support your family through this. All the worldly goods don't matter if you're not there."

During her first year at Dallas Children's, she'd worked with their social worker to put together a solid list of contacts for services that could help parents. Whether they were struggling with financial issues, mental health issues or grief, Dallas Children's had a printout. The social worker made sure that the list of contacts was regularly updated.

If Tessa's mother had known who to ask for help, she might be celebrating becoming a grandparent now. She'd give as many people as possible the opportunities her family hadn't gotten.

Adrian nodded. "Thank you."

"You're welcome. Someone will be in with all those papers in a little while. If Ryan gets dehydrated, please bring him back. And introduce new foods slowly. His digestive system is at war."

Adrian mumbled a few words before heading back into the room with his kids. And Tessa headed toward the employee bathroom to scrub off the room's germs.

Tessa's hands were red by the time Gabe found her. He knew the odds of fifth disease transmission were minuscule. But in the 1 to 3 percent of pregnancies it affected, the consequences were catastrophic. And those numbers didn't seem so tiny when it was your children.

"I don't think any germs could have survived that scrubbing, Tessa." Gabe tried to keep his voice light as he reached for the taps and turned off the water. He hoped she hadn't burned her skin. Even if she hadn't, the vicious cleaning was going to leave them sore. Gabe made a mental note to make sure they had aloe vera or some other cooling lotion at home.

She held up her wrinkled digits and swallowed. "We have to tell Human Resources."

Gabe was stunned by the reaction. After her vehement refusal last night, he'd expected to argue the point with her. To have to address why they needed to be open about this.

When his mother had been pregnant with Isla, she'd been put on bed rest toward the end. Some of the worst fights between his parents had occurred during that period. His mother had been determined not to lose her position at the marketing firm where she worked. She'd only taken time off when the doctor had told her if she went into labor again, she'd have to be hospitalized until delivery.

There was no need to get into the actual details with everyone, but for Tessa's and the twins' safety, they needed to keep her from highly infectious rooms. There were only a handful of diseases that Tessa wouldn't be able to treat anyway. It was standard protocol for pregnant medical staff. She wasn't asking for any special treatment.

There would be some whispers, but at least a few of their colleagues already suspected that they were seeing each other. And hospital gossip shifted to new topics with lightning speed.

"I'm up-to-date on all my vaccinations. It should have a minor impact." Tessa voiced the thoughts that were rattling around in Gabe's mind. "And I'll let Patrick know that this will have no impact on my decision to apply for Dr. Lin's position."

And we're back to the promotion.

"Sure." His voice was more clipped than he'd meant it to be, but Tessa didn't seem to notice. Gabe understood wanting to advance at work. He understood Tessa's drive to be successful. But she was already incredibly successful.

What if, after this promotion, there was another and another? He'd watched medical professionals chase glory during his career. Higher pay and more prestige always came with trade-offs. And they were usually borne by the families.

Was that what Tessa wanted?

No, Gabe forced the thought to the back of his brain. If that was all Tessa wanted, he'd have already seen it by now. She loved their little ones, even though they were barely bigger than a cherry.

She'd scrubbed her skin raw out of fear of a disease that she'd almost certainly been exposed to dozens of times as a pediatric physician—even if she hadn't had it as a child. He'd heard her telling Ryan's father that he needed to take care of himself, too. And Gabe had seen the papers outlining how to deal with parental stress and divorce in the discharge notes he'd pulled up for Ryan. Those were not the actions of a woman who would put her work before everyone else.

Gripping her hands, Gabe wanted to make her smile. To lighten the day's heavy mood. "So, since we are having identical twins, there is one serious issue we need to consider." He tapped the edge of her nose as her eyes widened. "How do we keep from mixing them up?"

"What?" Tessa laughed.

The sound sent joy ping-ponging around his soul. Her smile lit up the room and his life. He'd do anything to make that smile remain forever. Of course, life wouldn't allow that. But as often as possible, Gabe was going to ensure that he made Tessa happy.

Gabe dipped his head. "I was surfing some online twin forums last night."

"Really?" Tessa grabbed a paper towel and gently dried her hands.

He shrugged. "My brain was a little too hyped up to sleep." In truth, the initial searches he'd done had nearly sent him spiraling. There was a reason that physicians always warned their patients not to go searching the web; you could find some truly terrifying statistics that would do nothing but worry you.

And there were more than enough medical horror stories about multiples pregnancy out there.

He'd finally found an identical twin forum and searched out funny stories to ease his tumbling brain. "I kept worrying that we might get them mixed up. Since, you know, identical!"

He made a silly face, enjoying the giggle that erupted from her. "Several parents recommended choosing a color or pattern for the little ones. One in yellow, the other in green. One twin in stripes and solids for the other bean.

So you don't confuse who is who when they're newborns, though their individual personalities shine through pretty quickly, according to most of the parents."

Gabe had only meant to look at a few things, but he'd loved searching through the forums. Finding out new things about the next step he was taking. *With Tessa*.

It was easy to care about Tessa. Easy to be around her. Easy to fall in love—

No. That had not happened. But even as Gabe stared at Tessa's wrinkled palms, which were blessedly less red now, he knew that was wrong. He was already half in love with her.

Emotions swirled through him, a mixture of excitement, joy and fear as he looked at her. She was his second chance. What if he lost her?

His mouth was dry as that thought tossed around his brain. Losing the person he cared most about had nearly destroyed him before, and now it wasn't just Tessa he might lose.

No. He could protect Tessa and the twins. Make sure that nothing bad happened to them. Make sure that he didn't face the bottomless pit of despair he'd known when Olive passed. He could make sure everything was fine. And it would be easier as Tessa's—

Boyfriend was the wrong word. *Roommate* made his skin crawl. The correct word refused to materialize. But Tessa's hand on his interrupted his mental wanderings.

"I said, I never even thought that I might not be able to tell them apart!" Tessa enunciated words that he'd missed while trying to work out ways to protect his family. At least she was unaware of all the thoughts racing through his mind.

"Sorry, I guess the day is longer than I thought." He stroked her palm, glad that twenty minutes under scorching water didn't seem to have injured her. "I read an article by a mom who swears she might have mixed her boys up on the day they came home from the hospital."

"That sounds like the hook of a bad sitcom—and all too possible!" Tessa's chuckle echoed in the small room. "We should definitely have a plan!"

Gabe wrapped an arm around her shoulder. "That's tomorrow's worry. Why don't I stop by Maggie's after my shift and meet you after you've talked to Patrick?"

She cocked her head, "Expecting it to go poorly?"

"No." Gabe was almost certain that was the truth. "Just looking for a reason to get some cupcakes."

"You don't need a reason, Gabe."

His heart burst as she winked and headed for the door. "I cannot imagine a situation in which I would turn down a coffee cupcake. I may drink nothing but decaf right now, but I can at least enjoy that sweet treat!"

He offered another pretend salute and was rewarded with a brilliant grin before she exited. He'd bring her anything to make that smile appear. Seeing Tessa happy was the best part of his day. She and their children made him feel whole. It was as simple as that.

CHAPTER NINE

"I THINK IT's time you got a new comforter for your bed!" Isla winked at Tessa as she followed Gabe up the stairs carrying a box of his belongings. "This one is not pretty. Maybe Tessa can help you pick another."

"It keeps me warm, Isla. It doesn't really have another purpose." Gabe took the lamp from Tessa's hands and kissed her cheek before setting it on his beat-up dresser.

Isla dumped what Tessa had to admit was an ugly comforter on the bed that Matt and Gabe had carried up an hour ago. "It's brown. And not a pretty warm coffee color. It looks more like…" Isla held her nose and smirked at her brother.

Tessa covered her lips to keep her grin from showing, but she caught Gabe's knowing look.

"This is the last one," Matt stated as he set another box on the bed. "And the comforter looks fine to me."

Gabe nodded to his brother before Matt headed down the stairs again. The nonverbal sibling communication made Tessa's heart race. Gabe's family interacted with one another just like she'd always dreamed of. They were a family—a real family.

"Two against one." Gabe laughed as he hung up a stack of shirts.

"Nuh-uh!" Isla slipped her hand through Tessa's. "Back me up, Tessa!"

She felt her eyes widen as her gaze shifted between Gabe and Isla.

Crossing his arms, Gabe leaned against the wall. The smile he offered her sent desire spilling through her. Those dimples were a work of art.

"Do you think it's ugly?"

"No using the dimples." Isla stomped her foot. "He knows they have power."

Gabe threw his arms in the air. "Guilty."

Tessa laughed at the fun exchange. She hoped her kids would have this type of relationship. The love was clear between them, even as Isla judged her brother's bad taste in bedroom decor. This was the life she'd yearned for. The life her kids would get.

"All right." Isla nodded before facing Tessa. "Honest answers only, Tessa."

Biting her lip, Tessa glanced at Gabe and shook her head, "Isla's right. It is ugly."

Gabe flung a hand over his chest and playfully threw his body against the wall. Tessa's and Isla's laughs echoed through the room.

"I guess the vote's tied then." Tessa shrugged.

"Oh, no, it's not. You count as three votes."

"Isla! My family would like me home for dinner. You coming?" Matt yelled from downstairs.

She offered Tessa a quick hug and high-fived her brother. "I'll find some suitable choices and email you, Tessa. The perks of being a department store buyer." She waved and disappeared.

"She never did play fair." Gabe laughed as he swung Tessa into his arms. "She means it, too. She'll send you a few choices and expect you to make me choose another comforter. Determined doesn't begin to describe Isla."

"They're wonderful." Tessa sighed before kissing Gabe's cheek. "Really, really wonderful." Tessa hadn't been sure how they'd react to Gabe moving in with her and becoming a dad, but the Davis clan had been nothing but loving.

"How about we get the bed cleared off so I can sleep in it tonight, then we can pop some popcorn and watch a movie? A nice night at home."

Tessa ran her hand along his chest. "That sounds lovely." And it did. Her heart swelled.

Such a simple word, with so much meaning. *Home.* Just replaying the sound of the word on his lips was enough to make Tessa's heart sing. Maybe this could work—truly work. Despite expecting twins and playing get-to-know-you—*really* get-to-know-you—at the same time, maybe everything would be all right. If she hadn't been nearly in love with him already, today would have sent her over the edge.

The words were on the tip of her tongue, but their unorthodox start had already gone through so many twists and turns. The last thing it needed was her confessing that she was falling in love with him the day he moved into her spare bedroom.

Telling him she loved him could wait. *But the timing is perfect*, her heart whined as her brain refused to operate her tongue. *Not today!*

Her phone buzzed, and she quickly glanced at the text. Dr. Lin was asking if she could cover a shift or three for him for the next few weeks. If she said yes, she'd be at the hospital nearly every day for a while. But if she said no—

No. That didn't seem like an option. In a few months, she might not feel like adding extra shifts.

Instead, she typed back a quick response and then grabbed Gabe's hand. "We'll have to make tonight count." She pressed her lips to his again.

"Oh?" Gabe wrapped his hand around her waist.

She leaned into him, enjoying the feel of him, the knowledge that he'd be here when she came home. It calmed her. "Dr. Lin needs me to take a few of his shifts. I guess he's finally getting his retirement paperwork filed and starting some retirement courses that the hospital mandates its staff take before they out-process."

"How many shifts?"

Gabe's tone was light, but his gaze flickered with a touch of worry. The look disappeared behind a smile, but Tessa was certain she'd seen it.

"I'll be at the hospital most days. But it will give me another leg up when they fill his position. Plus, it means Patrick believed me when I said that my pregnancy wouldn't impact my work. I know he told a few of the staff and asked them to be discreet."

"But nothing is discreet among hospital staff." He kissed the top of her head before moving to grab a stack of pants from a box on the bed.

She couldn't control the giggle. "I think that may be one of the biggest understatements of all time. But I'm happy that my colleagues aren't treating me differently. At least for now, I can still take on extra shifts."

"I'm glad." He dropped the pants into a drawer.

Is he frowning?

When he looked at her, Gabe's eyes were bright. He grabbed the few remaining boxes and set them next to the bed. "I can sleep in there now. Let's get our movie marathon going. I don't want to miss a single minute." He smiled again, but there was a flicker of something in his gaze.

Another uncertainty pushed through her. Was he upset that the hospital was still relying on her? Had he hoped she'd take a step back after they found out about the twins, even though he'd told her he'd support her?

"Rom-com or horror flick?" Gabe's grin chased away most of her worries.

But not all of them.

"Are those our only choices?" Tessa folded her arms.

"Nope. The choice is yours, my lady." He playfully bowed, and the final flutters of worry drifted to the back of her mind.

She was looking for ways to worry. Looking for reasons her world might implode. Just because it always had did not mean this was destined for failure. She was going to have a family—a real family.

After weeks of extra shifts, Tessa was reaching levels of exhaustion she hadn't experienced since she was a resident. It must be the pregnancy, because she'd kept long hours since she'd started at Dallas Children's. Often it had been easier to be at work than at home.

Following her divorce, she'd increased her hours even more. Anything to avoid the daily reminder that she had a job she loved but an empty house. A few days of double shifts were normal for her, but today, she was dragging.

Her stomach let out a growl as she started for the cafeteria. The granola bars she'd always kept in her pocket for between-meal snacks at work didn't come close to satisfying her. In fact, most days, she felt like she could eat her way through an entire grocery store and not burst!

"You look like you could use a strawberry smoothie." Gabe's voice was bright as he held up the cup. "Complete with a meal replacement supplement for hardworking doctors."

"You don't need to spoil me." She cocked her head and playfully folded her arms across her chest.

"So, you don't want it?" He smiled as he held the smoothie.

"Of course I do!" She grinned as her belly let out a growl loud enough for Gabe to hear.

"What would you do without me?" Gabe winked and took a big sip of his smoothie.

The smoothie stuck to the back of Tessa's throat. His tone was playful. He was kidding with her. There wasn't an underlying unhappiness. It didn't mean anything.

He leaned as close as was professionally responsible, and her heart jumped. "I also put a few snacks in the employee fridge for when I'm off in a few hours."

"Thank you." Tessa squeezed his hand quickly before dropping it. Gabe had made sure that she had a packed meal and several snacks to get her through the shifts. He'd been great and so reliable.

Too reliable. Tessa hated that niggling thought. Over the last week, he'd taken on so much at home. More than she'd ever expected.

It would be easy to rely on Gabe—to let him handle so many things. But hadn't that driven Max away?

Why wouldn't that thought disappear?

No, her heart screamed. Tessa could let Gabe handle little things. That's what partners did. They shared the load—without complaining.

Besides, if everything fell apart, she was more than capable of remembering to pack snacks. But what about protecting her heart?

"We've got a burn victim en route!" Fran, a triage nurse, called.

Tessa took another giant swallow of her smoothie before dropping it on the nurses' station. Gabe had made sure that her name was written in bold letters on both sides. Even if it was melted, it would provide the calories she and the twins needed. The man thought of everything.

His smoothie dropped beside hers, too, and they quickly made their way to the ER bay doors. Burns were common in the summer and fall. Children touched hot grills and burned themselves roasting marshmallows, but those emergencies usually resulted in a frantic parent bringing their child in. If an ambulance had been dispatched...

Her chest was tight. The waiting was the worst. Knowing that a seriously injured or ill child was incoming and needed support sent your adrenaline into overdrive. But the wait made your body doubt the reserves it was pouring forth. Tessa rocked on her heels and felt Gabe's strong body right behind her. He didn't touch her; he was prepping for the arrival, too. But just knowing he was there calmed the electricity racing along her skin. They made an excellent team—and could handle whatever was coming through the door now.

"Amy fell next to a pit where her family was roasting a pig. Caught herself with her hands in the coals," the paramedic called as he pulled the doors open. "Parents were distracted with a work call and left her in charge. Amy is eight."

Gabe heard the collective gasp of the staff that was waiting. It was impossible to work in a children's emergency room and not see unfit parents. Far too many individuals prioritized things that could be replaced over their children, which could not.

His mother's choices hadn't resulted in any of her kids taking a trip in an ambulance. But only because Gabe had become hypervigilant watching his younger siblings. If he'd been younger or less responsible, things could have been much worse when their father hadn't been around to act the way a parent was supposed to.

Anger, tension and a hint of fear raced along his spine. How could anyone do anything other than treasure their family? Prioritize anything over their children?

He forced his emotions into lockdown as the paramedics pulled the gurney down and passed the paperwork to the waiting admitting nurse. Being mad at her parents wouldn't help Amy. Hopefully, this would be a wake-up call for them.

"Hi, Amy. I'm Dr. Garcia, but you can call me Tessa. And this is Nurse Gabe. We're going to make sure you're all right." Tessa offered the child a smile, but her knuckles were white as she gripped Amy's gurney.

They treated so many things that resulted from accidents. Things that couldn't be helped. Kids flipped on their bikes and skateboards, trampoline injuries, but it was infuriating when it was the result of neglect.

"I didn't mean to mess up." Her whimper was so soft, and it broke Gabe's heart. "My hands hurt."

Tessa ran a hand along Amy's forehead. "This is *not* your fault."

He watched Tessa shake a bit of the fury away before she met Amy's gaze. "We're going to give you some medication to make it feel better."

Gabe saw Tessa swallow as they turned into the room. Burn patients were a medical professional's worst nightmare. The risks of infection and loss of use of an appendage were much higher than with other wounds. Plus, patients had a tendency toward shock within the first twenty-four hours of injury.

But it was a good sign that Amy's hands hurt. It meant

that the nerves were still intact. Unfortunately, it also meant that she would deal with a significant amount of pain while she healed.

"Pain management first, then initial debridement," Tessa stated as she put the orders into the computer tablet before turning to check the child's wounds.

The paramedics had loosely dressed her hands. When Tessa removed the dressings, Gabe saw her cheeks twitch. Second-degree burns covered both her palms and most of her fingers.

Amy sniffled. The child had to be in significant pain, but she was doing her best to hide it.

Gabe got down on her level. Maybe no one paid much attention to her at home, but here she was their primary focus. "What's your favorite color?" Tessa was going to need to clean the wounds, and even with the pain meds she'd ordered, it was going to hurt. Distracting Amy was the best thing he could do for her right now.

Where are the child's parents?

"Purple." Amy's voice was wobbly but strong. She wasn't in shock—at least not yet.

Denise entered with the pain meds Tessa had ordered and quickly administered them to Amy. The child didn't even flinch as Denise placed the needle into the meaty part of her arm.

"You're very brave." Gabe smiled. "Not many adults can just get a shot and not flinch. I cried the last time I got one."

Amy's eyes narrowed, but she offered him a tiny smile. "Really?"

"Cross my heart!" Gabe grinned. "I was hiking and fell on some rocks. I got a big cut on my leg that got infected. They gave me an antibiotic called Rocephin. It hurt bad."

"But you're okay now?" Amy's words were quiet, but he could hear the real question behind them.

His throat was tight, but he forced out, "Yep. Even the scar is less noticeable now. And *you* are going to be okay, too."

Amy's eyes teared up as she nodded.

As she exited the room, Denise looked over her shoulder. "Your mom is here. She'll be in as soon as she finishes her phone call."

"My parents are always on the phone."

The resignation in the little one's statement cut across him. The few times he'd visited his mom after the divorce, she'd always been on the phone, too. At least he'd had his dad to make sure he knew that he was important. But it hurt to know that something else mattered more than you. It was a cut that might heal, but the scar on your heart never disappeared.

His children would never believe that anything was more important than them. They wouldn't have to beg for attention like he had from his mom. Never wonder if he loved him.

"Gabe's right. You're going to be okay, but we have to make sure your hands are clean." Tessa smiled at Amy, but Gabe saw the subtle twitch in her hand. This was going to hurt, even as the pain meds took effect.

Amy swallowed and looked at Gabe. "You'll stay."

"You bet." Gabe patted the top of her head. "I'm here for you." He knew those words would comfort Amy, but he also glanced at Tessa. He was here for her, too— whatever she needed.

Gabe started from his bed. His brain thought he'd heard something, but the town house was silent. He rolled his head from side to side a few times, straining to hear any sound.

Nothing. He blinked and rolled over to look at his clock. He'd tried waiting up for Tessa. After taking care of Amy's burns, he'd thought she might need someone to talk to. Particularly since she'd been vibrating with anger as she talked to the child's parents, who'd seemed more concerned with their jewelry shipments than their daughter being admitted to the burn unit.

He'd waited after his shift ended, but Tessa had needed to handle one of her additional duties as the senior attending. He hoped she found the Thai food in the fridge and his good-night message.

It had been their routine since she'd started taking on additional shifts. The quick kisses as he passed her in the morning and the occasional stolen time for a smoothie at the hospital were so unsatisfying. At least she only had two more days of these nightmare long shifts before she rotated back to her regular schedule.

Was this really the position she wanted? And how much time would it steal from their family?

Gabe glared at his ceiling and threw an arm over his eyes. This wasn't Dr. Lin's shift. It was his and most of Tessa's shifts combined. She was working all the hours she could legally muster to prove herself to Human Resources, for a position that they hadn't even sent out an official announcement for.

What would their lives be like when the actual competition started? Gabe had watched doctors contend for positions before. He knew how cutthroat the healing professions could be when positions that rarely opened were competed for. It would have been daunting anytime—but she was pregnant. *With twins.*

"So, what else can I do to help?" The walls gave no

answer to his whispered question as he tried to calm his mind enough to drift back to sleep. He was off tomorrow. At least he could make sure Tessa had a solid meal before she headed back to the hospital.

Assuming she'd even come home. She'd slept in the employee suite a few nights ago and quipped about it reminding her of her residency days. Gabe had nodded as she talked about it, hating the circles under her eyes and worrying about her increasing focus on the hospital. He was doing his best not to voice his worry that she was operating on too little sleep for a physician and a pregnant woman. Tessa knew her limits.

But would she listen to them?

"Argh!"

The scream echoed down the hall from Tessa's room. Gabe's feet hit the floor.

He didn't stop until he was next to her bed.

"Gabe?" Tessa's eyes were open, but her voice was dreamy. He wasn't sure she was really awake. She couldn't have been home for long, and asleep for even less time. She had to be exhausted.

"I'm here." He sat on the bed and stroked her hair as she lay back down.

"I dreamed there was an accident." Her hands flew to her belly, and she sighed. "Dream…" Her voice was soft as she shifted her head on the pillow.

He dropped a kiss along her temple. "Pregnancy hormones can make dreams more vivid." Stacy had talked about how crazy her dreams had gotten after her first trimester. From birthing cats to her brain pulling the most horrific things from her subconscious.

Tessa's subconscious had more than enough material to make her dreams grim. Especially following a nightmare scenario at the hospital, and the fact that she was already running herself into the ground.

He stroked her back. She looked so beautiful in the moonlight as it streamed through the window. *And exhausted.*

When her breaths became even, he dropped another kiss to her temple and stood. They both had Monday off. And Tessa was going to do nothing but be pampered. She deserved to be taken care of for at least twenty-four hours.

He'd make sure they had plenty of popcorn for an epic movie marathon.

"Gabe?"

Would he ever tire of hearing her say his name? He hoped not. "I'm still here," he whispered.

"Stay with me." She pulled the covers to the side and slid over. "I don't want to be alone. Please."

The quiet plea nearly undid him. He joined her in bed and pulled her close. "I'm here." He kissed her shoulder as he wrapped his arm around her waist. She fit snuggling against him, and his heart soared as she sighed and slid back to sleep.

He tried to stay awake a few minutes to make sure that she was all right, but his eyelids kept drifting closed. Soon he gave up and let himself drift away, too.

Tessa rolled over and smiled as she stared at Gabe's lips. He'd come running last night. She couldn't remember the dream that had woken her so soon after she dropped into bed. But she could remember asking him to join her in bed. And how safe she'd felt as he slid his arms around her. How safe she felt lying in his arms now.

She ran a hand along his jaw, enjoying the feel of the bit of stubble under her fingers. They hadn't seen much of each other outside the hospital lately, and she was surprised by how much she hated that. It had been normal for her to basically live at the hospital before she met Gabe.

The employee suite, where staff routinely caught a few extra hours of sleep, was a regular overnight stay for Tessa. Gabe had looked so shocked when she'd slept there on Wednesday that she'd made up a story about it reminding her of her residency days—which it technically did—but also it wasn't uncommon for her.

But last night, she'd driven home rather than stay. Even if they weren't sharing a bed, she wanted to wake up in the same place as Gabe. Wanted to have breakfast with him.

And she'd asked Dr. Killon to cover the final two shifts for Dr. Lin. She wanted the senior attending position, but she was too tired. It wasn't safe for her patients or for the twins for Tessa to be so exhausted.

For the first time in years, she had three days off in a row. And Tessa planned to spend as much of it as possible in Gabe's arms. She dropped light kisses along his jaw, slowly working her way toward his lips.

He stirred as her lips met his. "Good morning." Gabe managed to get the words out between kisses.

"I missed you." Tessa ran her hand along his back, enjoying the feel of his skin beneath her fingers. She doubted there was a better place to wake than in Gabe Davis's arms.

"We live together, you know." Gabe's fingers traced up her thigh as he kissed her nose. "But I missed you, too. It would be nice to share more than just a few passing kisses and smoothies." His lips pressed against hers as he shifted his hips.

Tessa pulled him back. She wanted him—all of him—this morning. She let her lips trail along his shoulder as her fingers wandered farther south, and she enjoyed the hitch in Gabe's breath as they edged ever lower. "That isn't exactly what I meant." Tessa slipped a finger along the edge of his boxers.

Gabe gripped her hand, stilling its advance. "There is nothing I want more. Promise." He sucked in a deep breath. "But the next time I make love to you, I want to take my time."

He nodded toward her nightstand. "Your alarm should go off any second. I'm a little surprised it hasn't already."

"Dr. Killon is taking Dr. Lin's shifts for me today and tomorrow." Tessa pulled his face to her and kissed him—deeply. His hands trailed along her back, creating tiny bolts of electricity with each light stroke. "I have the next three days off."

Before Gabe could fully react, Tessa rolled him onto his back and started trailing her lips down his body.

In the morning light, he was stunning. And he was hers. That sent such a rush through her as she listened to his breathing increase.

Gabe's hands wrapped through her hair as she worked her mouth lower. When she slipped his briefs down, Tessa grinned.

She'd been wrong. There *was* a better way to wake up than in Gabe's arms.

CHAPTER TEN

"YOU HAVE TO be gentle with the seeds." Tessa pulled his hands out of the pot she'd handed him and gently rearranged the seeds he'd pushed into the soil before tossing dirt on top of them. Then she patted the soil and set the small pot to the side.

Gabe watched the process for the fourth time. He kissed her cheek as she laid another small pot in front of him and handed him more seeds. "I hate to break it to you, sweetheart, but that was *exactly* what I was doing."

Tessa's light chuckle made happiness burst through him as she stepped into his arms. Her hands wrapped around his neck before she kissed him. "I am patting the dirt, Gabe. You were mashing it."

He really didn't see the difference, but he'd stand next to Tessa all day while she worked with seeds. She'd decided last week that they should have a winter garden. Tessa was intent on trying the small garden ideas she'd found in the books she'd been leaving all over their living room. It would be nice to have fresh veggies, though Gabe believed she might have more fun growing the plants than anything else.

The bedroom he'd briefly called his own was now a veritable greenhouse. Grow lights were set up on a few small tables with labels announcing each pot's seeds and the watering schedule that needed to be handled for each grouping. This made Tessa happy, and that made Gabe happy.

Happy. Gabe stared at Tessa as she darted between her pots. His heart sighed at the image as he drank it in.

Life had dealt him an unimaginable loss. He'd never expected to feel this again. To relish the simple days at home. To be part of a family outside of the one he'd been raised in.

It was a gift. One he planned to hold on to tightly. To protect.

He'd do anything for Tessa and the twins. Anything to earn a permanent place next to her. *Forever.*

She planted another kiss on his cheek as she stepped beside him. Then her brow furrowed. "I got dirt on your chin." She held up her hands, staring at the dirt splatted on them. "And I've no way to wipe it off."

"You've had dirt on you since we stepped in here. It hasn't stopped me from wanting to kiss you yet." He shrugged. "What's a little dirt when you—" Gabe managed to pull back, barely.

Clearing his throat, he gestured to all the seeds. "When you're having such a good time."

Blood pounded in Gabe's ears as her beautiful brown eyes stared at him. The words *when you love someone* had nearly slipped into the space between them. His heart screamed for him to finish the statement. To declare what he wanted to believe was between them.

The last few weeks of living together, working together, watching her belly expand together had been some of Gabe's life's happiest. The hole in his chest that had refused to seal when he lost Olive had closed more the closer he got to Tessa.

He'd always miss Olive. But finding love again was a precious gift. And he was going to protect his family as much as possible.

"I was thinking about the nursery." Gabe pushed the seeds into the pot, barely controlling his grin as Tessa monitored his motions. When she accepted his pot and set it with the other spinach plants, Gabe thought his heart might shoot from his chest. *Success!*

"I know you wanted to wait a little while longer." He accepted another pack of seeds and a pot as Tessa started watering the plants on the far table. "But I think it's pretty obvious what theme we should go with."

"Theme?" Tessa raised an eyebrow as she looked over her shoulder at him. "I wasn't aware that we were actually going to have a theme. Is that a little overboard?"

Tessa's hands rested on her belly, and he knew that her shirt was going to have a dirt stain just over where their children were growing. It only cemented his idea. Gabe gestured to the seed pods around them. "Gardening! Picture it." He squeezed her shoulder tightly. "A room with images of flowers, green blankets, maybe even a few of their mother's plants in the corner."

He pulled the loose plan he'd sketched from his back pocket. "See."

Her dark eyes misted over as she ran a finger over the paper. "You did all this?"

"Of course. I love doing things for you and the babies. As much as you enjoy dirt and seed pods." He kissed the tip of her nose—one of the few spots that was dirt-free.

"That is a lot! Because I do love dirt and seeds." She giggled as she looked at her fingers. "I think cartoon characters and woodland creatures are more standard."

He shook his head as he pointed to the sketch he'd

made. "Standard is boring. Besides, I think we should lean into the twin parent thing. Two peas in a pod and all." He kissed the top of her head.

Touching Tessa, being with her, watching the small bump where the twins—his twins—were blooming, was exciting. He'd go all out at being a twin dad. Double strollers, minivan and all.

Tessa pulled one lip to the side as she looked at him. "I like this, but we have to make one change." She put a finger against the dirt, then added another thimbleful of water on the plant. "What if we find someone to paint a snowy mountain hiking path into a garden? A combination of us. And that is as close to a hiking trail we will be—at least until the twins are older."

Gabe hadn't realized it was possible for his heart to expand more. But his chest bloomed as she pointed to where the mural would be on the paper. "That would make this design perfect."

Tessa's grin lit up the room. "I never expected you to be so involved in the entire process. Max hated any decorating. I was all prepared to have to pick out all the colors and furniture on my own." She rocked back on her heels as she stared at him. "You are amazing. I lo—" Her eyes darted to the pots as she folded her arms. "I love the fact that you are so invested in our little family."

His ears burned as he stared at her. It felt like there was more to that statement. Or at least he wanted to believe there was. But Gabe didn't want to push—at least not yet.

Handing her another pot, he smiled. "I enjoy picking stuff out. Helping you, researching car seat standards, safety regulations—protecting our family in the cutest way possible." Gabe winked. "Besides, I'd do anything for our kids." *And you.*

Tessa started toward him and then abruptly stopped. "Oh!"

It took him three steps to reach her, but Gabe's heart felt like it was dropping from his chest. "What's wrong? Do I need to call the doctor? Or Emergen—?"

She grabbed his hand and placed it on her abdomen. "The babies are moving." Her smile was bright as she laughed. "Oh, it feels so funny! Like dancing gas. Wow. Not the cutest description I could have chosen. Though accurate."

His skin felt clammy as the adrenaline leaked from his body, and his stomach twisted. There was no danger here. *Nothing to worry about.* "You scared me." He hadn't meant to say that, and he saw compassion and concern float in Tessa's eyes.

Her fingers were soft as they touched his cheek. "You can't jump to the worst case." Tessa leaned her head against his chest. "I know you lost Olive, but you couldn't have known that she had an aneurysm. And Dr. Fillery said just two days ago that at seventeen weeks along, I am healthy, and the babies are doing great. Breathe with me."

Pulling in a few deep breaths, Gabe tried to remind his heart to slow. It was still too early for him to feel the twins twirling around her belly, but Gabe didn't remove his hand from Tessa. The connection grounded him.

His leap to calling the emergency line was too much for a light comment. But when you'd lost everything once, the urge to protect what you could engulfed you.

Letting the worries float away, Gabe enjoyed the feel of Tessa pressed against him. The feeling of rightness that echoed through him in these small moments. The movies made grand gestures seem like the epitome of romance. But they weren't.

It was these simple moments, with a hand on the belly where your children were growing, surrounded by spinach, lettuce and winter squash seeds, that made the best memories. "Sorry. I just…" He shrugged as the words and worries refused to materialize.

Her lips were warm as they pressed against his cheek. "I understand." Tessa trailed her fingers along his jawline. "We're fine. Promise."

He dropped a light kiss along her lips, sighing as she deepened it. "I also know you'll refuse to let me wrap you in Bubble Wrap for the rest of your pregnancy!"

"Nope. No Bubble Wrap. Too much to get done!" She held up a tiny pot containing a winter squash and marked the bottom.

She was always on the go. They'd yet to have another movie marathon or spend more than a few minutes relaxing on the couch since his first night here. The woman seemed incapable of slowing down.

"What are you thinking for dinner?"

"Oh!" Tessa held up her hand before reaching in her back pocket. "That 'oh' was because my butt was vibrating." She held up her phone. "Finally!"

Gabe playfully put his hands over his ears as her shout echoed in the room. "I'm scared to ask." Though he suspected only one thing would have sent such an excited yell through the small room. The job was finally open. The thing she wanted so badly.

He swallowed the touch of panic clawing at his throat. *It will be fine.*

Tessa danced like she had all those weeks ago before holding the phone to his face.

Gabe tried to put on a cheerful smile as he read the

confirmation of what he already knew. "So, Dr. Lin's position is open."

"Yep!" Her voice was an octave higher than normal. "I'll probably put in for a few extra shifts here and there. Pad my application and all." She smiled.

More shifts. Did she really have to take on more work? Spend more time away? Wasn't her expertise enough to speak on its own?

He bit back an objection as Tessa's eyes roamed his. He cared about her, loved her. He wouldn't dampen this moment with his own fears.

"I'll pace myself. Promise."

Gabe pulled her to him and rested his head on hers. "I'll do anything I can to make this easier." Tessa wanted this position, and he wanted her to succeed. He did.

His throat closed as he tried to stop the flutter of worry arching its way through his belly.

"Anything and anytime, right?" Tessa kissed the tip of his nose.

"Right," Gabe responded, hating the tingle in the back of his skull. There was nothing wrong with wanting a promotion, with wanting to reach for everything. *Nothing.*

Tessa wasn't his mother. She'd protect herself and the twins. All these fears were the past. If only he could get his heart to listen to his mind. Stop the bead of worry that lit up in his chest any time Tessa talked about the promotion.

She wasn't going to choose work over her family. She wasn't. Besides, Gabe was going to be the best partner he could be. He'd make sure she was as comfortable as possible at home.

If he did everything for her, she'd realize that being home with him and the twins was just as exciting as being at the hospital.

* * *

Tessa had never felt as exhausted and achy by the long shifts as she had over the last week. Just walking the floor was enough to make her yawn.

Growing children is hard work.

Her stomach grumbled again, and she popped a few blueberries that Gabe had packed into her mouth. Then she playfully glared at her expanding belly. "I am literally feeding you now!"

Or so it seemed. She smiled as she rubbed her belly.

Tessa had begun showing. She was enjoying each of these new steps. Though with as much as she was at the hospital, it felt like she was in danger of letting it fly by.

Stroking her belly, she grabbed another mouthful of berries. The selection process for the senior attending should be completed before Tessa hit her third trimester. She could dial it back a little then.

Or you could withdraw your name from consideration.

Her stomach lurched as the idea tossed around her brain. It was just the fatigue talking. She'd given up one senior attending position. She wasn't walking away from another.

The twins...

Tess quashed that thought before her exhausted brain could finish it. Her mother had lost her career because of an unplanned pregnancy. Tessa wasn't relinquishing this chance because her path to motherhood had been unexpected.

She was just tired. That was all.

The twins moved, and Tessa's nerves quieted a little. During her third trimester, she was sure she'd be uncomfortable as they danced and battled for the ever-decreasing space in her abdomen. But for now, it was the best feeling ever!

Hopefully, Gabe would feel it soon. She planned to memorize every moment of that event. He was going to light up, with that big grin that made his eyes nearly disappear. She loved that smile. Loved how much he'd taken on without her even asking.

Being protected by Gabe was a blessing she'd never counted on. He'd made life so much easier. She'd missed being taken care of.

Though a tiny kernel of worry still hid in the recesses of her mind. She never wanted Gabe to resent all his help. For him to wish that she hadn't taken advantage of the job opening. But it was easy to ignore the tiny voice when he held her in arms.

Her buzzer went off, and Tessa grabbed a final handful of blueberries before heading for the nurses' station.

"We've got twin boys in room four. One needs stitches in his arm and cheek. The other has an ankle the size of a baseball. Triage ordered an X-ray." Debra passed over the tablet chart.

Tessa looked over the triage report. A pair of seven-year-old boys had jumped out of a tree house.

"The mother is beside herself. Just so you know."

"I bet." Tessa tapped the chart. Children never calculated dangers into their adventures. She knew her own two were likely to send her into a panic many times before they hit their teens. And then a whole new host of worries would likely begin.

"Daddy!"

The stereo echo hit Tessa as she closed the door and turned to greet her patients. Identical pairs of watery eyes hit her, and her heart exploded as her own future stared back at her.

Offering a smile, Tessa stepped toward the table where the boys were huddled together. "Nope. I'm Dr. Garcia."

"I want Dad," the one that had a large gash on his right arm stated, before glaring at his mother.

"Dad will be here when he can. But I'm here, DeMarcus." The woman's dark gaze met Tessa's. "We're separated. He always handled everything. Never complained—" She caught a soft sob and forced a tight smile. "Collin said he'd be here soon."

Tessa nodded. She'd seen all sorts of family dynamics during her medical career. "It's all right. Can you tell me what happened?"

"We tried to fly," the little one with an ice pack on his ankle offered.

"And crashed," DeMarcus finished.

"But next time—"

"There will be no next time, Dameon." Their mother's lips pursed as the statement echoed off the walls. "Sorry."

The door opened and a tall man with the boys' curly hair stepped into the room.

Both the boys' eyes lit up.

"I thought I heard you, Eva."

The twins' mom shook her head and gestured toward the boys. "They're already plotting how to jump off the tree house again."

"Without crashing," Dameon added.

Both parents sent a look toward their son, dutifully ignoring looking at each other.

"We are going to X-ray Dameon's ankle." Tessa raised her voice, trying to regain some control of the room. The tension between the boys' parents vibrated, and she saw the twins squeeze each other's hands. It was always difficult when marriages ended, but when children were involved, the stakes changed.

She'd dealt with many struggling parents and all sorts of custody issues as a physician, but the focus had to be on the boys right now. "And DeMarcus is going to need stitches in his arm and cheek."

"Guess it's a good thing I remembered the insurance card and snacks." Collin's words were clipped as he passed a bag to his wife. "You need to do some of these things, Eva."

"I'm trying." Her words were tight as she looked from Collin to her boys. "There's just so much."

"Which I've always done."

Tessa crossed her arms as she stared at the warring pair. This was not helpful. "Why don't you two take this conversation to the hall while I start DeMarcus's stitches." Tessa smiled, hoping the oncoming quarrel could occur away from the boys.

The radiology tech stepped into the room and moved aside as Collin and Eva took their argument to the hallway. "Who am I taking for a ride to the X-ray machine?"

"Me!" Dameon shouted, but when he moved, the color drained from his young face.

"Careful, little guy. Let's get some pictures of that ankle." He nodded to Tessa as he took the child out.

"Let's see if we can't get you stitched up." Tessa smiled as DeMarcus stared at the closed door.

"I miss Daddy living at home."

The sadness in his childish voice caused a lump at the back of her throat. There was nothing she could say. His parents weren't divorced—yet—but it hadn't sounded promising.

"You might feel me pulling on your arm, but if you feel any pain, let me know and we'll make sure we give you some more numbing." Tessa hoped her smile was comforting, but DeMarcus's gaze never left the door.

"Dad makes better mac and cheese than Mommy. But

he was tired of doing everything while she was at work. They yelled a lot. But I miss the mac and cheese."

"I bet," Tessa conceded. Children missed a lot less than their parents thought. "You're a very brave little boy."

The door opened again, and Collin stepped through. "Sorry, Doctor."

Tessa nodded. She wouldn't say that arguing in front of your kids while they were waiting on stitches and X-rays was fine.

"Are you coming home?" The wistfulness in De-Marcus's voice hung in the room as his dad's shoulders slumped.

"I love you, buddy. And I love Mommy, too." He choked back a small sob. "But…not right now."

"He needs to keep these clean and dry for the next two weeks. After that, the stitches should be fully dissolved. One of the nurses will give you information on infection. And once we have X-rays back, we'll see what we need to do for Dameon."

He nodded. He still wore his wedding ring. Maybe their marriage wasn't completely over.

You need to do some of these things.

His words sent a shiver through Tessa as she left the room. She was still independent. Wasn't she? Sure, she liked Gabe taking care of her. She'd let him take over so much while she took on extra shifts. He hadn't complained, but Collin hadn't, either. And neither had Max at first.

Her lunch rolled in her stomach as Tessa tried to think of anything she'd contributed to the household over the last few weeks. Her mind produced very little. She'd ceded so much to him…

Was she setting herself up for another disaster?

Her phone buzzed, and she felt her frown deepen as she stared at Gabe's words.

Oil changed! And I got the grocery shopping done. Don't worry, I didn't touch the plants. How about we do takeout? I'm exhausted.

She'd told him she'd take the car to the mechanic this weekend. And she'd planned to do the grocery shopping on her way home. Though after a long shift, could she really be upset about this?

She bit her lip as the realization struck her. Tessa was independent—she was. But hearing the twins' parents' argument highlighted how much she'd changed over the last few weeks. She'd been relying on Gabe. For *everything*.

That would not do. She didn't want her twins to live DeMarcus and Dameon's reality. Hadn't she learned from her marriage that people didn't always mean it when they said they didn't mind? She loved Gabe. She never wanted to see him exhausted because she hadn't pulled her weight.

She could make a few changes. Ensure that Gabe didn't resent her like Max had.

"Ouch!"

Gabe started toward Tessa as she put her soapy finger to her lips. "That can't taste very good." He reached over and turned off the water, trying to control the frustration in his belly. He'd told her he'd clean up, but she'd insisted that she do the dishes since he'd cooked.

It was one of the many things she'd asserted control over this past week. The more he tried to assist at home, the more she insisted that she didn't need it. How was he supposed to help, to show how much he cared for her? No matter how he tried to lighten her load, she seemed intent on doing more than her share.

And she brushed off all his offers of help. That stung. He was happy to do things for her. Happy to make sure that she was taken care of. She'd told him the night they'd reconnected that no one had protected her—cared for her. He was here to do that.

If she'd only let him.

"I'll admit that a mouthful of soap is not appealing. But when I broke my nail, it was just an automatic reaction." Tessa looked down at her fingers. "That's the second one I've broken today. Guess I need to pay better attention, huh?"

"Second one today? Do you think your iron levels are okay?" Dr. Fillery had warned them that moms of multiples often ended up with vitamin deficiencies that weren't serious if they were caught early. Tessa had put the list of symptoms on the fridge, even though as a doctor she knew them. Just as a reminder.

Gabe passed her a glass of lemonade. "This should cut the taste of soap."

"You have a bank of knowledge on the taste of soap?" Tessa smiled before taking a few deep swallows.

"It was one of my mom's favorite punishments for saying curse words. I only got the punishment once, but Isla received it several times." Gabe frowned as he glanced at the list of low iron symptoms. Tessa had several. But it could just be that she was working so much.

His brain wrapped around the worries as he tried to shake himself. History was not going to repeat itself.

"Why don't I finish the dishes?" Gabe sighed as she held up the last dish.

"All done!" She yawned again and looked at her watch.

"Can we postpone movie night? I'll just fall asleep in your lap."

He'd be fine with that. Gabe would never tire of holding her, but it was probably better if they went straight to bed. Leaning over, he kissed her cheek. "Of course." This was at least the sixth movie night they'd tabled.

His gaze drifted to the list once again before he focused on the woman in front of him. He was worried about her and the twins. Sucking in a deep breath, Gabe raised his concern. "I know you've been tired lately, and brittle nails can be a sign of low iron. Maybe we should talk to Dr. Fillery at your next appointment." He nodded toward the sheet on the fridge, hoping she'd understand.

"No, we don't need to raise this with Dr. Fillery." Tessa pushed a hand through her curly hair before stepping into his arms. "Deep breaths, Gabe. This isn't a medical crisis. I am working more right now and growing not one, but two babies. A little tiredness is to be expected."

Except this didn't feel like a little tiredness. She yawned several times an hour, despite regular naps and falling asleep as soon as her head hit the pillow. "And the nails?"

Tessa sighed before she met his gaze. "I broke two nails, Gabe. Relax. Please." She squeezed his hand. "I'm fine. This is just what happens when you fail to keep your nails trimmed. The prenatal vitamins are making my nails grow faster than normal."

Her hand rested on his chest, and she grinned. "There isn't anything wrong with me, Gabe. Other than your two children are sucking up all my energy."

"What about cutting back at the hospital?" Gabe knew they were the wrong words as soon as they left his lips. But there was no way to reel them in—and this was a conversation they needed to have. He knew she wanted

Dr. Lin's position, and Tessa wasn't the only physician doing their best to prove themselves indispensable to the hospital.

And Dallas Children's was more than happy to take on their extra labor. It was a script he'd seen play out several times throughout his career. A hospital exploiting a cutthroat competition to get the most out of its workforce was standard. He'd participated in it at his hospital in Maine, too.

But a job was not worth hurting yourself or your family for.

"That's not an option, Gabe." Her hands slapped the counter before she crossed her arms. She was preparing for battle.

He didn't want to fight, but he was concerned. "It is," Gabe countered. Tessa was exhausted, and if her record and résumé didn't stand on its own, did she really want the position? "You are not required to burn yourself out for Dallas Children's. Doing everything is not possible."

He watched her take a deep breath and tension seeped from her shoulders. Tessa sighed. "I appreciate the concern." She stepped beside him. "I really do." Her lips were cool as they pressed against his cheek. "I'm a physician. I know all the signs for low iron and a multitude of other ailments. I'm fine. I promise. I don't need you to protect me."

The words cut as he held her gaze. There was so little he could do right now. She'd started packing her own lunches and insisted on dividing the chores equally. She got upset if he did something that she'd declared was her job. Protecting his family and those he loved brought him the most joy. Helping was how he showed his love.

But if the woman he loved didn't want his help...

His sister's text ringtone echoed in the kitchen, and

Gabe was grateful for the interruption. He needed a few minutes to gather his thoughts.

Barbecue Saturday. Three o'clock. You bring the chips and salsa.

"Everything okay?"

No. But Gabe didn't want to discuss the divide that he felt was opening between them. Tessa was stressed enough as it was. Part of Gabe was worried that she'd tell him she didn't need him at all if he pushed her to take it easier. And he wasn't sure he'd survive that.

"Stacy is having a barbecue Saturday. I know you're working the evening shift on Friday."

"But my Saturday is still free. Unless Dr. Lin or someone needs…" Tessa shook her head. "No. I am free, and I won't pick up another shift then. I promise."

She was choosing family time. Choosing *him.* The ball of tension in Gabe's chest relaxed a little on those words. It refused to dissipate completely, but at least it was easier to breathe. For now.

"I'm going to hold you to that. And I need to raid the cilantro plant—we are supposed to bring chips and salsa."

Tessa kissed his cheek, and more of his worry slid away. "I'll cut some. Just tell me how much you need."

Before she could walk away, Gabe pulled her into his arms. Her shoulders were tight, but they relaxed as he kissed the top of her head. A tiny thump got his attention, and he pulled back. "Was that…?"

Tessa's brilliant smile warmed his heart as she put his hands on her belly. "Yes!" She placed her hands on either side of his cheeks. Her face was bright with happiness as her gaze roamed him. "I promised myself that

I'd memorize every moment of you feeling the twins for the first time."

"You did?" Gabe laughed as a foot or elbow pushed at the hand he had on her belly.

"I knew it was a memory I would never want to forget." Joyful tears hovered in her eyes. "And I was so right. I can't wait to watch you be a dad."

She released her hold and laid her hands over his as the twins twisted in her belly.

His children…*their children*. Tears coated his eyes as Tessa leaned her head against his shoulder. Most of his final worries slid away as she let out a soft sigh, and their children kicked his hands.

CHAPTER ELEVEN

"HOW ARE YOU DOING?" Isla handed Tessa a glass of punch.

Gabe was playing with his nieces and nephews on the lawn. He lifted a little girl high in the air, spinning around fast before collapsing with the child on the lawn. Peals of laughter rang across the patio.

Warmth and happiness bloomed in her chest. Tessa was watching a snapshot of the future—her future. Their children would never feel like they had lost their family. No matter what happened in their lives, they'd have a place here.

"I'm doing okay." It was the truth, mostly. She was tired, but that was the normal state for her now. No matter how many naps she took, she couldn't shake the exhaustion. But nothing was going to keep her from enjoying every moment today.

She loved watching Gabe with his family. He was going to be such a good father. And she was going to make sure that he never felt taken advantage of. *Ever.*

Her free hand rested on her belly as she took in the fun scene and sipped her punch.

"You know it's okay if you aren't." Isla laughed as a nephew jumped on Gabe's back and screamed for him to be a horsey.

Tessa barely controlled the yawn that pulled at the

back of her throat. She'd gotten eight solid hours of sleep last night and even taken a nap in the car on the ride over. There was no reason for her to be so tired. *Maybe you should talk to Dr. Fillery.*

"The Davis family can be a lot." Isla raised her glass to Stacy's husband as he carried their screaming toddler inside. "I swear I've lost a few girlfriends because I introduced them to my family. One didn't even make it to dinner before telling me that we had a nuthouse."

She wrapped an arm around Isla's shoulder and squeezed. "Your family *is* a lot. A lot of fun and love."

They cringed as a toddler, whose name Tessa hadn't learned, squealed. The sound echoed into the woods behind Stacy's house, and a group of birds took flight.

"And a lot of noise, too." Tessa winked at Isla. "Anyone who can't see the happiness here, and run toward it, isn't worthy."

This is what Tessa had always dreamed family was. The rowdy, joyful nature thrilled her. Her mother had done the best she could, but she couldn't magic a room of cousins for her to play with. No fun weekends with aunts or uncles. She sighed as she soaked it up.

Isla smiled as she raised her drink. "You're perfect for him. Even if you let him keep that ugly brown comforter."

Tessa laughed as Isla's pronouncement sent a thrill through her. Her eyes misted, and she ran a hand across them. *Hormones.*

The noisy Davis family was wonderful. And her children would be so loved here. With cousins galore!

"Thank you. I know this has been a different path." As the statement escaped her lips, Tessa wished she could withdraw it. Those words may have been right a few weeks ago—but they didn't feel accurate now. What did it matter how she and Gabe had gotten here?

"Your brother is special. He makes me happy." Those words brought another round of mist to Tessa's eyes. Second trimester waterworks were definitely stronger than first trimester ones. Her eyes might be constantly wet by the third trimester if this trend held.

"Yes." Isla leaned close. "Gabe is special, and *you* make him happy. I wasn't sure that was possible after—" Her voice died away.

"After Olive passed," Tessa finished for her. "You can say her name. It doesn't bother me. Gabe will always love her. I know that. But his heart is big enough for both of us."

Isla wiped a tear away from her cheek. "I'm so glad you're part of our family, Tessa. And you, too, little ones." She laid a hand on Tessa's lower belly. "Two more little girls!"

Tessa giggled. "I am delighted to be an honorary family member. But we decided not to find out what sex the babies are. Better to be surprised. Though I am wavering on that decision now."

Gabe had said it was her decision, and she'd wanted to be surprised. But she also wanted to know if Gabe was going to have two little girls to dote on or two boys they'd have to keep from trying to fly from tree houses. Though she'd patched up lots of little girls, too… They were going to be busy—and happy.

Isla shrugged as she looked back toward Gabe. "The twins are girls. I've guessed every one of my nieces and nephews correctly. Those are feisty little girls—*trust me*. And Tessa." Isla waited until she looked at her before continuing. "You aren't an honorary member of anything. The Davis clan is your family, too."

Her throat closed as she met Gabe's youngest sister's gaze. Isla really meant it. Before she could say anything, the babies twisted in her stomach, and suddenly she needed to find the restroom. "Thank you, Isla. You have no idea how much that means. But I need to find the bathroom. I think the twins have started playing hockey with my bladder!"

"Ahh, the joys of pregnancy!" Isla cooed. "At least, so they tell me." She winked again and quickly gave Tessa directions.

"I swear, you two need to find a better toy." Tessa joked while washing her hands. She knew that carrying twins meant even less space for the two of them to move around, but at twenty weeks along, she felt like she was constantly feeling them argue over who got to kick her kidneys.

She stepped into the hallway and yawned. This was out of control. She was *not* tired! At least not enough to yawn every thirty seconds.

"Isla has claimed Tessa as her new best friend. I think she plans to spoil your little ones to pieces. And she swears the twins are girls." The voice of Gabe's oldest sister, Stacy, was light as it traveled from the other room.

"Well, she's been right every other time." Gabe's laugh sent a small thrill through Tessa as she laid a hand over her stomach. If there were two girls in her belly, he'd be the perfect girl dad. But Tessa wasn't ready to buy girl dad stuff based on Isla's predictions.

"I don't care. As long as the twins and Tessa are healthy."

Tessa's heart expanded as the twins danced around her belly. Gabe had told her he didn't care what they were having, but hearing it repeated to his family was nice too. How had she gotten so lucky?

"I'm glad you found Tessa. She's perfect for you."

Tessa smiled. She really was part of the family. *Family.*

"She is. I just wish she'd relax some." Before Tessa could announce her presence, Gabe continued, "I'm worried about her getting this promotion."

Tessa's chest clenched and it felt like cold water was splashing across her dreams. *What?*

"Brett, stop practicing karate takedowns on your sister! I swear that girl needs constant attention." Dishes clinked, and Tessa heard Stacy turn the sink off. "I thought you said Tessa was really qualified."

She wasn't sure she wanted Gabe's explanation; eavesdropping wasn't a trait she wished to cultivate, but her feet refused to move. Maybe he was worried she'd be disappointed if the hospital hired someone else. Maybe it wasn't about Tessa getting the promotion.

Maybe this wasn't a repeat of Max. Gabe had said he was happy. Except he'd talked about her pulling back the other day. And he'd hesitated to date her because of the job.

Her brain rattled with worries as she twisted her palms together. *Please.*

"She's very qualified. That's the problem. If she gets it, well, I worry what that means for our family." His voice drifted away.

The happiness bubble in her chest burst. That Gabe could question her ability to be present for her family cut a deep wound across her heart.

Did he think her getting the promotion would make her less of a mother? She didn't want to answer that question. Tessa wasn't sure her heart was strong enough to handle it.

Squaring her shoulders, she rubbed away a tear before she stepped into the room. "Is there anything I can help with?" She hoped her smile looked real, even though it felt so false.

Gabe's gaze shot toward her. His jaw clenched, but he didn't ask if she'd overheard the conversation.

"Yes." Stacy smiled as she handed her a plate of cookies. "Can you put these out—but tell the kids they only get one!"

"Of course." Tessa's voice felt odd, and she couldn't quite bring herself to meet Gabe's gaze. Even as she felt it rake across her. If she looked back, Tessa feared she'd force him to explain his worry about the promotion now. This was not a conversation she wanted to have with an audience.

It wasn't a conversation she wanted to have at all. She loved him. Tessa was almost positive he loved her, too. But if her advancing at Dallas Children's was a problem—

She'd never live with someone who looked at her like Max had. She couldn't do that again.

"Oh, and we're doing ladies' night in two weeks. Friday night tacos while the boys watch the kids. It's not a late night anymore, just a few hours away from the madness. You should come." Stacy's smile made Tessa want to weep.

She wanted to go. Desperately. Wanted to belong to the Davis family. Fully. But this place would always be Gabe's. Their children would belong here, too. But if she got the promotion, and he left her...

Tessa barely controlled the sob clogging her throat. Her soul ached at the idea that she might not be welcome here someday. The Davis family felt like...like family. Her family.

Her heart screamed for her to say yes. To take the risk, to trust that Gabe hadn't really meant that it would be a problem if she got the job. But she would not make the mistake she'd made with Max's friends. If Gabe wasn't sure what would happen if Tessa got the promotion, she couldn't let herself get too close to them. No matter how much she might want to. "I have to work."

"The schedules aren't out yet," Gabe stated.

His eyes held a look that she couldn't quite read. But she already had a ready excuse.

"I promised Dr. Lin that I'd work a few final shifts with him." It was mostly the truth. Dr. Lin had asked, but she'd told him she had to think about it.

She saw Gabe's lips turn down, and her heart seized. How was she supposed to ask him about this? Until Tessa could find the right words, she was just going to pretend everything was fine. At least with the extra shifts, it would give her an excuse for putting it off.

Tessa smiled, and she caught Stacy's gaze. "Thank you for the invitation. It means a lot." *More than you could know.* She bit back that final statement as she lifted the plate of cookies.

Stacy smiled. "Don't let the kids talk you into more than one cookie. They are cute but diabolical!"

"I won't. Cross my heart." Tessa nodded to Stacy before she let her gaze drift to the man she loved. They'd never said that they loved each other, but her heart was his—completely. But if Gabe didn't feel the same way...

She forced those thoughts away. Now was not the right time or place. And the last thing she wanted to do was break down in front of Gabe's entire family. No, there'd be plenty of time to figure out what Gabe meant—and what it meant for their future.

"Cookies!" Her call was choked, but the kids came running. And Tessa let some of her fear go. Even if she wasn't destined to be part of this clan, at least her children would always have a place to call their own.

* * *

The sheets next to him were cold as he rolled over. Tessa hadn't come home—again. That made two nights in a row that she'd slept at Dallas Children's. Two nights she'd chosen an uncomfortable hospital sleeping room over their bed.

He flopped over and stared at the ceiling. His heart hammered as he tried to push at the doubt pooling in his belly. Something was wrong.

Tessa was putting distance between them, but Gabe didn't know how to draw her back. How to fix the situation. How he could help more when she seemed intent on proving that she didn't need it. Didn't want it.

Or maybe she was just too busy trying to ensure she got the promotion to notice the gulf between them. Maybe the promotion was more important than sleeping next to the man who loved her. His mother had felt that way.

Gabe pushed his palms into his eyes, willing the horrid thought away. But his brain refused to choose another track. What if this promotion wasn't enough? What if he wasn't?

He loved Tessa. Wanted to be with her. But waking up alone to cold sheets was not something he'd settle for. Being an afterthought to a parent left scars that never completely healed. He didn't want that for their children— or for himself.

He blew out a breath as he swung his feet from the bed. The few times he'd seen her this week had all been when they were on shifts together. There was no way to have a discussion during that time. No time to address whatever was bothering her.

And how could he help if he didn't know why she was avoiding him?

He started the coffeepot, adding an extra scoop of

grounds. He needed as much caffeine as the pot could create. Pulling open the fridge door, his heart squeezed as he looked at the meal he'd packed for Tessa. It was still sitting on the top shelf. It was ridiculous to get upset about a packed lunch. Particularly since he was sure she hadn't been home.

Maybe she didn't *need* his help, but why didn't she want it? It was a gesture of love; couldn't she see that? Didn't she want his love?

The garage door opened, and Gabe rubbed his palms on his blue jeans. She was home, and they needed to talk. But his fingers twitched as the worry ricocheted through him. What if he didn't want the answers?

So many thoughts and emotions chased through him. Ambushing Tessa as soon as she got home from the hospital wasn't ideal. But when else was he going to see her?

"You're awake." Her gaze hovered on the coffee cup in his hand.

The dark circles under her eyes were even deeper now than they'd been three days ago. *Is she okay?*

"I'm glad you're home." Gabe started toward her, but she barely paused long enough to let him kiss her cheek before she pulled open a cabinet and grabbed a granola bar and coffee mug. Gabe tried and failed to stop the pain that caused. When was the last time they'd kissed— really kissed, not just a peck on the cheek?

"That's not decaf," Gabe stated as Tessa poured the coffee and put a lid on it.

"It's okay." She sighed as she took a deep sip and ripped open the granola bar.

Having up to two hundred milligrams of caffeine a day was fine during pregnancy. But Tessa had refused to drink anything but decaf since finding out she was pregnant. He bit back his list of questions about her health and chose what he hoped was a safer topic.

"Rough night at the hospital?" He sipped his own drink as he slid next to her.

"Yes. Two car accidents and a trampoline injury that resulted in compound fractures of both tibias." She let out a sigh and took another sip of coffee before pouring the rest of it down the sink. "As much as I want to suck this down, I probably need a few hours of sleep first."

Yes! Gabe smiled and set his coffee mug next to hers. "Do you want me to tuck you in?"

Her gaze shifted as she stared at him. "I am working every day but Friday next week."

Her chin rose, and Gabe felt the air in the kitchen shift. There was a script—he was sure of it—but he didn't know which words she expected him to say. "I'm not sure what that has to do with my questions, but okay. Maybe after next week, you could take a day or two off."

"Why?" Her voice was tight, and there was a fire in her eyes that sent a shiver down his back.

She was exhausted, and there had to be a better time to discuss this. But he wasn't sure when the opportunity would show itself. "Because you will have been living at Dallas Children's for the better part of two weeks by the time those shifts are over."

"The other physicians are doing the same," Tessa countered, and straightened her shoulders. "Josh Killon has a newborn and two other little ones at home, and he is working similar hours."

"Working hours like that only proves that Josh Killon doesn't care about his wife or family. The man cares only about himself." Gabe wanted to kick himself as the words flew between them. That wasn't what he'd meant to say—though it was the truth.

Tessa looked like he'd slapped her. Gabe bit the inside of his cheek as he shook his head. "I know you aren't like Josh."

"Do you?" Tessa's eyes twitched as she met his gaze.

No. Yes. That had been an unfair statement. Even if Tessa was spending more time at the hospital than home, even if he hadn't seen her in two days, she didn't see people as stepping stones like Dr. Killon did.

If he could have pulled his words back, he'd do it. Swallowing, he took a step toward her. "Yes. Dr. Killon only cares about himself."

He took a deep breath and pulled on all his reserves. He shouldn't have compared her to Dr. Killon, but there was a topic they needed to discuss. "But you should understand better than most that working to exhaustion is a recipe for disaster."

Tessa's eyes narrowed. "Meaning?"

"You have dark circles under your eyes. You're exhausted. What if you had fallen asleep on the drive home? Your mom was working so hard that she fell asleep behind the wheel."

Damn it! He hadn't meant to say that, either. *Why is your brain refusing to provide better words?*

"Sorry, Tessa. I'm messing all of this up."

"You're wrong."

The cool tone of her voice sent a wave of panic down Gabe's back.

Her eyes were clear, and her shoulders were firm as she met his gaze. "My mother didn't die because she was working too hard. She died because she left med school to have me. She died because my father got tired of supporting everyone and abandoned us."

Tessa hiccuped as she wrapped her arms tightly around herself.

"But would she have wanted you to push yourself to the edge for a job? A promotion isn't more important than family. It isn't worth injuring yourself or the babies." Gabe pushed his hands through his hair as he caught the final words.

Tessa's eyes widened and the final bit of color slipped from her face. "Do you want me to get this promotion, Gabe? Or are you hoping that Josh Killon or Mark Jackson gets it?"

"No one wants Josh to get it." The joke fell flat as Tessa raised an eyebrow and tapped her foot.

Swallowing the fear, Gabe shrugged. "I want so many things, Tessa. I want to protect you and the twins. I want to provide for you. I want you." He tried to say he wanted her to get the promotion. Those were the words she wanted to hear—but they refused to materialize.

She was exhausted. She looked sick. No job was worth that. Why couldn't she understand that?

"I'm here for you. Let me carry some of the load." The plea fell from his lips. *Please.*

Tessa's eyes flashed with tears, but they didn't spill down her cheeks. "We can share the load, but I don't *want* you to do everything. I don't *need* you."

Gabe blinked as her words pummeled him. "I see." Helping others, protecting them, was what Gabe did. All the things he offered to do for her, she didn't want him to do. Didn't need *him*.

At least not like he needed her. That was a painful truth. His heart cracked as he stood next to her. The walls felt like they were closing in as he tried to push back the hurt. What was his role if he couldn't help the woman he loved?

"I need to get some sleep, but Patrick talked to me today.

I have an interview for Dr. Lin's position next week." Tessa walked past him. "I thought you should know.

"And I heard you say at Stacy's barbecue that you were worried I'd get the position." Her voice cracked. "I can do this, Gabe."

Her shoulders slumped as she stood in the doorway. The final bit of fight draining from her. "I will be a great senior attending."

She would. Gabe offered a small smile. "I'm sure you will. But Tessa, you can't do it all." *At least not alone. And you don't have to.* But his tongue refused to say the words his heart cried out.

Pulling at the back of his neck, Gabe tried to find a path forward, anything that let him be in her life as more than just the father of their children.

How had the dream shattered so quickly? He'd watched his mother pull away from her family for years. Watched her put a little more distance between her and their father. Gabe wouldn't wait around to watch history repeat itself.

"Maybe I should stay at Stacy's for a little while." The words fell into the space between them. The obstacles this conversation had highlighted radiated around them.

Her bottom lip shook, and Gabe swallowed. If she asked him to stay, he would. He would do almost anything for the woman in front of him. *Just ask me to stay.*

"If you think that's best." Then she turned and left.

A hole opened in his chest as he stared at the empty doorway. How were they supposed to cross this chasm? The clock ticked away, and his heart cracked with each step he climbed.

Tessa was already fast asleep. She hadn't even pulled the covers down on the bed. Gabe grabbed a bag and threw in as many of his clothes as he could. Then he grabbed a blanket and pulled it over her.

Running his hand along her temple, Gabe didn't try to stop the tears falling down his cheeks. "I love you." At least he'd gotten to say the words once. Then he turned and fled the place he'd hoped would be his forever home.

CHAPTER TWELVE

TESSA WATCHED GABE walk to his car from the shadows of Dallas Children's parking garage. Her heart screamed for her to run to him. To yell for him to come home. To plead that three lonely nights was more than she could take.

To tell him she loved him and see if that could right the chasms between them.

She'd given up one career opportunity for a partner. And he'd left her anyway.

But Tessa hadn't expected Gabe to leave. That was the part that pummeled her. She'd been exhausted and had needed a nap to regroup. To find better words to explain.

When she'd woken she'd smiled at the blanket he'd thrown over her. She'd gone to find him, hoping to work through the divide that had opened between them. To apologize for her harsh words.

But his things had been gone. His bed was still in the room where they'd first put it. Still covered with plants. But his clothes were gone. The pictures of his family had been taken from the fridge.

When he'd offered to go to his sister's, she'd assumed it was only for a night. Just to give them each a day to cool off.

Not for good.

She hadn't even spoken to him in three days. Three

long days of silence. She'd drafted and discarded so many text messages in the last seventy-two hours. Tessa grabbed her phone and pulled up Gabe's number. *Again.* She'd never realized how difficult it was to press Send.

She yawned and slid her phone back into the pocket of her scrubs. Even if she'd known what to say—what the proper apology was—she didn't have time right now.

Closing her eyes, she sighed. She'd been at the hospital nearly every day this month. Even before he'd left, she'd packed her lunches, handled her share of the household chores—made sure that she was carrying her part of the load. And it still hadn't kept Gabe in her life.

It had driven him away.

What if Gabe really had enjoyed taking on so much? Enjoyed picking up extra chores so she could rest? Truly enjoyed helping her, instead of resenting her? What if she'd been so concerned with the past that she'd ruined her future?

His crushed face hovered in her memory. Her words had done that. She'd told him she didn't need him. *Didn't need him.*

That was the biggest falsehood she'd ever spoken. She needed Gabe more than she'd ever needed anyone. Not to help her around the house, but to love her. To believe in her—and that terrified her. Instead of clinging to that amazing gift, she'd let fear rule. And lost everything.

Her chest clenched as she started for the hospital entrance. Tessa put her hand to her heart as she tried to catch her breath. Spots dotted her vision as she tried to force her feet to move faster, but it felt like she was wading through quicksand.

Her skin was clammy, and panic raced across her spine. This wasn't a symptom of the brokenhearted. Her hand reached for her belly as she crossed Dallas Children's threshold.

"Dr. Garcia?" Denise's voice was far away.

"I...need...an ambulance." Tessa's chest clenched as she tried sucking in air. Blackness pulled at the edges of her vision, and she tried to keep it away.

Gabe... She tried to say his name. *Maybe she had.* But as the darkness took her, Tessa wasn't sure she'd managed to get it out. *Gabe...*

Dr. Fillery offered a nod as she walked into Tessa's room at Presbyterian Hospital. She didn't remember being transported here, but Tessa didn't care about how she'd landed here. She had only one concern.

"The babies."

"Are fine. My concern is about you." She strode to the bed. "Your iron levels were dangerously low, Tessa."

Dr. Fillery's voice carried an authority that she recognized. It was the *I am a doctor and I need you to follow the orders I am about to give* voice. Tessa had used it many times in her career.

She didn't care what Dr. Fillery said she needed to do. The twins were fine. She let out a soft sigh as she let that knowledge wrap around her. The babies were okay. A kick to her ribs sent a smile to her lips. Tessa rested her hand over where the twins were wrestling.

"You're staying here at least overnight, Tessa. You will need to take an iron supplement for the rest of your pregnancy and likely through at least the first few months postpartum." Dr. Fillery took a deep breath and then offered the final order. "And you need to take at least the next two weeks off at Dallas Children's. I know your patients are important, but your hemoglobin levels were at four point two grams per deciliter. I can't believe you were still standing."

"I'll take time off." She meant it. Tessa wouldn't fight the orders, but the forced time off carried other consequences. She bit her lips as the tears coated her eyes. It was fine. *It was fine.*

"If we can't get your levels regulated, I'll recommend bed rest. But right now, I'm just going to tell you to stay home, rest as much as possible, eat lots of leafy greens and lentils. I'll see you in my office at the end of next week, and we'll see if you're strong enough to go back to work then."

Tessa nodded, but the blood was pounding in her ears.

She'd have to cancel her interview—pull her name from consideration. She'd worked so hard for the senior attending position. She was the most qualified. It hurt to step away from it. But Tessa wouldn't risk the health of her children—or herself.

Still, she let a few tears fall for the lost opportunity. There'd be other job openings, she knew that. But that didn't fully chase away the pain.

Her throat was tight, but she pulled up her phone. It wouldn't take long for the gossip network at Dallas Children's to rehash one of their doctors collapsing as they started their shift. She didn't want Gabe to worry.

Besides, he deserved to know that their children were all right. She typed a few words, then hit Send. Then she gave in to the exhaustion chasing her.

"Brett didn't eat all her lunch today. Do you think she's feeling all right?" Gabe put the cheese stick and uneaten grapes back in Stacy's fridge.

His sister's scoff echoed in her kitchen as she passed him a plate and a towel. "She's almost thirteen, Gabe.

Lunchtime is more about socializing than it is about eating lunch. Besides, she told you that she only wants tuna and carrots. I know you're bored, but let the preteen pack her own lunch."

The statement sent a pain down his back. The fissure over not speaking to Tessa for the last three days was bursting at the seams. But he took a deep breath and forced the feelings back inside. He wasn't going to break down—at least not right at this moment.

It was a constant battle to just pretend to be normal when everything seemed lost. Colors no longer seemed as bright, and food—even the sugary treats he loved— had no flavor. Without Tessa, the world was bland.

Leaning against the counter, he tried to shake off the despair that had clung to him since he'd walked out of Tessa's town house. *Keep moving forward*; it was the mantra he'd used after Olive passed. The one that had eventually broken him. But Gabe wasn't going to let that happen—not again.

Besides, Tessa was still alive. Still at Dallas Children's. Still pregnant with their children. Still so many things—but not his.

He needed to get control of himself. "I'm just trying to earn my keep. Brett's barely been home between school, martial arts and dance. I swear that kid is always gone!"

The excuses fell from his lips as the truth ate through him. Tessa hadn't wanted his help, hadn't needed it. He was trying to ignore the hole their argument had torn through him. Who was he if he couldn't help the people he loved? If the woman he loved didn't want his help?

Stacy raised an eyebrow before dipping her hands into the soapy water again. "Help is appreciated, but Brett needs to do things for herself—it builds character."

"Mom! We're going to be late to weapons class." Brett's voice was high-pitched as she raced toward the garage.

"No running in the house!" Stacy dried her hands before putting her hand on his shoulder. "And Gabe—" his sister's smile was tinged with an emotion he feared was pity "—you don't have to do everything for everyone. There's no need to earn your keep with family."

Gabe didn't move as his sister grabbed her purse and rushed to the car. Crossing his arms, Gabe stared out the window of the back porch. Memories of Tessa laughing with his family played out before him, and pain raced through him.

There's no need to earn your keep.

His sister's words ate through his soul. He wasn't trying to. Not really.

Except...

He squeezed his eyes shut as the truth settled within him. After his mother's abandonment, Gabe had taken on more responsibilities. To help his dad and make sure everyone was cared for. To be enough...

Enough that a job wouldn't be worth more than him.

Tears blurred his vision when he opened his eyes. He'd tried for years to be "enough," so his mom would come home. To be more important than the career she'd given everything up for. But Gabe would never be enough for her—no one would.

But that wasn't because there was something wrong with him.

A weight he hadn't known he was carrying lifted off his chest. He was enough—just as he was.

But now he had to address how he'd let that fear destroy his family.

Rather than tell Tessa he loved her, he'd tried to earn his place in Tessa's life. Tried to be more important than her promotion. Because he was worried that she'd choose that over him. Like his mother had.

And she had.

The specter of hurt raced across his heart. But the truth cried out, too. She'd said they could carry the load. *Together.* That she didn't need him to do everything. She'd wanted a true partnership. And he'd wanted more. To be the protector who rode to the rescue.

She'd asked for a partner, and he'd walked away because she wasn't looking for a knight in shining armor.

The woman he loved had asked if he wanted her to get the thing she'd worked hard for. A job that she would excel at, and that would enable her to help others. She had a passion for serving others that their children would see and learn from. A true partner would have screamed, *Yes!* But he'd walked away—because he'd feared that one day she might choose it over him. Because leaving felt safer than getting left.

But Tessa was not his mother. He'd lost love once. But this time he'd thrown it away on the minuscule chance that he might get hurt.

How was he supposed to fix this? He banged his head against the kitchen cupboards, trying to force some idea to present itself. This couldn't be fixed with cupcakes or some other treat. He needed some grand gesture— something to prove…

No!

Gabe was done trying to prove that he was enough. But he needed to figure out a way to show Tessa how much he loved her. How lost he was without her. How much he wanted to stand beside her as she achieved her dreams. *All of them.*

His phone buzzed. His hands were clammy as he ripped the smartphone from his back pocket. He still wasn't sure of the right words, but he didn't care. He needed her.

Always.

The twins are fine. I don't know if you heard, but I passed out at the start of my shift. I will be at Presbyterian overnight. Then two weeks of strict rest. I'm going to pull my name from consideration for the job. You were right. I can't do it all.

The words devastated him. She was brokenhearted over the job—and he'd contributed to that. He'd made her feel that she couldn't do it all. He could have tried to be more understanding. Tried to see her asserting her need to help him as wanting to be his partner.

Instead of seeing that as a blessing, he'd given in to his own anxiety. And he'd shown her that she might have to rely on herself in a world without him. Gabe slapped the top of his head. *God, he was a fool.*

But Gabe could fix part of this. He made a quick call, then grabbed his keys. There was one errand to run, and then he was going to see Tessa. He was going to apologize, to confess his love, and to promise he'd stand by her no matter what.

Presbyterian Hospital didn't have bright walls or pretty murals to ease the hospital feel like Dallas Children's did. As Gabe raced toward Tessa's room, his chest tightened. It had taken him almost two hours to get everything together.

A nurse brushed his shoulder, and his backpack shifted. He'd grabbed the items he'd thought might make her stay more comfortable. He didn't pause to make sure the one breakable thing was fine. If he had to buy another because her mouthwash leaked, Gabe would. He would not waste any more time getting to her side.

Her door was closed. Gabe took a deep breath to keep from rushing through. If Tessa was resting, he didn't want to wake her.

Only the small lamp was lit, but she turned as soon as he walked through the door. Her tentative grin sent a flash of hope through him. Even after everything that had happened, she'd reached out to him.

His heart leaped. He'd never walk away from her again. *Never*.

"You came."

Her whispered words cut across him. Gabe hated that she had doubted for even a second that he'd come to her. He never wanted her to worry about that again.

"I will always come. No matter what. Because I love you." The words fell from Gabe's lips as he slid in next to her bed. "I know there are a million other things that I need to say, apologies to make, but I need you to know that I love you, Tessa Garcia. All of you."

Her fingers wrapped through his, and tears coated her dark eyes.

Before she could say anything, Gabe rushed on. "I was trying to earn your love." He brushed his lips against her hand as the words rushed out. "All the chores, the dinners, the cupcakes—I needed to prove that I was worthy. But I never meant to make you feel like I didn't believe in you. Like I didn't think you could do it all, or that I wouldn't want to walk beside you from here to eternity. I am so sorry."

"Oh, Gabe." Tessa turned in the bed as much as the rails would allow. "You never need to earn my love. My whole heart is yours."

He thought his body might erupt from happiness as

she held his gaze. "I love you." He would never tire of saying those words.

Tessa bit her lip and squeezed his hand. "I was so concerned about making sure that you didn't feel like I was taking advantage of you that I pushed you away. Max may have hated when I leaned on him, but that was a fault in him, not me. I love you, Gabe Davis. What if we just promise to look forward now? Let the past stay where it belongs."

"That's the easiest promise I will ever make. I can't wait to spend each day with you, Tessa." Gabe ran his hand along her arm, unable to keep from touching her.

She wiped away a tear and gestured toward the room. "This isn't the best setting for a happily-ever-after, is it?"

The sterile room wasn't the location that he'd have chosen for this moment, either. Outside of their twins' birth, Gabe would be happy if he never had another night sitting next to Tessa in a hospital bed. But there was a bit he could do to brighten her room.

"I know you won't be here for more than a day or two—"

"One day, I hope." Tessa rubbed her belly as she interrupted him. "Though I'll stay as long as I have to."

How could he ever have doubted the woman he loved would choose anything over her family? If Gabe could kick his past self, he would. He knew the lifetime he planned to spend with Tessa was going to have valleys, but he was going to do everything in his power to make her happy every single day.

"I thought this might make it easier to stay overnight." Gabe pulled a small succulent from the front pocket of his backpack. "This was the smallest guy I could find— and you said they were hardy, so I figured a ride to the hospital wouldn't cause it too much worry."

Tessa grinned at the small plant. "You brought a plant. That's great. And it brightens the room."

"That isn't all I brought." Gabe took a deep breath and pulled out the router. He understood her raised eyebrow as she stared at the box. "It will make the internet at the house super strong. No dropped streaming videos."

"Oh." She nodded. "That will be helpful while I'm stuck at home. Lots of shows to catch up on. And movie marathons to enjoy."

"I can't wait for a movie marathon. I'm going to pop so much popcorn!" Gabe squeezed her hand and waited for her to meet his gaze before he continued, "Want some company in there?"

He sighed as she scooted over in the large maternity bed. When she curled into his chest, Gabe's world finally felt like it was nearly right. But it wouldn't be complete until Tessa had the chance to chase her dream. "But this isn't for movie marathons. At least, not completely. It's so there's no chance of your video freezing during your interview next week."

"Gabe." Her voice wobbled, but she sucked in a deep breath. "I'm not interviewing for the position."

"Why not?" He ran a hand along her side. "You're the best candidate, Tessa. Everyone knows it. I should have said it three days ago. I should have told you how great a senior attending I know you'll be. I should have encouraged you to get a little rest, but I should never have made you doubt yourself." He kissed her cheek as her lip trembled.

"I appreciate those kind words. I really do. And I'm not giving up on the dream. But there will be other positions. You and the twins come first. Always." She smiled, but he could see the hint of sadness still hovering in her eyes.

"Don't get mad." Gabe kissed the top of her head. "But I called Patrick before I went to get that router. There's no reason you can't do a video interview. They're even interviewing at least one outside hire that way."

"An outside hire!"

There was the fire he loved so much. "Yep. If you really want to pull your name from consideration, I will support you, whatever you want, but make sure it's because that's what you want, not because a crazy terrible week made you think you can't do it. Because you can."

"If I get the job, you'll have to take on more at home with the twins." Tessa looked at the router. "It won't be even."

The words were music to his ears. "No one's keeping score, Tessa. I promise."

"But I'll always handle the plants."

"Absolutely." Gabe ran a finger along her cheek and then bent his lips to hers.

The kiss was sweet and long. It spoke of all their hopes for the future. The years of love and happiness that spun out before them. *Together*.

EPILOGUE

"I'M HOME."

Gabe's deep voice echoed down the hallway, and Tessa smiled.

She would never tire of hearing him say that he was at home. However, today she was trying to surprise him. And she wasn't quite ready!

"Hold on!"

Tessa pulled the cake from the bakery box. It had flowers all over it—and Maggie's had promised that this green icing wouldn't leave stains on anyone's teeth. The sugary scent floated up as she set it in the middle of the small dining table, and one of the twins kicked.

Whoosh! At nearly thirty-two weeks along, they were almost out of room in her abdomen, but they still managed to level at least a few good jabs every day. But Tessa really didn't mind.

"Behave!" She glared playfully at her belly. "Or I might let Daddy eat all the cake."

Another rib shot.

"Tessa? Are you all right?"

"Fine," she called. Adjusting the silverware, she let her gaze wander to the decorations she hadn't had time to lay. *Oh, well.*

Swinging open the door, Tessa bowed as much as her belly would let her. "Dinner is served."

Gabe raised an eyebrow before dropping a kiss to her cheek. "This looks lovely. And that cake is making my mouth water. What's the occasion?"

She knocked his hip with hers as they walked to the table. "You pamper me. All the time!" After she'd taken over the role of senior attending, Tessa and Gabe had slipped into a routine that worked well, but he deserved some indulging, too.

"And you love it." Gabe's lips were soft as they brushed against hers.

Yes. She did.

"True." Tessa smiled. "But you deserve a night off, too. I'd have put up more decorations, but the delivery guy was running late."

"Decorations?"

She bit her lip as she gestured toward the cake. "Isla is driving me nuts with all the girl stuff. Figured we might want to know so we can get serious about choosing names! What better way than dinner and a gender-reveal cake."

The bristles on his cheek sent waves of need racing across her as Gabe pulled her close and kissed her. She leaned into him. Hope, excitement and love pulsed around them. And then the twins kicked.

"They're getting strong!" Gabe laughed.

"I know!" Tessa tapped his side as she gathered herself. "Do you want dinner or dessert first?"

"Like you even need to ask." Gabe ran a finger along her chin. His eyes held so much love that Tessa felt like she might take flight. "Cut the cake and tell me what we're having."

She quickly slid the knife through the frosting and smiled. *Pink*. "Isla's winning streak holds true. Girls!"

Turning, she barely managed to set the piece of cake on the table. Gabe was down on one knee. His smile was so big as he held the ring out to her.

"I love you so much."

"Yes!" Tessa yelled.

He shook his head, and a small chuckle escaped his lips. "I didn't even ask yet." He pulled the ring from the box and slid it on her finger.

"I love you." Tessa smiled at the ring, and then at him. "But if I don't feed your little girls, I think they might start rearranging my ribs."

He pulled her close as the twins kicked. "Definitely a dessert-before-dinner night!" He bent and kissed her belly. "But don't get used to it, girls."

* * * * *

MEDICAL
Pulse-racing passion

Available Next Month

How To Win The Surgeon's Heart Tina Beckett
Caribbean Paradise, Miracle Family Julie Danvers

Larger Print

....

Stolen Nights With The Single Dad Alison Roberts
Fling With The Children's Heart Doctor Becky Wicks

....

Falling For The Brooding Doc Annie Claydon
The Paramedic's Secret Son Rachel Dove

6 brand new stories each month

MEDICAL

Pulse-racing passion

MILLS & BOON

Keep reading for an excerpt of a new title
from the Medical series,
REUNITED WITH THE HEART SURGEON
by Janice Lynn

PROLOGUE

NURSE NATALIE GIFFORD unlocked Dr. Will Forrest's door and let herself into the luxurious New York City penthouse. She'd never known money had a scent, but the condominium they'd shared the past six months reeked of it. Money. Wealth. Extravagance. The finest of everything.

Just like Will.

But not her. How had she ever thought a girl who'd grown up in a poor North Jersey neighborhood could fit into his life? That they could be a couple and function as equals in their relationship? If nothing else, her birthday party had proved to her that she'd just been fooling herself.

"Rough night?"

Startled, Natalie jumped. She'd expected Will to have left to make early-morning hospital rounds and she hadn't noticed where he stood by a row of windows overlooking Central Park.

As usual, he'd dressed his six-foot frame impeccably, wearing dark gray pants and a crisp white shirt with the top couple of buttons undone. Perhaps it was because he had grown up as the only child of one of America's wealthiest blue-blooded families that he had such an air of power and allure. Or it could be his rich dark brown hair and vivid green Harroway eyes which graced the most handsome face she'd ever looked upon that made him so appealing. Even after spending a tearful night at Callie's, asking herself why she'd had to fall for someone so beyond her world, seeing him made her pulse pound so fast her breath could hardly keep up.

That's why she'd fallen for him. Despite their many differences, her silly heart had led her to believe they could have a happy-ever-after. That dreams really did come true, and although not quite a Cinderella story, she could have the fairy tale with a real-life Prince Charming.

Despite his silverspoon upbringing, Will worked hard, genuinely cared about others and had completely wowed her when they'd met. Watching the kindness and compassion he showed while interacting with others had stolen her heart from the beginning and still gave her aww moments.

Watching Will stirred her no matter what he was doing. Quite simply, the man took her breath away.

He'd yet to turn toward her, but didn't question that it was her. The building's doorman had probably called to let him know she was on her way up before she'd even stepped foot into the elevator. Usually friendly, the doorman had given her messy bun, the ill-fitting jeans borrowed from her best friend, sandals, T-shirt, and the paper bag containing her party dress and heels a disapproving shake of his head. Yes, she had stayed out all night, but not because she'd been up to no good. She'd been nursing a broken heart. How horrible that her surprise twenty-fifth birthday party had ended with her crying on her best friend's sofa.

"You might say that," she admitted, pushing a stray auburn hair behind her ear as she stared at his stiff back. Did he regret their fight as much as she did? Was he ready to admit that his mother had intentionally used Natalie's birthday party to drive home the differences in their socioeconomic backgrounds? Not that Natalie needed any help in recognizing the stark contrast. These days, she felt it more often than not. To put the icing on the cake, Rebecca Harroway Forrest had invited Will's "perfect for him" ex-girlfriend and kept throwing them together. When Will had given in to his mother's urging and danced with the woman, Natalie had had enough.

"How about you?" she quipped. "Rough night or did your mother send Stella over to comfort you?" She wouldn't have put it past Rebecca.

What had Natalie ever done other than love Will? But Rebecca's issues with her had nothing to do with how Natalie felt about Will and everything to do with the fact Natalie wasn't good enough for her precious son. Natalie didn't have the right pedigree or back account.

Will turned and the coolness in his eyes just about undid Natalie. She knew he was mad that she'd left her party without telling him. He'd made that clear during their brief phone exchange which she'd ended by hanging up on him. But she'd been mad, too. Livid. How dare he be so blind to Rebecca's meddling in their relationship, so tolerant of how she took every opportunity to let Natalie know she wasn't a welcome part of Will's life or their upper-crust family?

"Then you agree I was wronged and needed comforting?" His tone matched his gaze. She couldn't recall having ever seen that particular hue to his eyes before. Who knew green could look so cold?

"Not at all," she corrected. He'd been the one dancing with Stella Von Bosche. Yes, it had only been after Rebecca's urging, but *he should have said no.* "It was my night that was ruined."

His gaze narrowed. "Was something at your birthday party not up to your expectations?"

"A lot. For example, I expected my family and real friends there." She didn't attempt to hide her anger at the poor choices he'd made. For such a brilliant man, when it came to his family, he could be so clueless. "Not a bunch of strangers invited to purposely make me feel as if I didn't belong. And, you dancing with your ex-girlfriend absolutely wasn't something I expected."

Guilt flashed across his face, momentarily replacing the ice.

"If I'd realized it would bother you, I wouldn't have danced with Stella," he admitted.

Relief rushed through Natalie. His admission was a start in the right direction to soothing the unease she'd been experiencing more and more over the past few weeks. They never fought. Her gut twisted that they were now. Natalie's nature was to keep the peace, even to her own detriment. But not this time.

"You should have talked to me, not left without a word."

He wasn't wrong. She should have talked with him. At the time logic had been beaten down by her own emotions, and her self-doubts worsened by Rebecca's cooing over how wonderful it was that Stella was back in her son's life, how much they had in common and how no couple had ever been more perfect for each other. Natalie had had to leave. Either that or she'd have done something she would have regretted—like tell Rebecca what she thought of her.

"Do you know how I felt when I realized you were gone?" Raw emotion harshened Will's words. "That I had to make excuses at your own party for why you were no longer there?"

Nausea churned the few bites of breakfast she'd forced down at Callie's insistence. The entire night had been such a mess.

"I dare say you didn't feel nearly as upset as I

did that leaving appealed more than staying at my birthday celebration. Then again, that party wasn't about me."

"If you'd stuck around, you'd have realized it was." Any semblance of calm was gone as he stepped away from the window. "I wanted to spend my night with you, and you left. *You left me.*"

His reactive, accusatory words both hurt and soothed her inner ache, but not enough to sway her sharp, defensive reply.

"You were barely with me when I was at the party." She lifted her chin, daring him to say otherwise.

"My father is up for reelection for his Senate seat. Spending a few minutes talking with his supporters shouldn't have been a problem." His brow arched. "Mother said you didn't appreciate—"

"That she invited your ex-girlfriend? That she planned my birthday party that you said was a surprise from you?" Natalie's anger surged. "Or that while I was listening to her go on and on about how perfect you and Stella were together and she just knew wedding bells were in your future, you were on the dance floor with said ex-girlfriend hanging all over you?"

"Natalie—"

"You seriously think I'm wrong to be upset?" she interrupted, gripping the sack she held tighter and crinkling the paper as her hand fisted. Part of her wanted to whack him with the bag to knock some sense into him.

Stopping to stand just in front of her, Will's gaze narrowed. "Stella's family are longtime friends of my family and she's Mother's goddaughter. I'll be cordial to her for that reason, if no other. Have I ever given you reason not to trust me, Natalie?"

He hadn't. That is, until she'd seen him laughing with Stella and felt the sharpest stab of pain she'd ever known, and all her doubts about their compatibility had exploded within her. After seeing him with Stella and Rebecca's words ringing in her ear, she'd felt so emotionally defeated she'd begged her only actual friends present, Callie and Brent, to get her out of the pretentious party.

"I don't appreciate not being trusted," he continued.

She jutted her chin upward. "I don't appreciate that your ex-girlfriend was at my birthday party."

"My mother—"

"Don't get me started about what I don't appreciate where that woman is concerned," she huffed, glaring at him.

Warning flashed in Will's eyes. "Stop right there, Natalie. You're treading on thin ice."

No doubt. Which was why she'd let Rebecca get away with her jabs time and again. Because Will would defend his mother to his dying breath. Why was Natalie bothering? They were so close that Will couldn't imagine his mother as anything other than Saint Rebecca. If Natalie told him everything the woman said and did, he wouldn't believe that Rebecca continually insinuated he was just passing the time until Stella returned.

And now, much to Rebecca's joy, Stella was back.

Natalie's stomach lurched. Her belly had been on edge the past few weeks as she'd felt Will's distraction, knowing he was keeping something from her and had grown withdrawn. Had Stella's return triggered the change in him, or had he just grown bored with Natalie?

The writing was on the wall. She could cut her losses or she could continue to live on edge, waiting to be tossed aside when Rebecca succeeded in driving a wedge so deep between them that they couldn't recover. Was that what the night before had been about? His mother smiling so happily as she'd surprised him with Stella's appearance?

No doubt anyone who'd looked their way would have thought Natalie and Rebecca were having a pleasant conversation as Rebecca smiled at the dancing couple while verbally inserting a knife into Natalie's heart and twisting it. For all Rebecca's gouging at her happiness, Natalie blamed Will as much, if not more, than she blamed his mother.

"Fine. I'm on thin ice, but guess what?" she spat back, months of biting her tongue unleashing. "So are you for being blind to the way your mother treats me. Thin, *cracked* ice."

"You're wrong," he defended, his brows furrowing. "Mother tries to reach out to you, but you're so biased you don't see that you push her away. That you let your insecurities about your background be a barrier to your relationship with her."

"Seriously?" Natalie rolled her eyes. "Is that what she tells you?"

"She asked to help me with your party because she wanted to do something special for you, to introduce you to our friends, and welcome you to the fold to let you know you're welcome."

"Of course she did." Natalie snorted. "And lucky for her that Stella came home to make the night even more welcoming."

Hands trembling, she turned to go. She really had had enough. If he'd loved her, she'd have been invincible to anything Rebecca tossed her way and would stay forever, but Will had never said he loved her. The one time she'd braved saying those three words out loud to him, he'd feigned being asleep. She should have known right then that they weren't meant to be.

Maybe she had, because wasn't that around the time she'd started feeling him pull away from her? Becoming more and more distant the weeks that followed?

She'd been such a fool. Love really was blind.

"Natalie!" Her name came out a bit ragged as he reached for her arm, stopping her from leaving. "You're behaving childishly."

Probably. The tears in her eyes certainly made her feel less adultlike.

"I can't believe you've allowed your bias about my mother to ruin your birthday party and lead us to spend a night apart." He sounded incredulous as he gently turned her to face him. "Nor can I believe we're fighting over my mother and Stella when there's no need."

Battling her tears, Natalie's heart thundered against her ribcage as he traced his finger over her cheek. Every nerve ending within her sparked to life like a Fourth of July show finale. Lord help her. It was no wonder she was putty in the man's talented hands. He touched her and she turned to mush. Only, she didn't want to be mush.

Not anymore. She wanted…

"Surely you know you have nothing to worry about where any woman is concerned?" he continued, his touch gentle as he cradled her face, forcing her to look up at him. He looked sincere, looked upset that they were at odds. Good. It upset her, too.

"How do I know that, Will?" she pressed even as tingles of awareness shot over her body just as they always did when he touched her. One little touch and she instantly wanted to kiss him until they were both breathless. Their chemistry was intense and had been from the moment they'd first met at the hospital when she'd dropped off lunch and a drink for Callie.

Will studied her, seeming surprised by her continued antagonism. "Because I want you."

Want. She needed more than want. Their explosive attraction was what had gotten her into this mess. One sexy I-want-you smile and conservative, play-it-safe, gonna-have-a-better-life-than-my-parents Natalie had been his for the taking. To be fair, all she'd had to do was give him a flirty look and he'd been hers for the taking, too. That Will had been so smitten had stunned her. When the good-natured cardiac surgeon, who also happened to be the only son of Senator William Forrest Sr. and business icon Rebecca Harroway Forrest, could have anyone, why Natalie?

Maybe that's why it was so easy for Rebecca's barbs to dig in.

Most days Natalie barely believed one of the city's most eligible bachelors wanted ordinary her.

"I'm tired of doubting myself, feeling as if I don't belong here, in your apartment, and in your life. I'm not willing to live like this, questioning myself all the time, questioning us, anymore. I deserve better."

"Questioning us?" He frowned. "I'm sorry you misunderstood about Stella, but if you'd stayed, you and I would have had an amazing night celebrating your birthday rather than a miserable one."

Natalie's insides shook. She might have misunderstood his dance with Stella, but there was nothing to misunderstand about what Rebecca had bluntly said. Nor the fact that Will refused to acknowledge that his mother had never approved of their relationship.

"I was miserable long before your dance with Stella," she admitted, realizing it was true and wondering how a person who made her so happy could also leave her feeling so unsure of herself. "It just took seeing you with her for me to admit to myself that I'd had enough."

To say he looked stunned was an understatement, and Natalie just stared as he asked, "You were miserable with me?"

Natalie put her hands on her hips as anger, frustration and so many emotions batted for pole position within her. Disgusted with herself, she flipped her hair back and spoke with more bravado than she actually felt.

"In case your memory is foggy, I wasn't with you," she pointed out, refusing to back down as all the things she'd been holding in poured from her. "I haven't been with you in weeks. Longer. You've been so busy and distracted that, other than at the hospital or at the Cancer Society for Children committee meetings, we've barely seen each other. You come home tired and distracted and won't talk to me about what's bothering you, even though I know something is. I feel the change in you and want to help and yet, you shut me out. Do you think I'm incapable of understanding? Or that I haven't felt the changes in our relationship? You and me—" she gestured to his chest, then her own "—we don't fit. I thought we did, but I was wrong."

The words gushed from her and, deep down, maybe she'd always known they were true. Maybe that's why she hadn't interrupted his dance or rebutted Rebecca's barbs, but had retreated to lick her wounds. Because part of her had always acknowledged Will would never be hers long term.

His face losing color, he took a step back. When his mouth opened, likely to remind her just how well they did fit together physically, she continued.

"At least, not outside the bedroom, we don't." Because there was no denying how perfectly their bodies melded. Maybe that's all it had ever been, phenomenal sexual attraction and she'd been too naive to see the truth. "I thought we did—" oh, how she'd believed that "—but your mother was right and I was only fooling myself that we ever could. Whatever was between us is over. I'm done with trying to fit into your world and pretending that I ever could."

The skin on his face pulled tight, his cheeks flushing to an angry red.

Before he could tell her to get out, she said, "I'll pack a bag to take to Callie's and be back for the rest of my things."

Tell me not to go. Tell me you want me to stay. Tell me your mother will eventually approve of me despite my lack of pedigree and hefty bank account and that someday we can be a family. Tell me you love me.

He said none of those things.

What did she say to the man she loved when she didn't want to go, but when even on the verge of goodbye, he couldn't find words to convince her to stay?

Natalie sighed as she battled with the surrealness of what was happening. She was leaving Will. He was letting her go. They were ending. How could her fairy-tale romance have turned into a nightmare heartache?

"I'll have your other things delivered to Callie's later today."

"Okay," she choked out. "Thank you."

Heart breaking, she headed to the door.

"Natalie?"

Thank you, God.

She turned back, hoping he was going to tell her not to leave, that he'd make his mother understand how important she was, that he couldn't imagine his life without her, and then she'd run into his arms, they'd kiss and figure this out. They couldn't be ending.

They just couldn't.

Her gaze connected to his. His usual polished persona faltered and she got a brief glimpse that he wasn't as calm about her leaving as he'd appeared, but his next words shattered that illusion.

"Goodbye, Natalie. Have a nice life."

MILLS & BOON

Book Club

Have your favourite series
delivered to your door every month
with a Mills & Boon subscription.

**Use code ROMANCE2021 to
get 50% off the first month of
your chosen subscription PLUS
free delivery.**

Sign up online at
millsandboon.com.au/subscription-2

or call Customer Service on

AUS **1300 659 500** or NZ **0800 265 546**

**No Lock-in
Contracts**

**Free
Postage**

**Exclusive
Offers**

For full terms and conditions go to millsandboon.com.au
Offer expires June 30, 2021

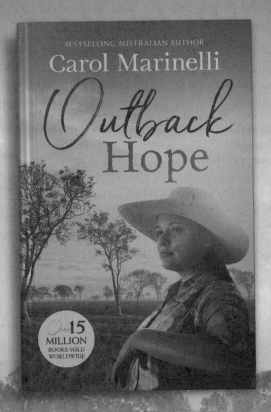